NOW WE ARE DEAD

Stuart MacBride is the No.1 *Sunday Times* bestselling author of the Logan McRae and Ash Henderson novels. He's also published standalones, novellas and short stories, as well as a children's picture book. In 2017 he won *Celebrity Mastermind* (which surprised him more than anyone) – his specialist subject was the life and major works of A.A. Milne.

Stuart lives in the northeast of Scotland with his wife Fiona, cats Grendel, Gherkin, Onion, and Beetroot, some hens, horses, and a vast collection of assorted weeds.

For more information visit StuartMacBride.com
Facebook.com/stuartmacbridebooks
@StuartMacBride

STUART MACBRIDE

NOW WE ARE DEAD

HarperCollins*Publishers*

This is a work of fiction. Any references to real people, living or dead, real events, businesses, organisations and localities are intended only to give the fiction a sense of reality and authenticity. All names, characters, places and incidents are either the product of the author's imagination or are used fictitiously, and their resemblance, if any, to real-life counterparts is entirely coincidental. The only exceptions to this are a number of characters who have been named after people from A.A. Milne's life, but, aside from this homage, all behaviour, history, and character traits assigned to their fictional representations have been designed to serve the needs of the narrative and do not necessarily bear any resemblance to the real person.

HarperCollins*Publishers*
1 London Bridge Street,
London SE1 9GF

www.harpercollins.co.uk

This paperback edition 2018

18 19 20 21 22 LSCC 10 9 8 7 6 5 4 3 2

First published by HarperCollins*Publishers* 2017

A catalogue record for this book
is available from the British Library

ISBN: 978-0-00-825710-1 (PB B-format)
ISBN: 978-0-00-828804-8 (PB A-format)

Set in Minion Pro by Palimpsest Book Production Limited, Falkirk, Stirlingshire

Printed and bound in the United States of America by
LSC Communications

For more information visit: www.harpercollins.co.uk/green

To
Alan Alexander Milne
for writing the book
that made me
a reader

'Er-h'r'm!'

In the autumn of 2016 I did a Very Foolish Thing: I allowed myself to be talked into appearing on *Celebrity Mastermind*.

Now that might not sound so Very Foolish to you, because you're a sophisticated person-about-town type who can remember Important Things, like when the Battle of Hastings was and what you had for breakfast yesterday. I'm not, I've no idea, and I think it was an egg (but I can't be certain). I have a terrible memory and I *really* don't like quiz shows, because watching them just makes me feel thick.

But I let myself get talked into it anyway. Tried to back out when I came to my senses. And was talked back into it again. Oh dear.

Then came the Big Question – what would my specialist subject be? I picked 'The Life and Major Works of A.A. Milne' because the first book I can ever remember reading is *Winnie-the-Pooh*. It's the book of *me*: the one that sits at the core of my being, way down there in my dark and sticky heart. The first book I loved. The book that made me into a reader. So off I went and studied and crammed and revised and Worked Very Hard not to make a complete and utter goat-squirrelling bumhole of myself on national television.

Now, I am a great believer in recycling and there was no chance in hell I was going to let all that studying go to waste after the horror of sitting in the Big Black Leather Chair had faded (I still get flashbacks), so I decided to channel it all into a book.

It just so happened that there was a story I wanted to tell that I thought would probably fit quite well with this newfound A.A. Milne-flavoured knowledge swirling around in my head.

It's the story of what happens to Detective Chief Inspector Roberta Steel after she was caught being Very, Very Naughty in *In the Cold Dark Ground*. After all, I did rather leave her hanging and she's been impatient to be getting on with things.

Logan, on the other hand, was adamant that he'd Worked Very Hard in the last two books and he'd really much rather go on holiday somewhere nice and sunny: where no one ever got murdered, beaten with a claw-hammer, threatened by criminals, slapped by their sister, or had to frisk Extremely Smelly People for weapons and/or drugs. So he won't be appearing in this book (except for a tiny cameo, where he wandered into a chapter or two by mistake {then wandered right out again, when he realised this story isn't about *him* [because it's about Roberta]}).

But don't worry, she's got Detective Constable Stewart Quirrel to keep her company and stop her from doing anything we'll all regret. Or at least he'll Do His Best, and that's all we can ask of anyone...

Oh dear: Roberta's glaring at me and tapping on her watch. She clearly thinks I've spent quite enough time on this introduction and I should get my finger out and actually start the book.

She's probably right.

S. B. MB

are you sitting comfortably?

CONTENTS

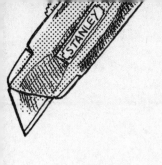

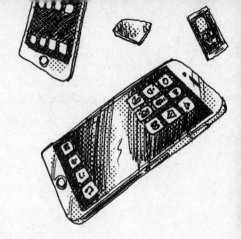

HALFWAY DOWN THE STAIRS

Jack whistles as he works his way downstairs, one step at a time: the 'Funeral March', but the tune falls apart because he can't – stop – grinning.

OK, so today started out pretty bad, but it's going to end absolutely perfect. Class one. Grade A. Whoop-de-bloody-doo. *Terrific.*

It's a nice house, maybe a bit on the frumpy side, but big. Bet it's worth a *lot* of money. No way an honest cop can afford all this. But then she isn't honest, is she? No, she's a dirty lying, corrupt, BITCH.

Jack shifts his grip on her ankles and looks back over his shoulder. Keeps hauling her down the stairs, nice and slow so the Bitch's head bounces off each and every step.

Bump. Bump. Bump.

Could she be dressed more like a dyke if she tried? Dungarees? Honestly, some people have no sense of style at all. She's even wearing comfortable shoes, for Christ's sake. What a cliché.

And what's with the hair? Looks like someone tumble-dried a Scottie Dog then stapled it to a wrinkly chimpanzee. Lesbians in porn films look nothing like that. They're all lithe and young and pert. Compliant. Willing. Grateful. *Completely* unlike Detective Sergeant – Oh I'm So Special

1

– Roberta Bloody Steel in her bulldog-dyke dungarees.

Still, she'll not be wearing them long.

Her eyes flicker open as her head bumps against the next step down. Mouth moving like it's not been wired up right. 'Unnnngggghhhh…'

Gwah… The *smell* coming off her: like someone drowned a tramp in cheap chardonnay and cheaper perfume.

Still, Jack's prepared to overlook all that, cos he's a gentleman. And this one's been a *long* time coming.

He gives her a smile. 'Oh, we're going to have so much *fun!*'

Bump. Bump. Bump.

CHAPTER ONE

*in which we are introduced to Roberta Steel
and her Horrible New Job*

I

Tufty lunged, arm outstretched, fingertips just brushing the backpack … then closing on thin air. Too slow.

The wee scroat laughed, shoved his way through a couple of pensioners examining the pay-as-you-go phones, and exploded out through the doors. His mate hurdled the fallen oldies, hooting and cheering. Hit the pavement and ran right, twisting as he went to stick both middle fingers up through the Vodafone shop window.

Tufty sprinted after them. Burst through the doors and out onto Union Street.

Four-storey buildings in light granite lined the four-lane road, their bottom floors a solid ribbon of shops. Buses grumbled by, white vans, taxis, cars.

The foot traffic wasn't nearly thick enough for the pair of them to disappear into a crowd. They didn't even try. Running, laughing, hoodies flapping out behind them. A couple of mobile phones clattered to the paving slabs, screens shattering amongst the chewing-gum acne.

Look at them: neither one a day over thirteen, acting like this was the most fun they'd ever had in their lives. Expensive trainers, ripped jeans, one bright-blue hoodie – violent orange hair – one bright-red – dark with frosted tips – both with stupid trendy haircuts. Earrings and piercings sparkling in the morning sunlight.

Tufty picked up the pace. 'Hoy! You!'

The clacker-clack of Cuban heels hammered the pavement behind him.

He glanced back and there she was: Detective Sergeant Steel, *actually* giving chase for once. Didn't think she had it in her. Her dark-grey suit was open, yellow silk shirt shimmering, grey hair sticking out in all directions like a demented ferret. Face set in a grimace. Probably hadn't done any serious running since she was a kid – trying not to get eaten by dinosaurs.

A man wiped coffee off his jacket. 'You rotten wee shites! I was drinking that!'

An old woman grabbed at her split bag-for-life, its contents rolling free. Off the kerb and into the road. 'Come back here and pick this up, or I'll tan your backsides!'

Up ahead, the one in the blue hoodie barrelled through a knot of people stopped in the middle of the pavement chatting, sending one bouncing off a solicitor's shop window with a resounding '*boinnnngggggg*', the others clattering down with their shopping. Another couple of mobile phones, still in their boxes, joined them, spilling out of the open backpack.

Hoodie Red sprinted past the e-cigarette shop where the granite buildings came to an abrupt end. A pause in the street, marked by a short row of black iron railings, a small gap, then a sort of fake two-storey-high neo-classical frontage thing, with a graveyard lurking behind its Ionic pillars.

A grin and Red jinked right, into the gap and down the stairs.

Tufty gritted his teeth. Come on: *faster*.

He scrabbled to a halt in front of the railings.

Red was still there, dancing from foot to foot on the stairs, unable to get any further than a quarter of the way down due to the bunch of mothers wrestling pushchairs up.

The stairs descended about fifteen/sixteen feet to a narrow cobbled road that disappeared under Union Street.

Ha! Got you.

Red pulled a face, gave Tufty the finger again, then jumped. Clearing the handrail. Dropping six foot onto the top of a Transit van, parked below. A *boom* of battered metal. Then he rolled off, landed square on his feet and took off into the tunnel. Still laughing.

The driver leaned out of his window, shaking his fist. 'Hoy!'

Blue clearly didn't fancy his chances. Instead he went left, sprinting across the bus lane, hooting away as car horns blared – a taxi and a truck slammed on their brakes, inches away from turning him into five stone of hoodie-wearing pâté.

Blue or Red? Blue or Red?

Steel's voice cut through the horns. 'Shift it! Police! Coming through!'

A quick look – she shoved her way through a couple of gawkers and some well-meaning souls helping pick up the old lady's shopping.

Blue or Red?

The stairs were still jammed with mothers and pushchairs. Red.

Deep breath. 'Oh God...'

Tufty stuck one hand on the rail and swung his legs up and over into thin air.

It whistled past him, then, *boom* onto the Transit's roof, just as it pulled away. He had time for a tiny scream as the world flipped end-over-end, then the cobbles broke his fall with a lung-emptying *thud*.

Argh...

They were cold against his back. Little flashing yellow lights pinged around the edges of the bright-blue sky, keeping time with the throbbing high-pitched whine in his ears.

Steel's face appeared over the railings, scowling down at him. 'Don't just lie there, get after the wee sod!' A shake of the fist, and she disappeared again.

Urgh...

Tufty struggled up to his feet. Shook his head – sending the little yellow lights swirling – and lurched into the tunnel.

Roberta shook her head. Silly sod. Having a wee kip in the middle of the road while the thieving gits got away. Never trust a stick-thin, short-arsed detective constable. Especially the kind with ginger hair – cut so short their whole head looked like a mouldy kiwi fruit – and watery pale-blue eyes the same colour as piddled-on Blu-Tack.

That's what she got for taking the new boy out on a shout.

Well Tufty had better sodding well catch Hoodie Number Two, because if Tufty didn't Tufty was in for a shoe-leather suppository.

And in the meantime...

She charged across the pavement and out into mid-morning traffic, one hand up on either side of her eyes to shut out the view. 'Please don't kill me, please don't kill me, please don't kill me...' Horns blared. Something HUGE slammed on its brakes – they squealed like pigs, hissed like dragons.

An angry voice: *'YOU BLOODY IDIOT!'*

And pavement! Beautiful, beautiful pavement.

She dropped her hands.

Wasn't difficult to see which way Hoodie Number One had gone – just follow the trail of swearing people sprawled across the beautiful pavement, leading west along Union Street.

Roberta dragged out her phone, dialling with one hand as she ran past McDonald's. Jumped over a young woman with a screaming toddler in her arms, sprawled beside the bus shelter.

A bored woman sighed from the mobile's earpiece, followed by: 'Control Room.'

'I need backup to Union Street, *now!*'

'*Nearest car is two minutes away. How severe is the situation? Do you need a firearms team?*'

Roberta threaded her way through a clot of idiots outside Clarks, all staring after Hoodie Number One. 'Shoplifter: early teens, blue hoodie, orange hair, ripped jeans—'

'*Oh you have* got *to be kidding me. We're not scrambling a patrol car for a shoplifter!*'

The tunnel under Union Street spat Tufty out between two tall granite buildings. Cold blue-grey in the shadows, the windows at ground level either bricked up or barred. He limp-ran to the end, making little hissing noises every other step. Like his left sock was sinking its teeth into his ankle.

Oh let's go after the *red*-hoodied shoplifter. Let's jump off a bridge...

That's what you got for being brave: a whack on the cobblestones and a carnivorous sock.

He burst out from between the buildings and into the Green. Aberdeen Market was a massive Seventies concrete hatbox off to the left, making the stubby end of a blunt triangle – old granite buildings on the other two sides and...

There he was: Red. Jumping up and down behind a line of big council recycling bins. Still laughing. Twirling around on the spot, middle fingers out again. Waiting for him. Taunting him.

Then off, running down the middle of the Green. Getting away.

Not this time.

Tufty put some welly into it. Onward brave Sir Quirrel!

He jumped, hip-sliding across one of the bins marked 'CARDBOARD ONLY', *Starsky-and-Hutch* style. Landed on his bad ankle. Hissed.

Started running again.

Red looked back, grinned at him, barrelling headlong towards a fenced-off eating area outside a wee bar/restaurant full of loved-up couples eating a late breakfast in the sun. Red jumped the barrier, feet clattering on top of the tables, sending plates and glasses flying.

Diners lunged for him.

A man jerked back as his Bloody Mary introduced itself to his lap. 'Hey! What the hell...?'

A woman bared her teeth. 'Get your manky feet out of my eggs Benedict!'

Then bang – Red was out the other side.

Tufty pumped his arms and legs harder. Leaned into the sprint as he skirted the dining area. Ignoring the sock eating his ankle. Closing the gap...

Horrible Hoodie Number One did a wee dancy twirl around an old man with a walking stick, showing off, hooting. Then disappeared around the side of Thorntons.

Sodding hell...

Roberta gripped her phone tighter. 'He's gone down the steps to the Green.'

Another sigh from the bored woman on the other end. *'I don't care if he's gone down on Nelson Mandela's ghost, you're not getting a patrol car.'*

The wee sod's face popped back around the corner again, joined by a double-handed two-fingered salute. He jiggled the V-signs in her direction, then vanished.

'But—'

'You're not a child, for goodness' sake. Surely you can catch a shoplifter without a SWAT team!'

Roberta wheeched around the corner, grabbing onto a big bearded guy to stay upright. 'Well bugger you, then!'

The big guy flinched back. 'What did I do?'

She jammed her phone in her pocket and skidded to a halt at the top of the stairs.

Oh … wow, that was a *long* way down.

The stairs weren't far off vertical, at least three-and-a-half-storeys'-worth of thin granite steps, with a handrail at either side and one down the middle. Fall here and it'd be bounce, crack, bang, wallop, thump, crunch, scream, crash, splinter, *THUD*. Followed by sirens and nine months in traction.

Hoodie Number One was already halfway down the stairs. Taking them two at a time.

A boxed iPhone spilled from his backpack and bounced off the granite steps.

Gah…

She stuck both hands out, hovering them over the railings. And ran.

Going to die, going to die, going to die…

Down at the bottom of the stairs, Hoodie Number Two – the one dressed in red – hammered past, laughter echoing off the grey buildings.

And Hoodie Number One was nearly at the bottom too, grinning over his shoulder at her.

Where the hell was Tufty when you actually needed him?

How could one detective constable be so completely and utterly, *totally*—

He ran into view, staring straight ahead. Which was a shame, because Hoodie Number One wasn't watching where he was going either and smashed right into him.

BANG!

They both hit the cobblestones in a twisted starfish of arms and legs. Thrashing and bashing and crashing as she hurried down the last two flights of stairs and into the Green.

They rolled into the 'Pedestrian Zone ENDS' sign with a faint clang.

'Aaaargh, gerroffus gerroffus!'

Roberta skidded to a halt at the foot of the stairs. Looked right.

Hoodie Number Two was just visible as a red smudge – running deeper into the tunnel that led under the St Nicholas Centre and out to the dual carriageway. He turned and treated them to his middle fingers. Then his voice thrummed out, amplified by all that concrete and granite, 'CATCH YOU LATER, MASTURBATOR!' That red smudge vanished into the gloom.

'Sodding hell…' Roberta bent double, grabbing her knees and puffing like an ancient Labrador.

Tufty hauled Hoodie Number One to his feet, both hands cuffed behind the wee sod's back.

A cough, then Tufty wiped a hand over his shiny forehead. Gave his prisoner a shoogle. 'You are *comprehensively* nicked.'

The wee sod just grinned and stood on his tiptoes, shouting after his friend: 'IN A WHILE, PAEDOPHILE!'

Kids today.

Tufty pushed through the scabby grey doors into a scabby grey room. Voices echoed up from the cells below, bouncing off the breeze-block walls – some singing, some shouting, some swearing, some crying. Call it 'NE Division's Custody Suite Symphony' in arrested major.

He tightened his grip on the blue-hoodied shoplifter, manhandling him over to the custody desk – chest high with a selection of that season's Police Scotland posters and notices Sellotaped to the beech laminate front. 'Bogus Callers, Scammer, And Thieves', 'Have You Seen This Man?', 'Domestic Violence Isn't Love', '"No" Means "No!"'

A huge man was hunched over the desk, wearing the standard-issue black T-shirt with sergeant's stripes on the epaulettes. No need to call in Hercule Poirot to investigate 'who ate all the pies' – the answer was elementary, my dear Morse: Big Gary. He had his tongue poking out the side of his mouth as he scribbled away at something.

Steel sauntered up, popped onto her tiptoes and peered over the desk. 'Aye, aye...' Her hand snaked out and she snatched whatever the sergeant was scribbling on. 'Colouring-in for adults?' She flipped through the pages. 'This no' a bit advanced for you, Gary? You're supposed to stay *inside* the lines.'

Big Gary grabbed for it, but she skipped back out of reach. Grinning.

'Tufty, do the honours. I'm going to draw willies on all Big Gary's pictures.'

Another grab, another miss. 'Don't you dare!'

Tufty gave Blue a nudge, propelling him closer to the desk. Then mimed pinging a hotel bell. '*Ding*. Single room with en suite and a view of the lake, please.'

A tiny smile flirted with the corner of Big Gary's mouth. 'And what name's the reservation in?'

Silence.

Tufty poked Blue again. 'The nice man wants to know your name.'

Blue's shoulders came up. His voice: small and sulky. 'No comment.'

A sigh. Then Big Gary took a form from beneath the desk and slapped it down on the top. 'Very good, son. But you're supposed to save that bit for when your lawyer gets here. Now: name?'

A grin. 'Wanky McSpunkbucket. The third.'

'Oh be still my splitting sides.' Big Gary pointed at another of his many, many posters.

'IT IS AN OFFENCE TO GIVE FALSE DETAILS TO THE POLICE'.

'Let's not make it any worse, eh?'

Blue shrugged again. Looked down at his shiny white trainers. 'Charles Roberts.'

'Thank you. And where do you live, Charles Roberts?'

'No com...'

Big Gary pointed at the poster again.

'Thirteen Froghall Crescent.'

'There we go.'

Tufty snapped on a pair of nitrile gloves and dug into the knapsack, still strapped to the kid's back.

'Hey, gerroff us!'

He stuck a pair of iPhones – brand new and still in their boxes – on the custody desk. Followed by half-a-dozen Samsungs: boxed, three Nokias: boxed, eight assorted smart-phones: used, and four wallets. Another wallet and two smartphones: used, from the pockets of the blue hoodie.

'I never seen them before in my life. You planted that lot.'

'Really?' He took hold of one of the hoodie sleeves and pulled it up. A row of three watches sparkled in the romantic overhead strip lighting.

'You planted that as well.'

'Don't be a—'

The double doors banged open and in marched a heavy-weight boxer in a dark suit and pale blue tie. Broken nose, narrow eyes, hair swept back from a widow's peak. Two plainclothes uglies followed in his wake, both in matching grey suits and red ties, hipster haircuts, and I'm-So-Hard-

14

And-Cool expressions. Like a two-man boy band. The uglies frogmarched a little guy with a grubby face up to the custody desk. The cuffs of his shirt were ragged and stained a dark reddy-brown, more stains on the front of his tattered jumper.

The boxer pointed at Big Gary. 'Sergeant McCormack, I want Mr Forester processed, seen by the duty doctor, given a solicitor, and placed in an interrogation room within the hour.'

Steel bristled. 'Hoy, wait your turn. We were here first.'

He turned a withering glare on her. 'Did you say something, Sergeant?'

'Aye. Back of the queue, mush.'

The boxer stepped closer, looming over her. 'You seem to be a little confused, *Sergeant*. You're not a detective chief inspector any more.' He poked her with a finger. 'And while you're running around after shoplifters and druggies, I'm out there catching murderers.'

One of his sidekicks sniggered.

Steel's face curdled.

But he just smiled. 'I outrank the hell out of you now, and if I say my suspect goes first, he goes first. Understand?'

She glowered back, lips and jaws moving like she was chewing on something horrible.

'I said: do – you – understand?'

The reply was barely audible. 'Yes, Guv.'

'Or would you like another visit to Professional Standards?'

She narrowed her eyes. Bared her teeth.

Oh God, it was all going to kick off, wasn't it?

But Steel swallowed it down. Cricked her neck to one side. 'No, Guv.'

'Good. I'm glad we had this little chat, aren't you?'

Please don't hit him, *please* don't hit him…

* * *

Tufty stuck a finger in his other ear and leaned back against the meeting room wall. Next to the whiteboard with a huge willy drawn on it in black and red marker pen. 'Yes. … No. … I think that's OK, isn't it? … Were we? Sorry, didn't know.'

Idiot.

Roberta let her head fall back, over the back of her leather chair, and stared up at the ceiling with its regular grid of toothpaste-white tiles. OK, the view was a bit dull, but it was still better than looking at Harmsworth.

She snuck a peek anyway.

He was sitting on the other side of the long oval meeting table, feet up on one of the big blotter-sized notepads, peering at a copy of the *Aberdeen Examiner* like someone who'd forgotten his glasses. Chubby wee sod that he was, with his receding hairline and a face that looked as if it'd never smiled in its life. A miserable balding bloodhound in a rumpled brown suit. Picking his nose when he thought no one was looking.

Oh she got all the 'special' ones on her team, didn't she?

Roberta's phone *ding-ding*ed at her. Incoming text:

> I beat Lizzy Horsens by eight strokes! She's moaning about it like a whiny little bitch! It'll kill her when I win the trophy again!
> I'm a golfing NINJA!!! :)

She smiled and thumbed out a reply:

> Golfing ninja Susan!
> So I take it we're celebrating tonight? You wear a sexy nightie and I'll pretend I'm there to fix the washing machine.

Send.

Harmsworth was digging away in his nose again. Well if he was searching for a brain he was excavating the wrong end of his body.

Ding-ding:

> Don't be naughty. Logan's coming over to
> see the kids tonight, remember? I'm doing
> chicken casserole, so don't be late.

Sit down and break bread with Logan Traitorous Scumbag McRae? Rather break the casserole dish over his sodding head.

Then make him eat all the jagged broken bits…

Oh for goodness' sake: Harmsworth was *still* at it.

He glanced up and caught her looking. Popped his finger out. Sighed. Then droned on in that depressing Marvin-the-Paranoid-Android voice of his, 'Listen to this:' he ruffled his newspaper, '"Blackburn residents live in fear of sex pest pervert. 'I can't even cook dinner with the blinds open,' said Janice Wilkinson, brackets, thirty-one. 'What if one of the children look out of the window and see him?'"' Another sigh. 'You'd have to be a bit funny in the head, wouldn't you?'

Roberta grimaced back at him. '*I* used to be the one catching murderers. And *now* look at me. Stuck here with you pair of neeps.'

Tufty laughed. 'I know. … Yeah. Probably.'

'I mean, who wakes up one morning and thinks, "You know what I fancy? Sticking on a superhero mask and having a wank outside someone's kitchen window while they're doing the dishes."'

The boy idiot put a hand over the mouthpiece of his phone. 'Sarge? That's our boy ready to interview.'

'Oh joy.' She let her head fall back again, then blew a big wet raspberry. 'Urgh…' A drizzle of cold spittle drifted back down across her face. She sat up and wiped it off.

Tufty went back to his phone. 'Yeah, we'll be right down.'

Harmsworth gave his paper another theatrical ruffle. 'Speaking of wankers, did you see this?' He turned it around, showing off a two-page spread. A photo of a skinny wee nyaff sat beneath the headline '"POLICE CORRUPTION BLIGHTS ABERDEEN" CLAIMS MISCARRIAGE OF JUSTICE VICTIM'. Jack Sodding Wallace, wearing his going-to-court suit, standing outside the council offices on Broad Street. He was holding a sheet of paper up, as if that meant anything, looking all serious and concerned at it. Raping wee shite.

Harmsworth sniffed. 'Jack Wallace says we're all a bunch of useless dodgy bastards.'

'Jack Wallace can roll himself up sideways and shove it up a llama's bumhole!'

'Says all we do is fit up innocent people and take bribes.'

She stabbed a finger in Harmsworth's direction. 'I'm no' telling you again, Constable.'

A huff and he went back to his newspaper. 'Don't know why I bother. No one *ever* appreciates it.'

Tufty put his phone away and pointed at the door. 'Sarge?'

Harmsworth was still groaning on. 'I should just go jump under a bus. Give you all a laugh. Oh look at Owen, he's all squished and dead. Isn't that funny? Ha, ha, ha.'

'Well, we can all dream.' Roberta stood. Twinged a bit, then had a dig at her treasonous left underwire. Whoever designed bras to have sharp pokey bits of metal in them needed a stiff kick up the bumhole. 'Meantime: get your backside in gear. Two teas, interview room…?' She looked at Tufty.

'Three.'

'And see if you can scare up some biscuits too.'

A groan, then Harmsworth made a *big* show of folding his paper and stood. Smeared a martyred expression across his miserable face. 'Oh, just order Owen about, why not? Not as if he contributes anything to the team, is it? No. Make the tea, Owen. Find some biscuits, Owen…' He slouched from the room, leaving the door to swing closed behind him.

Idiots. Morons. Whingers. And tosspots. Why couldn't she get dynamic go-getting sex bunnies in her team? How was that fair?

She glowered at the ceiling. 'I swear on the sainted grave of Jasmine's gerbil, Agamemnon...'

The door opened again.

For God's sake!

Roberta turned the glower into a glare. 'Two sodding teas and a couple of biscuits! How difficult can it—' But it wasn't DC Moanier-Than-Thou Harmsworth, it was a lump of uniformed officers all clutching notebooks and clipboards.

The guy at the front had inspector's pips on his broad shoulders. He looked over the top of his little round glasses at his watch. Oh, I'm so *important*! 'What are you doing in here?'

'Inspector Evans. It's been yonks, hasn't it? How's your piles these days?'

He stiffened. 'I've got this meeting room booked till five.'

'Just keeping it warm for you.' She stood and hooked a thumb at Tufty, then at the door. 'We're leaving anyway.'

Tufty followed her out into the corridor, and as the door swung shut Inspector Evans's voice went up an octave. *'Oh for goodness' sake! Who keeps drawing willies on all the whiteboards?'*

II

'No comment.' Charles Roberts shoogled in his seat, setting his white Tyvec suit rustling. Even the extra small was *way* too big for him, the sleeves and legs rolled up about six inches so they didn't flop about. Cleaned up and out of his shoplifting gear, he looked even younger. Nine years old, maybe ten at a push?

Interview Room Three had more stains than carpet on the floor. A weird wet patch in the corner by the window that looked a bit like Joseph Merrick if you squinted. A radiator that gurgled, pinged, and whistled away to itself.

Roberts was on the naughty side of the chipped Formica table, his appointed solicitor sitting next to him in an ill-fitting suit. She looked about as bored as it was possible to be and not die from it. Apparently being a middle-aged lawyer doing Legal Aid wasn't the non-stop party bus it was cracked up to be.

A sad older man in a baggy grey cardigan was squeezed in at the end of the table in a chair nicked from the office across the hall. Grey cardigan. Grey hair. Grey moustache. Grey face.

Steel dunked a chocolate Hobnob into her tea and sooked the molten brown off.

She was braver than Tufty. No way he was risking a

sip of the suspiciously milky beverage DC Harmsworth had banged down on the table with a sinister mutter about how nobody ever appreciated him. Five people. Two teas.

Tufty picked up an evidence bag from the blue plastic crate at his feet. Held it out. 'I am now showing Mr Roberts Exhibit Nine.' One of the brand new iPhones, still in its box and cellophane wrapper. 'What about this one, Charles, do you recognise it?'

A rustly shrug. 'Never seen it in me life before.'

'You stole it this morning, didn't you?'

Rustle. 'No comment, yeah?'

Steel finished her Hobnob and sooked her fingers clean. Shifted in her seat. Yawned. Didn't say a word.

'You and your accomplice in the red hoodie stole a large number of phones from the shops on Union Street. I saw you do it.'

'Nah you didn't.' He turned to his solicitor. 'They're totally lying. Me and Billy never nicked nothing.'

Steel slumped forwards, hands covering her face. 'Oh God, I'm so *bored*.'

Captain Cardigan sighed. 'Come on, Roberta, play nice.'

She sagged back again. 'It's all right for you, you don't have to do this day after day. "No comment." "It wasnae me." "A big boy did it and ran away." Over and over and over… You social workers don't know you're born.'

Roberts' solicitor shuffled her paperwork. 'Perhaps this would be a good time to take a short break?'

Steel closed her eyes and jerked forwards, arms straight, palms flat down on the table, head hanging. 'Ooooooooooooooo… OOOOOOooooooo…'

Everyone stared.

The solicitor shrank back a bit in her seat. 'Is she OK? Do we need to call a doctor?'

But Steel's voice belted out, 'Big Chief Lionel Goldberg, are you there?'

'Is this meant to be some sort of joke?'

'Knock once for yes, twice for no.'

Captain Cardigan rolled his eyes. 'Come on, Roberta, this isn't helping anyone.'

'Big Chief Lionel Goldberg, I beseech you: guide me from the spirit world!'

Roberts' solicitor scowled. 'Whoever heard of a Red Indian chief called "Goldberg"?'

'Ooooooo-oooo-oooooh… OOOOOOooo…'

'For goodness' sake.' A sigh from Captain Cardigan. 'I could've retired last year. Could be on the golf course right now.'

'Tell me, oh wise and powerful spirit, what does the future hold?'

The solicitor's papers got stuffed in a satchel. 'I'm going to make a formal complaint. This is simply *not* acceptable.'

Steel held up a hand. 'Big Chief Lionel Goldberg him say, "Hud yer wheesht, quine." The future … yes, I can see it now!'

Charles Roberts grinned. 'She's mental. Proper in-the-head mental.'

'We shall sit in this stinky wee room for the next hour and a half, wasting our time, listening to him denying everything. Then we'll stick him in a cell and … and we'll get the CCTV footage from Union Street, and the security camera stuff from the shop, and do him for nicking all those phones anyway…'

'Nah, you planted them, like. Remember?'

'What's that, Big Chief Lionel Goldberg? And then we'll check the records for the last three weeks? What will we find, oh mighty spirit?'

'I *insist* you stop this ridiculous charade, right now! My

client will not answer any further questions under these circumstances!'

Tufty shared an apologetic smile with the other side of the table. 'Sorry about this.'

'OOOooooo... We'll find that the six phone shops on Union Street have reported over twenty grand's worth of stock stolen? And they're certain it was Charlie-boy here and his mate Billy that did it?'

'Nah.' Roberts shook his head. 'And you can't do nothing about it, cos we're just kids. We ain't responsible.'

'And Charlie will get three years in a young offenders' institution? Maybe a nice comfy borstal?'

Roberts' solicitor slammed her hand down on the table. 'All right, that is ENOUGH!'

Steel sat back. Had a scratch at her armpit. Stared at their junior-issue shoplifter. 'Where's your mum and dad, Charlie? How come we had to get a social worker in to be your appropriate adult?'

Roberts pulled up the hood of his rustly suit, shrinking into it. Looked away. All bravado gone. 'No comment.'

Steel thumped Tufty on the arm. 'Call it.'

'Interview terminated at twelve twenty-six.'

The sound of voices floated up the stairwell from somewhere below. The rattle and clank of cutlery and crockery coming from the station canteen, joined by the smell of cauliflower, sausages, and chips.

Steel tugged her jacket on, fighting with the sleeves. 'Lunch, lunch, lunch, lunch, lunch.'

Tufty followed her downstairs. 'A fiver says they're going to make a complaint.'

'I'm feeling a bit pizza-ish. That or noodles.'

'I thought you were trying to keep a low profile?'

'Maybe a baked tattie?'

Tufty sighed. 'The boy was right: you're off your head. You know that, don't you?'

'What's wrong with baked tatties?'

'Not baked potatoes, the complaint!'

A small man in a sharp suit was on his way up the stairs. Short, but wiry and powerful looking. The kind you always had to watch in a fight, because he had something to prove. He looked up, raised an eyebrow. Then stopped in the middle of the stairs, reached out, and took hold of both handrails. Blocking their path. 'Detective Sergeant Steel, what's this I hear about you holding a séance in Interview Three?'

'Oh, Detective Chief Inspector Rutherford, can you believe it?' She bit her bottom lip and put the back of one hand against her forehead, looking a bit like a B-movie damsel in distress. 'DC Quirrel here thinks there's something *wrong* with having baked tatties for lunch.'

'"Big Chief Lionel Goldberg"?'

'They were all out of Native Americans at the spirit guide shop.'

There was a hint of a smile. 'Witnesses from beyond the grave aren't admissible in court, Sergeant. And you can consider yourself lucky Charles Roberts' solicitor isn't making a formal complaint.'

She frowned. 'I think I was right in the first place: ham-and-mushroom pizza, with extra cheese.'

'I'm serious, Roberta.' All hint of that smile disappeared. 'The last thing you need is another visit from Professional Standards. Might not get off so lightly next time.'

Her expression hardened. 'Thank you, Guv.'

'And what about the other shoplifter, this "Billy" character?'

Steel shrugged. 'That'll be Billy Moon. Him and Charles Roberts have been tag-team nicking things since they could walk. He'll lay low for a few days, then he'll be out on the

24

streets again, five-finger-discounting everything he can grab. Don't worry, we'll get him.'

'Excellent. In the meantime we have twenty-three thousand, eight hundred and sixty pounds' worth of missing phones out there somewhere. That would be a significant amount of stolen property to recover, don't you think?'

'Guv.' All the warmth of a fridge freezer.

'Then you'd better go recover it, hadn't you?'

She stuck her hand against her forehead again, bottom lip trembling. 'But... But pizza?' Ham-and-mushrooming it up.

'Remember: the road to redemption is paved with little victories.' He let go of the handrails and stepped past her.

Tufty slunk back, out of his way. Watching as the detective chief inspector disappeared up the stairs.

Then his voice echoed down from the floor above. 'And no more séances!'

Tufty waited until the sound of a door shutting rang out. 'So... We still can has pizza?'

Steel sagged. 'Sodding hell.'

III

The police van rattled and squeaked its way past a big red-brick building with a pagoda sticking out the middle of it.

Tufty indicated right and drifted the van into the turning lane. Waiting for the traffic on the other side of the dual carriageway to open up.

Sitting in the passenger seat, Steel had her feet up on the dashboard, digging away at some itchy spot at the back of one knee.

The Proclaimers sang away on the radio, boasting about how many miles they'd walk for the honour of collapsing, knackered, outside someone's front door – when surely it would make a lot more sense to just *drive* over there, leaving you with plenty of energy for a nice cup of tea, a fondant fancy, and a bit of frisky naughty business.

But it was fun to hum along to.

Steel held up a hand. 'Warrant?'

DC Barrett scooted forward in his seat, bringing with him a waft of aftershave mixed with cheese-and-onion. He held out a sheet of paper. 'Signed, sealed, and dated.' In the rear-view mirror he looked bigger than he was. Blond, snubbed nose. Prominent ears. A bit more overbite than was healthy in a grown man.

'Thanks Davey.' She stuck the warrant in her pocket without so much as a glance. 'Now, anyone set on doing a formal recap of the *whole* plan, or can we just get on with the important bits?'

Right, then up the hill and over the railway bridge.

The van was fitted out with a cage at the back for ferrying the very naughty from arrest to the station. In front of that were two rows of seats, facing each other. And when Barrett sat back down again, Harmsworth and DC Lund were revealed in the mirror. Harmsworth looking like someone had just told him he had twenty-four hours to live, but all the shops were shut. And Lund looking like someone's mum had gone on a fitness kick and then fell asleep at the hairdresser's.

Tufty drove into a big housing estate of terraced council flats, built in the standard Aberdeen configuration: blocks of six, sharing a front door, stitched together in a long, featureless row. The front doors had been painted in jaunty primary colours, but the buildings themselves wore a coat of faded dirty white.

Barrett consulted his clipboard. 'Thirteen Froghall Crescent – address supplied by one Charles Roberts when questioned about the large quantity of stolen mobile phones in his possession at time of arrest. Flat's owner is one Miss Harriet Ellis, currently residing in a residential care home in Portlethen. Early onset dementia. No relation to young Master Roberts. And I couldn't find any next of kin for her on the system, so the place is probably being used as a squat.'

Lund leaned forward. 'Dogs?'

'Not that we know of. But I'm definitely taking my can of Bite Back with me.'

'Yeah... Bags being the one to batter down the door. You three can charge in and get bitten first.'

Harmsworth groaned. '*I* should go last. It's not my fault dogs find me extra tasty.'

'Tough.' Lund picked up a riot helmet from the seat next to her and held it out, upside down to Steel. Little bits of blue and red paper were just visible in there.

Another right and Tufty pulled onto a street where the terraces gave way to twin rows of squat granite semis with tiny front gardens. Some paved over to provide off-road parking.

'Are we ready?' Steel turned and rummaged in the helmet, one hand covering her eyes. She came out with two bits – unfolded and peered at them. Held them out at arm's length to get them into focus. 'Right. Today's expletive of choice is…'

Tufty gave a little drum roll on the steering wheel. 'Tant-ta-ta-taaaaa!'

'"Motherfunker." And if something's good it's, "Snake-alicious."'

Another groan from Grumpy Harmsworth. 'Oh not *again*.'

Barrett nodded. 'Got to love the classics.'

'Why can we never have the ones I suggested?'

'Because the ones you suggested are crap.'

Tufty tightened his grip on the steering wheel. 'And three. Two. One!' He jammed his foot down on the accelerator and the Maria surged forward, then a hard left brought the front wheels up onto the pavement outside a semidetached with an overgrown front garden and all the curtains drawn.

He slammed on the brakes before they hit the short brick wall.

Flicked off his seatbelt.

And, 'Go! Go! Go!'

Steel hit him. 'Hey, *I* say that!'

Too late. Harmsworth lunged, snatched the riot helmet

from Steel's hands and stuck it on his head, bits of paper flying free. Barrett hauled open the big sliding door and Lund jumped out. Then Barrett. Then Harmsworth – grabbing a riot shield on his way, strapping it on as he ran. Tufty joined them, charging up the path to the front door.

But Steel just popped out into the afternoon sun and leaned against the van, hands in her pockets.

Lund got to the house first. Squared up to the door with the Big Red Door Key and swung it back while Barrett and Harmsworth flattened themselves against the wall to either side.

She grinned. 'Hot potato!'

The mini battering ram slammed into the door, just below the handle. A solid crack morphed into a *BOOM* as the whole thing burst inward, taking most of the frame with it.

She ducked back out of the way and Harmsworth pushed past, shield up.

'POLICE! NOBODY MOVE!'

Barrett hopped in after him, followed by Lund and tail-end Tufty. Because the better part of valour is not getting your nadgers bitten off.

The hallway stank of rancid cheese – probably coming from the knee-high stack of filthy trainers piled up against the shabby wallpaper. Crayon graffiti laced its way around and overhead, complete with stick figures. Some of whom seemed to have been based on a naked Pamela Anderson. Junk mail made a slippery mat on the lino.

Lund took the first door on the right, bursting through with her truncheon out. 'EVERYONE DOWN NOW!'

Barrett barged into a room on the left. 'POLICE!'

And at the far end of the hall, Harmsworth kicked the door open and lunged inside. 'YOU! ON THE FLOOR! I SAID— AAAARGH! MOTHERFUNKER!'

Oh crap...

Tufty legged it, slithering over the junk-mail slick and into a kitchen that looked like it hadn't been cleaned in months. Harmsworth lay in the middle of the filthy floor, hands clasped over his eyes. Bright-red stains covered his skin, his shirt rapidly turning a very dark pink.

The back door hung open, and through the gap came a flash of someone legging it. Male, six foot, dressed in cargo pants and a green Action-Man jumper. Crew cut. He snatched a look over his shoulder, showing off a short Vandyke and a worried expression.

Tufty turned and bellowed back into the house, 'OFFICER DOWN! REPEAT, OFFICER DOWN!'

Then leapt over Harmsworth's whimpering body and thumped out into the back garden.

Action Man had already crossed the yellowed patchy grass – clambering over the fence into the garden of the house behind this one.

'POLICE! COME BACK HERE!' Tufty cleared the garden in eight strides and leapt, swinging himself over the fence and into a much nicer space with fruit trees and patio furniture.

Where was… There: Action Man, he'd nipped down the side of the house, shoving out through a full-height gate towards the front.

Oh no you don't.

A burst of speed and Tufty was only six, seven feet behind him.

BANG, through the gate and out onto the driveway.

A young woman in a yellow summer dress was frozen in the middle of unloading an armful of shopping from the boot of a little hatchback. Staring at the two men charging towards her.

Action Man grabbed her arm and sent her spinning, practically throwing her right at Tufty.

She hit with a squeal and down they both went, crashing to the lock-block in a clattering hail of tins and packets. They rolled to a halt against the grey harling wall. Which was when she started slapping him. 'Get off me, you pervert! HELP, POLICE!'

Thunk – that was a car door slamming. Then the engine roared into life.

Tufty struggled free, just in time to see Action Man stick the car in gear and look back over his shoulder. The hatchback's tyres screeched and it jerked backwards, off the driveway in a cloud of blue smoke… *BANG* – right into the side of a Volvo parked on the other side of the street.

A piercing shriek filled the air: the Volvo's car alarm screaming in indignation, hazard lights flashing.

Then the sound of grinding gears and the hatchback lurched forwards again, just as Tufty reached the kerb, swinging round and— Too close! Too close! He jumped back and the bumper snatched at the leg of his trousers. Missed by about half an inch. Then away, engine and tyres squealing in protest.

Miss Sundress staggered into the road beside him. 'Come back with my car, you bastard!' She grabbed up a fallen tin of beans and hurled it after the departing hatchback. But it fell too short, buckling against the tarmac as the car screamed down the road, round the corner, and out of sight.

'Can you smell that?' Barrett looked up from his clipboard. 'For some reason, I've got a strange craving for stovies.'

Harmsworth scowled at him. 'Oh ha, ha. Very funny. Let's make jokes at poor Owen's expense.'

The living room was … OK, it was a hovel. Piles of pizza boxes on the floor, heaps of shoplifted clothes in the corner – most with the security tags still on. A carpet that… Aye, well, probably best no' to think about what made it so *sticky*.

But for all the overwhelming mank they had an impressive collection of kit. A huge TV and just about every games console going. Roberta settled into the leather couch, arms along the back. Probably the only clean thing in the entire house.

Harmsworth dabbed at his face with a towel again, turning more of it scarlet. 'You're all horrible to me.'

'We do our best.' Barrett noted down the details of another iPad, sealed it into an evidence bag, then placed it into one of his blue plastic evidence crates. Happy as a wee squirrel, gathering nuts for winter.

The boy, Tufty, was on the phone again, standing in the corner with one finger in his ear. Presumably to stop his brain from falling out that side. 'Yeah. …. Yeah, OK, thanks.' He hung up. Pulled a constipated face. 'Nothing from the lookout request.'

Roberta shook her head. 'Motherfunker…'

'Hmph.' Harmsworth made a big thing of wiping his eyes. 'I'm *fine*, by the way. Thanks for asking.'

Barrett slipped a mobile phone into another bag. 'Got to be thousands and thousands of quids' worth here.'

'Not as if someone tried to *blind* me or anything.'

Then Lund's dulcet tones came screeching down from somewhere upstairs 'SARGE? SARGE, YOU BETTER COME SEE THIS!'

No thanks.

Roberta stretched out a bit. Enjoying the farty squeak of the leather.

'SARGE, I'M SERIOUS!'

Wonderful.

She hauled herself up from the couch's leathery embrace and stepped around the soggy pink figure of Harmsworth. 'Don't be such a crybaby, Owen. He chucked a jar of beetroot at you, no' sulphuric acid.'

'Pickle vinegar really stings!'

'Blah, blah, blah.' She slouched out of the manky living room and up the manky stairs to a manky landing decorated with more stick-figure-porn graffiti.

Lund poked her head out of a room at the end. 'Sarge?'

'Why can no bugger do anything without me holding their hand?'

But Lund just ducked back inside again.

'Swear to God...' Roberta dragged herself down to the end of the landing and into a bedroom that stank of socks and sweat and something a bit sweet and funky smelling. Cannabis hiding beneath the BO.

Five single mattresses were lined up on the floor: some with duvets, some with sleeping bags. All surrounded by drifts of dirty clothes.

A built-in wardrobe with mirrored doors took up nearly the whole wall opposite the curtained windows. Lund was hunkered down in front of it, peering in through a gap between two of the sliding doors.

'You better no' be coiling one out there, Veronica. You're no' in Elgin now.'

Lund held out a hand to the wardrobe, voice low and gentle. 'It's OK. No one's going to hurt you.'

Roberta frowned, then shuffled around till she could see what Lund was looking at.

Oh...

Two wee boys cowered in the wardrobe, between the coats and things. The pair of them *filthy*, wearing nothing but grubby T-shirts and grubbier underpants. Five, maybe six years old? Poor wee sods.

She crouched down next to Lund. 'Hey, guys, are you OK? Want to come see your Aunty Roberta? We've come to take you home to your mummies.'

The wee boys didn't say anything. Then one of them

33

reached out, took hold of the wardrobe door and slid it closed. Leaving Lund and Roberta staring at their own reflections.

Great.

The back garden looked like the kind of place plants went to die. And then get widdled on. Nowhere to sit. So Roberta turned a bucket over and sat on that instead. A modern-day version of Oor Wullie, only much sexier.

She took a long draw on her e-cigarette, dribbling the vapour down her nose as she chased an itchy bit around her left armpit. Mobile phone clamped between her ear and shoulder. 'No, they're no' saying. But the snottery one in the SpongeBob T-shirt's got a Belfast accent, so maybe no' even local.'

'*Hmmm...*' DCI Rutherford sounded a bit distracted, as if he had something more important to do. Tosser. '*You'd think someone would miss a five-year-old boy...*' The clickity sound of a keyboard being fingered rattled out of the earpiece. '*We've got nine missing children in Aberdeen-slash-Aberdeenshire right now: four girls, five boys. Six of them "allegedly" abducted by a parent. Remaining three are early teens.*'

'Social Services are on the way. Maybe if we get them cleaned up and photographed...?' Roberta rubbed at her eyes as the weight of it all dragged her shoulders down another inch. 'Wee kids, hiding in a wardrobe.'

'*We just have to do what we can.*'

She took the e-cigarette out of her mouth and spat into the yellowy grass. 'Yeah. Suppose so.'

Didn't make it feel any better, though.

CHAPTER TWO

in which it is a Braw, Bricht, Moonlicht Nicht
and Tufty Has a Clever – and then a bath

I

Steel stopped on the stairs for a scratch. 'Will you stop whinging?'

Division Headquarters was surprisingly quiet for a change. Peaceful. Probably because everyone else – all the *lucky* people – had actually managed to go home.

Tufty peered over the stack of evidence bags, shifted the large plastic crate in his arms. Biceps already wobbling with the strain. 'This weighs a ton!'

'Whinge, whinge, whinge, whinge, whinge.' She gave up on the scratch and started up the stairs again. 'And when you've signed that lot in, you can sit down with Lund and get an e-fit done. I want to know who our kidnappy scumbag is.'

He groaned.

Sergeant McRae was right – the woman was a nightmare.

He manoeuvred the heavy evidence crate around the half-landing, puffing. 'Shift ended two hours ago...'

Steel paused at the top of the flight of stairs. 'You're no' in uniform any more, Dorothy; CID doesn't go home till the job's done. And just for that, when you've finished the e-fit you can...' Her eyes bugged, mouth hanging open as she stared at something Tufty couldn't see.

'What?' He struggled up beside her.

She was staring at the double doors that led off to the third floor. Muffled voices came from the other side.

Then one of the doors *twitched*.

'Quick!' Steel grabbed him, hustling them both into a room just off the stairwell.

She stood there, one eyebrow raised as the trough urinal along one wall flushed, fresh water glistening across the suspicious limescale streaks that striped the stainless steel. The sound echoed around the gents' toilet. A row of cubicles lined the wall opposite the trough, a row of sinks down the middle. That eye-nipping smell of urinal cakes and ancient piddle. 'Oh.'

She didn't… Did she? Was this supposed to be some sort of *sex* thing? Dragging him into the gents to have her wicked way with him?

Noooooooooo!

Not that she wasn't – well, let's be honest she *really* wasn't – but it was still sexual harassment!

Tufty backed off a couple of paces. 'Er… It… I mean, I'm flattered and I'm sure you're a lovely—'

She slapped a hand over his mouth. Stared at the toilet door.

Which began to open.

'Eek!' She dragged him and his box backwards, thumping open a cubicle door and shoving him inside. Squeezed in there with him and swung the door shut, catching it at the last moment so it wouldn't bang.

Her body was warm, pressed against him like that – the toilet roll holder digging into the small of his back.

He opened his mouth to complain but she just tightened her grip on his face and pulled panicked faces.

'Shhhh!'

A voice bounced back and forth against the tiles outside their cubicle. *'Inspector McRae.'*

And then the Sarge's voice: *'Charlie.'*

Well, not 'Sarge' any more, not since the promotion, but old habits and all that.

Piddling noises joined the echo chamber.

Steel adopted a hissing whisper, the words barely audible. 'What the hell is *he* doing here? Supposed to be in Bucksburn with the rest of his Satan-worshipping mates!'

Tufty tried for: 'I don't think you're being very fair to Sergeant McRae,' but all that came out was, 'Mmmphnnn, gnnnnphnnn innng, pfffnnnnggg,' muffled by her hand. And where was that weird garlicky-onion taste coming from?

Steel shook her head. 'Well, I don't know, do I?'

Someone's phone burst into an upbeat ringtone.

McRae answered it. *'Hello? … Hi, Susan. … Yes, looking forward to it. Erm, will* she *be there?'*

OK, another go: please get your stinky oniony hand off my mouth. 'Mmnnff, ffnnnphm mnnnnfffnn nnnnnnffn mmmmnf ff mmnnfff.'

She shrugged, keeping her voice low. 'Well … look on the bright side: at least he's no' in the cubicle next to us making smells. Bloody place stinks like a dead tramp's Y-fronts as it is.'

'No, not a problem for me, but you know how she gets. … Yeah.'

'Mmnph?'

Steel glowered at him. 'Don't you dare!'

A hand dryer roared, drowning everything else out. Then *clunk*, the door closed.

Steel peeled her oniony hand from Tufty's mouth. 'Is he gone?'

Urgchhhh. He machine-gunned out a barrage of teeny spits. 'Your hands taste horrible!'

She stuck her ear against the cubicle door, just next to a

bit of biro graffiti about what a lovely bottom some PC named Mackintosh had. 'Maybe we'd better wait a bit? Just in case.'

He shifted his grip on the evidence crate. 'Listen, while we're here—'

'Don't care what freaky sexual fantasy you've got, the answer's no.'

'Shudder!' He shook his head. 'No: the Blackburn Onanist – I've been thinking. They say the events are all random, right? But I has a clever!'

'Shhh!' She slapped a hand over his mouth again. 'Was that the door? Did you hear the door?'

He wriggled free. 'The first time he goes out for a wank, he has another one the very next day. Then it's twenty-five days till he does it again. Then twenty-eight days. Then seven—'

'All right, Rain Man.'

'—Then sixteen. Then one. Then eleven— Ow!'

The rotten sod hit him.

Steel's voice went back to its smoky whisper. 'There's someone out there!'

He copied her, so quiet even *he* could barely hear it. 'Then sixteen, then one, then six—'

And again with the oniony hand, squeezing his cheeks so he couldn't escape this time.

The cubicle door swung open and there was Inspector Evans, with a copy of the *Racing Post* tucked under one arm. A look of horror spread across his face. 'What the *hell* are you doing in here?'

Steel let go of Tufty's face, reached out, and grabbed the door. 'Do you mind? I've got this meeting room booked till seven.' Then pulled it shut again and snibbed on the lock.

'*Hello?*'

'Anyway...' Tufty gave up on the whispering. 'There was

this article in *New Scientist* about some new open-source pattern recognition software they're using to re-examine the data from the Large Hadron Collider – which is completely super cool – and I thought, why not apply it to the Blackburn wanking dates?'

She sighed at him. 'I need a big success, Tufty, no' a bunch of wee kid shoplifters. No' some pervert playing slap-the-Womble in other people's back gardens. A *big* success.'

Inspector Evans's voice took on an imperious tone. '*I insist you come out of there this instant!*'

'Yeah, but listen: I modelled the whole sequence with the days and dates. He never plays with himself on a Monday or Wednesday, or at the weekend.'

'Do you have any idea how hard it is to work your way back up to detective chief inspector?'

'And he's got these blocks where nothing happens at all. So I thinks to myself, "What if he's a shift worker?" Eh?'

Evans knocked on the door, rattling it. '*You can't be in here, this is the gents!*'

Steel bared her teeth. 'Use another cubicle, this one's occupied!'

'*Right, that's it – I'm calling Professional Standards. We'll see what* they *say about this.*'

She opened the door and stepped out. 'OK, OK, we were just leaving anyway.' Snapped her fingers. 'Detective Constable Quirrel: heel!'

Inspector Evans stared after them. Then ruffled his copy of the *Racing Post*, shuddered, and stepped into another cubicle.

Tufty dumped the evidence crate alongside the other ones – pretty much covering the creaky desk in the corner. 'So, anyway: if it's just him working shifts it'd be a more straight-forward pattern, wouldn't it?'

Did the wee sod *never* shut up?

The CID office had all the charm of a cat with diarrhoea: the paintwork peeling from the walls and woodwork, the carpet tiles an archaeological record of every spilled cup of tea and coffee going back decades. Half the ceiling tiles were missing too, showing off an impressive collection of spiders' webs, speckled with teeny black fly carcases.

Wasn't like this when she was a detective chief inspector, was it. No, course it sodding wasn't. Office of her own. A coffee machine that worked. A window you could crack open if you fancied a crafty cigarette. All the minions stuffed into a different room so they weren't underfoot and asking stupid questions the whole time.

Roberta pulled on her coat. Keys. Keys. Keys… Where the hell were her keys? 'Have you seen my keys?'

'There wouldn't be all this numerical variation to the pattern.'

'Who moved my keys? Why does everyone have to fiddle with things?'

'But what if there's someone else in the house who works nights sometimes? And *that's* when he slips out to bash Uncle Bulgaria. Spank Madame Cholet. Tug the Tobermory.'

There they were! Hiding under that stack of crime statistics she was technically supposed to have finished last week. 'Do you *never* shut up?' She stuck them in her pocket along with various bits, bobs, and her phone. Which made a *ding-ding* noise as soon as she picked it up.

A text message from Susan:

Come home, Roberta. Don't do this again.

J&N need to see their father.

Humph… She wasn't stopping them, was she? No. She was being nice and staying away. If anything Susan should be thanking her for *no'* coming home and ramming one of those golf trophies right up Logan Sodding McRae's backside.

Tufty still hadn't taken the hint. 'Our wanky little friend did it last night. And I'll bet you a fish supper he does it again tonight. We can catch him pink-handed!'

She scowled at him. 'It's red-handed, you neep. *Red*-handed.'

'Nah, think about what he'll be holding, Sarge. We're only going to catch him red-handed if he's squeezing *really* hard.'

Idiot.

And why was it suddenly *her* fault? She wasn't the one who'd clyped to Professional Standards. She wasn't the traitorous bastard.

'Sarge? Are you all right? Only you look like something's just thrown up in your mouth.'

'Being a sperm donor doesn't count.'

He stared at her. 'O – K…?'

She thumbed out a reply on her phone:

I'll be late home. Got a pervert to catch.

Then stuck it in her pocket. Sniffed. 'Go down to the desk and book out a pool car. We'll see if you owe me a fish supper or no'.'

Steel curled her top lip, shifting in the passenger seat, elbows in, hands curled so she wouldn't touch anything. 'Could you no' have picked a cleaner one?'

'This was all they had. And you're welcome.' Though, to be fair, the pool car was a bit of a tip. It rustled with discarded crisp packets, chocolate wrappers, biscuit packets, polystyrene takeaway containers, paper bags from Burger King and McDonald's, crushed Irn-Bru tins, Coke, Fanta, ginger beer… They littered the footwells and piled up on the back seat. And crumbs – crumbs *everywhere*.

'Hmph.' She crossed her arms and stared at her own reflection in the passenger window. Ungrateful lump.

Woods reared up to the right of the dual carriageway, its greenery burnished with gold and amber as the sun sank its way down to a hazy horizon. A patchwork quilt of fields, stitched together with drystane dykes, blanketed the land. The pointy bits of Bennachie just visible in the distance.

Tufty snuck a look at his sulky passenger. 'Er, Sarge?'

Grunt.

'I kinda noticed ... you're avoiding Inspector McRae?'

She crossed her arms even tighter, putting a bit more freckly cleavage on show, and grunted again.

'Only, I worked with him for what, two and a half years? And he was a good boss. A bit obsessed with his cat, and God knows he could put away the lentil soup, but he stood his hand in the pub. Didn't play favourites.' Shrug. 'He's a good guy.'

'Don't make me wash your mouth out with soap and water, Constable.'

'He always said nice things about *you*.' Sort of. If you didn't count all the horror stories.

'Because I will if you don't shut up.'

Ah. Fair enough.

He cleared his throat. 'OK, so you want to know how I *know* the Blackburn Womble-Spanker's going to spank again tonight?'

She turned and scowled at him. 'And for your information: Logan Scumbag McRae can away and crap in his hat. Then wear it.'

Roberta sat forward and rubbed a clear patch in the fogged-up passenger window. Scowled out at the identikit houses. No' one hundred percent identical, but imperfect clones of each other. With grey harled bits, stonework details, grey tiled roofs. New enough for the gardens to still look as if they'd just been planted yesterday.

She sighed. 'Bored.'

'I wanted to play I Spy, but noooo, that was too childish.'
Tufty didn't even look up from his mobile phone. Just sat
there like an idiot playing some stupid game – it binged
and wibbled to a backdrop of irritating plinky-plonky music.
'And when I *tried* to discuss quantum chromodynamics,
suddenly quarks and gluons were "stupid and boring". Do
you remember that bit? Because—'

She hit him. 'Where is he then? The World's Wiliest
Womble Walloper?'

More bings and wibbles. 'Patience, Grasshopper.'

'And it's cold. Cold and boring.' Roberta thumped back
into her seat. Then did it again. Like a petulant teenager.
Hamming it up with a big long-suffering sigh.

Should've brought a book.

She folded her arms. Unfolded them again.

It killed five or ten seconds.

Gah…

Roberta poked a finger at the dashboard, making a dull
thunking sound. 'You know what? We should go visit every
house he's wanked outside. At least then we could scam a
cup of tea and a bit of a warm. Maybe even a biscuit or two?'

Roberta dunked her Jaffa Cake in her tea. Bone china,
believe it or no', the tea poured from a pot, with milk in a
wee jug. Biscuits in a porcelain dish. Very swish.

It was a nice wee conservatory. Right at the back of the
house, it had a view out over stubble fields, angled just right
to catch the setting sun. All reds and yellows. Blue shadows
reaching out from the drystane dykes. A comfy set of
couches flanked a glass-topped coffee table artfully littered
with the kind of magazines normally reserved for dentists'
waiting rooms. A couple of wicker chairs with chintzy
cushions.

Mrs Rice sat in one of them, fiddling with the pearls

around her throat. Couldn't have been a day over thirty and she was *actually* wearing a twinset to go with it. Pastel blue. As if she was ninety. She shifted, making the wicker groan. 'Honestly, I didn't know where to look. Standing right there in the back garden ... *pleasuring* himself.' She pointed out at the manicured lawn and shuddered. 'We had to throw the garden gnomes out in the end. I couldn't bear to look at them *leering*.'

Tufty nodded, making a note in his book. Swot. 'And he was...' He stared at Roberta as she licked the chocolate off to get at the orangey bit in the middle. 'Sorry. And you say he was wearing a superhero mask?'

Mrs Rice pulled a face. 'About all he *was* wearing. I ask you, when you're making spaghetti Bolognaise for four, is that really what you want to see through your kitchen window? Spider-Man playing with himself?'

Another note went in Tufty's book. 'And did he...?' A euphemistic hand gesture. 'You know?'

'What?'

Thick as two shorts.

Probably better help the poor thing. Roberta leaned forward and put a chocolaty hand on her knee. 'Did he arrive? Did he succeed in his endeavour? Did he finish his fun?' A wink. 'Did he squirt his filthy man-mayonnaise all over your begonias?'

Mrs Rice stared back, horrified.

Roberta popped the remaining half biscuit in her mouth. 'Cos if he did, then my constable here can scoop it up and we'll run some tests. Maybe find out who your saucy wee friend is.'

'Oh...' Her face curdled for a moment, then she forced an unconvincing smile and reached for the pot. 'Oh. Er... More tea?'

* * *

The kitchen was minuscule, nearly every flat surface covered in carrier bags and boxes of cereal and plates and pots and pans. More carrier bags on the floor.

Mrs Morden shook her head and poured boiling water into four mugs, sending up the burnt-toast scent of cheap instant coffee. Her tracksuit looked nearly as tired as she did.

Tufty shuffled his feet in one of the few patches of clear linoleum. Pen poised.

'Urgh…' She stirred the burnt brown liquid with a fork. 'Well, it's not every day you see the Caped Crusader having a batwank in your back garden, is it? The security lights came on and everything.'

The kitchen spotlights glittered back from the polished black granite worktops. Oak units. Slate tiles on the floor.

A man in jeans, a Jeremy-Corbyn-as-Che-Guevara T-shirt, and flip-flops handed Steel a mug of tea. 'Yeah, he was wearing this Incredible Hulk mask. Only the Incredible Hulk is meant to be big and green. And he was neither.' A wink. '*If* you know what I mean.'

Kids' toys littered the living room: Lego, Night Garden, SpongeBob, Transformers, My Little Ponies, balls, ray guns, teddy bears… Mrs Allsop wrapped her arms around herself and shuddered as Steel helped herself to yet another Penguin biscuit. 'Oh it was horrible.'

Tufty nodded. 'I know. I'm sorry, but you say he was wearing a mask?'

II

Tufty checked his notebook, with his back to the lay-by, reading by the pool car's headlights. 'So: that's one Incredible Hulk; one Iron Man; three Spider-Mans ... Spider-Men? no, definitely Spider-Mans; an Asterix the Gaul; two Batmans; one of "those horrible Ninja Turtle things"; and, for some unknown reason, a Peppa Pig too.'

The car's engine was running, radio on, volume turned up, newsreader booming out her local reports, but it still couldn't cover the disturbing sounds coming from the bushes at the side of the road.

Steel groaned. 'Oooooh... that's better.'

'*...outside the Music Hall from six tomorrow.*'

'Oooooohhhhh... Bit steamy, mind.'

Urgh. The shudder rippled all the way through Tufty wearing cloggity boots. 'Too much information!'

'*Complaints are pouring in after farmers threatened to bring Union Street to a halt this weekend in protest against the proposed changes to farm subsidy payments.*'

'Should've nicked some toilet paper from that last place.'

A man's voice growled from the car's speakers. '*We're sorry it's had to come to this, but the government's left us no choice. If farming's going to survive in this country, we need this sorted now!*'

Tufty stared straight ahead. 'Could you not have just gone when we were there?'

And the newsreader was back. *'Finally, miscarriage of justice victim, Jack Wallace, is to sue Police Scotland for what he calls its gross negligence and culture of lies.'*

'Oh don't be such a girl, Tufty. The bladder wants what the bladder wants.' Steel emerged from the bushes, wiping her hands on her trousers. 'Better out than in.' She froze, staring at the car as Jack Wallace came on the radio.

'The only way Police Scotland are ever going to change is if we, the people, stand up and sue them. They think they can get away with murder and I'm here to say, "No, you can't!"'

Steel snarled at the car. 'Dirty wee shite.'

The newsreader took over again. *'Police Scotland have declined to comment at this time. Weather now, and there's sunshine on the way this weekend as high pressure...'*

'Turn it off.'

Blackburn glittered in the darkness – ribbons of yellow streetlight coiling around each other, windows glowing as people settled down to a night in front of the telly. All visible through the windscreen of their wheelie-bin pool car, parked on the outskirts of the dormitory town. Only 'town' was stretching it a bit. If you sneezed while driving through the place you'd miss half of it.

Roberta let out a long, slow breath. Sod this for a game of soldiers.

She took her feet off the dashboard. 'I'm calling it. This was a complete waste of time. Why on earth did I listen to you?' A quick backhand to the arm had him flinching. '*You* are a detective constable of Very Little Brain!'

'Ow! Hey, no fair...'

She was gearing up to hit him again, when her phone launched into the theme tune from *Cagney & Lacey*. The caller ID was enough to make everything taste bitter and coppery. Like sucking on a dirty penny. 'Traitor Bastard'.

Tufty pointed. 'You going to answer that?'

'How did you work out tonight was wanking night?'

'Might be important.'

She turned in her seat to face him. 'It's no' important. It's that tosser McRae.'

'Oh… OK. Well, when I figured out there was probably *two* shift patterns involved I put one set on one side and one set on the other and shoogled them about till there was a match with the nights he… I thought you wanted to know this?'

Roberta stared past him, through the driver's window at a little path that snaked away from the road, skirting the back gardens at the edge of Blackburn. There was a shape in the darkness, just visible in the pale grey moonlight that oozed its way through the clouds. A figure, picking its way through the gloom. 'Over there. By the trees.'

Something must've triggered the security light in the garden beyond, because it cracked on.

The figure froze. A man, middle-aged, paunchy, parka jacket with the hood pulled up. Two steps and he was in the gloom again.

Roberta narrowed her eyes. 'He look suspicious to you?'

Course he did.

She declined the call on her phone and stuffed it in her pocket. Clambered from the car. Closed the door without making a sound.

Her breath fogged around her head.

Tufty got out of the driver's side and joined her. Standing there in plain view like a vast twit. At least he was bright enough to keep his voice down: 'What now?'

The guy in the parka jacket was hunched over, fiddling with something at groin height.

She whispered, nice and quiet. 'Think I owe you a fish supper.'

They crept across the road, sticking to the cover of the whin bushes that grew like massive rustling beasts along the pavement. Closer. Closer.

What was he fiddling with? Please be his willy. Please be his willy...

The moon broke through the clouds – full, heavy, and round – casting its ghostly light over everything.

Closer...

Then her phone launched into *Cagney & Sodding Lacey* again.

The wee man gave a little squeak, flashed a glance over his shoulder at them, then *ran*.

Tufty jumped up from his crouch. 'Come back here!'

Idiot.

She hit him again. 'Don't just stand there!'

He lurched into a run, giving chase. Getting faster with every stride.

That was more like it.

She hammered after him, following their pervert across the road, away from the streetlights and back gardens. Over a drystane dyke and into a stubble field. Into the brown, heavy scent of wet earth that squelched beneath her feet.

Moonlight turned the world into a shadow play – silhouettes in shades of blue and grey, the trees: spidery ink blots. Shining patches of silver where puddles reflected back the lunar glow.

The masturbating wee turd had a head start and he was fast, but Tufty was faster. Closing the gap.

Water sploshed up Roberta's leg as she charged through a hidden puddle. 'Gahhh!' Cold. *And* wet. Slippery too.

A handful of sheep stopped doing whatever it was sheep

did at half nine on a Monday night to watch the three of them squelch past. Tufty almost on him. Roberta bringing up the rear. 'Sodding horrible, muddy, clarty, slippy...'

The filthy sod jinked left, then right, just as Tufty made a grab for him.

Tufty's hands closed on sod-all. A brief squeak of terror, and he windmilled his arms, trying to stay upright. Then went splattering down in a dark muddy patch, skidding to a halt flat on his back with his arms and legs in the air like a tipped-over tortoise. 'Aaaaargh!'

The pervert glanced back at the muddy scream, which was why he didn't see her cut right in front of him, one hand out to snatch at the parka's hood. She grabbed a handful of furry collar and dug in her heels.

'Ulk!' His feet kept going forward, but the rest of him stayed where it was, suspended in mid-air for a breath ... before slamming down into the mud with a wet squelchy *thump*. Right on his backside at Roberta's feet.

She loomed over him, grinning. 'Your Womble Whapping days are over, sunshine!'

Tufty dragged their prisoner back across the squelchy field, over the drystane dyke, across the road, and under a streetlight. Ooh, yeah. Tufty was *filthy*. No' just a wee bit grubby, but completely and utterly clarted in mud. All up his back. And most of his front. Kind of a funky smell about him too...

Roberta gave him a sniff, then recoiled – wafting a hand in front of her face. 'Aye, don't take this the wrong way, but I think you fell in more than just mud.'

He grimaced, looking down at his filthy, filthy self. 'Argh...'

Under the streetlight, their prisoner emerged from the shadow of his parka's hood. No' exactly George Clooney.

No' even George Clooney's ugly brother. A forgettable wee man with a forgettable face and squint glasses.

Roberta fluttered her eyelashes at him. 'Do you come here often? Pun intended.'

The nasty wee wanker drew himself up to his full five-foot-four and stuck his chin out. 'Let go of me, or … or I'll call the *police!*'

'That's a coincidence: me and my sharny little friend here *are* the police.' She patted the whiny sod on his shiny cheek. 'Now, how can we help you? Having difficulty getting it up? Trouble deciding which house to wank outside?'

He pulled that forgettable chin in again. 'What?'

'We know it's you, sunshine. Now, let's get you down the station, into a cell, and onto the sex offenders' register.'

'But I haven't done anything!'

Tufty spun him around a half turn, so they were face to face. 'Oh yeah? Then why did you run?'

'It's the middle of the night and you were chasing me. Of *course* I ran. You could've been anyone.'

Tufty loomed. 'We're the *police.*'

'Well why didn't you say anything? I thought you were muggers.' He dug into his parka's pockets and came out with a dog lead and what looked like a filled plastic poo-bag. 'I was walking Sheba, and next thing I know I'm being attacked by you pair of maniacs!'

'Ah…'

Still, could be a ruse. She pointed at the bag. 'Detective Constable: examine the evidence.'

He stared at her. 'You're kidding.'

'Just give it a squeeze or something. Make sure it's really poo.'

'Oh for…' But he curled his lip and reached out anyway. Gave the bag a quick squeeze. 'Urgh, it's still *warm.*'

'I see.' Roberta cleared her throat and looked away. 'You were walking your dog?'

'And God knows where she's got to now. Greyhounds are *incredibly* sensitive.'

'Well, you can understand why we thought—'

'Probably spend half the night looking for her. Thank you *very* much.'

Roberta shuffled her feet. 'Yes. Well, no one's perfect, are they?' She straightened his jacket. Brushed a bit of mud off his shoulder. 'Still no harm done, eh?'

'I'm going to make a complaint, just you see if I don't!'

Of course he was.

'Oh joy.'

It just wasn't fair. Here she was, knocking her pan in, trying to make a difference, and what did she get? Lumbered with a mud-slathered idiot for a sidekick, a night stuck in a manky pool car that smelled like the inside of a wheelie-bin, and a complaint from a poo-gathering member of the public. Because she needed *more* complaints on her file, didn't she? Because there weren't enough on there already.

Pffffff…

Roberta groaned, letting one arm flop across her face. Lying draped across the back seat of the car, one leg dangling over the edge. Making rustling noises in the garbage with her boot.

Tufty had himself another whinge. 'Come on, it's freezing out here.'

'No' till you're dry. We're in enough trouble as it is without—'

Her phone launched into *Cagney & Lacey* again.

'Gah…' She pulled it out and peered at the screen.

Same caller ID as last time: 'TRAITOR BASTARD'.

The orchestra joined in with the tooty horns as the theme tune really got into its stride.

Tufty knocked on the car window. 'You're going to have to talk to him sometime.'

'Where did it all go wrong, Tufty?'

'Might have been when you tried to fit Jack Wallace up on kiddy-fiddling charges? Just a guess.'

'I'm in my prime here.'

'*Please* can I get back in the car? I can't feel my toes.'

'Arrrrgh!' She covered her face with both hands, as the phone belted out its tune. 'Should be catching killers and getting commendations and medals. Nothing snake-alicious ever happens to me...'

'Look, I'll answer it if you like?'

'I am *no'* talking to that back-stabbing, two-faced, Judas-licking ... motherfunker.'

The phone fell silent. Finally.

Ding-ding. Incoming text. She snuck a glance:

> I heard about Wallace suing Police Scotland.
> Do you want to talk about it? I'm still at yours.
> Logan.

No she sodding wouldn't. You're getting deleted, sunshine. Delete.

Then the car's police radio had a go. *'All units: anyone in the vicinity of Blackburn? Got reports of an unidentified individual performing a solo sex-act in the caller's back garden.'*

Ha!

She sat up, grabbed her phone before it disappeared into the drifts of crisp packets. 'We're on!'

Tufty jammed on the brakes and the patrol car screeched to a halt outside an identikit house at the end of an identikit street. He flicked off his seatbelt and jumped out into the night. Steel scrambled out of the passenger side, puffing after him as he sprinted up the driveway.

She grabbed the back of his muddy jacket and pointed. 'Go round the back: catch the bastard!'

He peeled away, running along the front of the house and around the side. A six-foot wooden fence blocked the way. Damn it: gate was locked too.

Two steps back, then lurch forward and jump … clambering over the top and dropping down into the back garden. The whole thing was lit up like a football pitch, a cordon of security lights blazing away. Tiny shed on one side, a collection of kids' plastic tat toys: Wendy house, tipper truck, swingset, a rocking horse in the shape of a dinosaur – all of it glowing in its Technicolor splendour.

A man stood on the other side of a rotary dryer, in a dressing gown, waving a spade, shouting over the back fence and into the darkness. 'AND THERE'S MORE WHERE THAT CAME FROM, YOU PERVERT FREAK!' He spun around and the dressing gown flared out, revealing a Darth Vader T-shirt and a pair of tartan jammie bottoms. Bared his teeth at Tufty. Then jabbed the spade at him like a rifle with bayonet fitted. 'Another one, eh? Come on then!'

Tufty skidded to a halt, hands up. 'Woah, woah. Police. I'm the police.'

Steel barged out through the kitchen door. 'Did you get him?'

Mr Spade grinned. 'Oh I got him all right.' He jiggled his spade, swinging it about. 'Right in the face. *Pang!*'

Tufty went for the back fence, foot on the centre rail, and up… Coming to a halt with one leg straddling the top.

The houses stretched away to the left, hiding behind their own timber fences, but on the right it was nothing but fields bathing in the moonlight. Sinister grey shapes moved across the stubble, their eyes gleaming like jackals'. Sinister sheep.

Sheeping sinisterly. But they were the only living things out there. No sign of anyone else.

Sod.

He hopped back down again. 'Gone.'

'Damn it!' Steel did a three-sixty, fists clenched. 'Mother*funker*!'

Mr Spade backed off, nostrils flaring as he grimaced at Tufty. 'What have you been rolling in?'

Steel grabbed at the guy's dressing gown. 'Did you recognise him? The man you hit?'

'He was wearing a mask. One of those cheap plastic kids' things.'

She let go of the dressing gown and snatched the spade off him instead. Holding it under the nearest security light, turning it back and forth. 'Can't *see* any blood. Might get some DNA off it, though.'

So close.

Tufty got out his notebook, flipping it open at the last marked page. Pen poised. 'Right, let's start at the beginning.'

III

The manky pool car was still slewed half on the road and half on the pavement. Steel slouched back against the bonnet, puffing away on her fake cigarette, making a fog bank all of her own. It gleamed like a solid thing in the moonlight.

Tufty's phone was warm against his ear, notebook pinned to the roof of the car. He wrote the word 'MAYBE' in it and underlined it three times. 'Yeah. OK. Thanks. Bye.' He hung up. 'Maud says she'll do her best, but the lab's backed up as it is.'

Steel pulled the e-cigarette from her mouth for long enough to spit in the gutter. 'Which is secret SEB code for "no' a chance in hell". Sod.'

'This still means you owe me a fish supper, though, right? I mean, I predicted he'd be out and about tonight. And, ta-daaaa!'

But Steel just stared off into the distance, eyebrows knitting away at something just inside her head. 'You fiddled about two shift patterns to work it out?'

About time she took an interest.

'Told you: I has a clever.' He leaned over the bonnet at her. 'It was pretty obvious he was on a two-week cycle, so probably works offshore. The tricky part was the *other* shift pattern, but then I had an even cleverer!'

She stared at him. 'Did your mum drop you on your head when you were a kid?'

That was the trouble with old people – no appreciation of popular culture.

'See, it had to be a really weird shift pattern to match up them being on nights while he does his thing. And the only shift pattern I could think of that's *that* screwed up is the one I had to do for three years up in Banff, back when I was divisional police officer. So…?'

A slow smile dawned as the penny dropped.

'He's living with a cop. Some spod in uniform's boyfriend is the Blackburn Womble Whacker!' Steel hauled out her phone and dialled, puffing away. 'Come on, come on, come— Ernie? How many uniform we got living in Blackburn? … Uh-huh.' She looked up at Tufty. 'He's got three.' Back to the phone. 'How many off duty tonight? … Two? Oh Ernie: you're a *sexy* wee fish, you know that, don't you? Now give me a name and address for the one who's working.'

The house wasn't as big and grand as the last one they'd visited, but it'd been squeezed out of a similar mould. Grey harling, stonework features around the windows, grey tiles on the roof. They'd put the effort in and planted a tree right in the middle of the teabag-sized front garden, though. It didn't look healthy.

Steel thumped her car door shut with a flourish. Then held her arms wide, beaming. 'Isn't it a lovely night?' She swaggered up the path, leaving a trail of vape behind her that glowed in the moonlight.

Woman was insane. But Tufty followed her anyway.

At the front door she gave a couple of hoppity-skippity dance steps then swept into a curtsey, one hand gesturing at the letterbox. 'If you would be so kind, my dearest Constable Quirrel?'

Completely crackers.

He rang the bell.

She rocked back and forth on her heels. Hands in her pockets. Grin on her face. 'Oh, the excitement!'

A shadow moved on the other side of the frosted glass pane set into the middle of the door. Then a muffled mushy voice joined it. *'Hello?'*

Steel pressed the doorbell again.

'This better not be Jehovah's Witnesses! I told you lot last time.' The door opened and there was Mr Parka, only he'd ditched the jacket for a Winnie-the-Pooh sweatshirt, boxer shorts, and slippers. He had a bag of frozen sweetcorn in one hand, holding it over his nose and mouth.

He took one look at them and his bloodshot eyes widened. 'Oh...'

Steel grinned at him. 'Mr Corbet? Mr *Alan* Corbet? Your wife's at work tonight, isn't she? Pounding the beat, while you're out pounding your meat.'

He lowered the sweetcorn, showing off two swollen lips and a pair of nostrils with toilet paper sticking out of them – bright red where it disappeared up inside his head. He licked his top lip, setting a crack bleeding again. 'It...' A deep breath, then Mr Parka stuck his chest out, chin up. 'Have you found my dog yet?'

Steel's grin got even wider.

Steel whistled a happy tune as she swaggered her way out of Interview Room Four, paused on the threshold and cast a wink back at the room's remaining occupants. 'I'll leave you two lovebirds alone for a minute. No inappropriate touching though, this is a family show.'

Alan Corbet sat on the other side of the interview table, the skin around his eyes darkening to a lovely shade of reddish-purple. Bottom lip trembling. Shoulders quivering.

He reached up with cuffed hands and wiped tears from his cheek.

Sitting next to him, his solicitor sighed and dug a hankie out of her suit pocket. Handed it over as Tufty closed the door.

Steel beamed. 'Oh, I *enjoyed* that.'

Tufty sagged and little flakes of dried mud tumbled from his filthy suit to the grey terrazzo floor. 'Can we go home now?'

'Don't be daft: it's time to celebrate!' She grabbed him by the shoulders like she was going in for a kiss, then cringed back a bit. Sniffed at her hands. 'Pfffff... On second thoughts, you really, *really* need a wash. Gah...' She wiggled her fingers, then wiped them on the wall. 'Just make sure you get Mr Corbet back to his cell, before—'

'ALAN!' An officer stormed up the corridor in full uniform kit, complete with stabproof vest, utility belt and high-viz waistcoat. Her hair pulled back in a severe ponytail. Face like the underside of a hammer as it whistles down towards a nail. 'Where is he, I'LL KILL HIM!'

Steel hissed at Tufty out the side of her mouth. 'Run away!'

Ahh... Water lapped across Tufty's chest, bringing a cloudscape of bubbles with it. Frothy white bubbles. Warm and lemony-scented. He reached out and picked his mug of tea off the toilet lid. Had a sip.

Bliss.

OK, so it wasn't the biggest bathroom in the whole world – wasn't the grandest either – but right now there was nowhere better. Four walls of off-white tiles, a medicine cabinet, a sink, a wee plastic doodah for holding your toothbrush, a heated towel rail, a toilet of his very own, and a bath. A lovely, luxurious, bubbly bath. Just the thing to share with an old friend.

Mr Einstein floated out from the cumulonimbus foam, orange beak first, followed by his tubby yellow body. Tail last to emerge from the bubbles.

'Hello, Mr Einstein.'

Tufty put on a high-pitched pirate voice. 'Arrrrr Jim lad. Ye better watch yerself, there be a vast scary beastie lurkin' in the water, right next to the hairy islands! Arrrrrrr...'

'Oh noes, Mr Einstein! What if it's – dan, dan daaaaaa! – the *Cockness Monster*? What if—'

The phone on the toilet lid buzzed, then launched into its generic ringtone.

'Ah ... bums.' He dried his hands on the towel lying by the bath and answered the thing. 'Hello?'

Steel's voice grumped out of the phone at him. *'For your information,* Constable, *I didn't fit Jack Wallace up. ... OK, so maybe I did, a little, on the paedophile charges, but he's still a raping scumbag, understand?'*

Great. Because Tufty wasn't allowed to have five minutes' peace, was he?

'I'm in the bath.'

'Four women. That's how many he brutalised. And we couldn't lay a finger on him for it. So yes, I fitted him up. Does that make me a bad person?'

'Well, *technically* '

'I mean, what was I supposed to do, let him get away with it? Let him attack more women? Is that what you want?'

Tufty shared a look with Mr Einstein, rolling his eyes and pulling a face. 'I didn't say anything! I'm an innocent bystander here. In the bath!'

'That's right, avoid the question. Just like a bloody man. And while we're at it: have you done that sodding e-fit yet?'

'What? *No.* We went out to Blackburn and caught—'

'For God's sake, Constable, do I have to do everything? I want that on my desk seven a.m. tomorrow morning!'

Silence.

She'd hung up.

Lovely.

Tufty put his phone down on the toilet lid, clutched Mr Einstein to his chest, and slowly sank below the bubbles. 'Motherfunker...'

And then there was nothing but foam.

Roberta scowled out through the windscreen. The sky licked at the roofs of the buildings – granite terrace on this side of the road, granite semis on the other. Trees making the whole place look quaint and olde-worlde. Sulphur-yellow streetlights painting it in shades of yellow and black. Like a wasp. Dangerous.

Her MX-5 was a lot tidier than the pool car, but then she wasn't a complete sodding pig.

She cracked the window, letting in the cool night air. A faint whiff of decomposing leaves oozed out from Victoria Park, down at the end of the street. A hint of roses from the garden she'd parked outside.

The house on the other side of the road was dark.

Expectant.

Waiting.

Her phone *ding*ed at her.

Susan:

> Roberta, please. He's gone. COME HOME!!!

She thumbed out a reply:

> Can't. Busy.

Ding-ding:

> You're not brooding outside Jack Wallace's house again, are you? We talked about this: it's not healthy. COME HOME!!!

Oh for God's sake...

'All right, all right.' She stuck the key in the ignition

and turned it. Sat there for a minute with the engine running.

Wherever Jack Wallace was, he wasn't here.

Just had to hope he wasn't off attacking some poor bloody woman somewhere. Because, right now, there was sod-all she could do about it.

One last glare, then Roberta put her MX-5 in gear and drove away into the night.

CHAPTER THREE

*in which we find out what happens when
you microwave a Small Yorkshire Terrier*

I

Tufty stifled a yawn.

Barrett was up at the whiteboard, droning on about something, everyone watching him. Lund and Harmsworth were at least *pretending* to pay attention – between slurps of coffee – but Steel just fiddled with her phone. The stack of evidence crates had migrated to the middle of the office carpet, hiding one of the many, many stains that called the CID office home.

Barrett took the cap off a red whiteboard marker. 'So remember, don't be afraid to shout.' Then underlined the words 'STRANGER DANGER!!!' 'And last, but not least...' He picked up a police cap off the desk and rummaged inside it, pulling out two bits of paper. One red, one blue. 'Right: our expletive of the day is "fudgemonkey", and if something's good it's, "Get down with your bad self". OK? OK.' He scribbled something on his beloved clipboard, then turned to Steel. 'Sarge?'

'Hmmmph?' A blink. 'Oh. Aye. We've still no' IDed the wee kids we found yesterday. But our very own Tufty came up with this.' She pointed at him.

Tufty held up the e-fit of the Action-Man wannabe he'd chased from the slum/squat yesterday. The one who'd nearly ran over him in a stolen hatchback. Really good likeness too. Which was even more impressive given that he'd been half asleep while putting the damn thing together.

Steel had a dig at her wrinkly cleavage. 'Anyone want to take a guess?'

'Yes.' Harmsworth put down his coffee cup. 'And I *know* no one cares what I think, but that looks like Kenny Milne to me.'

'Well done, Owen, ten points to Hufflepuff.'

He looked hurt. 'Hufflepuff?'

She nodded. 'Kenneth Milne: form for assault, possession with intent, and breaking into pensioners' houses and nicking everything he can carry. I want him found and I want him found today. I'm no' having kidnappy scumbags making off with wee kiddies in *my* town. Understand?'

The resulting wave of apathy was overpowering.

'I CAN'T HEAR YOU!'

A lacklustre 'Yes, Sarge' rippled around the room.

Harmsworth stuck out his bottom lip. 'Why do I have to be a Hufflepuff?'

She ignored him. 'Kenny Milne is a rancid wee fudge-monkey and we are putting his arse behind bars, so—'

The door opened and DCI Rutherford stepped into their humble office. 'Ah, DS Steel, glad I caught you.' He pointed at their collection of mobile phones. 'This stolen property, it's been entered into the system?'

Barrett snapped to attention, clutching his clipboard. 'Did it last night, sir. I'm taking them down to the evidence store after the briefing.'

'Hmm...' The detective chief inspector made a show of thinking about that. 'Well, given that your young man has pleaded guilty, and the fact that he's a minor, I've spoken to the Procurator Fiscal and I'm delighted to say that we've been cleared to return these items to their rightful owners.'

Steel snapped her fingers. 'You heard the man, Davey, bung that lot down to Lost-and-Found and we can—'

Rutherford held up a hand. 'I favour a more proactive approach, Roberta. We want people to know that Police Scotland are here for them. That we care.'

'Aye, but—'

'I want you and your team to return these items to their *rightful* owners.' Big smile.

Her face drooped an inch. 'But—'

'This is what community policing is all about, Sergeant. Imagine how delighted people will be to get their property back! We'll see a massive PR boost from this. Hop to it.' He turned and swept from the room.

Silence.

Barrett grimaced. 'Oh my ears and whiskers...'

Steel stuck two fingers up at the closed door. 'Sod that. We've got a Kenny Milne to catch.'

Roberta shifted in the passenger seat. What the hell was taking Tufty so long? Go in, ask a couple of questions, buy some butties, and come out again. How hard was that?

The baker's window was all steamed up, the words 'MRS JOHNSTON & DAUGHTERS ~ QUALITY BAKED GOODS EST. 1985' looming through the fog. Sausage rolls and broken legs a speciality. Ask us about our protection-racket specials.

Susan's voice took on that sharp, waspy tone it got when there was a fight brewing: *'Are you even listening to me?'*

'Course I am.' Roberta shifted the phone so it stayed pinned between her ear and her shoulder, keeping both hands free for the important task of drawing devil horns on Jack Wallace's smug little rat face.

Look at him, smugging away beneath the headline. 'MY CAMPAIGN TO CLEAN UP POLICE SCOTLAND STARTS HERE!' Aye, right. The *Aberdeen Examiner* should be ashamed of itself, giving a raping wee shite like him front-page coverage. Or any coverage at all, come to that.

'*Well how about an answer then?*'

'I'm no' saying Jasmine can't have a party, Susan, I'm saying Logan McRae can pucker up and kiss my sharny arse if he thinks he's getting an invite. OK?'

'*Oh for all that's… Do you have any idea how unreasonable you're being?*'

'Yup.' She blacked out a couple of Jack Wallace's teeth, for luck.

'*Honestly, Robbie, you're going to have to talk to him some-time.*'

'Nope.'

The pool car's door creaked open and Tufty got in, clutching a couple of greasy paper bags and two Styrofoam cups with lids. He held out one of each. 'Sausage butty with red, and a flat white.'

Steel dumped her pen on the dashboard and took both. 'Sorry, Susan, got to go. Official business.'

'*You do know I can hear him, don't you?*'

'OK, love you.' She hung up and opened her paper bag. Took a big bite of butty: an instant hit of flour and tomato sauce, silky butter and soft bap, then the dark-brown savoury crunch of deep-fried sausages. Ooh, hot. But tasty. She chewed around the words 'Any news?'

Tufty unwrapped his own butty. Bacon from the look of it. 'They haven't seen Kenny Milne round here for about a month. Sodded off and didn't pay his tab, so if he turns up again they'll definitely tell us. After he's fallen down a few times.'

'He didn't pay his tab? God, Milne's a braver man than me.' Another bite of rich sausagey goodness. 'You do *not* screw with Alice Johnston and her girls.'

The car's radio crackled. Bleeped. Then, '*Control to DS Steel, safe to talk?*'

'No. Sod off.' Creaking the lid off her coffee.

But Tufty had to go ahead and pick it up anyway, didn't he? Twit. 'Go ahead.'

'You're in Cornhill, aren't you? We've got a call – vulnerable adult not been seen for a few days. Can you check in on her?'

Roberta grabbed the handset off the soft sod. 'Get uniform to do it. We're busy.'

'Can't. There's a riot kicking off at the crematorium, a four-car pileup on South Anderson Drive, and we're still searching for that old dear with Alzheimer's. Tag: you're it.'

'Gah…' Rotten bunch of sods. But it wasn't as if she had a choice. 'Fine. But I'm finishing my butty first!'

The tower block loomed over the surrounding housing estate, monolithic and grey. Sixteen storeys of miserable Lego, dirty streaks leaking down from the corner of every single window. The other three blocks in the development were just as slab-faced, but at least they were clean. This one was like the stinky kid at school no one wanted to be friends with.

Tufty locked the car and held a hand above his eyes, blocking out the sun, counting his way up from the ground. 'Ten. Eleven. Twelve. That's us: Cairnhill Court, twelfth floor.'

Steel scowled at him. The effect was a bit undermined by the sausage butty's aftermath: a tomato sauce smile over flour-whitened cheeks. Like the Joker had really let himself go. 'How much do you want to bet the lifts don't work?'

The lifts did work. Well, one of them anyway. Yeah, it was covered in graffiti, but it *was* working. Not very quickly, though. It creaked and groaned upwards, the little lights above the door marking their snail's pace up to the twelfth floor.

A lurch, then the thing gave a particularly loud groan.

Steel curled her top lip, nostrils twitching. Trying to hide a smile. 'That better no' have been you.'

Tufty pulled on his best offended look. 'Of course it wasn't!' Then leaned to one side and squeezed one out. Grinned. 'But that was.'

'Urrrgh! You filthy wee sod!'

Tee hee.

The lift doors pinged and Steel stumbled out. 'Air! Fresh air!'

Someone had painted the corridor institution-green at some point long, long ago. Now it was cracked and scuffed. Peeling in the corners. A patch of magnolia almost managing to conceal some spray-paint graffiti. 'ENGLISH SCUMMERS ~ FREEDOME!!!'

Think if you were going to be a bigoted arsehole you could at least get a friend to check your spelling.

Steel turned and thumped him on the arm. 'What the hell have you been eating?'

'You've got to admit the timing was lovely.' He led the way down the corridor to the flat at the end. The front door was gouged and darkened around the bottom. Like it'd been given a stiff kicking. 'And the embouchure! A perfect middle C.' He knocked on the door, raised his voice to carry through the dented woodwork. 'Mrs Galloway? Hello? Can you come to the door please?'

'It's no' wholesome.'

'You started it.' Another knock. 'It's the police, Mrs Galloway. We just want to check you're all right.'

'I did not!'

'Did too. Mrs Galloway? Can you hear me? Mrs Galloway, can we come in and speak to you please?'

A rattle, and a tracksuited wifie poked her head out of the flat opposite, puffing away on a rollup. A large woman with yoghurt-pale skin and her ponytail hauled back in a

Torry facelift. But when she opened her gob it was like your favourite aunt: full of care and concern. 'I've not seen her for three days. Normally she's out walking her wee dog, regular as clockwork. And they haven't seen her down the shops either, I checked.'

Tufty tried a jaunty, friendly *rat-tat-a-tat-tat* knock. 'Mrs Galloway?'

Steel nodded at the door. 'She got family? Maybe she's staying with them?'

'Got a son, but he's in P.R.I.S.O.N.' Spelling it out nice and quiet. 'Drugs. Very sad.'

One last go. 'Come on, Mrs Galloway, *please* open the door! Pretty please?'

Steel sidled over to the neighbour. 'Haven't got a key, have you?'

'Give us a second.' And she disappeared.

Steel sniffed. 'I still say there's something wrong with your bumhole if it produces smells like that.'

'You're just jealous.'

'If smells like that came out of me, I'd be straight down the doctor's demanding—'

'Here you go.' The neighbour appeared again, a toddler balanced on her hip. Holding out a key with a little rubber bone as a fob.

'Thanks. We'll take it from here.' Steel gave her a smile, took the key, then slipped it into the lock. Twisted. Pushed. Whistled. 'Wow...'

Tufty peered over her shoulder.

The hallway was a complete and utter tip. If a tornado had touched down in here it couldn't have made more of a mess. Pictures torn from the walls. Coats and shoes hurled around. Holes gouged in the plasterboard.

Steel backed up a step. 'You better go first. In case it's dangerous.'

Oh that was *fair*. Because detective constables were a hundred percent more disposable than detective sergeants, weren't they? Even saggy old wrinkly ones.

He squeezed past and crept down the hall, feet crunching on broken glass from the picture frames. Scuffing through a duffle coat. 'Mrs Galloway?'

A door led off to one side. Tufty pushed it open: bathroom. The medicine cabinet lay in the middle of the floor, its contents spilled out like pill-bottle confetti.

Another door opposite: bedroom. The mattress was up on its side, blocking the window, its underside exposed and slashed, nylon fibre guts hanging out in long dangling swathes.

One door left, at the end of the hall.

Sobbing filtered through from the other side.

Tufty eased it open. 'Mrs Galloway?'

It was a living room, or at least it used to be. Now it was more like a day at the dump. Even with the curtains closed, the devastation in here was obvious. Broken furniture lay sprawled across the floor. The smallest member of a nest of tables poked out of the smashed screen of an old-fashioned cathode ray tube TV.

That sobbing was coming from a little old lady, sitting on the floor in the corner, surrounded by her wreckage, rocking back and forwards with one hand clasped against her chest and the other clenched over her eyes.

He squatted down next to her. 'Mrs Galloway, are you all right?'

OK, so it was a stupid question, but what else was he supposed to say?

Steel picked her way through the debris and pulled the curtains open.

Light flooded in.

Mrs Galloway flinched back into the corner. 'Aaaaaaagh…'

Almost every visible inch of skin was covered in dark purple bruising, already starting to yellow and green around the edges.

Steel's face darkened. 'Who did this?'

Mrs Galloway perched on the edge of an armchair, curling away from the sunlight. The room didn't look a lot better with the furniture the right way up, but at least they'd made the effort. Even if it had taken that idiot Tufty ages to sort it out.

Roberta hunkered down at the side of the armchair, placed a hand on Mrs Galloway's knee. It was like squeezing a lump of bone, but hot – a bone that been left too long in the oven. 'Shh… It's going to be OK. You tell me who did this and we'll take care of it. OK?'

Mrs Galloway just shook her head.

'You'll feel better with a nice cup of tea in you. Then we can all go take your wee dog out for a walk. You'll like that, won't you? Bit of fresh air?'

A gulping noise, then Mrs Galloway blinked at her. Mouth trembling. An acre of pain and longing in those watery bloodshot eyes.

Cup of tea, cup of tea, la, la, la, la, cup of tea.

Tufty turned the cold tap and filled the kettle.

At least the kitchen hadn't been trashed. Everything clean and tidy. All nice and easy to find. So now three china mugs sat in a row, each with a budget-brand teabag in it. He stuck the kettle on to boil.

Sniffed.

Funny smell in here, though. Sort of meaty and gritty. Maybe a bit burnt?

Now: milk and, indeed, sugar.

The fridge was bare, except for a can of dog food – the

top covered with tinfoil. Which had to be the only food in the place. All the other cupboards were empty. Well, except for the crockery and pots and pans and things. Not so much as a digestive biscuit.

He wrinkled his nose again.

Maybe it was the dog food?

He peeled back the tinfoil and sniffed.

Smelled like mystery meat mixed with BO and manky socks, AKA: dog food. So nope.

It had to be coming from somewhere though.

He had a peek in the bin while the kettle boiled.

Nope.

Tufty did a slow three-sixty. Maybe…

A microwave sat in the corner, by the toaster. That's where the stink was coming from. There were dark stains underneath it too, spreading out along the worktop. Brown and sticky looking. Yeah, definitely the microwave.

He reached out and opened the door.

Oh shit.

He shut it again.

Shit, shit, shit, shit, shit.

It took two goes to get his voice to work. 'Sarge?'

Roberta leaned both hands on the windowsill and stared out at the day. Look at it. All bright and shiny. Green on the trees, blue in the sky, sunlight sparking back off the windscreens of passing cars. And out, past the rooftops and the wiggly streets, the North Sea was a hazy shade of sapphire, a couple of cheery-coloured offshore supply boats waiting their turn to come into harbour.

She clenched her teeth tighter, jaw trembling with the pressure.

How? How could anyone do that?

How could *any* human being—

76

'Sarge?'

She looked back, over her shoulder. Tufty stood in the kitchen doorway with a bin-bag dangling from one hand. There was something in it – no' big, but heavy enough to pull the black plastic tight.

Mrs Galloway covered her eyes. 'I… Please…'

Roberta took a deep breath. Turned to face the window again. 'What was its name? Your wee dog.'

'Pudding. Had him … since he was a puppy.'

Tufty's voice was soft and gentle. 'There isn't a scrap of food in the house. When did you last eat?'

'What kind of dog was he?'

'Yorkie.' Mrs Galloway dragged in three or four jagged breaths. 'He's … he's a Yorkshire terrier.'

Roberta nodded. Turned. Tried *very* hard no' to growl it out: 'So someone kicked their way in here, beat the crap out of you, and did *that* to your dog. And you won't tell me who it was?'

'I … can't.'

'Do you want them to get away with it?' Getting harder and sharper with every word.

Tufty shifted the bin-bag behind his back, where Mrs Galloway wouldn't see it. 'Come on, Sarge, maybe this isn't the best—'

'Do you want them to do this to someone else? To someone *else's* dog?'

Mrs Galloway shrank into her armchair, hand over her eyes, tears running down her cheeks. 'Please. I… I just want to be left alone.'

II

Steel stormed out of the flat and into the corridor, slamming the door behind her.

Tufty shuffled his feet. Cleared his throat. 'Sorry about that, she gets a bit ... involved.'

Mrs Galloway just kept on sobbing.

'Right. Yes.' He shuffled backwards towards the lounge door, keeping himself between her and the bin-bag. 'Don't worry about Pudding. We'll take good care of him.' Poor little thing. 'Anyway, I'd better ... you know.'

He let himself out.

Steel was pacing up and down the corridor, face like a ruptured haemorrhoid, mouth moving like she was chewing on something bitter. She marched straight past him to the window at the end of the corridor and turned back again. 'Screw this. I'm no' letting this one go. Not a chance in sharny Satan's shiny hell!'

She marched the three steps to the neighbour's door and hammered on it. 'A wee dog.'

The neighbour opened it and frowned across the hall. 'She OK?'

'Course she bloody isn't! Who did it? I want a name.'

'He wasn't well, you know: Pudding. Had to have this operation. Really expensive.'

Steel jabbed a finger at Mrs Galloway's door. 'Someone killed her dog. Who?'

'How's an old lady like Agnes supposed to afford something like that? Vets think we're all made of money.'

That stopped her. Steel narrowed her eyes. 'She borrowed the cash, didn't she? She borrowed it from someone who doesn't do credit checks, they break your legs.'

'He was a lovely wee dog.'

Steel leaned in, dropping her voice to a theatrical whisper. 'So tell me who it was.'

And at that, the neighbour's face set like cement. 'Mrs Galloway had a wee dog. I've got a wee boy. And I'm saying nothing more than that.'

Tufty pulled away from Cairnhill Court, driving nice and steady, but Pudding's bin-bag still slithered across the back seat when he turned onto the main road.

Steel scowled back through the rear window at the tower block as it faded into the distance. 'I want this bastard, Tufty. I want him really, really—'

Her phone launched into its Eighties cop-show tune.

She sighed, then answered it, stabbing the speaker button. 'This better be important!'

DCI Rutherford's voice crackled out into the car. *'I don't think I quite got that, Sergeant.'*

Steel slumped in her seat and mouthed a very rude word. 'DCI Rutherford. Sir. Thought it was someone else.'

'I see… Well, I need to know how you're getting along with returning those stolen phones. The Chief Superintendent wants to put out a press release.'

'Working on it as we speak, Boss.'

Fibber.

'Good, good. Well, keep me informed. I expect to see some real results ASAP on this one.'

She forced a smile. 'Will do.' Then hung up. Sagged even further into the passenger seat. 'Sodding fudgemonkeys.'

Tufty checked the sign fastened to the corridor wall: 'WILDLIFE CRIME OFFICER'. He shifted his grip on the bin-bag and knocked.

'*Come.*'

OK.

The room was about the same size as his bathroom back at the flat. Only without the bath, Mr Einstein, sink, or toilet. Or tiles. Instead it had a row of five filing cabinets that took up one entire wall. Opposite them was a desk, crammed in under the window, leaving just enough space for a saggy office chair that you probably had to wheel out into the corridor if you wanted to open the filing cabinets. A stack of box files filled the last available corner, beneath a whiteboard covered in tiny blocks of perfect handwriting.

A young woman sat at the desk, poking away at an antique computer – beige with a state-of-the-ark monitor that took up nearly a third of the available space. The Wildlife Crime Officer turned and looked up at him, a little row of creases between her eyebrows. Dishwater-blonde hair in a loose half-ponytail thing. Glasses. Cute, in a fellow-police-officery, mutual-respect, let's-not-have-any-sexual-harassment-in-the-workplace kind of way. Quirky smile...

The smile slipped a bit.

Oh, yeah, he was probably staring like a creepy person. Tufty cleared his throat. 'Hi.'

Not a bad start. The smile was back at least. 'Can I help you...?'

Was it getting hotter in here?

'Erm, Stewart. I mean, Detective Constable Quirrel.' Definitely getting hotter. 'Or "Tufty" if you want? You know, to my friends? Ahem.'

Nowhere to sit, so he stayed where he was.

'And what can I do for you, Constable Quirrel?'

'Oh, right. Yes. Reason for visit.' He held up the black plastic bag. The weight inside set it swinging. 'I'm kinda new here. We found an old lady's Yorkshire terrier, and I...' A shrug. 'Look, I know this is going to sound daft, but is there a council cemetery for people's pets or something? She's not got any money and someone killed her dog and...' He licked his lips. 'Name was Pudding. The dog's name, not the old lady's.' The tips of his ears were ablaze. 'Sorry. I didn't know who else to ask. Because you're the Wildlife Crime Officer...'

And babbling like an idiot was a *great* way to make a first impression.

She looked from him to the bag and back again.

Now would probably be a good time for a meteor to hit the earth and wipe out all life on the planet.

Then she sighed. 'Poor wee thing.'

Not entirely certain if she was talking about *him*, or the dog.

The Wildlife Crime Officer pointed to the stack of file boxes. 'There's a chair under there. Why don't you dig it out and tell me all about Pudding?'

Definitely the dog then.

Every single desk in the CID office was a spaghetti-nightmare of phone-charger cords and extension leads. Barrett had his clipboard out again, checking that everything still in its original packaging was correctly entered and cross-referenced before loading it into a plastic crate marked, 'RETURN TO PHONE SHOPS'. Lund scrolled through the contacts on an old Sony, tongue poking out of the side of her mouth.

Harmsworth was hunched over his desk, forehead an inch

from the wire-strewn surface, face scrunched up in obvious mental distress, a big Samsung job pressed to his ear. 'Yes, we've recovered your mobile phone. ... No, it's right here. ... No, I know it is, because I'm *talking to you* on it.'

The woman on the other end of Tufty's phone sighed. *'OK, OK, I'll come in tomorrow and pick it up. Happy?'*

'That'd be great.' You ungrateful lump of lumpiness. He hung up and slid it back into its little brown cardboard box. Scribbled 'OWNER COMING IN TOMORROW' on the form printed onto the outside.

Look at them all, working like a proper team. All pulling together for the same goal.

Made you proud.

Even *Steel* was on the phone. Mind you, it wasn't one of the stolen ones, it was her own, but it was the thought that counted. She swung her feet up on the desk and rubbed at her forehead. 'I'm no' asking you to clype on the Cosa Nostra, Bobby, I'm just asking who's loansharking in Cornhill these days?'

Harmsworth groaned. 'No, I'm *sure* it's your phone. That's how I got your number, you saved it under "Home".'

'There must be *someone*, Bobby!'

'Yes, I know that means you're paying for this call, Miss, but ... Yes, I *do* understand that...'

Tufty dumped his re-boxed phone in the 'COMING TO COLLECT' crate and wandered over to the array of mobiles charging on his desk. Picked a slabby Nokia smartphone at random, unplugged it from its lead, and powered it up.

'Bobby. ... No, Bobby it's— ... Bobby! I'm looking for a scumbag who microwaves people's dogs if they don't pay him back. He's no' going to be easy to forget.'

Lund settled back in her seat. 'Hello? Who am I speaking to please? ... Mr Morrison, this is the police, we've found your mobile phone...'

The Nokia came to life with a *binglety-bing*. Wasn't even locked. He poked at the screen, selecting 'PEOPLE', and scrolled through till he found the entry called 'HOME'.

He set it ringing.

'Yes, I know. … No, we just need you to come down to the station and pick it up, Mr Morrison.'

A click sounded in Tufty's ear. Then, *'Yes?'*

'Hello?'

'Hello?' A man's voice. Not all that bright sounding.

Harmsworth bounced his forehead off the desk. 'I *know* money doesn't grow on trees, Miss, but we're *trying* to return your phone.'

Tufty stuck a finger in his other ear and moved away to the opposite side of the office, by the whiteboard, where it was *slightly* less noisy. 'Who am I speaking to?'

'Look, is this some sort of PPI marketing nonsense, because—'

'It's the police. Was your phone stolen recently?'

'Oh? You found my phone? Right. Well, don't suppose it really matters now: got a replacement. Was due an upgrade anyway.'

'If you come down to Queen Street you can fill in a claim form and get it back.'

'But I don't really need… Actually, you know what?' Doing his best to sound super nonchalant. *'There's probably photos and things on there.'* He cleared his throat. *'Sentimental reasons. That kind of thing.'*

Which probably meant filthy, filthy pics of his girl-and-or-boyfriend.

'You'll need proof of purchase and the serial number so we can make sure it's definitely yours, otherwise we have to go through a whole big red-tape exercise to prove owner-ship.'

'Right. Yes. I'll pop down tomorrow-ish and pick it up. Thanks.'

Tufty hung up and waved at the others. Pointed at the phone and gave them a big cheesy grin. Then wrote the words 'DIY PORN!!!' on the whiteboard in big red letters.

Steel's eyes widened. She got up from her desk and hurried over, still on the phone. 'Yeah well, ask around, Bobby, and maybe those parking tickets will disappear.'

Harmsworth pointed at the mobile in his hand and rolled his eyes. 'Yes, I *do* understand that, Miss, but— ... No. ... Yes.'

Lund gave them the thumbs up. 'Just come past tomorrow and that'll be grand.' She stuck the phone back in its little cardboard evidence box and dumped it in the 'TO BE COLLECTED' crate. Joined them at the whiteboard. 'Come on then.'

Tufty opened up the 'PICTURES' menu and a bunch of folders filled the screen. No names, just dates. He picked one at random and opened it. Flicked through the contents.

A bunch of blokes staggered their way through a drunken night out. Next folder: a middle-aged couple taking a Rottweiler for a walk along Aberdeen beach.

Steel hit him. 'You said there was porn!' Then back to her *own* phone. 'No, no' you, Bobby. This idiot here.'

He tried the next folder... 'Bingo.'

The screen filled with a topless woman in a fancy tiled bathroom – long blonde hair, mole on her right cheek, pouty red lips. Then the same woman from various intimate angles all the way to bare-arse naked as he scrolled through the pics. Then the same woman unzipping the photographer's trousers.

Barrett blushed. 'Oh my ears and whiskers.'

The next ones were even more explicit.

'Ooh, no wonder he wanted his phone back!'

Steel widened her eyes, eyebrows raised all the way up to her disastrous hairline. 'Bobby? I'm going to have to call you later.' She snatched the mobile from Tufty's hand and leered at the screen. 'I may need some alone time...'

Duncan sat on the park bench, rubbing at his forehead while Ellie banged on and on and on and on...

Didn't matter what day it was, she always had *something* to bitch and whinge about.

Little children squealed and roared and laughed and giggled as they chased each other around the playground. Hung upside down from the swings. Scooted down the slide on their backsides. Twirled and yelled and screamed on the spinning roundabout.

Look at me, Mummy! Look at me, Daddy!

Oh to be five again. When the only things you had to worry about was how many marbles you could fit up your nose and how dinosaurs brushed their teeth with those stubby wee arms of theirs. When the scariest thing in the world was running out of chocolate biscuits and the monster that lived under your bed.

Well you know what? The monster that lived under his bed had *nothing* on Ellie.

God knew how something as lovely and warm and wonderful as Lucy came out of that frozen, frigid monster's fanny.

She was still at it. '...*you should've known better. For Christ's sake, Duncan!*'

'How is this my fault, Ellie? You're the one who—'

'*And if you think you're getting her for the holidays, you can bloody well whistle.*'

'No. No, that's not fair and you know it!'

Lucy roared past, both arms held out, making aeroplane noises, curly blonde hair bouncing out behind her. 'Look at me, Daddy! Look at me!'

'Yes, Daddy can see you, darling.' Back to the phone. 'You're being *completely* unreasonable, Ellie.'

'*Don't you take that tone with me, Duncan Nicol. She's my daughter and if I say she's coming with us to France, she's coming with us to France.*'

Lucy made another pass, strafing the dog-poo bin. 'Rrrrrrraaaaaawwww… Dugga-dugga-dugga-dugga! Neeeeewwww… *BOOOM!*'

'It's called "joint custody", Ellie. Joint!'

'Are you watching, Daddy?' Lucy was looking back at him, eyes so big and bright, smile so wide. Not paying any attention to where she was running. 'Are you watching—' She crashed into the bushes and went headlong, disappearing into the greenery with a squeal.

Duncan jumped to his feet. 'Lucy? Lucy!'

'*What's happening? Has something happened?*' Ellie's voice got even shriller as he ran over to the bushes. '*Duncan, what have you* done *to our baby?*'

'Lucy! Lucy, are you… Oh thank God.'

She crawled out of the bushes on her hands and knees, little bits of rhododendron poking out of her curls.

He swept her up. Kissing her on the forehead and cheeks. 'You silly sausage. Are you OK?'

She nodded at him, eyebrows down, mouth clamped into a line – her serious face. 'I fell down.' Then she glanced over her shoulder at the undergrowth and back again. 'Daddy? There's a lady in the bushes and she's all crying and *sticky.*'

Lucy held up her hands. They were clarted with blood.

Oh no. No. Oh no…

She almost slipped out of his arms. The phone bounced off the grass at his feet, Ellie's voice barely audible.

'*Duncan? Duncan! I demand you tell me what's happened this instant!*'

The bushes.

A woman.

Blood.

Duncan swallowed. Then inched his way forward, one hand on the back of Lucy's head, keeping her face snuggled in against his neck so she couldn't see anything. He peered in through the leaves.

Oh Christ. Oh dear, bloody Christ.

The woman lay on the dirt, between the rhododendron branches and roots, twisted, crying. Most of her clothes were gone, bits, like the cuffs of her shirt, still attached – the fabric tattered and frayed where the rest had been torn off. Blood oozed down her arms and legs, deep red gashes carved into pale skin.

She looked up, right at him. Reached out with a filthy hand. 'Help … help me…'

Duncan screamed.

Dirty, rotten, useless, halfwit *bastards*.

Roberta stormed down the corridor, uniforms flattening themselves against the walls, getting the hell out of her way. Good. Tufty scuffled along behind her, trying to play the voice of reason. Aye, good luck with that.

Time for reason was past.

'Come on, Sarge. Maybe if you had a cuppa or something? Calmed down a bit before you…'

She barged through the door to DCI Rutherford's office, letting go of the handle so the thing banged off one of the filing cabinets. The git himself was behind his 'look how important I am' desk, DI Vine taking up one of the visitors' chairs, one of Vine's sidekicks over by the whiteboard. Case notes and photos spread out across the desk.

Everyone stared at her.

Tufty grabbed her arm, hissing in her ear. '*Really* don't think this is a good—'

She shook him off. 'It's Wallace, isn't it? He attacked that woman.'

Vine looked down his nose at her. 'We're in a meeting, *Sergeant*.'

'Victoria Park, same place he attacked Claudia Boroditsky—'

'You've got a bloody cheek bursting in here!'

'—in the bushes with a sodding knife. Do I have to draw you a diagram before you'll get it through your thick skulls?'

Vine stood. 'That is ENOUGH!'

He was right, it was. Time to rearrange some teeth.

She stepped forwards, fists curling, but Tufty grabbed her again with a little *eek*ing noise.

From the safety of his desk, DCI Rutherford held up a hand. 'Now, now, let's all just take a deep calming breath before we do or say something we can't take back.'

No one moved.

'Good.' Rutherford pointed at the chairs. 'Sit down, John. And Roberta, I know you mean well, but you need to walk away from this one.'

'He raped that—'

'We don't *know* that yet. We can't *prove* it.' He lowered his hand. 'But I can assure you DI Vine will liaise with the Divisional Rape Investigation Unit and we *will* find the man responsible.'

Oh yes, that was *such* a comfort. 'Jack Wallace is a vicious, raping, scheming little—'

'And given your history with the man, I would hope you're bright enough to never get involved with him again!' Rutherford screwed his face up for a moment. Took a deep breath. Spread his hands out on his desk. 'Look, Roberta, it almost cost you your career last time. Leave this one to DI Vine. Walk away. That's an *order*.'

It was like swallowing broken glass.

But she bared her teeth and did it anyway. 'Yes, Boss.'

* * *

The hospital room had that throat-catching disinfectant stink: slightly smoky, laced with iodine and Jeyes Fluid. They had the blinds down, shutting out the harsh morning sun, leaving the place cloaked in gloom. The only light, other than what seeped through the blinds, came from the array of machinery hooked up to every one of the four patients in here.

The starchy sheets crackled as Roberta shifted her bum along the edge of the bed. A little whiteboard was fixed to the metal frame at the head end, just big enough to have 'BEATRICE EDWARDS AB RhD –' on it, a laminated sheet of paper Blu-Tacked up beneath with: 'NIL BY MOUTH' in thick laser-printed letters.

Roberta squeezed Beatrice's hand, the skin cool and clammy like the recently deceased. Bandages wrapped around Beatrice's wrists, reaching all the way up to her elbows – yellow and red stains leached out into the fabric. Defensive wounds. She'd fought back.

They'd taped a wad of gauze across the gash in her face and the dressing stood out bright white against the bruises. Her eyes, hooded and heavy, the pupils dilated like shiny black buttons.

Roberta cleared her throat. Swallowed. Tried again: 'Are you *sure*, Beatrice?'

It took a while for her to respond and when she did the words were thick and slurred. 'Was dark… So dark… Knife.'

'How about his voice, did he threaten you? Did he say anything?'

A slow-motion blink. 'Tired… Sleep…'

'Did he have an accent? Anything?'

The word, *'There!'* hissed out from somewhere over by the door, followed by, *'There she is.'*

Roberta glanced up from Beatrice's bandaged wrist. A fat nurse in pale blue scrubs stood in the doorway, nearly filling it, fists on her hips. Nose in the air. She dwarfed her companion – a weedy uniformed PC with greasy hair Brylcreemed into a hard side parting as if he'd just fallen out of the 1950s.

The wee sod jabbed a finger at Roberta, then at his feet. He adopted the same hissing rasp. 'You: get over here! What do you think you're doing?'

She took out one of her Police Scotland business cards and put it in Beatrice's hand. Closed the cold fingers around it. 'If you remember anything, anything at all. You call me, OK?'

The weedy PC bustled up. 'You can't be *in* here! This woman's been attacked!'

His lardy sidekick was right behind him. 'It's not even visiting hours! You should be ashamed of yourself.'

Roberta gave Beatrice's hand another gentle squeeze. 'It gets better. I know it doesn't seem like it, but it does. There comes a time when you won't flinch if someone touches you. When your heart doesn't feel like you're going to die if you hear footsteps coming up behind you. When the darkness doesn't make you want to scream.' She stood, leaned forward and kissed her on the forehead. 'Trust me. I know.'

The nurse folded her arms, chin up. 'I demand you leave this ward at once!'

Roberta stuck two fingers up, blew a very wet raspberry, then sauntered from the room, pausing to grab the PC by the ear on the way, taking him with her.

He squealed like a wee piggy. 'Ow, ow, ow!'

A disdaining sniff as his sidekick turned to watch them leave. 'Horrible woman. How anyone could—'

The ward doors clunked shut behind them, cutting her off.

Roberta dragged the weedy PC across the corridor to the vending machines, keeping a plier-like grip on his lug. 'You know who I am?'

His face contorted for a moment or two, then it must

have dawned, because his eyes bugged. 'DCI … I mean Detective Sergeant Steel. You— Ow!'

She gave his ear another twist for luck.

'Ow!'

'Let's try that again. Do – you – know – who – I – am?'

His face creased, little hands twitching at his sides. Then finally he got it. 'No?'

There we go.

'Good boy. Keep it that way.' She released his ear and patted him on the cheek. 'Now buy me a KitKat.'

Tufty stood in front of the pool car, scuffling from foot to foot. Face all creased and fidgety.

Roberta polished off the last of her pilfered KitKat. 'You look like a dog with worms. Been calling you for *ages*!'

'Nice people switch their phones off in Hospitals, you wormy wee spud.' She crumpled up the KitKat wrapper and lobbed it in through the open passenger window. 'Come on then: out with it.'

'Mrs Galloway's next-door neighbour: she says there's two big thugs round there right now hammering away on the old dear's door, yelling at her to open up!'

Roberta stared at him. 'So get some sodding backup sorted!'

'We're closest. Going to be *at least* fifteen minutes till anyone else is free.'

Thugs.

Mrs Galloway. A grin spread across Roberta's face, hard and sharp. 'Get down with your bad self!'

Tufty backed away, chin pulled in. 'Sarge? Why are you smiling?'

Because the dirty wee sods that beat up an old lady and microwaved her dog were about to come down with a serious dose of police brutality. 'In the car, now!'

III

The lift juddered to a halt on the twelfth floor. Soon as the doors creaked open, shouting boomed in from the corridor outside.

'*Open up, you old bitch!*'

'*Don't be stupid, Agnes, you're only making it worse on yourself!*'

Roberta cranked her smile up a notch and charged out of the lift, Tufty right beside her.

Two massive bruisers, dressed all in black, battered on Mrs Galloway's door. Boxers' noses and rugby players' ears. They could've been twins, except one was boiled-egg bald while the other had a stringy blond mullet and sunglasses. Both with Seventies' porn star moustaches.

The bald one thumped on the door again. 'I'm not kidding around here!'

His mate kicked it. 'Open the bloody door!'

Roberta dug into her jacket and removed the extendable baton lurking there. Clacked it out to full length. 'HOY, CHUCKLE BROTHERS!'

Tufty did the same with his baton, a wee canister of pepper spray in his other hand. 'POLICE! NOBODY MOVE!'

Chuckle Brother Number One turned and peered at them over the top of his sunglasses. 'Here to back us up, are you?'

She thwacked her baton off the corridor wall, adding to the scuffs and dents. 'Oh, I'm going to enjoy this.'

Number Two held up his hands. 'Nah, you got the wrong end, like.'

'You battered an old lady. You wrecked her flat. YOU KILLED HER DOG!'

They both backed away at that, chins pulled in where their necks should've been.

Number Two frowned at Number One. 'Dog?'

A shake of the head sent lanky blond wisps floating at the back of Number One's head. 'Nah, we're *totally* not that.' He pulled out a sheet of paper. 'Bailiffs. Got a court order to seize goods worth two thousand pound, don't we?'

'We never killed no dog!' Number Two's face contracted around his broken nose. 'What kinda people you think we are?'

Roberta stared at them. 'You're *bailiffs*?'

'I got two cocker spaniels!'

The bailiffs stood in the middle of the living room, heads bowed, feet shuffling, hands clasped in front of them – a pair of schoolboys waiting for a thrashing from the headmaster. Only bigger. And more muscly. With the occasional tattoo poking out from the necks of their black T-shirts.

Mrs Galloway sat in her wonky armchair, somehow even thinner and older and frailer than she'd been this morning, a fibreglass cast on her arm. Trying no' to make eye contact with anyone. Especially the massive pair of thugs who'd been battering on her door two minutes ago.

Roberta poked Bailiff Number One. 'Go on then.'

He cleared his throat. Looked at his mate. Then back at the poor battered auld wifie sitting there like a broken sparrow. 'Erm... Mrs Galloway? Rick and me got this warrant and...' He swivelled his head from side to side, taking in the shabby wee room. 'And I'm really sorry to hear about your wee dog.'

Bailiff Number Two, AKA: Rick, nodded. 'That's a shitty thing to do. See if I ever get my hands on the bastard what did that, I'll—'

'Anyway, we can see you got nothing worth two grand. So I'm gonna go back to the office and see what we can do about a payment plan, or something, right? Spread the costs?'

Rick tightened his fists. 'A wee dog...'

The pair of them were waiting for the lift as Steel and Tufty stepped out of Mrs Galloway's flat.

Tufty closed the door, pulling on the handle till the Yale lock clicked into place. 'Think she'll be OK?'

Steel marched over to the lifts.

Baldy shook his head, jaw tight and clenched. 'I mean, what did a wee dog ever do to anyone? I tell you, Marty, I'm *seriously* gonna end that scummer.'

Mullet nodded. 'Bastard.'

Ping: the lift doors slid open and Steel stepped inside, a small pause, then the bailiffs joined her. Tufty squeaking in just as the doors started to shut.

Steel stared at Baldy and Mullet. Cracked her knuckles. 'You're getting one chance to answer this, then I'm kicking both your arses for you: who are you working for?'

'Landlord.' Mullet nodded his head at the lift doors. 'Owns about half the flats in the block. The old lady's not paid her rent in, like, four months.'

Baldy shrugged. 'Sent her dozens of letters, hasn't he? But these auld biddies?' A grimace. 'Wishful thinking, innit? You don't open the post, it don't count. Maybe the Denial Fairy makes all that back rent you owe disappear. Then me and Marty got to pay them a visit.'

She poked him in the chest. 'Someone's loansharking down here. I want to know who.'

Baldy growled. Bared his teeth. 'He the one microwaved that poor dog? Cos if it is...'

Mullet folded his massive arms across his chest, like a big red-neck genie. 'Can do you better than a name. I'll show you where you can find him.'

'Here youse go.' Chuckle Brother Number One, AKA: Marty, opened the door, revealing the lounge bar in all its retro glory. Red vinyl on the seats, a sticky lino floor, dark wooden tables and bar. A line of optics for Bell's and Grouse and own-brand vodka. The pub's name spelled out in red-and-blue on the mirror behind the bar: 'THE BROKEN SPIDER'.

Roberta stepped inside, Tufty tagging along like an idiot puppy.

Jimmy Shand's accordion diddledy-twiddled out of the jukebox, competing against the bings, squeaks, and electronic sirens coming from the puggy machine at the end of the bar. A knot of wee loons were poking away at it in their mismatched tracksuit tops, bottoms, hoodies, and baseball caps – most of which were on the wrong way around. All ten of them looking as if they'd failed the audition for *Crimewatch*.

The remaining patrons were never going to see forty again. Drinking pints of Export, having a game of dominos, keeping an eye on the racing playing quietly on the telly.

Bailiff Rick closed the door and stood in front of it, blocking the exit.

Then Bailiff Marty raised a hand and pointed at a table in the corner, by the gents. 'That's him: Phil Innes.'

A bruiser sat there on his own, back to the wall, nursing a Guinness and a nip. Big bloke. Expensive-looking leather jacket, silk shirt, side parting in his blond hair. Designer stubble and a diamond earring.

'Right, you wee shite.' Roberta marched over and flashed her warrant card. 'Philip Innes, I'm detaining you under Section Fourteen of the Criminal Justice, Scotland, Act, because I believe you to have committed a crime punishable by imprisonment.'

Innes took a sip of stout. Nodded at Rick and Marty. 'Rosencrantz, Guildenstern.'

Oh, aren't I so cool?

No' this time.

Roberta hooked a thumb at the ceiling. 'On your feet.'

He stayed where he was. 'And what is it you think I've done?'

'Constable,' she snapped her fingers, 'handcuff him.'

And nothing happened.

Typical Tufty: paying no attention to what was *actually* going on. Instead he was frowning at the troop of wee schemie neds playing the puggy machine. Useless sod.

She pulled out her *own* cuffs and dangled them in front of Innes. 'You killed an old lady's dog. You wrecked her flat. You beat the crap out of her. Now: on – your – feet!'

Innes had a sip at his nip. Pursed his lips. 'She told you that, did she?'

Tufty inched closer to the tracksuit baboons. Could the boy no' focus for two sodding minutes?

'You're a loanshark, Philly-boy. You prey on the weak.'

'Let me get this straight – you're saying some little old lady accused me of killing her dog? That right?'

Tufty turned back and grabbed at her sleeve. 'Sarge?'

'Get off me you idiot.' She pulled herself free. 'I said, on – your – feet.'

'I never laid a finger on anyone's dog. I like dogs. She must have been thinking of someone else.'

'Sarge!' The wee sod grabbed her again, pointing at the guy feeding pound coins into the puggy. 'Kenny Milne!'

At the name, the guy looked up, and it was. Kenny Milne. Nasty kidnappy, child-abducting scumbag that he was.

Oh you wee *dancer*. They'd got themselves that most sexy of arrests: a twofer – Milne and Innes, both in custody in the one shout.

One by one Milne's gang of underaged neds turned to stare. None of them looked a day over twelve, and each and every one of them held a tin of extra-strong cider.

That made it a threefer – the landlord was coming down the nick too.

Kenny Milne's mouth snapped shut. Then, 'Shite! Splinter!'

And that's exactly what his troop did, baying like dogs as they ran for it.

Rick grinned at them, chest out, massive arms stretched wide. Get past me, if you can.

They leapt on him, dragging him to the ground, whooping.

Milne sprinted for the exit, only this time Tufty was faster. He launched himself into a rugby tackle, smashing into Milne's waist and sending him staggering sideways.

The pair of them crashed into a table, sending pints and dominos flying.

An auld mannie in a tweed jacket shook his fist. 'I wis winning!'

His mate threw his bunnet at him. 'You wis cheating!'

'You dirty wee…' He lunged at his bunnetless mate. They grappled with each other, all false-teeth snarls and muttered swearing. There was a half-arsed attempt at a headlock and they lurched against someone else's table. A pint of lager tipped over, flooding into its owner's lap.

She reared upright, eyes glassy, face red. 'HOY!' Her fist swung wide, missed the old blokes, and clobbered the back of someone else's head instead.

And that was it: instant bar brawl. Everyone throwing punches, kicking, biting.

Tufty and Milne rolled around on the sticky floor, grunting and grappling.

Someone thumped the drunk woman with a bar stool, only it didn't break like they did in the movies. She did. Avalanching down on top of Tufty and Milne.

An auld mannie hurled a chair over the bar – shattering optics and The Broken Spider's mirror.

Innes just stayed where he was, taking sips from his pint. He nodded at the wrestling match taking place on the floor between the tables. 'You going to help your little friend?'

One of the neds went flying, following the chair. Cleared the taps and crashed into the till.

The auld mannie in the tweed jacket landed a solid right hook on his bunnetless opponent – walloping him backwards to bounce off the puggy machine – his knees wobbled then gave way, spilling him across the floor as the machine bleeped its tinny fanfare and paid out an avalanche of pound coins.

Roberta glared at the ceiling for a heartbeat. 'Fudgemonkeys.' She yanked her extendable baton free and whipped it out to full length.

Innes raised an eyebrow. 'And I thought you were just pleased to see me.'

'Stay there.' She jabbed it in his general direction. 'I'm no' finished with you!'

Deep breath, then Roberta turned and waded into the fray.

'Ow...' Tufty wobbled on his bar stool, a tea towel full of ice clamped to his face. Poor wee sod. Blood smeared one side of his collar, turning the blue fabric a dirty reddish-purple.

Blue-and-white light flickered in through the pub's front window, as if someone had set up a miserable disco right outside.

Roberta glanced around the room. Upturned tables, broken bottles, spilled pints, smashed chairs, the mirror behind the bar all cracked and broken – reflecting back a jagged patchwork version of the wreckage. 'Get the feeling we're probably barred?'

'Urgh...'

She picked up a bar stool, brushed off the dust, and set it next to Tufty's. Slumped herself onto it. 'Susan'll kill me when she sees the state of this suit. Look at it.' She held up an arm – the thing was rumpled and stained with beer. The shirt beneath it hung down over her fingertips, torn and dirty. Ah well. She still looked a hell of a lot better than Tufty. Roberta patted him on the back. 'The world stopped spinning yet?'

He poked at the inside of his mouth with his tongue. 'Think I chipped a tooth.'

'You're supposed to arrest people, no' bite them.' She peeled the tea towel from his grip and he blinked back at her, one eye no' *quite* in time with the other. So she flipped him the Vs. 'How many fingers am I holding up?'

'Three?'

'Yeah, you're going to hospital.'

He weebled round on his stool, till he was squinting into the corner where Philip Innes used to sit. 'What happened to the dog-murdering fudgemonkey?'

Her teeth clenched, but she forced a smile. 'Come on, let's get you into the car. And if you're *really* lucky, a nice nurse will take your temperature the naughty way...'

The doctor eased the ward door shut, then turned and gave Roberta a little smile. 'Sorry about that.' Tall and wide, with freckles and big hands – a traditional Northeast farmer's quine. The kind of daughter you could trust with the lambing, hurling bales of hay, or lifting a whole tractor by herself. She led the way down the corridor to the nurses' station where she flicked through a set of notes. 'OK, well, he's definitely got concussion, and I think he's probably in for a lovely black eye, but other than that he'll be fine.'

Roberta nodded at the ward, with its array of auld mannies laid out beneath their itchy blankets. Tufty was in the far corner, one eye screwed shut, the other staring at a wee individual carton of fruit juice. 'Fine enough to go back on duty?'

They watched him for a minute, trying to get the straw in through the little circle of foil in the top. And failing.

The doctor sucked a breath in through her teeth. 'Yeah… I think we'd better keep him in overnight. Unless you're going to stay up with him in case something happens?'

'Aye, that'll be shining. I'll pick him up tomorrow.' Roberta sniffed. Looked away. 'Take care of him, OK? He's an annoying wee spud, but he's ours.'

That got her a warm smile and a squeeze on the arm from one of those massive hands. 'We'll do our best.'

The same weedy PC was on guard outside Beatrice Edwards' room. Which didn't pose much of a challenge in itself, but that tosser DI Vine was there with one of his Eighties-reject sidekicks too. Honestly, the ugly lump was two rolled-up jacket sleeves away from being in a *Miami Vice* cover band.

So maybe best *no'* to pay a visit.

Roberta backtracked down the corridor to the lifts, then up a couple of floors, along a squeaky corridor lined with questionable art, and left into another ward. The nurses on station were all sitting drinking tea and reading dirty novels.

She rapped on the desk and a thin birdy one looked up from *Fifty Shades of Anti-Feminist Smut.* 'Aye?'

'Kenny Milne.' Roberta flashed her warrant card.'

A larger nurse put down *The Story of O*. 'He's sedated. *Strictly* no visitors. It's disgraceful how much police brutality that poor man's suffered. Violence solves nothing!'

'Says the woman getting all hot and bothered reading about BDSM.'

Her nose came up. 'It's called a book club, thank you very much! *Some* people are interested in literature.'

'Dirty nurses!' Roberta wagged a finger at them, then turned, sauntering from the room, singing:

'Whips and chains excite me,
They make my love life spicy,
We spank both hard and lightly,
And dream of Aphrodite,
Spreading jam on Keira Knightley...'

Roberta frowned at the form on her computer screen. Who the hell came up with this rubbish? Just because one little officer had been bashed on the head and hospitalised for the night, suddenly three tons of sodding paperwork needed filling out.

☐ Did you do a risk assessment?
☐ Did you appraise the chain of command before commencing operations?
☐ Did everyone present sign the appropriate warrants before it/they were executed?

Presumably they were talking about the warrants there, no' the people.

☐ Did you enter all command decisions into your Decision Log?

And *of course* they were all yes/no tick boxes so you couldn't even type 'SOD OFF!' into them.

Bloody Tufty and his delicate useless head.

Bet he did it on purpose, just to make more work for her.

See when she got her hands on him tomorrow—

Someone knocked on the door.

Pause. One. Two. Three. Four…

For God's sake.

Roberta took a deep breath and bellowed it out, 'WELL? DON'T JUST STAND THERE LIKE A NEEP, COME IN!'

The door opened and a rather sexy young hottie stepped into the CID office. Pert. Fresh. Browny-blonde hair all the way down to the perky swell of her gorgeous breasts. Naughty-librarian glasses, and I've-been-a-bad-girl-spank-me smile. Dressed in a PC's black T-shirt and standard-issue itchy black trousers.

Come in, my precious, let me relieve you of those nasty itchy things.

The delicious perky wee constable blinked at her. 'Sorry, did you say something?'

'No' out loud, I hope.' Roberta slid her keyboard to one side. 'Now, what can I do to you?'

She checked her notebook. 'I was looking for Detective Constable Quirrel?'

'Oh, were you now.' Disappointing. 'And what do you want our wee Tufty for? He's no' got you in the family way, has he? He's a scamp that one.'

Was that a blush? It *was.*

Roberta settled back in her seat. 'Of course it's my fault really: kept meaning to have him fixed, but you know what they're like at that age.' A shrug. 'We'd definitely have to make him wear the Cone of Shame, though. He'd have his stitches out otherwise.'

'No! No. I mean … no, it was…' She took a couple of breaths to compose herself. It made exciting things happen underneath her T-shirt. 'He came past earlier with a Yorkshire terrier's remains. Wanted to know if there was some way to get Pudding a proper burial…' Frowning just made her sexier. 'What? Why are you smiling at me?'

Roberta shrugged. 'He asked you that?'

'He said the old lady who owned Pudding couldn't afford a funeral.'

OK, so Tufty was a pain in the backside, an idiot, and a total waste of skin, but organising a burial for Mrs Galloway's poor wee dog? Right now Roberta could've kissed him. She held a hand out. 'Detective Sergeant Roberta Steel. You'll have heard rumours of my sexual prowess.' A wink. 'Tufty's no' here right now, but you can leave a message after the beep.'

'Right. Well. Detective Sergeant Steel.' The blush deepened a couple of shades. 'When Constable Quirrel gets back, can you tell him that PC Mackintosh came past about Pudding? I'm the Wildlife Crime Officer.'

Roberta grinned at her. 'And does the lovely PC Mackintosh have a first name?'

The blush went nuclear. 'Kate.'

'Don't worry, Kate, I shall make sure Constable Quirrel gets your message first thing tomorrow.'

'Thank you, Sergeant.' Then for some bizarre reason she did a proper about-face turn and marched from the room, back straight, arms swinging as if she was back on the parade ground at Tulliallan.

Nice bum too.

Before she'd managed to close the door behind her, Roberta launched into, 'Kate and Tufty, sitting in a tree, H.U.M.P.I.N.G.'

Ah young love…

The cursor blinked at her on the computer screen.

Should really get back to those forms.

Nah, sod that. It was half six on a balmy Tuesday in Aberdeen. Time to go home, crack out the barbecue, get Susan a bit squiffy on sauvignon blanc and take advantage of her.

There'd be time for crappy paperwork tomorrow.

CHAPTER FOUR

*in which Roberta learns an Important Lesson
About Friendship and we meet a lawyer*

I

Sunlight washed in through the French doors, making the kitchen work surface gleam like an oiled stripper.

Susan took a sheet of paper and pinned it to the fridge door amongst all the other kids' pictures: frogs, princesses, unicorns, dragons, and monster trucks. All of which looked as if they'd been done during Picasso's Off His Face period. The new one was some sort of dinosaur/unicorn hybrid wearing a pirate hat.

She still had a lovely arse – Susan, no' the dinosaur – firm and round and spankable. The kind of bum you could really sink your teeth into. The rest of her wasn't bad either. A curvier Doris Day in her heyday, wearing a sundress covered in little pink flowers. Shame about the Crocs, though.

The perpetrator of the fridge's latest artistic travesty was sitting at the breakfast bar, shovelling cornflakes into her gob and swilling down the orange juice. Her wee sister, on the other hand, wheeched round and round the floor with a toy truck, making roaring noises.

The toast went *chlack!* and Susan fished it out. Dumped both slices on a plate. 'Come on, Robbie, it wouldn't kill you to speak to the man.'

Roberta took hold of the litter tray and gave it a shake, evening out the wooden pellets and making dark things rise from the depths. She scooped them out with a plastic bag. Held it up for the world to see. 'Oh look, Mr Rumpole's made a little Logan McRae! Isn't that clever? Looks just like him.'

'The girls need to see their father.'

The turd went in the bin, and her hands went under the tap. 'Am I stopping them?'

'I'm *serious*.'

'And I'm late.' She kissed Jasmine on the head—

'Gerroffus, Mum.'

—swept Naomi up for a hug and a kiss.

Giggles.

Then groped that magnificent arse of Susan's, gave her a smooch, accepted the proffered slices of hot buttered toast and swept from the room.

Susan's voice thumped out from the kitchen as Roberta marched down the hall. 'Don't be late tonight! We're going to see that play. And remember to pick up my trophy from the engravers!'

'Love you.'

Photos of every family holiday they'd ever taken lined the walls. Just the two of them in Benidorm, Margate, Normandy, Shetland, Edinburgh, Wales. Half a dozen pictures of Susan on her own, showing off her latest golfing trophy. That trip to New York when Susan was six months pregnant. Then more holidays with the addition of a teeny weeny Jasmine – getting bigger and bigger. And finally: all four of them on the sands at Lossiemouth, everyone but Naomi grinning at the camera – she was too busy trying to eat a flip-flop.

Roberta grabbed her jacket from the coat rack, chomping on toast as she plucked car keys from the bowl and pulled out her phone. Bumping out the front door, dialling and chewing all at the same time. Multitasking.

Sunlight dappled through the trees, making leopard-spot

shadows undulate across the garden. Next door were getting their roof redone – the whole place shrouded in scaffolding, their builders far too well behaved to wolf whistle. Well, Rubislaw Den was a classy area. Couldn't have riff-raff swinging from the scaffolding with their sexual harassment and hairy arse-cracks on show.

Barrett's voice sounded in her ear, all efficient and polite. *'CID office, can I help you?'*

'Aye, aye, Davey. Is everyone in?'

'In and working, Sarge.'

'God, that'll be a first.' She plipped the locks on her MX-5 and clambered in behind the wheel. Propped the toast up on the dashboard. 'What about Beatrice Edwards?'

'Your rape victim? Nothing so far.'

She started the car and pulled away from the kerb. 'But they've arrested that crenelated fudgemonkey Wallace, right?'

'Actually, the word of the day is—'

'Don't mess with me today, Davey.'

'Sorry, Sarge.'

She turned left at the bottom of the street, past rows and rows of pale granite homes. 'I'm off to pick up Tufty. With any luck that bash on the head will have dunted some sense into it.'

'Well, we can always dream, can't— Oops. Hold on, got a visitor.'

A muffled voice in the background sounded suspiciously like Detective Chief Infector Simon Stinky Rutherford. *'Where's Detective Sergeant Steel?'*

'Don't you dare, Davey!'

'Sir. She's just left to collect Constable Quirrel from the hospital.'

'Oh. Good. And what about these phones and things: progress?'

'Tell him to jam them up his fundamental orifice.'

'*Got our first batch of people coming in to collect their property later today.*'

'*Excellent. Well, keep up the good work, and tell DS Steel I need to see her as soon as she gets back. Top priority.*'

'*Will do, sir.*' He lowered his voice, all conspiratorial. '*You get that?*'

'Oh I can hardly wait.'

She locked her MX-5 and sauntered across the car park, puffing away on her fake cigarette. Making clouds of watermelon steam. That was the trouble with real cigarettes, they didn't come in fun fruity flavours. And 'menthol' didn't count. That was just like smoking a rolled-up old person.

Anyway: twenty to nine and the hospital car park was already crowded with the usual collection of rustbuckets and massive four-by-fours that never had to deal with anything more 'off-road' than the potholes on Great Western Road.

Nice day, though. Warm and sunny.

What was that, four days in a row? Probably due a monsoon by the end of the week, then. Or snow. After all, it was only July. Probably be sledging down School Hill in—

The harsh *breeeeeeeeeeeeeeeeeeeep* of a car horn made her jump, then scuffle off to the side as a hatchback growled past on lowered suspension and alloy rims. Peugeot 208 with an oversized spoiler and a neon-orange paintjob. The wee turd behind the wheel couldn't have been much past seventeen: a baseball cap on backwards and a pair of oversized dark sunglasses perched on a long nose. Young woman in the passenger seat.

The words 'TOMMY & JOSIE' were printed on a strip at the top of the windscreen. Did people *really* still do that?

And it was a bit early in the day for boy racers too.

The Peugeot stopped at the end of the row, as close as you could actually get to Aberdeen Royal Infirmary in a car these days. Then the passenger door popped open and the young woman got out. Blonde hair long enough to reach the small of her back, a mole on her right cheek. She turned and blew a kiss back into the car, with pouty red lips.

Well, well, well. If it wasn't the star of Tufty's erotic bathroom photo shoot – the one on the stolen phone. Which meant the guy behind the wheel was the phone's owner. Just as well he was barely out of nappies, because in real life, with her clothes on, his photographic model didn't look a day over fifteen. Skin-tight jeans, bright-red crop top, denim jacket, and shiny-white trainers with three-inch soles.

Little Miss Porn Star trotted around to the driver's side and he buzzed the window down, letting out his horrible *Bmmmm-tsh-Bmmmm-tsh-Bmmmm-tsh* techno music. She gave him a quick snog, winked, then blew him another kiss, hopped over the wooden barrier and skipped across the road towards the hospital's main entrance. 'Tommy' watched her all the way. Probably ogling her fifteen-year-old backside, having nasty filthy thoughts about what he'd do to it later.

Roberta marched over, narrowed her eyes, leaned forward and stared into the car.

'Josie' disappeared through the automatic doors and 'Tommy' faced front again. Saw Roberta staring at him and flinched.

'The hell you looking at, Granny?' He gave her the finger, cranked up the tunes, and drove off. *BMMMM-TSH-BMMMM-TSH-BMMMM-TSH…*

Who the fudgemonkeying motherfunker was he calling 'Granny'?

She whipped out her phone and took a photo of the Peugeot's number plate before it disappeared. Little sod was about to find out what happened when you screwed about with the Sexual Offences (Scotland) Act 2009.

Roberta thumbed out a quick text to go with the picture:

> Gordy: I need you to look up a wee shite
> for me
> Possible first name "Tommy"
> Drives a sharny neon-orange Peugeot GTI
> Registration number in the pic
> ASAP

The Peugeot *BMMMM-TSH*ed its way along the road skirting the car park, then zoomed off with a boy-racer roar of oversized exhaust.

Dick.

Her phone launched into *Cagney & Lacey*.

'Gordy?'

'Aye, hold on. System's running like a one-legged dog the day... OK. Registered owner is Angela Shand, sixteen Oldfold Gardens, Milltimber.'

'He didn't look much like an Angela.'

'Checking insurance details... Here we go: named driver is Thomas Corona Shand, seventeen, resident at the same address.'

'Seventeen? Insurance must be costing them a sodding fortune.' Still, if 'JOSIE' was *fifteen* instead of fourteen, Tommy would have a decent chance of getting off when it came before the Procurator Fiscal. A less than two-year difference got him a free pass under Section Thirty-Nine.

Two years *and a day* got him a stint at Her Majesty's Pleasure and his very own place on the Sex Offenders' Register.

Roberta looked back towards the hospital entrance – a dirty-grey cantilever overhanging a clot of smokers in their hospital dressing gowns, at the end of a turning circle marked 'NO ENTRY' and 'BUSES ONLY'.

OK, so 'JOSIE' hadn't exactly looked as if she was being coerced in the photos, but that didn't mean Tommy Shand hadn't pressurised her into it. Or that the photography session was the first time. Or that she wasn't fourteen in real life.

And it'd only take a minute to check.

'*We done?*'

'Aye. Thanks, Gordy.' She hung up and hurried across the road. Skirted the smoky clot, and stepped in through the automatic doors. No sign of 'JOSIE' in the wee shop just inside the main entrance. Roberta peered over the balustrade at the stairs leading down to the lower level. No sign of 'JOSIE' there either.

There were rows of plastic chairs, bolted to the floor in front of the reception desk at the far end of the lobby. A half-dozen wheezy-looking men and women peppered the rows ... and there she was, sitting on her own, head down so her hair hung forward over her face nearly into her lap. She was fiddling with the ends, knees together, one leg jumping up and down on its own.

Roberta sank into the seat next to her. 'Aye, aye.'

She flinched upright, eyes wide and startled.

'It's OK, I'm a police officer, no' a pervert.' Roberta flashed her warrant card. 'See?'

'Hello?' A wee voice, wobbly, nervous. Like the smile.

'You OK? Cos you look—'

'Dad's got cancer.' The smile slipped a little. One shoulder came up in a lopsided shrug. 'It's moved to his lungs and his spine.'

'Sorry to hear that.' Roberta cleared her throat. 'So ... you in visiting?'

A nod. 'Waiting for Mum, Aunty Vicki, and Uncle Pete.

113

Don't want to go in on my own.' She shrank a little in her seat, her voice shrinking too. 'He's going to die.'

'That sucks arseholes.'

She nodded. Blinked a couple of times. Ran a hand across her eyes.

'I'm Roberta, by the way.'

A sniff. Another nod. 'Josie.'

'How old are you, Josie?'

'Fifteen.' She went back to fiddling with her hair. 'But I'll be *sixteen* in January.'

So Tommy probably wasn't going on the register. But the randy wee sod was still getting charged. Shagging a fifteen-year-old. There were things you could turn a blind eye to, and things you couldn't. Plus there was the 'Granny' thing. But mostly the underage sex.

Roberta pointed towards the entrance. 'Your boyfriend drop you off?'

Another nod. 'We grew up next door to each other.'

'No' easy being fifteen, dealing with stuff like this.' She dug a business card out of her pocket and wrote her mobile number on the back. Held it out. 'If you're ever in trouble, I want you to give me a call, OK?'

Voices came from the lobby behind them: *'No, Pete, I don't have to agree with you. You know nothing about it.'*

'I'm not fighting with you, Vicki, I'm just saying that if I'd taken Anderson Drive we would've got stuck at the road-works.'

Josie looked over her shoulder. Stood. Pulled on her wobbly smile again. 'Mum.'

Roberta creaked to her feet and turned.

Two women and a man were bustling towards the seating area.

The women couldn't have looked more different if they'd tried. One was short, with a shoulder-length tumble of

114

nearly-blonde curls, with half an inch of roots showing. Round cheeks and a *slightly* piggy nose. Terrible clothes, though, as if she'd bought the entire outfit from Frumps-R-Us. The other woman was tall, with long features and a short brown bob, tweed jacket and jeans. Oh aren't I so *stylish*?

Josie hugged the frumpy one, while Aunty Vicki had another go at Uncle Pete: 'For goodness' sake, could you not have put on a tie? Why do you always have to look like a slob?'

Pete sighed. 'I don't need to wear a tie to visit my own brother!' A tie probably wouldn't have helped, he'd still be a middle-aged man with greying sideburns and a pair of steel-rimmed glasses. High forehead. A little chubby. The kind of person who coached under-fifteens' football and spent his life ferrying his kids to dance class and chess club. The kind whose neighbours ended up on *Crimewatch* saying what a *nice* guy he was and how no one could have guessed that he'd finally snap and bury his dismembered wife under the patio.

Josie's mum gave one last squeeze and backed away a couple of steps. Put her hands on her daughter's shoulders. 'Did you have a nice sleepover at Emma's, sweetheart?' Then she seemed to notice Roberta, standing right there beside her daughter. 'I'm sorry, are you...?'

Josie pointed. 'Mum, this is Roberta, she's a police officer.'

Her mum paled, reached out a hand and grabbed the back of a seat. 'Is Dan... Is... Did he...?'

'Nah, I was just passing and Josie looked a bit worried. Thought I'd see if I could help.'

Aunt Vicki stuck her hands on her hips. 'If you're looking for something to do, *Officer*, I'd suggest tracking down the animal that attacked that poor woman yesterday!'

Cheeky tweed-wearing cow.

Roberta took a step towards her, but Uncle Pete got in the way.

'Come on, Victoria, she was only trying to be nice to Josie.'

'Don't *fawn*, Peter.' Aunt Vicki couldn't even look at him. 'If the police did their jobs properly that kind of thing would never happen!'

'She doesn't mean it.'

'Yes I bloody do!'

Roberta sniffed. 'It's OK. I was just leaving anyway.' She gave Josie a wee hug. 'Don't lose that number.' Then turned and sauntered off, hands in pockets.

With any luck Uncle Pete would snap sooner rather than later. And there wasn't a jury in the land that would convict him for it.

Meantime, she had a detective constable to collect.

Tufty stepped out of the ward and gave her a smile. 'I did has scrambled eggs for breakfast.' They'd taped a bit of gauze to the back of his head and his left eye was aubergine-purple around the outside – the white marred with a fingernail-sized splodge of red – but other than that he looked OK. Or as OK as he ever did. Scrawny wee spud that he was.

Roberta stuck her hands in her pockets and slouched against the wall. 'No Cone of Shame, then?'

'Don't know what they did to it, though. Tasted like lino leum laced with furniture polish.'

A nurse hurried out of the ward, pretty in a pneumatic, spank-me-Matron, jolly-hockey-sticks kind of way.

She bustled up to Tufty and handed him a bit of paper. 'Just in case.' She winked, then sashayed away, putting a bit of bum into it.

Unbelievable.

Roberta raised an eyebrow. 'Oh aye?'

Tufty stuck the note in his pocket and grinned. 'So, what we doing today?'

'Nurses by the look of it.' She shook her head. 'What the hell do perky young things see in you? Two in two days. Look at you: a whippet that's been bashed by the ugly stick.'

'Jealous much?'

'I'll never understand heterosexual women as long as I live.' She led the way down the corridor, making for the lifts. 'Back in the real world – your mate and mine: Kenny Milne. Going to lean on him a little bit.'

'Ah…' Tufty pulled a face. 'Without a lawyer?'

'I don't give a toss about "admissible in court", I care about the wee kids he had hiding in his wardrobe. And if we're lucky, he'll be too off his face on painkillers to remember we did it.'

Tufty sneaked up the corridor to the ward door. Checked both ways. No one else in sight, just him and Steel. She'd done something different with her hair today, like comb it with an angry badger. 'Clear.' He opened the door and slipped inside.

Steel followed with a very rude groaning noise.

The ward beds were nearly empty, just an old man snoring away and a young man playing something on his iPad, headphones on. Kenny Milne was in the bed by the window. And going by the state of him, it was clear he wouldn't be messing with Grand Master Police Ninja Tufty ever again. He had one leg in plaster, one arm too. His face was a road map of bruises, and that nose of his would *never* be straight again.

'Bloody hell, Tufty, what kind of animal are you?'

A shrug. 'Can't take all the credit. Those two auld mannies had a go at him while I was fighting off that drunk wifie. Think they battered him with the RNLI collecting tin.'

She grabbed the privacy curtain and hauled it around Kenny's bed, setting the rail rattling, sealing them in. 'Kenny. Kenster. Ken-fit-I-mean. How they hanging?'

Milne's head came around slowly, eyes big as dung beetles and twice as shiny. That was a *lot* of painkillers. He blinked at them. 'Mmmm… Thirsty…' Ooh look, missing teeth.

Seriously injured and off his face on drugs. There was no *way* questioning him was legal. 'Sarge, you sure about this?'

'Go wait outside, then. Kenny and me's having a wee chat.' She settled on the side of the bed. 'So, Kenny, be honest now: have you been fiddling with the wee kiddies we found at your place?'

'Sore.'

'Good. Where'd you get the kids from?'

'You wanna know a secret?' He leaned forward, wobbling, one bruised hand coming up to put a finger to his battered lips. 'Shhh… See when a prozzie has a kid? No one cares about them, right? No one cares… So, I care. Yup. Care, care, care…'

'You saying their mums don't mind you interfering with them?'

'Not *interfering*!' A scowl. 'I'm… I'm, you know, running a day care centre! Should get a medal. Looking after … after prozzies' kids… No one cares, but me.' He grabbed Steel's hand. 'Teaching them a trade, aren't I? Looking after them and teaching them a trade. Something to fall back on.' He nodded, agreeing with himself. 'So what if their mums are on … on the heroin and smack? I'm teaching them a *trade*.'

'You sure you're no' interfering with them?'

'Gotta pick … pick a pocket…'

Steel let out a little sigh, clearly a bit relieved by that. 'The two wee kids, I need their mums' names.'

'Is a secret.'

'No' between us though, right, Kenny? You and me are best mates.'

His face made a passable impersonation of someone thinking. 'Oh… OK. I forgot. Yeah…'

'Come on then, Kenny, the mums' names, soon as you like.'

'Right. Daphne … Daphne McClellan and … and Sally Gray.'

She glanced over at Tufty. 'You get that?'

Oh. Right. Erm… 'You don't want me to write it down in my *notebook*, do you? The one that could get seized as evidence if anyone found out that we did,' Tufty waggled a finger in a circle taking in the curtained-off bed, 'this?'

'Fair enough.' She prised Kenny's hand off her own and pushed him back into his pillows. 'Me and my performing monkey here are off to do important police things. You don't be a stranger, OK?' Then she hopped off the bed and swept out through the curtains.

Tufty wiggled his fingers in front of Kenny's face, putting on a ghosty-hypnotist voice. 'You are sleeeeping and you dreeeeamed all this. Weeee were never heeeere…'

Worth a try anyway.

By the time he escaped the curtains and then the ward, Steel was already halfway down the corridor.

He hurried after her, catching up as she marched straight past the lifts. 'Thought we were going back to the station?'

'Soon as we've made a wee stop.'

Yeah… Why did that sound ominous?

II

Steel marched through the warren of corridors, boot heels clacking out a drumbeat against the patchwork floor.

Tufty trotted along beside her. 'Wherever we're going, it's not going to get me into trouble, is it?'

'Let's no' spoil the surprise, eh?'

Yeah... That was ominous.

They turned a corner and there was a lanky wee PC poking away at a vending machine, a plastic cup of coffee in his other hand. The machine whirred and clunked, something falling down into the retrieval tray. He collected his purchase and stood, turned, clapped eyes on Steel and flinched like he'd been slapped.

She grinned at him. 'Hope that Twix is for me.'

'I didn't tell anyone!'

'Good boy.' She helped herself to his coffee. 'Beatrice Edwards said anything yet?'

Lanky sent Tufty a pleading look: help me. Help me!

Tufty shrugged back. You're on your own, sunshine.

Steel poked him on the arm. 'Sometime today would be good, Constable.'

Lanky sniffed. 'It... She still can't remember anything. Doctors say it's the trauma.'

Another poke. 'Aye, well, you won't mind if I have a wee chat with her, will you? Maybe she'll speak to—'

A voice growled out behind them. Big and extremely hacked off. 'Detective Sergeant Steel! What *exactly* do you think you're doing here?' DI Vine.

Oh lovely.

They were going to get fired for certain now.

Steel had a sip of her stolen coffee. 'Needs more sugar.'

Vine stormed up, dragging his two sidekicks with him in all their silly-haircutted glory. 'I'm talking to you, Sergeant!'

Sidekick Number One sniggered.

'Were you, Guv? Sorry, didn't notice.' Another sip. 'DC Quirrel and me were just on our way past and the constable here stopped us to ask a question.' She stared at Lanky. 'Didn't you, Constable?'

'Er... Yes?'

Vine crossed his arms and loomed. 'And?'

'Er...' There was that look again: help me. HELP ME!

Oh all right, then.

Tufty stood to attention like a good little boy. 'He wanted to know about the new minimum sentencing tariffs for possession with intent.'

'Yes. Right. That's what I was asking! Sentencing tariffs.'

Steel patted him on the shoulder, then stole his Twix. 'Glad I could help.' Before marching off in a hail of clattering boot heels.

Tufty shared a wee pained smile with Lanky, then hooked a thumb over his shoulder. 'I'd better... Yeah.'

Escape!

Steel waltzed into the CID office, arms out like she was about to bless them all. 'Davey, my little man, what news from the coalface?'

The desks were still covered in phone chargers and extension leads, Lund and Harmsworth making calls on other people's mobiles.

'...Hello? Yes, this is DC Lund, I'm calling about a stolen mobile phone?'

Harmsworth folded forward and banged his head on the desk. 'No. No, we don't want to arrest your neighbour just because he's English...'

'No, sir, I didn't steal your phone. This is the police? ... That's right.'

Barrett pointed at his precious evidence crates. 'That box are contacted and waiting pickup. That one's phones we can't unlock. And that—'

'Yeah, blah, blah, blah.' Steel hauled up her trousers. 'What about my look-out request on Philip Dog-Murdering-Fudgemonkey Innes?'

He checked his clipboard. 'They're still looking. And "fudgemonkey" was yesterday. Today we're saying "felch-bunny" for bad stuff, or "sproing!" if it's good.'

'Hmph, takes all sorts.'

Another thump as Harmsworth dunted his head off the desk again. 'Because I'm calling about your *mobile phone*, remember? ... No.'

Steel settled on the edge of her desk. 'Chase up the look-out. And remind me to check in on Agnes Galloway too. Make sure she's doing OK.'

Barrett made a note. 'Are you remembering DCI Rutherford?'

Yet another thump. 'Because being English isn't a crime, that's why!'

'Don't spoil my good mood, eh, Davey? Who's in charge of working girls these days?'

'DI Beattie's team.'

Steel groaned. 'God help us.'

'Look, do you want this phone back or not?'

Barrett checked his clipboard again. 'Oh, and Tufty? A PC Mackintosh came past wanting to talk about some Yorkshire terrier's funeral arrangements?'

Steel nudged him in the ribs with an elbow. 'She's a bit of a hottie too. Nurses *and* Wildlife Crime Officers chasing after you? You're like ugly catnip for short-sighted women.'

Tufty beamed. 'I has a popular!'

'Aye, well, there's no accounting for taste. Now get your arse on those phones, I want as many of them reunited with their rightful owners as possible before I have to brave DCI Rutherford and his Horrible Meeting of Doom.'

You could tell a lot about a police officer by looking at their office. Which was why Detective Inspector Beattie's office was a complete and utter craphole. Piles of paperwork on the desk. Piles of paperwork on the floor. Piles of paperwork on the filing cabinets. Evidence bags heaped on *top* of the piles of paperwork on the filing cabinets. A whiteboard solid with scribbled stuff. And sitting behind the desk, five-foot-eight of pure useless in a saggy suit. Biscuit crumbs mixed with beardy dandruff all down the front of his off-grey shirt. What was probably egg yolk on his brown tie.

He was on the phone, one hand scrunched over his eyes as Roberta barged in. 'I don't care. … Do I look like I care? No. … No, because I don't. Now get your finger out!' Beattie looked up as Roberta collapsed into the only visitors' chair no' covered in crap. Scowled and hung up. 'You're supposed to knock. And if this is about that sponsored swim, I'm skint, OK?'

Rude little fudgemonkey.

She stretched out her legs, hands linked behind her head. 'You're in charge of the Prozzie Patrol, Beardie. I need details on two of your congregation: Daphne McClellan and Sally Gray. And a cuppa wouldn't go amiss either.'

His face darkened. 'I do not make tea for *sergeants*, Sergeant.'

Roberta let her smile grow cold. Stared right back.

He held her gaze for a couple of beats – three seconds tops – before looking away. Then stood and rifled through a filing cabinet. 'Daphne McClellan; AKA: Daphne Macintyre; AKA: Natasha Sparkles, back when she was lap-dancing at Secret Service.' He pulled out a file and held it out.

She stayed where she was, hands behind her head.

Beattie shuffled forward and placed it in her lap. Then went back to the files. 'Sally Gray, AKA: Sally Anderson. Moved over here from Northern Ireland in the noughties.' He pulled out another file. 'Just bring them back when you've finished.'

Had to hand it to the useless hairy wee lump – he IDed both girls off the top of his head. Didn't mean she was letting him get away with that *'I don't make tea for* sergeants' dig, though.

She nodded at the files. 'Why don't you summarise them for me.'

A blush reddened the skin beneath the beard. Beattie gathered up both files and scampered back to the safety of his desk. Clearing his throat as he flicked through them. 'Pretty much identical. Form for soliciting, possession, assault, shoplifting… Social services. Methadone. Relapse. Possession again. And again. And again. Public urination…' A sigh. 'If it wasn't for the drugs, maybe? But life's not like that for these girls.'

'What about kids?'

Beattie checked the files again. 'Sally's got four. Two in care. Daphne has three: they stay with her mother in Stonehaven.'

124

Aye right.

Roberta had a dig at her underwire. How come no bugger could make a bra that fitted properly? Wasn't as if boobs were a new invention. 'We picked up two wee kids at Kenny Milne's house, day before yesterday. Kenny says they're Daphne and Sally's. He's been training them up Fagin-style and—'

The office door battered open and a PC scuttered into the room, nearly colliding with a pile of boxes. He was far too young to be shaving, never mind wear a police uniform. A tenner said he couldn't get served in a pub. Probably didn't even have *pubes* yet. He completely ignored Beattie, which was nice, and turned to Roberta instead. Face all shiny, breathing like a pervert in a changing room. 'Sergeant ... Sergeant Steel? ... The DCI's ... looking for you ... and ... and he's ... I mean a hundred percent *right* now.'

Pff...

Ah well, better get it over with.

And hopefully, by now, the team had been in touch with enough stolen-phone owners to make DCI Rutherford shut up about his stupid press conference.

She creaked to her feet. 'Thanks for the info, Beardie. Get some biscuits in for next time, though, eh?' She poked the panting PC. 'Come on then, sweaty, don't want to keep the big man waiting, do we? He might blame you.'

The nervous, sweaty wee PC hopped from one foot to the other as Roberta pushed through into the CID office. 'He really did say it was urgent!'

'Blah, blah, blah.' She frowned. 'Where's everyone gone?'

The only person in the room was Tufty, with his stupid gauze and stupider black eye. He tossed a re-boxed phone into the crate marked 'CAN'T UNLOCK'. 'Harmsworth was moaning so much that Lund wheeched him off for a cup of tea and a Wagon Wheel. Barrett's taking the latest batch of mobiles down to Lost-and-Found for collection. And *I* am working away like the brave little soldier I am.'

'I mean, really, really, *really* urgent!'

She sighed. 'Everyone with a pip on their shoulder says it's urgent. Whatever they want, they want it now. Does them good to wait for it every now and then.' She pointed at Tufty. 'Did Barrett leave his Blessed Clipboard of all Knowledge?'

Tufty nodded. 'Yes, Sarge.'

'Good: grab it and follow me. You can pretend to know what you're talking about when the DCI starts asking questions about all the mobile phones we've returned.'

The nervous, sweaty, wee PC's bottom lip was trembling. 'Please?'

'All right, all right, I'm coming.' She shoved him towards the door. 'Honestly, you're panicking over nothing. It's just a wee meeting. Nothing to worry about.'

Nothing to worry about at all.

The sweaty wee PC opened the meeting room door and Roberta sauntered in, hands in her pockets. Be nice to get a pat on the back for a...

She stopped.

Sodding *cockwombling* hell.

Jack Wallace was in here, sitting at the oval meeting table right next to Hissing Sid. The lawyer's suit probably cost more than Roberta made in a month, grey and well cut, a scarlet hankie poking out of the top pocket, matching silk tie. Grey hair swept back from a high forehead. A nose that never really went straight again after getting broken.

Which, incidentally, was a magnificent highlight of an otherwise miserable year. And all caught on camera too.

Wonder if the footage was still on her hard drive some-where? Hadn't watched it in *ages*.

Anyway… What the hell were Tweedle Rape and Tweedle Sleaze doing here?

DCI Rutherford had the head of the table, jaw clenched, little twitchy bit going at the side of one eye. No' a happy Weeble. The dick Vine was in the seat beside him, looking smug and vindictive all at the same time.

Sod.

She slumped down into one of the spare chairs. 'Sorry we're late, Boss, Constable Quirrel had a bit of a dizzy turn, but he's all right now. Aren't you, Tufty?'

Tufty nodded, retreating behind Barrett's clipboard as if that would save him. 'Yes, Sarge. Thank you, Sarge.'

Rutherford didn't even look at him. 'Mr Wallace is here with his legal representative. But then you know Mr Moir-Farquharson, don't you, Sergeant?'

She gave Hissing Sid a wee wave. 'Sandy. You here to get this raping scumbag off?'

That got her a thin smile. 'I don't remember you being quite so hostile when I was representing you, Sergeant Steel.' He held up a hand. 'If we can take the righteous indignation and acerbic banter as read, please, some of us have other appointments.'

Dirty wee fudgemonkey.

'Now: to business.' He took the top off a fountain pen and laid it next to a leather-bound notebook. 'Detective Chief Inspector Rutherford, my client is aware that a number of your officers erroneously consider the unfortunate attack on that young lady in Victoria Park yesterday to be his fault. He is here to assure you that it was *not*.'

The raping wee scumbag shook his head. 'Wasn't me.'

'And, as your officers have a rather unsavoury track record when it comes to framing my client for crimes he didn't commit, we're rather keen to make sure that doesn't happen in this instance.'

Wallace did his best to look sympathetic. It was like watching a dog hump a pillow. 'When was this poor woman raped? Between nine and midnight, wasn't it?'

Silence.

He shrugged. 'Cos I was at the pictures with friends.'

'Oh aye?' Roberta gave him the 'that'll be shining' stare. 'And you can prove that, can you?'

Hissing Sid opened his briefcase. 'Indeed we can, Sergeant.' He pulled out a slimline laptop that *bing*ed into life at the press of a button. Twisted it around so the screen faced out into the room. Then reached over and pressed a key.

The screen filled with four sets of security camera footage – all different views of a shopping centre. Union Square from the look of it. No sound, just pictures.

Window Number One: upper level of the car park. Wallace and two blokes were getting out of a Range Rover, laughing. One of them, the fat bald one, pointed a fist at the car and the lights flashed.

They walked towards the exit.

But Wallace stopped, turned, looked right into the security camera and waved.

A line of text at the bottom of the window displayed yesterday's date and a timestamp that ticked through the seconds as the footage played, '18:28:40'.

Window Number Two: upper concourse. The same three men wandered past a line of restaurants and into the cinema. More laughter. Wallace waved at the camera again.

'18:30:16'.

Window Number Three: cinema lobby. They walked up to a man standing at a wee podium in front of the doors to the screens and handed over their tickets. Then disappeared through the doors. A small pause, then Wallace popped back into the lobby, smiled and waved at the camera. '18:31:25'.

Window Number Four: the same view as Number Three, only this time the timestamp read '21:55:04'. A crowd of people surged out through the double doors: laughing, shoving. Wallace stopped right in the middle of the flow, forcing people to walk around him. He looked *right* at the camera again, smiled and waved.

Hissing Sid pressed a key, freezing all the windows. 'As you can see from the timestamps, my client was nowhere near Victoria Park at the time of the attack. You are, of course, welcome to examine the footage for yourselves. It will only confirm what we've told you.'

DI Vine poked a finger at his notes. 'I've looked into it and the Union Square footage is correct. We've got witnesses confirming that Mr Wallace remained in the cinema for the duration of the film—'

A nod from Wallace. 'All three hours of it.'

'—and then went to Frankie and Benny's for several drinks and dinner. They left when it closed at eleven and went to the Secret Service gentlemen's club on Windmill Brae till one a.m.'

'Yeah, and I went home with one of the dancers, didn't I? Kept me up all night. Haven't got any CCTV of that though.' He winked at Roberta. 'Sorry. Know you've got a thing for dirty pictures.'

Hissing Sid placed a sheet of paper on the table. 'I have here a sworn statement from the young lady in question, a Miss Strawberry Jane.'

Vine poked his notes again. Dick. 'Do you understand, Detective Sergeant Steel?'

Ooh… It was like squeezing out a pineapple suppository. She gritted her teeth and pushed. 'Yes, Guv.'

'Good.' Wallace spread his hands on the table, leaning

forward. Oh, look at me, I'm so concerned. 'I have nothing but sympathy for this poor woman. I hope you do everything in your power to catch the monster who did this.'

And how the hell were they supposed to do that when the monster was sitting *right there* in front of them with an airtight alibi?

III

Yeah, that wasn't awkward, was it? Watching Steel eating a dirty big jobbie sandwich and having to pretend it tasted lovely. No prizes for guessing who she'd take it out on either. Him. Muggins. Alas, poor Tufty! I knew him, Horatio…

He huffed out a breath.

Look at her, sitting there, fuming like an undersea vent as the meeting broke up.

DCI Rutherford was talking to the lawyer, Moir-Farquharson, the pair of them keeping their voices down – so probably up to something. Going by the body language, Rutherford was begging *not* to be kicked in the crotch again.

The nervous little PC who'd fetched Steel from the CID office shifted against the wall next to Tufty. 'It wasn't my fault she wouldn't come when I said.' He blinked watery eyes. 'You'll tell them that, won't you? It wasn't my fault? I didn't…' His mouth snapped shut as DI Vine approached. Stood to attention. 'Boss.'

Vine ignored him. 'Detective Constable Quirrel. How's the head?'

'Bit rattly at the time, but OK now, Guv.'

There was a pause as Vine stared at PC Weenie. 'Don't you have some *work* to do, Constable?'

'Yes, sir. Thank you, sir.' He scurried off.

'Should think so too.' Vine lowered his voice and leant back against the wall beside Tufty. Nodded at Steel. 'That, right there, is a disaster waiting to happen.'

She was sitting on her own, still chewing on a wasp, glowering at Wallace's lawyer.

'A land mine. A tripwire.'

Wallace got up from the table and wandered round to where Steel was sitting.

'An unexploded bomb. And if you're standing too close to it...' Vine mimed an explosion, mouthing the word '*Boooooom.*'

Wallace stuck out his hand and, when Steel refused to shake it, he leaned in and said something to her. Something too quiet to hear from here. But from the expression on Steel's face, whatever the something was, it wasn't very nice.

Vine pulled his chin up. 'I was impressed by your work on the Blackburn Onanist case, Constable Quirrel – figuring out the shift patterns like that. Other teams had been trying for weeks and got nowhere.'

'Thanks, Guv.' Playing it cool. But deep inside? *Totally* woot!

Nice to be appreciated for a change.

Steel flinched, but Wallace kept talking.

One of Vine's hands thumped down on Tufty's shoulder and gave it a squeeze. 'DS Steel might not be with us for that much longer. And when she goes, I want you to come work for me.' He gave Tufty a little shoogle. 'Put that brain of yours to work in a decent team for a change.'

Steel sniffed, scowling out through the glass-fronted reception area at the sunny day outside.

Tufty grinned. 'If the wind changes, your face will stay like that.'

Not so much as a flicker.

She didn't even look at him. Just kept on scowling. 'What were you and Arsebucket McVine talking about behind my back?'

Outside, DCI Rutherford stopped half a dozen paces from the front door. He said something to Moir-Farquharson, face all serious and ingratiating, then shook the lawyer's hand. Did the same with Jack Wallace.

Wallace patted him on the arm, like they were old friends, then walked away, hands in his pockets. Down the slope and out onto the street. Leaving the DCI and the lawyer standing on their own.

More talking.

Steel swung around and poked Tufty. 'Well?'

A shrug. 'He thinks I has a genius for catching the Blackburn Womble Whapper. Thinks I should go work for him instead. Thinks I'm totally sproing!' Wink.

'He's sodding welcome to you!'

DCI Rutherford grimaced, then shook Moir-Farquharson's hand again, before marching back through the station entrance and right up in front of Steel. Trembling slightly. Eyes bugging a bit. Voice like a hammer covered in razor blades. 'I meant what I said, Sergeant, you will stay *away* from that man. You will track down your phone owners. You will busy yourself with bits and bobs. You will stay – away – from Jack Wallace! Are we clear?'

She just looked at him.

'I said, ARE – WE – BLOODY – CLEAR?' Little flecks of spit gleamed in the light.

'Guv.'

'Good!' He stormed off, thumped through the key-code door and away into the station. No doubt to spread his very own brand of joy and happiness.

The lawyer still hadn't moved, stayed where he was, basking in the sun. Like a crocodile.

Tufty put on his innocent voice. 'Speaking of which: what did he say to you? Wallace. At the end of the meeting?'

Her face hardened. 'Nothing.'

Earlier ... (in which Roberta has a flashback)

Look at them all, congratulating themselves like the smug bunch of turdmagnets they were. Roberta tightened her grip on the arms of her chair, teeth grinding.

Hissing Sid was off talking to Rutherford, probably doing some sort of dodgy deal to stitch her up again. The idiot Tufty, talking to Vine. More dodgy deals. The only one no' talking was the raping sack of vomit sitting on the other side of the meeting-room table, fiddling with his phone.

Jack Wallace.

Six months in HMP Grampian hadn't done him any harm. He was leaner. A bit more muscle on that nasty wee frame of his. Must've spent a lot of time in the prison gym. Maybe so he could enjoy the communal showers with his fellow perverts.

He looked up from the phone and caught her staring. Smiled. Stood. Then wandered around the table and sat on it, right next to her. 'No hard feelings?'

Wallace stuck his hand out for shaking. No way in hell she was touching him.

He leaned in close, voice dropped to a whisper. 'It's you gave me the idea. After all, if Mr Moir-Farquharson can get a guilty, lying piece of shit like *you* off, what's he going to do for a *properly* innocent client?'

She bared her teeth at him, matching his whisper. 'You're no' innocent. You're a raping cockwomble and I'm going to prove it.'

'No you're not. Cos I know you've been hanging about outside my house at night. I've got proof. You're harassing

134

me.' His smile became a grin. 'And if you don't sod off, I'm going to tear your little world to pieces. Understand?'

Tufty raised his stupid eyebrows at her. 'Wallace didn't say anything at all?'

Roberta shrugged. 'Nothing important.'

Hissing Sid was still out there. As if he was waiting for something. Or someone. He raised a hand and waved at her.

Fair enough.

'Tufty, get your arse back to the office and light a fire under your fellow halfwits. You heard the DCI – phones, back with their owners.'

'Sure you don't want me to—'

'*Now*, Constable.'

'OK... Wow.' He backed off, hands up. 'I'm going, I'm going.'

She turned her back on him and pushed out through the reception door, into the sunshine. The rumble of traffic punctuated by screeching seagulls.

Hissing Sid just stood there, smiling at her. 'Ah, DS Steel. I'm sorry our reunion had to be under such unpleasant circumstances.'

Unpleasant? She'd give him sodding *unpleasant*.

'How could you, Sandy? How could you represent that nasty raping wee bawbag?'

He tilted his head to one side. 'I make no moral judgement of my clients: a criminal act is a criminal act. Whether it's *yours* or *his*.'

What?

'You did *not* just compare me to Jack Bloody Wallace!'

'So it's all right for me to have you found "not guilty" when you perverted the course of justice, but not for me to defend Wallace for a rape he didn't commit?' A tiny theatrical frown. 'That's a bit hypocritical, isn't it?'

Gah!

She marched off a couple of steps then back again. 'Who's paying for all this? We know you're no' cheap, Sandy, where's Jack Wallace getting the cash?'

'You know I can't tell you that. Let's just say that as *your* friends came to your aid during your hour of need, so did his. Isn't it nice to have friends?' He turned his face to the sun and sighed. 'Now, if you'll excuse me, I think I'm going to pick up some ice lollies on the way back to the office. Give everyone a bit of a treat. In the meantime…' Hissing Sid put a warm hand on her shoulder. '*Try* and stay out of trouble.'

Aye, well… Going on past performance that wasn't very likely.

Gloom shrouded the CCTV room, the only light coming from the bank of TV monitors that covered nearly one entire wall. Lots of little views of Aberdeen and its citizens going about their business. A control desk ran down the middle of the room, manned and womaned by three support staff, each one fiddling with a wee joystick – shifting the cameras by remote control.

Tufty looked as if he was bursting for the toilet: shuffling from foot to foot, making uncomfortable faces, constantly glancing towards the door. Big girl's blouse that he was.

'Right, here we go.' Inspector Pearce pointed at a screen mounted on its own at the back of the room, behind the consoles. She tucked a strand of hair behind her ear. Then poked a couple of buttons on her keyboard. 'And then Wallace comes out *here*.'

Roberta leaned in for a better look.

The camera was mounted about halfway up Windmill Brae, the cobbled street sweeping downhill from there until it finally disappeared under Bridge Street. Nightclubs, kebab shops, and bars stretched all the way down one side; more nightclubs on the other. Knots of drunken men and women staggered in or out of them. A couple opened and shut their mouths in unison – could be singing? – but no sound came out of the speakers. Probably just as well.

The timestamp clicked off the seconds, '23:10:05', '23:10:06', '23:10:07'.

Wallace and his two mates appeared around the corner from Bath Street. As they passed beneath the camera Wallace paused, smiled, and waved at it. Then followed them into Aberdeen's classiest titty bar: Secret Service.

Inspector Pearce set the scene flickering into fast forward. 'He doesn't leave till six minutes past one.'

Revellers came in pulses then thinned out as the time-stamp passed midnight. By the time she slowed the footage back to regular speed again there were just the stragglers left. Everyone wobbling their weary boozed-up way home.

Wallace emerged from the strip club with his arm around a young woman's shoulders. She had a long fur coat on over a *very* short skirt and sparkly top. Heels high enough to give Sherpa Tenzing a nosebleed. Long blonde hair and lots of make-up. That would be Strawberry Jane then. She staggered a bit as they crossed the road, climbing the hill. Probably a bit blootered.

And again, Jack Wallace stopped beneath the camera to smile and wave. '01:06:46'.

Inspector Pearce fiddled with her keyboard again and the scene jumped to the corner of Crown Street and Union Street, looking across the box junction towards the columned portico of the Music Hall.

Wallace and his 'date' hurried across the road. As soon as he reached the opposite pavement, he turned and gave them a wave. '01:08:02'. Then he wrapped Strawberry Jane in an arse-groping snog and led her away down the side of the Music Hall towards Golden Square.

'And the last time we see them is on Rosemount Viaduct.'

One more go on the keyboard and they were looking across the junction as Wallace and Strawberry strolled arm-in-arm past the Noose & Monkey. He stopped. Nipped back to the traffic lights, gave them one last wave, then hurried after his drunken pole dancer. '01:12:56'.

Roberta leaned in even closer, till her nose was inches from the screen. 'How does he know?'

Tufty tugged at her sleeve, like a wee kid. 'Can we get out of here now? What if DCI Rutherford finds out?'

'All the smiling and waving: how does he know? No' just where the cameras are – that's easy enough – but he's doing this to be seen. How did he know he'd need an alibi?'

And how the hell did they break it?

CHAPTER FIVE

in which Roberta and Tufty go on An Adventure,
Tufty has another bath,
and Roberta gets her bottom spanked
(but not in a Good Way)

I

The sound of happy munching filled the CID office, joining the heady scents of a team lunch from the baker's in the Castlegate. Welcome to Buttytopia, population: five. Well, four and a bit, because Steel hadn't touched her bacon-egg-and-black-pudding yet. Instead she was hunched over her desk, phone clamped to her ear, completely ignoring the lovely cup of tea Tufty had made for her.

He picked up his butty and wandered over. 'I'll eat that if you don't want it?'

'Come on, Agnes, pick up the phone...'

'No luck?' He took another bite. All crunchy and meaty and chewy, with slatherings of butter, English mustard, and tomato sauce.

Steel hung up. 'She's a little old lady, living in a tower block, with no friends and no dog. Where's she going to go?' A frown. 'What the hell are you eating?'

'Maybe she can't pay the phone bill?'

'No seriously, what *is* that?'

He held it up, every millimetre the proud father. 'Steak pie butty. That's what Tufties like best.'

'Freak.' She pulled her own butty over and took a big bite. The egg popped, dripping yolk onto her desk as she chewed through the words. 'We'll swing by Cairnhill Court while

141

we're out chasing down Beattie's prozzies. Make sure Mrs Galloway's OK.'

Tufty had a quick look around. Everyone else was busy stuffing their faces. He put on a whisper anyway, just in case. 'Sarge? Erm… The CCTV room. That's it, isn't it? We're done? No more Jack Wallace?'

'Maybe take her a packet of biscuits. Some milk. A decent box of teabags. And I need to pop past that trophy shop on Rosemount Place too.'

'Only I'd *really* like not to get fired.'

Another massive bite got ripped out of her butty. Egg all down her chin. 'Pshaw, little Tufty, would I ever get you into trouble?'

Of course she would.

Today's pool car was a bit cleaner than yesterday's, but it had a weird plastic-floral kind of smell. Like someone was trying to *hide* something. And in a police car, that usually only meant one of three things. None of which were in the least bit hygienic.

Tufty drove them down the Kirkgate and up onto Schoolhill. Past the graveyard.

Lunchtime had brought out all the office workers, some lay sunning themselves on the gravestones, others marched along the street, sipping iced lattes and being all smiley. Enjoying the Costa del Aberdeen. Skirts were getting shorter, tops getting smaller, trousers swapped for shorts, shoes for flip-flops, exposing more and more Nosferatu-pale skin. They'd probably head back to the office in an hour with all that milky-white flesh turned baboon's-bottom red.

And for once, Steel wasn't having a good ogle at all the young ladies on display. Instead she was slouching in the passenger seat with her feet on the dashboard, mobile phone clamped to her ear. 'Oh, aye, and before I forget,

Davey: give Social Services a shout. See if they can get Agnes Galloway into a nice sheltered housing unit somewhere. Poor old soul deserves a bit of peace. ... Yeah, OK. ... Thanks. ... Bye.' She put her phone away, then turned and grinned at him.

Creepy.

Suspicious.

Tufty pulled his chin in. 'What?'

'Pop quiz, Tufty: Sexual Offences, Scotland, Act, 2009. Section Twenty-Eight. Go.'

'Ah. OK...' He dredged it up from the last refresher course. 'If someone *older* than sixteen has sex with someone *younger* than sixteen it's an offence. Having intercourse with an older child?'

'Ten points to Slytherin. For a bonus, and a chance to go through to the semi-final, what's a relevant defence?'

'Erm... Section Thirty-Nine? If you genuinely thought they were older than sixteen at the time you did it.'

She made a loud buzzing noise. 'Childhood friends, so no: try again.'

'If the difference in your ages isn't more than two years?'

'And you win the cuddly toy!'

'Yay!'

They passed the art gallery and the Cowdray Hall – two kids had climbed on top of the big granite lion sitting outside the hall, riding it like a pony and eating bags of crisps.

The lights were red, so Tufty coasted to a halt at the junction. Then frowned at her. 'I know it's an honour just to be nominated, but *why* are you asking?'

'Because a little birdie called Davey just told me Tommy Shand is twenty-six months older than Josie Stephenson. Two months past the expiry date on his get-out-of-jail-free card. And I'm going to nail the randy wee shite to the wall by his *balls*.'

'Ah!' Tufty nodded. 'Right. OK. Got you.' A small pause as the lights turned green. 'Who's Tommy Shand?'

The woman in the grey green overalls curled her top lip at Tufty's warrant card. Folded her thick arms over her thicker torso. Hair swept back from her face. Little flecks of magnolia paint on her cheeks and overalls. 'Sally Gray doesn't live here any more. Do you have any idea how hard it is to evict someone these days?'

He took out his notebook. 'Where's she living now?'

'She was using the place as a drug den and a brothel! I can't even *begin* to describe what that does to property values.'

'Mrs Webber, please, we just need to speak to her. Did she leave a forwarding address?'

'Do I look like the Post Office? I served the eviction notice and she disappeared. Oh yes, but not before trashing the place.' A full-on shudder made everything wobble. 'You will not *believe* what she smeared all over the walls. Filthy cow.'

Tufty climbed back in behind the wheel. 'Isn't it lovely when members of the public *help*?'

Steel didn't look up from her phone, kept poking away at a text with her thumbs. 'She give you an address?'

'Gave me an earful about how the law cares more about the scumbags who trash their landlords' flats than the poor landlords who have to paint over the dirty protests they leave behind. No forwarding address.'

'Pffff...' A shrug. 'Nothing for it, then: to the docks, dear Tufty. We've got some ladies of wobbly virtue to question. One of them's bound to know where Sally Gray's got to.'

The lunchtime rush for an illicit kneetrembler can't have been that great on a sunny Wednesday, because only a couple of girls were out plying their trade. Well, not so much girls as middle-aged women with hollow eyes and sunken cheeks. Lank hair. Spots around their mouths. Short black skirts in cheap-looking fabric. Arms and legs that were just bones covered in bruise-speckled skin. One with dyed blonde hair, the other in an unconvincing auburn wig.

Steel puffed away on her e-cigarette, sending out pineapple-scented smoke signals. 'Come on, Sheryl, have another look at the picture. You *know* Sally Gray.'

Tufty held the picture out again and the woman in the wig glanced at it, biting at the skin around her fingernails. They were a mass of raw flesh and scabs. 'I don't... Don't... Haven't. No.'

Steel's shoulders dropped an inch. 'When did you last eat, Sheryl?'

'Just trying to get by. That's... Get by. Yup.' A nod. 'Get by.'

'How about you, Lynda? You know where Sally's rinsing out her fishnets these days?'

Lynda's long-sleeved lacy top wasn't quite thick enough to hide the trackmarks tattooing her veins. 'Maybe... Maybe if, you know, you could lend us a couple of quid I'd remember?' Eyes glittering away in the darkness of her skull. 'Just a twenty or something?'

'Aye, cos there's no way you'd just go spend that on smack, is there?'

'A tenner then. Just a tenner. You can afford it, right?'

'I'm no' giving you money to spend on drugs, Lynda.' Steel sighed. 'God's sake. Come on.' She hooked a thumb over her shoulder. 'Follow me.'

Tufty backed out of the chipper, a paper parcel in each hand trailing the enticing scent of hot batter, chips, and vinegar. He hurried around the corner and there were Steel, Lynda,

145

and Sheryl, right where he'd left them: sitting on a low wall behind the chandler's yard.

'I stuck a couple of pickled onions in there too. *Bon appétit.*' He handed one parcel each to Lynda and Sheryl.

They unwrapped them, picking away at the fish suppers, peeling off chunks of battered haddock.

Steel held out her hand to Tufty. 'Hoy: make with my change, you thieving wee sod.'

'Give us a chance.' He dug out the one pound twenty she was owed and dropped it into her palm.

'Is that *it*?'

'Yes. And you're welcome.'

'Pfff…' She stuck the cash in her pocket. 'Right, you two. I need to speak to Sally Gray. Where is she?'

They shared a look. Then Lynda shrugged. Popped a chip in her mouth and chewed. 'Don't know where she's living, but I know who she gets her gear from. He might?'

'Last chance, Shawn.' Steel leaned in close. 'Either you tell us where Sally Gray lives, *right* now, or I'm going to make your miserable wee life a living nightmare.'

Shawn licked his lips and hunched his shoulders forward, like someone had hollowed him out. He didn't look like a big-time drug dealer, he looked like a schoolkid trying to grow a beard. The result was a sparse smattering of wiry black hairs. More scrotumy than anything else. 'I… It's not… I mean, I don't really know her or anything. You know. I've got a girlfriend and that.'

'You sell her gear, Shawn, you *know* where she lives.'

'Gear? No, no. Not me. I don't sell gear. Nah, that's illegal, man. Definitely not.'

She lowered her voice. 'A living nightmare.'

'Who says I sell gear? Cos I've never sold gear in my life…'

'In five. Four. Three.'

Shawn stared at Tufty. 'But—'

'I'd be terrified, if I was you. Seriously bricking it.'

'Two. One—'

'OK! OK. Yeah. Sally. She's got a place in Torry, belongs to an aunt or something.'

Steel patted him on the cheek. 'Saved by the bell, Shawn. Now give us the address.'

The street was a canyon of depressing grey. Two identical rows of terraced flats faced each other across a strip of fading tarmac – the usual set-up of six flats to one door copy-and-pasted until they ran out of road. Rows of once-black wheelie-bins standing to attention between the pavement and the thin strip of unloved grass that passed for a front garden.

More like a gulag than somewhere for human beings to live.

Austere and soulless.

Roberta had a wee dig at her itchy bra as she clambered out of the pool car.

A mangy greyhound was tethered to a stake in the middle of the grass – it trotted round and round in the biggest circle the chain around its neck would allow. Whining and yowling.

Tufty led the way up the path to a door halfway down the street. He peered at the intercom. 'Here we are: Sally Gray. Top floor left.' A wee grimace. 'Aren't neighbours lovely? Someone's written "Dirty Prozzie Bitch" on her name tag.' He poked the button, making it buzz.

Buzz, buzz, buzz.

Roberta frowned at the greyhound. 'What did Hissing Sid mean?'

'Nope, no idea who that is either.'

More buzzing.

'Hissing Sid, AKA: Sandy Slithery Moir-Farquharson, AKA: Greasy Lawyer-Faced … what's the word of the day?'

'"Felchbunny."'

Buzz.

'Oh, he's definitely that.' She slapped Tufty's hand out of the way. 'Don't be so damp. This is how the grown-ups do it.' She mashed all the buttons with her palm, holding it there. Making them *all* buzz. 'Hissing Sid said Wallace's friends "came to his aid" when he needed them. "Just like mine." What's that supposed to mean?'

The door hummed, then clicked open.

'Told you.' She let go of the buttons and gave the door a shove, stepping into a shabby hallway. Stairs marched up to the floors above, the scent of lemon furniture polish overlaying a bleachy note. Shabby, but clean.

A little old lady peered out of the ground-floor flat on the right. 'Hoy, Quasimodo: stop ringing that bloody bell! This isn't nineteenth-century Paris!'

Roberta marched past and up the stairs, Tufty trotting along at her side. She thumped him. 'And for the record, no one "came to my aid".'

Tufty shrugged. 'Well … he's a swanky expensive lawyer, right? Maybe Wallace's friends all chipped in to cover the legal costs?'

'First sign of trouble, my so-called sodding "friends" dropped me like a radioactive jobbie.' Round the landing and up the next flight of stairs.

'I mean, he's got to be really expensive, right? Lawyer that swanky.'

'And then some.'

Tufty stopped on the top step. 'So how did *you* afford him?'

'Didn't. He did it pro bono, on account of all the times

148

he'd been a pain in my arse in court, getting murderers and rapists off. Guilty conscience.' A sniff. 'Even *lawyers* do the right thing now and then.'

The top floor was shabbier than down below, the scent of furniture polish joined by the chemical-floral hit of too much air freshener – making the air thick enough to cut with a spoon. A child was crying somewhere inside one of the flats, the sound echoing back from the bare walls.

Roberta pointed and Tufty wandered over there and knocked. 'Miss Gray? Sally? Can you come to the door please?'

No reply. But the crying got louder, so that was something.

The theme to *Cagney & Lacey* blared out into the stairwell. Roberta answered her phone. 'Who's this?'

'*Sarge?*' Barrett.

'Davey, my little disaster-monkey, what have you got for your lovely Aunty Roberta?'

'*Dug up some dirt on Tommy Shand, Sarge. Been complaints about his vehicle hanging round the car park behind Airyhall Library late at night. Local residents think he's dealing. There's a bunch of unsolved break-ins at the community centre too.*'

Tufty tried again. 'Miss Gray? It's the police. I need you to open up.'

'You wee dancer, Davey. Who's investigating?'

'*Let me check… OK. DI McPherson's running that one.*'

'McPherson? He couldn't catch a fart in a bubble bath. But I can. Cheers, Davey.' She slipped her phone back in her pocket. 'You giving up already?'

Tufty wasn't knocking any more, he was bent double, hands on his knees, sniffing at the letterbox. Then backed off a couple of paces, face all wrinkled. 'Can you smell that?'

She inched forward and gave the letterbox a sniff. Recoiled. No wonder the whole landing stank of air freshener, someone was trying to cover up the rancid-meat stench coming from Sally Gray's flat. 'Kick it in.'

Tufty slammed his boot into the door. It battered open, bouncing off the wall inside.

That wailing child's cry got louder, accompanied by the dark heavy buzzing of far too many flies.

'Oh Jesus…' Tufty stuck a hand over his mouth, pinching his nostrils shut. 'You want me to call it in? Sarge?'

She stepped over the threshold into the flat.

There was nothing in the hall. No carpets, no coats, no shoes, no mail, just bare floorboards scuffed with dirt.

'Sarge?'

The door at the end of the hall was shut. She tucked her hand into the sleeve of her jacket and turned the handle. Pushed it open.

That rotting meat stench collapsed out through the doorway like an avalanche, burying her in its greasy embrace.

Her bacon-egg-and-black-pudding butty lurched… But stayed down.

A bare mattress sat on the bare floor, bathed in the sunlight streaming in through the living-room window. And right in the middle of that warm spotlight was a body: female, half naked, skeletally thin. Skin blackened and furred with mould. Stomach swollen.

Fat bluebottles made lazy circuits of the room – probably startled when Tufty put the door in. One by one they settled back onto the body.

A couple of needles lay on the floor beside the mattress. A blackened teaspoon. A lighter. Some cotton wool. A bottle of distilled vinegar.

Tufty appeared at Roberta's side, staring down at what was left of Sally Gray. 'Sarge?'

What a waste.

What a stupid, bloody, sodding…

The crying. It was coming from the corner behind them.

150

She turned. 'No, no, no...'

A rickety crib sat in the corner. A little boy was imprisoned inside it – couldn't have been more than nine or ten months old – standing on the bundled-up jacket that covered the bottom of the crib, holding onto the bars and wailing. Wearing nothing but a filthy T-shirt and a filthier nappy.

Roberta lurched over, legs stiff as boards.

Little red cuts covered the wee boy's fingers, the tip of his nose and chin – semi-circular scrapes on his cheeks and around both wrists.

A lump of brambles knotted in her throat. Made it hard to swallow.

A bunch of those sports drinks bottles with the flip-top caps lay suckled dry and crumpled in the corners of the crib.

Empty tins of dog food littered the floor around the cot. All licked clean.

No...

A few of the ring-pull lids sat further out, crusted with dried brown lumps, too far away for a wee arm to reach.

She stared. Blinked as the world went a little blurry.

Do *not* cry in front of Tufty.

Do not.

A deep, shuddery breath.

Poor wee thing...

Roberta reached into the crib, pulled the toddler out, and hugged him tight.

II

'Sarge?' Tufty knocked on the bathroom door. 'Sarge, you in there?'

The child's wails boomed out from the other side of the scarred wood.

He knocked again. 'Sarge?'

Yeah. Probably better go in and hope she wasn't on the toilet.

He pushed the door open.

The flat's bathroom was *manky* filthy. Dirty grey-brown water in the sink, a thick black tidemark around the inside of the bath. The jagged yellow reek of a toilet that never got cleaned. Discarded crap littering the cracked lino floor.

Steel was on her knees, in front of the bath. She'd got a bright-red jumper from somewhere – dipping it into the sink then dabbing it at the screaming little boy's naked bottom. 'I know, I know. Shhh… Who's a brave wee soul?'

Tufty cleared his throat. 'Ambulance is here.'

The little boy screeched again.

'There's no hot water and he's all covered in sores. Shhh…'

Which explained the colour of the water in the sink. Tufty pulled the plug, letting the scummy water swirl away. Then filled it again. 'Next door say they haven't seen her for five days.'

'Five days.' Steel screwed up her face. Then dipped the jumper in the fresh water. 'Five days in a filthy nappy, scraping dog food from tins, while your mum decomposes into a mattress...' She blinked. Sniffed. Took a deep breath. 'Right. Ambulance.'

Tufty indicated left, taking them out onto the main road. Something upbeat and cheery bingled out of the car radio – a woman singing about how it was a lovely day for love and everyone should get out there and dance.

He glanced across the car at Steel.

She was slumped in the passenger seat, staring out of the window. Hands loose in her lap. Face dead and expressionless.

He forced a smile. 'Well ... look on the bright side. Imagine what would've happened if we hadn't gone round and kicked the door in!'

No reply.

'He would've died, wouldn't he? We saved that little boy's life today.'

Still nothing.

'He's only alive because of—'

'They didn't call the police.' Her voice was as dead as her face. 'They sat in their flats and they listened to that poor wee boy crying his arse off and didn't do a thing about it.'

'Yeah, but—'

'And then, when Sally started to smell, they still didn't call us. They got out the air freshener and tried to hide the stench.' Steel's head dipped. 'You know what, Tufty? I sodding *hate* human beings.'

The window at the end of the corridor was half boarded-up, the remaining half a mess of cracked grey glass. Graffiti crawled down the walls. Not the fancy arty type either – the type that was all swearing and crudely scrawled genitals. Bin-bags stacked in stinky heaps along the skirting boards.

The guy who'd opened the ground-floor flat's door squinted one eye shut, the other had a pupil black as treacle and big as a bowling ball. He scratched his crotch, ruffling his dirty Y-fronts and stained T-shirt. One grey-brown sock with a toe poking out. Dirt and bruises mingling on the pale hairy skin of his arms and legs.

Tufty held up the photo. 'Try again.'

Steel nudged a bin-bag with her boot. 'Come on, Shuggie, it's no' hard: where's Daphne McClellan? Two of you are shacked up, aren't you?'

He wobbled a bit, staring at the picture, holding onto the doorframe. Then a slow smile dawned across his filthy face. 'Nah, you mean Natasha, right? Natasha *Sparkles*.' Jazz hands. 'Not in, is she. Out. Out. Out.'

'Of *course* she is.' Steel gave him a glower. 'Where?'

Music oozed through the Regents Arms: Kylie encouraging everyone to do the Locomotion. Which was *never* going to happen here. Most of the gloomy bar's denizens looked like they'd struggle to walk in a straight line, never mind pretend to be choo-choo trains.

Ten to four on a Wednesday and the regulars were well into their fourth or fifth pint – the empties littering their tables. Some hadn't even bothered changing out of their overalls before coming in to quench the demon thirst.

The wall behind the bar was covered in apostrophes, all of which looked like they'd been stolen from other signs. At least three of them had definitely spent time attached to the front of a McDonald's. The guy in charge of the collection took one look at the photo in Tufty's hand and sighed. Then pointed at a table over by the cigarette machine.

Steel hunched her shoulders and marched over.

Tufty gave the barman an apologetic smile. 'She's having a bad day.'

'Hmmph.' He went back to stacking alcopops in the fridge.

Fair enough.

Tufty hurried over to catch up with Steel as she came to a halt in front of the table.

Daphne McClellan was there, sitting with an older man – grey hair, grey jumper on over a white shirt and grey tie. He had his eyes closed, both hands on the tabletop. Daphne was all done up in knee-high PVC boots, a short skirt and lacy top that showed off a skeletal figure so lacquered with fake tan she could've been one of those mummies they fished out of peat bogs.

She had one hand inside the flies of her friend's trousers. Working. A bored expression on her face as her arm jiggled up and down.

Steel gave the table leg a kick, setting the glasses on top clinking. 'Hope you're wearing gloves, Daphne. Practising safe sex and all that.'

She snatched her hand back. 'Urgh, not this again.' Daphne rolled her eyes, then sagged. 'I'm not doing nothing!'

Her friend scrabbled at his flies and jumped to his feet. 'I wasn't... This isn't... We—'

'You: Old Aged Pervert.' Steel hooked a thumb over her shoulder. 'Go spend your pension somewhere else.'

He legged it, straight out of the pub.

Steel hauled out a chair and sat in it. Staring across the table at Daphne McClellan. 'How many kids have you got, Daphs?'

A shrug rearranged the bones beneath that leathery skin. 'What's it to you?'

'You've got three.' She leaned in, growling it out. 'And you're supposed to be their sodding mother! Where are they?'

'At... At my mum's. The court gave her custody. I see them when I can, but it's—'

'THEN WHY DID WE FIND YOUR WEE BOY COWERING IN A CUPBOARD AT KENNY MILNE'S HOUSE?' Steel's voice echoed around the bar. Everyone stopped what they were doing to stare at her.

Then Daphne lowered her eyes, those formerly busy hands of hers picking at the tabletop. 'No comment.'

Steel barged through the station's back doors, slamming them against the walls with an echoing *BOOOM*...

Yeah. Her mood *definitely* hadn't got any better.

Tufty marched Daphne into the custody suite, struggling to catch up. Getting there just as Steel banged her hand down on the desk.

'Shop!'

Big Gary put down his colouring book. Sighed. 'And what can we do for *you* today, Your Royal Rumpled Majesty?'

The words came out like she was chewing on sick: 'Child endangerment. Neglect. Soliciting. Sex in a public place. And anything else you can think of.' She turned to go.

Big Gary reached for her. 'Wait, aren't you going to—'

'No. I'm done. No more.'

Tufty stared after her as she stomped out through the double doors back into the sunshine again. Then the doors swung shut, and they were alone at last.

'Hmph.' Big Gary shuffled his paperwork. 'What the hell's got into her?'

'Yeah ... sorry about that.' Tufty wheeled out the same apologetic smile he'd been peddling since the shift started. 'She's having a *really* bad day.'

Roberta wound the passenger window down another inch, letting the cloud of cherry-flavoured steam escape out into the sunny afternoon.

Sunlight sliced across one half of the Rear Podium car

park, leaving the row of patrol cars bathed in the shadow of Division Headquarters – it's bulk towering seven storeys above her. Someone lumbered up the stairs from the mortuary, still wearing their green scrubs and white wellington boots. Escaping the stink of death to enjoy some fresh air and a fag.

Roberta poked away at the screen of her mobile phone:

Sod the diet. Let's get a great big Chinese

for tea and watch Groundhog Day!

Send.

Her phone did its *ding-ding* incoming message noise.

We're supposed to be going to that play,

remember?

She thumbed out a reply:

AAAAAAAAAARGH!!!!! Sod... Sorry.

HORRIBLE day.

Send.

The driver's door opened and Tufty sank into the seat with a sigh. 'Lund and Barrett say they'll interview her soon as she's seen a duty solicitor.'

Roberta shook her head. 'I swear to God, Tufty, if I have to deal with one more scumbag today...'

Ding-ding:

OK, forget the play. We'll break open a bottle

of wine when you get home. Put the kids

to bed. Then get all naked and naughty!

She smiled. Ah, Susan, you saucy, lovely, cuddly minx.

You had me at naked.

Send.

Ding-ding:

You did remember my trophy, didn't you?

Sod. No.

Tufty pulled on his seatbelt. 'So where are we off to?'

'Mrs Galloway's. And don't forget to stop off for milk,

157

tea and biscuits. We can pop in by that trophy shop on the way.'

Tufty shifted the carrier bag from one hand to the other, going for the punchline as the lift juddered to a halt. 'So the *other* nun says, "If that's the case, why's he been shagging a penguin all night?"' He grinned at her.

Nope.

The lift doors juddered open.

'You see, because the bishop thought the *penguin* was the Mother Superior.'

Roberta stepped out into the corridor. 'Don't give up the day job.'

'Oh, come on. It's funny.'

'You keep telling yourself that.' She sauntered down the corridor to the flat at the end. Stopped.

Mrs Galloway's front door hung squint from one hinge, the wood all buckled and scraped. Someone had kicked it in.

Oh sodding hell…

Roberta knocked on the splintered doorframe. 'Mrs Galloway? Agnes? Are you OK?'

She stepped inside, Tufty right behind her.

'Mrs Galloway? It's DS Steel. Hello?'

A voice behind them, cold and hard: 'You're too late.'

Roberta turned, peering past Tufty.

The woman from the flat across the hall stood there in her disappointed tracksuit, arms crossed, face pinched and creased.

'What happened?'

'What do you *think* happened? You were supposed to save her! Instead, she's in intensive care, half dead, because *you* screwed it up!'

'She's…' A lump swelled in Roberta's throat, like a tumour. She swallowed it down. 'Intensive care?'

'Should be ashamed of yourself!' The neighbour slammed a hand against the twisted door. 'HE – CAME – BACK!'

She was so tiny, lying there on the other side of the glass, in her crisp-white hospital bed, dwarfed by the machines gathered around her. Everywhere no' covered in bandages, casts, or dressings was covered in bruises instead. The almost imperceptible rise and fall of her chest was the only sign that she was still alive.

Roberta put a hand against the window through to the High Dependency Ward, its glass cool beneath her palm.

The doctor flipped the page in her notes and kept droning on in a flatline nasal monotone: '…four broken ribs, punctured lung, ruptured spleen, broken ankle, dislocated shoulder…'

So small. So fragile. So broken.

'…fractured cheekbone, detached retina, broken wrist, internal bleeding—'

'She going to be OK?'

The doctor sighed. Scrubbed a hand across her face, tugging the bags beneath her eyes out of shape. 'No. Maybe. Someone her age… It's a lot of trauma. She'd be better off if he'd run her over with a car.'

The neighbour was right: it *was* all her fault.

She'd screwed up and Agnes Galloway had paid for it.

'Look, I know I'm not meant to say this, but speaking as a medical professional…' The doctor put a hand on Roberta's shoulder. 'If you catch the bastard who did this, I want you to batter the living crap out of him.'

Tufty was waiting for her, fiddling with his phone as she marched out of the ward. He stuck it away in his pocket and fell into step beside her. 'Is she all right?'

Idiot.

'Of course she's no' all right! How would she be all right?

159

Philip Innes nearly killed her.' Roberta curled her hands into claws and glowered at the ceiling. 'AAAARGH!'

An old man pushing a drip on a stand stopped to stare.

'Keep moving, Grandad!' She stormed past him, down the corridor and into the waiting lift. Mashing the button with her thumb. Glowering at the numbers as the doors slid shut. 'We should've had uniform watching the place! Why didn't you remind me to get someone watching the place?'

Tufty shrugged. 'Concussion, remember?'

Useless git.

'Oh, come on, Sarge: this isn't our fault! We didn't do it, Phil Innes did.'

She hauled out her phone and called Control. 'What the hell's happening with my lookout request? You were supposed to find Philip Innes! Why isn't he in *sodding* custody?'

Ding.

She swept out into yet another bland corridor. 'Well?'

There was silence from the phone. Then, *'For your information, Detective Sergeant Steel, we are not here for you to yell and shout at. If you want an update you can ask nicely!'*

'Fine!' Roberta clenched her teeth, squeezing the words out: 'Can I *pretty please* have an update on my lookout request?'

'There, that wasn't so hard, was it?'

'I swear to God I'll come down there with a claw-hammer!' She barged through a set of double doors, and up to a reception area where a lumpy male nurse in green scrubs squinted at a computer screen.

'Philip Innes hasn't been spotted. Patrol cars and foot patrols have been asked to keep an eye out.'

'AAAAARGH!' She hung up. Rammed the phone back in her pocket. Poked a finger at the nurse. 'Police. Wee boy, brought in earlier. Eaten nothing but dog food for days.'

The nurse didn't even look up from his computer.

'Antibiotics for the sores, fluids for the dehydration, social workers for the rest of it. No visitors.'

'Well ... *sod* you then!' She turned on the spot and stormed out again, grabbing a handful of Tufty's sleeve on the way, hauling him with her. 'We're going to find Philip Innes. We're going to arrest him. And somewhere along the way he's going to fall down a LOT of stairs!'

III

Cairncry Drive was a nice street, very fancypants. The houses were of the semidetached-bungalow-with-attic-conversion type in pink granite. Neat and tidy front gardens with crisp-edged box hedges and artistic shrubs.

Tufty locked the pool car and followed Steel up the path to number thirteen. A Jaguar sat out front. A new-looking one with leather seats and bags of extras. And they said crime didn't pay? Had to admit, standing outside Phil Innes's fancypants house on his fancypants street with his fancypants car parked outside, loansharking looked a hell of a lot more lucrative than police work.

Steel's face was set like angry concrete, both hands clenched into fists.

Yeah, *that* was a good sign.

Tufty rang the bell. 'Erm… Sarge? You're not going to do anything silly, are you? You were only *joking* about him falling down stairs, right?'

'No.' She hammered on the door. 'PHILIP INNES! POLICE! GET YOUR BACKSIDE OUT HERE, NOW!'

'Only, you know, Professional Standards—'

'EITHER YOU OPEN UP, INNES, OR WE KICK THIS DOOR DOWN!' More hammering.

'He's probably not even here. I mean, surely if you've got a

162

lookout request out for you someone checks your house first, right? A patrol car or something?' A shrug. 'Stands to reason.'

'INNES!'

The door swung open, and there was Phil Innes, dressed in a denim shirt and tan chinos. Very preppy. 'What's all the shouting— Hey!'

Steel grabbed him, spun him around, slammed him against the side of the house and pinned him there. Pulled out her handcuffs and snapped them on. 'Want to know what happens to scumbags who beat up old ladies? They're going to tear you apart in prison.'

She shoved him towards Tufty. 'Get this piece of crap in the car. We're going for a drive.'

Interview Room Four had the same sharp cheese-and-vinegar smell as a pair of manky old trainers left out in the rain, then brought in to dry on a radiator. The only upside was the expression on Philip Innes's face as he sat there breathing it in.

His solicitor was a baby-faced young man in a slightly crumpled suit. His hair cut short to try to hide the baldiness happening on top of his head.

Roberta sat back in her seat and shared a look with DC Lund. 'That sound like a lie to you, Veronica? Sounds like a lie to me.'

Innes pulled an affronted face. 'Well it's *not*.'

'You seriously expect us to believe you had nothing to do with it? Nothing at all?'

'Yes, I've visited Mrs Galloway from time to time, but only to help out with shopping or if she needs a hand. Ooh, I don't know … changing a plug? That sort of thing. I would *never* attack her. She's an old lady, for goodness' sake!'

'You're a loan shark, Phil-pot.'

Baby Face tapped his pen against the desk. 'Do you have any evidence of that, Detective Sergeant Steel?'

'Ask anyone.'

He smiled at her, making little dimples form in his chubby wee cheeks. 'That's not *evidence*, that's hearsay. And it's *not* admissible in court.'

Cheeky sod. 'He put Agnes Galloway in hospital!'

'Do you have any witnesses, Sergeant? No. Do you have any CCTV? No. Do you have any evidence against my client whatsoever? No.' He rocked his baldy wee head from side to side. 'No. No. No. No evidence at all.'

She leaned forward, snarling it out. 'Then we'll *get* some.'

'Yeah...' Tufty leaned back against the wall, and swapped his phone to the other ear. 'Nothing so far.'

Steel's voice growled out like an angry bull terrier that smoked sixty a day. *'How could no one see anything?'*

Down at the end of the corridor, Barrett and Harmsworth knocked on the last doors on this floor. Stood there waiting for the occupants to answer.

'We're doing everything we can, Sarge.'

'Philip Scumbag Innes is going to walk.'

'Yeah, but DNA—'

'Oh he's already covered that *one. He "pops round from time to time" doing "odd jobs" for her.'*

'And my bumhole's a mariachi band.'

'Then stop buggering about and find me some sodding witnesses!' She hung up.

Got to love a well-crafted motivational speech.

He stuck his phone in his pocket and went back to work.

A thin woman with nervous, watery eyes peered out at him through the tiny gap between her door and the frame – she hadn't even opened it wide enough to pull the chain tight. 'I didn't see anything.'

Tufty held up the photo of Phil Innes again. 'Are you sure, because—'

'Why would I see anything? Because I didn't. I didn't see *anything*.'

Of course she didn't.

The old man adjusted his glasses, fiddled with his hearing aid. Squinted at the photo Tufty handed him. Sniffed. Fiddled with his glasses again. From somewhere in the flat behind him came the sound of a TV quiz show turned up far too loud.

He handed the photo back. 'I don't know anything. Stop asking me questions.'

Then slammed the door.

The toddler was dressed up in a paleontologically-inaccurate dinosaur onesie, staring up at Tufty like he was the – most – exciting – thing – *ever*!!! His mum, on the other hand, did pretty much everything she could not to look at him at all. Her mop of Irn-Bru curls was fraying at the edges, dark bags under her eyes. The end of her nose had a faint pink glow to it, her eyes puffy and red. Another shrug and she handed the photo back to Tufty.

'No, I didn't hear anything.' Shrug. 'Nothing at all.'

He pointed upwards. 'Mrs Galloway's flat is *right* above yours and you didn't hear anything? It looks like a bomb went off in there! How could you not hear anything?'

She hugged her dinosaur baby closer and looked away again. Shrugged. 'I didn't hear anything.' One last shrug for luck. 'Please, I have to go. I can't help you.'

The flat door swung closed, shutting Tufty out in the corridor.

Ten down, fifteen to go.

* * *

Steel stormed the length of the CID office then turned around and stormed back again. 'Bloody, felchbunny, fudgemonkeying, motherfunkers!'

Phones, chargers and extension leads still cluttered everyone's desks, but Tufty, Lund, Barrett, and Harmsworth all sat with their chairs facing the middle of the room, watching Steel storm up and down and up and down.

She did another circuit. 'None of them? No' a single sodding one?'

'Well,' Harmsworth flared his nostrils, 'why would they want to *help* the police? It's not as if we do anything, is it? No, we just sit about on our fat backsides eating doughnuts all day.'

Barrett checked his clipboard. 'Every single household spoken to.'

'No offence,' Lund held up a hand, 'but maybe you were doing it wrong? Maybe a woman's better at—'

'Oh please, don't start *that* again.'

'I'm just saying, Davey, it's—'

'AAAAAAAAAARGH!' Steel screamed at the patchwork ceiling tiles. 'FOR GOD'S SAKE!' She grabbed the plastic crate marked 'CAN'T UNLOCK' and hurled it at the whiteboard. It split open, showering the floor with Nokias, iPhones and Samsungs.

No one made a sound as she stood there, glaring at the fallen phones.

Then Tufty sighed. 'They're scared. They've seen what Innes can do and they don't want it happening to them or their families. It's not their fault.'

'Then whose sodding fault is it?'

'Phil Innes.'

DCI Rutherford really didn't look the same, dressed in lounging jammie bottoms, furry slippers, and an Aberdeen

Football Club T-shirt. He stood in the doorway to a two-up-two-down in Cults.

His mouth tightened as he turned over the last photograph: Agnes Galloway, taken by the hospital before they got to work patching her up. Her frail wee body crippled and twisted.

Roberta leaned forward and poked the picture. 'Philip Innes.'

'What have we got on him?' The DCI's hands shook, his words terse and clipped. 'Witnesses? Forensics? Anything?'

'I want a warrant to go through his place with a nit comb. He's got to have something incriminating in there.' She counted them off on her fingers: 'Payment books for the loan-sharking, the shoes he used to kick an old lady half to death, the gloves he punched her with, the bloodstained clothes he wore.'

'We can't get a warrant without probable cause,' DCI Rutherford stared down at the photo, face souring, 'you *know* that.'

'So give me a warrant and I'll find some!'

A teenager drifted by on a bike, waving as she passed. 'Evening, Mr Rutherford.'

He pulled on a smile. 'Kerry.' It disappeared as soon as she was out of sight. 'I want this bastard caught, prosecuted, and banged up. But to make it stick in court we need *corroboration*. I need a complaint from the victim or I need a witness. Get me something I can use!'

Airyhall Library looked a lot better from the front.

The bit round the back was more functional: a big block of council recycling bins sat beside a wee recess where the back door was. Beige walls with brown trim. A Rorschach inkblot stained the tarmac, where some poor librarian's car had been dripping oil. They were all gone now, of course. Twenty to nine and the car park round the side was empty.

Airyhall Community Centre looked pretty empty too. Or

at least the lights were off. The side that faced the library was a featureless grey-beige wall, with a wee sticky-out bit where a red door led into the building proper. The whole thing lurking on the other side of a chest-high wall, topped by a handrail.

No' the greatest of views.

Probably wasting her time sitting there, but after today even a *tiny* success would be terrific. A minute achievement. A microscopic win. *Anything* to dull the image of that poor wee boy, standing in his crib, bawling his eyes out.

All those tins... Were his teeny fingers strong enough to lever the lids off himself, or had his darling mother done that for him before shooting up?

And what sort of scumbag fed their toddler dog food? Even if it was the expensive stuff you didn't need a tin-opener for. After all, if you're going to shoplift, why no' shoplift the best?

Aye, well. Wasn't as if she'd be doing it again, was it?

Or anything else, come to that.

Overdosing in front of her wee boy – what was *wrong* with people?

For once in his miserable life, DI Beardie Beattie was right: *if it wasn't for the drugs...*

Stop it.

Sitting here brooding wasn't helping.

Roberta puffed on her e-cigarette, billowing out clouds of strawberry-and-lime-flavoured steam.

Come on, Roberta: focus.

There was a perfect view between the recycling bins and the back of the library. If anyone turned up to do something dodgy, she'd be on them like stupid on Tufty.

Mind you, twenty minutes parked here and what did she have to show for her one-woman surveillance operation? Sod, and indeed, all.

No sign of Tommy Shand or his horrible orange Peugeot.

Pfff...

Well, it'd been a long shot anyway.

Should probably just show that mobile phone to the Procurator Fiscal and do Tommy for making indecent images and having sex with an older child. But getting him for possession with intent as well? That would be the bacon in the butty.

She pulled out her phone and poked at her contacts, setting the thing ringing.

'Control Room.'

'Aye, Benny: Tommy Shand. If anyone phones up to complain he's dealing behind Airyhall Library again, I want you to call me. OK?'

Benny tutted at her down the phone. *'You do know that's DI McPherson's case, don't you? He's first point of—'*

'Do you want me to tell your boyfriend what you get up to on those Police Scotland team-building away days?'

'Ah... I thought we had an ... understanding about that. After last time? You promised!'

'You hear anything, you call me, Benny.'

A groan. Then, *'All right, all right. Jesus.'*

'Good boy.'

She hung up. Drummed her fingers on the steering wheel.

Sodding Tommy Sodding Shand. Here she was, ready to take this crappy, *crappy* day out on him and he didn't even have the common decency to bother showing up. Selfish felchbunny.

Her phone *ding-dinged* at her:

> I've got the chardonnay in the fridge and
> the takeaway menus out waiting for you.
> Now slipping into something slinky...

Naughty old Susan.

Poor old Susan too. She deserved better than a grumpy wife, stomping about the house, swearing about how people were all scumbags.

Roberta thumbed out a reply:

Be there soon. Got a quick stop to make.

After all, just because Tommy Shand was a no-show, didn't mean she couldn't take her crappy day out on somebody else. And one person in particular deserved it more than anyone.

Jack Wallace was out washing his fake four-by-four as Roberta pulled into the residential street.

He scrubbed away at the car's roof with a big yellow sponge. Headphones on. Oblivious as she drove by his house in search of a parking spot. A Hoover sat on the pavement, under one of the trees lining the road – an extension lead snaking up the path and in through the raping wee shite's open front door. Very suburban and domesticated.

No' the sort of thing predators were meant to do.

And who washed their car at five to nine on a Wednesday night anyway?

People trying to get rid of evidence, that's who.

She pulled into a spot on the other side of the road, about four houses down. Sat there, watching him in the passenger wing mirror.

Couldn't arrest him for washing his car. Couldn't arrest him for anything at all.

But that didn't mean she couldn't rattle his cage a bit. See what fell out.

Roberta climbed out of her MX-5 and balled her fists. Marched up the middle of the road and—

A hand grabbed her arm.

She spun around, fist at the ready...

Tufty let go and danced back a couple of steps, eyes wide, even the black one. 'Whoa!'

She lowered her fist. 'What the hell are *you* doing here?' Then turned back towards Wallace. 'You know what? Don't care.'

Tufty grabbed her again. 'Don't!' He scurried around

170

till he was in front of her. Blocking the way. 'DCI Rutherford will mount your head on a pike outside the castle wall. You heard him: we have to stay away from Jack Wallace!'

'Get out of my sodding way.'

'I followed you, OK? Because I knew you'd do something daft.'

She stepped forward, but he didn't move.

'What happened to Agnes Galloway wasn't your fault. What happened to Sally Gray's kid wasn't your fault either. Doing what you're doing won't help them!'

She closed her eyes. 'Felchbunnies...' For once Tufty was right. Fronting Wallace up was about as bright as punching a wasps' nest. Her shoulders slumped. 'The poor wee sod was living on dog food, in a five-day-old nappy.'

'I know. But—'

'Well, well, well.' A voice behind her. 'What have we got here?'

She turned, and there was Jack Wallace, smiling at them, headphones around the back of his neck, bucket of soapy water in one hand, frothy sponge in the other.

'Have to admit, I really didn't think you'd be stupid enough to come back here, Detective *Sergeant* Steel. My lawyer's going to be very upset when I tell him you've been harassing me again.'

She glared at him. 'We're just leaving.'

'So soon? You don't want to come in and plant some evidence? Like you did last time?'

'How did you know?'

'That you planted evidence?' He laughed in her face. 'I knew, because I'm not a kiddy fiddler.'

'No: how did you know you needed an alibi that night? All that waving at the cameras: how did you know?'

'You never learn, do you?' He walked back to his car and

placed the sponge on the roof. Hefted the bucket. Time to rinse off the bubbles.

'How did you know you needed an alibi, *Jack*?'

Tufty tugged at her sleeve. 'Don't get drawn in. Let's go.'

'Well? Come on, Jacky Boy: impress us with your brilliance.'

'OK.' He swung the bucket at the car, swivelling at the very last moment, swinging wide. The soapy water arced out like a big wet tongue.

Roberta scrambled sideways and the whole lot went splosh – all over Tufty. He stood there with his arms out, dripping. 'Aaaargh…!'

She hauled out her handcuffs. Grinned. 'You just assaulted a police officer! Jack Wallace, I'm detaining you under Section Fourteen—'

'You don't even know how much trouble you're in right now.' He grinned right back at her. 'But you're about to find out.'

DCI Rutherford glared at them from behind his desk. At least he'd changed out of his T-shirt and jammie bottoms. Tufty stood to attention in the middle of the room, his fighting suit two shades darker than it had been at the start of the shift. Damp as a dishcloth.

'Well?' Rutherford's voice was just this side of shouting, his face just this side of aneurism-red. 'What the *bloody* hell did you think you were playing at, dragging this soggy idiot along with you? Is chucking your own career in the septic tank not enough? Do you have to ruin his as well?'

Tufty *eek*ed.

Roberta patted the silly sod on the back. 'Constable Quirrel was there trying to stop me. He had just succeeded when Jack Wallace attacked us with a bucket of soapy—'

172

'DON'T INTERRUPT!' Rutherford was on his feet now, fists resting on his desk, spittle gleaming on his bared teeth. 'Your reckless, *idiotic* antics have made NE Division look like a bunch of bloody halfwit amateurs!'

She shrugged. 'To be fair—'

'You were given a second chance, Sergeant. We could've fired you for what you did, but we thought, for some godforsaken reason, that you'd learn from your mistake. Well, apparently we were wrong!'

The only sound came from the radiator, pinging and gurgling like an unfed stomach.

Outside, in the corridor, someone laughed.

The mobile phone on Rutherford's desk buzzed twice then went silent.

She pursed her lips. Maybe a bit of contrition would make him feel a bit less shouty? 'Actually, Guv, if you—'

'ENOUGH!' He stabbed a finger at his office door. 'Get out of my sight. I need to decide what to do about you.' Rutherford curled his lip in disgust and turned away. Couldn't even look at her. 'You're an embarrassment.'

Sunset painted the granite houses in fiery shades of amber and peach. The trees glowed. And Roberta sat there, in her car, parked outside her *own* house for a change.

She closed her eyes and curled forward till her forehead came to rest on the steering wheel. Let her arms dangle either side of her knees.

'Sodding, felchbunnied, fudgemonkeying…' Deep breath. 'MOTHERFUNKER!' Bellowing it out into the footwell.

Was there ever a crappier day?

One: Agnes Galloway battered into intensive care. Two: Philip Sodding Innes sitting happily at home while half the idiots in NE Division were out looking for him. Then having to let him go! Three: Jack Wallace walking free. *Again.* Four:

a full-on bollocking from DCI Rutherford. And last, but crappiest of all, Five: Sally Gray's poor wee boy.

Dog food.

No' just the fact he'd been fed on it, but that he'd eaten the lot. Every last scrap. How long had he stood there, in his filthy nappy in his filthy cot while his mother rotted into a filthy mattress in that filthy hole of a house? Starving. Licking the tins out again and again till his little fingers and wrists and nose and cheeks were a network of sharp little cuts from the metal edges.

And the *sores*... All up and down his legs and bottom.

No child deserved that.

No one did.

Roberta's phone *ding-ding*ed at her.

She hauled it out.

> If you're not home in the next 5 minutes
> I'm putting on joggie bottoms and that
> sweatshirt you hate.

Great.

A long hard sigh, then she climbed out of the car. Got the box with Susan's trophy in it out of the boot. Plipped the locks. Slouched up the path to the front door.

It swung open and there was Susan, posing in a low-cut lacy negligée, bottle of fizzy wine in one hand, champagne flutes in the other. 'I cheated: saw you parking when...' Little creases formed across her brow. 'Oh, Robbie, what's wrong?'

The hallway got all wobbly, the breath sharp and lumpy in her throat.

Susan opened her arms and swept her up into a hug. Warm and soft and comforting. 'Shhh... It'll be OK. I promise.'

Roberta just stood there and cried.

CHAPTER SIX

in which it is shown that PC Harmsworth should Never Get Naked In Public, we find out if rubber willies float, and Tufty catches someone red-handed

I

'Gah…' Roberta pushed the scrambled eggs around her plate some more. It'd gone all cold and congealed, greyed by the liberal application of Worcestershire sauce, the toast beneath it turned to soggy linoleum.

Which pretty much summed this whole week up.

Susan pushed a cup of coffee in front of her. 'What's wrong with my scrambled eggs?'

A shrug.

'Honestly, some people.' She clapped her hands. 'Right, Naughty Monkey Number Two: do you want more soldiers?'

Naomi squealed in her high chair, a big smile on her face as she painted herself with baked beans.

'No. OK, then. Naughty Monkey Number One, what do you fancy for your packed lunch: peanut-butter-and-banana, or cheese-and-pickle?'

Jasmine stuffed another spoonful of Rice Krispies in her gob, chewing as she talked. 'Chicken jam!'

'Chicken jam it is. And don't talk with your mouth full.' Susan reached for the chicken pâté, spreading a thick layer onto a round of soft white bread. 'Robbie, are you going to be late tonight? Because I thought we could go to that new French place on Holburn Street. Cheer us up a bit. Dolly says she'll watch the kids.'

Roberta stared into the lumpy grey mess clarting her plate. 'Mmmph.'

'Robbie!'

When she spoke the words came out all flat and dead. 'Sorry. Not really hungry.'

Susan put down the knife, sooked her fingers clean, then took hold of Roberta's face. Stared right into her eyes. 'Do you want to quit? Because if you do, you march in there today and you tell them to take their horrible job and ram it *so* far up their backsides a spelunking team couldn't get it out.'

Her mouth twitched. 'That far?'

'Further.' Susan leaned in and gave her a kiss, soft and warm and faintly chickeny. 'Sod them.'

Barrett was up front at the whiteboard again, that clipboard of his clutched to his chest like a teddy bear. '...so keep an eye out if you can.'

Harmsworth slouched in his seat, digging away at one ear with a relentless finger. Lund stifled a yawn, both hands wrapped around a mug of coffee. Steel, on the other hand, wasn't really there. She sat staring out of the window, face droopy as a basset hound, drumming out a funeral beat on her desk jotter with her hand.

Only Brave Sir Tufty was paying any attention to the morning briefing. He'd taken notes and everything.

'Finally...' Barrett dug out the upturned police cap and went a-rummaging. Pulled out one blue bit of paper and one red. Unfolded them both. 'Today's word of approbation is "Spanktastic" and for *dis*approbation we have "Funkbiscuits". And that concludes morning prayers. Sarge?'

Everyone turned to look at her.

No reply.

Barrett tried again, only louder. 'Sarge?'

She sighed. Shrugged. 'Finish with the phones.' You could've ironed your shirt on those words, they were *that* flat.

'OK, you heard the lady: phone time!'

While everyone else picked a new mobile to try, Tufty stuck his heels into the carpet tiles and backward-walked his office chair over to Steel's desk. Put on a bit of a whisper: 'Are you OK, Sarge? Only you seem a bit … suicidal.'

She sagged a bit further. 'Ask no' for whom the bell tolls, Tufty, today it tolls for me.' Steel checked her watch. 'In five, four, three, two…' She pointed at the office door.

It opened bang on time and the nervous PC from yesterday stuck his head into the room. God knew what facial expression he'd been aiming for, but he'd wound up with a cross between a smile and a grimace. Like he'd tried for a fart and got an unpleasant surprise instead. 'DS Steel? They're ready for you.'

'Course they are.' She stood, slapped a hand down on Tufty's shoulder. 'Come on, then. You can hold me back if I try to kill anyone.'

They'd arranged themselves down one side of the meeting room table, like this was some sort of job interview. Or a firing squad.

DCI Rutherford, DI Vine, Jack Wallace, and his solicitor Moir-Farquharson. The first two looked like someone had just rammed a lit Catherine wheel up their backsides, Wallace smugging it up big-time in the middle, the lawyer deadpan.

Leaving Steel and Tufty to stand on the other side of the table.

Rutherford scowled at them. 'Detective Sergeant Steel, do you have anything to say in your defence?'

'Aye. Constable Quirrel had nothing to do with it. He was there trying to talk me out of confronting Jack Wallace.'

'I see.'

She nodded. 'He did good. This is all on me.'

Which was really nice of her. Given the option, most senior officers would shoot you in the kneecap so the bear would eat you while they ran away. Wouldn't even blink.

Rutherford poked the table. 'I *specifically* ordered you to stay away from Mr Wallace and you went there anyway.'

She bared her teeth. 'All that smiling and waving at the CCTV cameras – he knew we'd check, so—'

'Stop – right – there!' The finger stopped poking and pointed right at her. 'You had no business harassing Mr Wallace. You were *ordered* not to.'

Steel shrugged. Her shoulders might have been all nonchalant and 'whatever', but her face looked one red button away from going intercontinental. *BOOOOOOOOM...* At least three megatons.

Tufty hissed it out the side of his mouth, as quietly as possible so no one but her would hear. 'Please don't.'

DI Vine opened the manila folder in front of him and pulled out three sheets of paper. 'The results of Miss Edwards' rape kit came back from the lab. The DNA they found doesn't match Mr Wallace. He has an alibi for the evening. He has a witness who stayed with him until eight in the morning. Do you understand, Sergeant?'

Steel's chin came up. 'So whose DNA *did* it match?'

'Say it with me: "Mr Wallace had nothing to do with it."'

'Then how come he *knew* he'd need an alibi?'

Wallace spread his hands, palm up. 'Didn't. But I know you and your wee mates like to keep an eye on me, so I smile and wave when I pass a CCTV camera. Just to show there's no hard feelings.'

The lawyer glanced at his watch. 'If I may, gentlemen, time is moving on.' He smiled at Steel. 'Detective Sergeant: my client has very generously asked your superiors not to demote or fire you for your actions. In exchange for which he will not sue Police Scotland for harassment.'

OK, *that* was a bit unexpected.

Tufty smiled.

Woot – they were going to get away with it!

So how come Steel didn't look so happy?

She stared back, one eyebrow slowly creeping its way up her forehead.

Hissing Sid nodded. 'This is on one condition: you apologise.'

The eyebrow slammed back down again, joining its neighbour in a scowl.

Sitting there, flanked by Vine and the lawyer, Wallace grinned. 'And you do it like you mean it.'

Oh God…

Time to sound the four-minute warning…

DCI Rutherford thumped down behind his desk and treated Steel and Tufty to a family-sized portion of the evil eye. Morning sunlight streamed in through the office window, turning the whole room into one big microwave oven, great sticky waves of heat making sweat prickle across the back of Tufty's neck. Or maybe it was the upcoming bollocking?

Steel moved towards one of the visitors' chairs.

'Don't even *think* about it!'

She slouched to attention instead. 'Boss.'

Rutherford shuffled some paperwork out of his in-tray and back again. 'I think you understand what's coming next.'

'Aye, got a fair idea.'

'You will not go anywhere near Jack Wallace. And Constable Quirrel here is going to be held responsible if you do.'

What?

No, no, no, no, no.

Tufty pulled his chin in. 'But that's not—'

'You clearly don't give a toss about your own career, Roberta, so let's see if you care about *his*. Your crimes will be *his* crimes. One more complaint from Jack Wallace and DC Quirrel gets a black mark on his record so big they'll be able to see it from the International Space Station. Are we clear?'

He held up a hand. 'Boss, sir, can I just—'

'No you can't.' Rutherford leaned forwards, half out of his seat, fists on the desk again. 'Well, Sergeant?'

Tufty stared at her. Tell him no! Tell him it's not fair to lumber poor Tufty with the sins of the Sergeant! Tell him—

Steel nodded. 'Guv.'

Nooooooooooooooo!

'Good.' A nasty little smile appeared beneath Rutherford's nose. He selected a sheet of paper from his in-tray. 'And to make sure: I have a very special assignment for you and your team. Maybe this time you'll learn your lesson?'

Something inside Tufty curdled a little.

It was going to be one of *those* days, wasn't it?

'Now, children, we've got a real treat for you.' Mrs Wilson clapped her hands and beamed out at the rows and rows of little kiddies sitting cross legged on the gym hall floor. Standing there on the little stage, she looked more like the kind of person who sold life insurance than ran a primary school – black suit, purple top, kitten heels, hair piled up in a plume of smoky curls.

Had to be at least a hundred kids in here, all staring up at her. About thirty of them were dressed as Disney princesses – boys as well as girls – all sitting in a sequin-and-lace clump at the back. Clearly, St Henry's Primary was a lot less strict with its dress code than the school Tufty went to.

A dozen teachers sat in plastic chairs dotted around the

room. Eyes scanning the kids like the searchlights on a prison watchtower.

Steel slumped against the wall bars at the side of the stage, with her head in her hands. 'Susan was right: I should've just resigned.'

Harmsworth and Barrett shifted from foot to foot, like they were getting ready to bolt at any minute. But Lund was rubbing her hands, a cheery smile on her face. Was she *actually* looking forward to this?

She was.

Freak.

Mrs Wilson pointed at the five of them. 'These nice police officers have come here to talk to you all about staying *safe*! Isn't that lovely?'

The kids chorused back, 'Yes, Mrs Wilson.'

'Look at them.' Steel curled her top lip, like she'd caught a whiff of something stinky. 'Sticky wee children. *Thousands* of them.'

Tufty nudged her in the ribs. 'Thought you liked kids?'

'This is all Jack Raping Turdbadger Wallace's fault.'

'Is it? I thought we were being punished because you were round his place harassing...' Yeah, the look on her face meant it probably wasn't a good idea to finish that sentence. Tufty cleared his throat. 'I mean, look on the bright side: they could've fired you. *And* me. Both of us. And I don't want fired.'

Harmsworth sniffed. 'You know what they say, don't you? Kids are the Fifth Horseman of the Apocalypse. War, Famine, Plague, Death, and the Under Twelves.' He shuddered, making his chins wobble. 'This'll all end in tears. Doom, disaster, horror, the dead rising from their graves...'

Mrs Wilson clapped her hands. 'So come on, children: let's have a big St Henry's welcome for Detective Sergeant Steel and her police friends!' Then she led everyone in a round of applause as Lund dragged Steel up onto the stage.

The two of them stood there, Steel all droopy, Lund grinning out at the evil horde.

Tufty, Barrett, and Harmsworth stayed right where they were, thank you very much.

So Lund launched into get-over-here-you-lazy-sods! hand gestures, bugging her eyes at them, and mouthing, 'Now!'

'It's the End of Days, I swear to God.' But Harmsworth lumbered onto the stage anyway.

Barrett and Tufty followed him.

The sea of wee faces had a … *predatory* look to them. Even the ones dressed up as Disney princesses. Actually, they were the worst of the lot. Six-year-olds with glittery dark eyes to match their glittery costumes. Like someone had rolled a load of hyenas in sequins and lurid nylon.

Hungry and ready to feed.

Harmsworth was right.

Lund stepped to the front of the stage and held her arms wide. 'Hello, boys and girls! Who wants to learn all about "Stranger Danger"?'

Squeals of delight throbbed up from the audience.

Steel mimed gagging on her own vomit.

Soon as the nine o'clock bell went, the teachers all vanished. One second they were there, the next it was like the rapture had come early and decided it'd forgotten to install child seats, so the kids would all have to stay behind. After all: the police dealt with riots and football hooligans all the time, didn't they? What could possibly go wrong?

The Disney princesses crowded in around Tufty, Steel, Barrett, Lund, and Harmsworth, making a multi-coloured sea of gap-toothed smiles, magic wands, tiaras, fairy wings, and sticky fingers.

Harmsworth shrank back, bumping against Tufty. 'Oh God. It's like a George Romero film...'

A little girl, dressed as Belle from *Beauty and the Beast*, held up her wand. 'I can make nasty boys turn into frogs! I *can!*'

Lund pulled an impressed face. 'Ooh, that's *very* clever. I've got a magic wand too, do you want to see it?'

Lots of happy squealing as the kids jumped up and down. 'Yes! Yes! Yes!'

Harmsworth curled his hands against his chest, elbows in, not touching anyone. 'You know they're just walking disease vectors, don't you?'

'Ready? Here we go!' Lund pulled out her extendable baton. 'Abra-ca-dabra!' She flicked it out to full length with a hard *clack*.

The unisex princesses ooh-ed and ahh-ed as they shuffled closer, eyes wide.

Yeah, Harmsworth was right. This was *way* more *Night of the Living Dead* than *Balamory*.

Closer. Closer. Sticky hands out like horrid little—

A hand grabbed Tufty's arm. 'Aaargh!' He spun around... but it was only Steel.

She hauled him away from the pack, leaving Harmsworth, Barrett, and Lund to their fate. 'What we need is a plan.'

Ooh, good idea.

'Finish up here and go for tenses?'

'No, you neep. A plan about Jack Raping Funkbiscuit Wallace.'

Tufty backed off, hands up. 'No – no – no – no – *no*! We are *not* having a Jack Wallace plan!'

Harmsworth's voice carried across the princesses' squeals. 'Colds. Flu. Salmonella. Botulism. Bubonic plague...'

A little boy Snow White jumped up and down in front of him. 'Do you have a magic wand too, Mr Policeman?'

Steel poked Tufty in the chest. 'He *knew* he'd need an

alibi for that night. How? How did he know? Because he's involved, *that's* how.'

Not this again. 'You heard DCI Rutherford: if we go within a million miles of Wallace, we're screwed.'

Harmsworth curled away from Snow White, hands and arms raised like he was trapped in a nettle patch. 'And don't get me started on C. difficile and MRSA. Kids are an Ebola outbreak waiting to happen.'

'Mr Policeman? Do you have a magic wand like the lady?'

'Rutherford can kiss my sharny hoop. Jack Wallace is up to his armpits in this and I'm going to sodding well prove it.'

'*No!*' Tufty stared at Steel. 'Do you even *listen* to yourself? You're obsessed! He wasn't there. He didn't do it. It's not his DNA.'

'I'm no' saying he *did* it, I'm saying he's involved. He knew!'

'Mr Policeman? Magic wand, Mr Policeman! Magic wand!'

'Urgh,' Harmsworth curled away again. 'Get off me. You're getting sticky fingerprints on my suit.'

'We can't just go around arresting everyone you think is dodgy.' Tufty chucked his hands in the air. 'Rutherford was right, you're unhinged! You're—'

'Don't you speak to me like—'

'—walking nightmare who ruins *everything*!'

' pasty-faced wee turd-sniffer. Wallace is guilty.' Glaring back at him. Teeth bared. Toe to toe and nose to nose.

The kids launched into a chant. 'Magic wand! Magic wand! Magic wand!'

'Get off me, you little horrors!'

Tufty's ears fizzed, blood whoomping in his forehead – burning in his throat. And OK: it was probably career suicide to shout at a senior officer, but if she was going to get him fired anyway, what difference did it make? Might as well throw in a poke for good measure.

So he did, right on her collar bone. See how *she* liked it

for a change. 'I'm not chucking away four years in the police just because you can't take a funkbiscuiting telling!'

She poked him back. Harder. 'Did you see what happened to Beatrice Edwards? Did you see what he did to Claudia Boroditsky? Wallace has to be stopped!'

The princesses crowded in on Harmsworth, forcing him to retreat. 'I'll arrest the lot of you!'

Lund sighed. 'Oh for goodness' sake, Owen, just play along for once in your life.'

'I will *not* be bullied by a bunch of snottery wee kids!'

Another poke. 'It – wasn't – him!'

'He *knew* about it! He…' Steel wasn't glowering at Tufty any more, she was staring at the group of kids as Harmsworth stumbled back, tripped and went down with a thump.

Nobody spoke. The princesses froze.

The sound of the older kids whooping it up in the playground filtered in through the windows.

Then a little girl Pocahontas stabbed her fairy wand up into the air sideways, William-Wallace-broadsword style. 'PILEY-ON!'

They did. All of them. Leaping onto Harmsworth. Burying him beneath an avalanche of Disney princesses.

'GET OFF ME! HELP! HELP!'

Steel ran a hand across her face, still staring. 'Why did he need an alibi, then? Why did Jack Wallace need an alibi for a crime he didn't commit?'

'Just because your career's nearly over, doesn't mean I want mine chucked away too!'

'AAAAAAARGH! NO BITING!'

'My career's no' "nearly over", you cheeky wee shite!'

One of Harmsworth's shoes came flying out of the piley-on, bounced off the gym floor and skittered four or five foot before coming to a halt. His other shoe followed the first. Then a sock.

'FOR GOD'S SAKE, LUND, GET THEM OFF ME!'

Lund moved, but Barrett grabbed her arm.

'Actually we're not supposed to have any physical contact with the kids.'

She smiled. 'You know, I think you're right.'

'AAAAAAAAARGH!!!'

Steel escalated the poking war. 'Well, come on, then: how did Wallace know?'

'It… I…' Yeah, she had a point. 'Look, I've no idea. Maybe he *is* involved, somehow, but we still can't do anything about it. It's DI Vine's case, we have to let it go.'

'And what happens when another woman gets raped?'

'AAAAAAAAAARGH! STOP BITING ME! LUND! LUND, HELP! BARRETT!'

Barrett shrugged. Grinned. 'Sorry, we'd love to, but it's the rules.'

'GET OFF ME! HELP! HELP!'

A suit-jacket sleeve went flying, fluttering to the ground like a wounded bird. It was followed by a chunk of trousers. Then more scraps of clothing – bits of shirt, a vest, another sleeve, more trousers.

Steel shook her head. 'It has to be him.'

'It isn't! Didn't you learn *anything* from last time? Just because you want Jack Wallace to be guilty, that doesn't magically make it happen!'

'NO! DON'T YOU DARE, YOU WEE SHITE! AAAAAAAAARGH!'

Tufty jabbed a hand at the far wall, indicating the entirety of Aberdeen. 'I want to *be* something, OK? I want to catch killers. I want to make a difference! You are *not* dragging me down with you!'

Steel turned. Teeth bared. Snarling like a police Alsatian.

'HELP! SOMEONE HELP ME FOR GOD'S SAKE!'

He backed away a step. 'You know when I first wanted

to be a policeman? Five years old. Dad ran off with a traffic warden to Paisley and Mum climbed up on the roof of our tower block.' Tufty wrapped his arms around himself. 'This policeman came and talked her down and I thought: that was it. That was what I wanted to do with my life. Make people better. *Help* people.'

Steel's face softened. 'Five?'

'Please don't make them fire me.'

'NO! NOT THE PANTS! NOT THE PANTS!'

A wee boy dressed as Elsa appeared from the depths of the piley-on, holding a pair of Y-fronts above his head, triumphant grin on his freckled face. They weren't the newest or whitest; Harmsworth's underwear had the perished-elastic sag that marked them out as antiques.

'GIVE ME BACK MY PANTS!'

'NEVER!' Elsa ran off, Harmsworth's Y-fronts held high like a captured enemy flag. The rest of the Disney Princess Posse hammered out after him – all squealing and giggling – clutching various torn bits of Harmsworth's clothing.

They banged through the door to the playground, disappearing outside.

Tufty, Steel, and Lund *stared*.

There, left all alone, lying on the gym floor between the lines for netball and tennis, was a stark-naked Harmsworth. His uncooked-cookie-dough skin was covered in little red bite marks. Both hands clamped over his intimate masculine area. Eyes screwed shut. A high-pitched keening noise coming out of his mouth.

He had a hairier back than expected. Hairier bum too.

A smile broke across Steel's face. She snorted. Sniggered. Then creased up, hands on her knees, hooting it out. Lund guffawed, pointing at Harmsworth's poor furry backside.

Tufty tried not to laugh, he really did.

Didn't help, though.

'You're all a bunch of *bastards!*' Harmsworth struggled to his feet, one hand still clutching his original sin, bottom lip trembling. His head snapped left and right, eyes raking the school gymnasium, then he scurried across the wooden floor, his other hand shielding his furry bottom as he ran for a stack of gym equipment. He dived behind a pile of blue floor mats, hauling them over himself.

Then a pasty, hairy arm poked out from beneath the makeshift fort, pointing at the doors to the playground. 'Don't just stand there, go get my pants back!'

Steel hammed-up a massive grin at Lund, Barrett and Tufty and they all rushed over to the window – noses pressed against the safety glass.

The princesses paraded around the swings, marching like the soldiers of a strangely-dressed sparkly-sequinned army. Once round the roundabout, across the hopscotch squares, and back around the swings again. Following Elsa and his triumphant trophy – held aloft on the tip of a magic wand, the grey fabric flapping in the breeze as they chanted their victory cry in unison: *'PANTS! PANTS! PANTS! PANTS! PANTS!'*

Lund wiped a tear from her eye. 'Some days, I *love* my job.'

II

Everyone sat facing the front in the police van. No one making eye contact with anyone else. Because every time they did...

Barrett sniggered. Coughed. Cleared his throat.

Lund bit her bottom lip and blinked a few times, shoulders quivering.

Steel let out a shuddery breath.

Tufty glanced in the rear-view mirror.

And there was Harmsworth, all crunched down into himself on the very back row of seats, a hairy grey blanket pulled tight around his hairy bare shoulders. A foul scowl on his face. 'I bloody *hate* the lot of you!'

And that just set them all off again.

Roberta leaned back against the metalwork and munched her way through a cold sausage roll. The bridge wasn't huge, only big enough for three people to stand side by side on the wooden decking, but it thumped straight out through the trees and across the River Don. The water crawled by underneath, sparkly and blue.

Metal crossbeams made three-foot-high asterisks above the handrail, leaving just enough space between them to squeeze your head and shoulders. No' the prettiest of bridges in the world, but it was nice and quiet, and lovely and warm in the sun.

Tufty dipped into the Tesco carrier bag and came out with two tins. 'You want Irn-Bru, or Coke?'

She polished off the sausage roll and held out greasy pastry-flecked fingers. 'Bru. And a gentleman would open it for a lady.'

He looked skyward for a moment, shook his head a little, then did the business and handed over the Irn-Bru.

'Why thank you, kind sir.' She knocked back a scoof of fruity fizz. Belched. 'You know what? Seeing Owen diving for cover, wee wrinkled willy flapping in the breeze, kinda makes life feel worthwhile again.'

Tufty dipped back into the bag again. 'Samosa, or mini pork pie?'

'Pie me.'

He did.

'We should make a tradition out of it. Every time we have a crappy day, Harmsworth has to run around naked.'

'Yeah,' the word was mumbled through a mouthful of samosa – no manners at all, 'maybe not. I never want to see that ever again. Can you believe how *hairy* he was? Like a bar of prison soap.' A shudder.

'Don't be such a killjoy.' She ripped a bite out of her pie, all savoury and crumbling pastry and jellified pork bits. Chewing through the words, 'Did your dad really sod off when you were five years old, or was that just a cunning lie to—' Her phone blared out its theme tune. 'Oh, what fresh hell is *this*?' She took another bite of pie and answered it. 'What do you want?'

'*That what passes for manners in your house?*' Big Gary.

'Make it quick, Gary, I've got a pie on the go.'

'*You wanted to know when someone came in to pick up a stolen mobile phone.*'

'I did?' Frown. Mobile phone. Mobile phone... Aha: Tommy Shand's phone. The one with the dirty photos of Josie Stephenson on it. The one that was going to get him sent down for three or four years as a sex offender. 'So I did.' Another bite of pie.

Could just get Lund or Barrett to detain Shand under a Section Fourteen...

But why deny herself the pleasure of making the dirty wee sod squirm? Tommy Shand would keep.

She popped the last chunk of pie in her mouth. 'We're going to be a while, tell him to come back later. I want to be there when he gets it.'

'But of course, Your Majesty. Anything else while I'm running around after you?'

'Bye, Gary.' She hung up. Frowned down at the water crawling by underneath.

Tufty stuffed a couple of Skips in his mouth. Sooked the prawn-cocktaily dust off his fingers. 'Problem?'

'Tommy Shand wants his phone back. Because *of course* I'm going to let him get away with an amateur porn shoot starring a fifteen-year-old model. Trouble is, if I do him for the phone *now*, I can't catch him dealing drugs round the back of Airyhall Library and do him for that as well. Decisions, decisions.'

'A sex offender in the hand is better than two in the bushes.'

Roberta sighed. Picked up a stick lying on the bridge deck. 'Why does the world have to be full of perverted funkbiscuits?' She turned, reached through the metalwork and dropped her stick on the upstream side. Sauntered over to the other side to watch it float by. 'You really think we shouldn't go after Jack Wallace?'

Tufty nodded. 'They'll fire you and they'll screw me. Besides,' a shrug, 'DI Vine's a professional pain in the bumhole:

no way he's going to let whoever raped Beatrice Edwards get away with it. Even just out of sheer bloody-mindedness – he'll get them.'

'Yeah. Probably.' Maybe.

She sent a second stick after the first. 'Doesn't mean we can't go after Philip Dog-Murdering Innes, though.'

'True.' Tufty tried a stick of his own. Scuttling over to the other side and poking his head and shoulders through the metalwork railings. 'Mind you, it'd help if we had some evidence. Maybe we could try going door-to-door again? Someone *might* change their mind and talk to us.' He made a wee boat out of the paper bag his samosa came in and dropped it at the exact same time Roberta released Stick Number Three.

They looked at each other for a heartbeat, then raced to the other side.

'Come on, Boaty McBoatface!'

'Come on Sticky McStickface!'

Tufty stuck his arms in the air. 'I has a win!'

'What else have we got?'

He dug into the carrier bag and came out with two Eccles cakes.

She took her one and held it out through the railings. 'On three, two, one ... go!'

Rush to the other side.

'Ha: two-nil to the Magnificent Detective Constable Quirrel!'

'Yeah? Well I know something that'll wipe the grin off your smug wee face.' Roberta marched back to the car and popped the boot. Rummaged through the bits and bobs gathered there. Where the hell were... Ah. Bingo. She grabbed two of them and hurried back to the bridge. Held one out to Tufty.

He recoiled. 'That's a *massive* dildo!'

194

'Don't be such a wet blouse, it's no' been used.'

He stuck his hands into his armpits. 'Why...? What?'

'From the Great Rubber Willy Burglary last year. Two blokes broke into Ann Summers and filched half the stock. I sort of forgot to sign three or four into evidence. Oops.'

'Never been used?'

'No' so much as a dry humping.'

'OK, then.' He took the big purple one and they rushed to the side of the bridge again.

'On three, two, one...'

Sploosh!

'Oh.' He leaned out through the railings, frowning down at the water below. 'I was expecting them to float.'

Roberta hit him. 'Waste of two perfectly good—' *Cagney & Lacey* wailed out from her phone. 'No' again! Leave me alone, it's lunchtime!' But she pulled it out anyway, holding her other hand above the screen to block out the sunlight. 'UNKNOWN NUMBER'.

She pressed answer. 'Hello?'

'Miss me?'

Took a second to place the voice, but there it was – like a sour taste in her mouth: 'Wallace.' Dirty raping wee turd. 'What the hell do you want?'

'Did you enjoy grovelling this morning? Feel good to be on your knees?'

'Listen up, sunshine, you're going to screw up sometime and when you do I'm going to ram my boot so far up your...'

Tufty was staring at her, pointing at the phone and mouthing, 'Jack Wallace?'

She pressed the button to put it on speaker.

'—never learn, though. Do you really think I'm stupid enough to...' Pause. *'Did you just put me on speakerphone?'*

'Course no': I'm in the car. Hands free.'

'Yeah, I'm not a moron, Sergeant.'

195

And the line went dead. He'd hung up.

Roberta wiggled the phone at Tufty. 'You heard that.'

'Yeah… Well, I heard you threaten him, then him say he wasn't stupid. It's not exactly Watergate, is it?'

Of course it wasn't. Because there was no way Jack Wallace was going to say anything incriminating with witnesses present.

'Sodding hell.'

'No chance.' Mrs Galloway's neighbour crossed her arms and jerked her chin up. Her toddler clung to her tracksuited knee, staring at them – thumb in his mouth.

Tufty held out the photo of Phil Innes again. 'Please, just think about it, OK?'

Steel sniffed. 'Come on, Helen, you know who this is, and I know that you know, so why no' save us all a heap of time and talk – to – me.' Really leaning on the words, forcing them in like a blunt knife.

'You don't get it, do you?' She nodded at the sooking toddler. 'I've got a wee boy. You think I'm putting Justin at risk?'

'Has Innes threatened you?'

The round cheeks darkened, pink spreading upwards from the neck of her T-shirt. '*No one*'s threatened me. And they won't, because I'm not doing your bloody job for you!'

'*My* job? Have you forgotten what he did to Agnes Galloway?' Teeth bared. 'Have you?'

Tufty stepped between them. 'OK, let's all just calm down a little.'

Steel thumped him on the arm. 'Calm?' She marched away a couple of paces, then back again, arms jabbing away for emphasis. 'How can I do my job when none of you buggers will say a sodding word? They won't give me a warrant unless I've got corroboration! Witnesses! Evidence!'

The chin came up a little higher. Voice a little louder. 'That's not *my* fault!'

'You won't bloody speak to me! I can't even search the bastard's house because of you lot!'

The toddler made whingy gurning noises.

Steel shoved Tufty out of the way. 'I can't get forensics from Innes without a warrant. No forensics, no evidence. And I can't arrest him with no bloody evidence! Help me! If you don't help, we can't do anything!'

'Don't you dare!' They were almost nose to nose now, eyes bugging. 'You're the *police*, you should know what you're doing! That poor woman's nearly dead because you poked your noses in and didn't arrest the bastard!'

Steel's right hand curled into a fist.

Tufty grabbed her sleeve. 'All right, come on, this isn't helping.'

'Do you want him to keep doing it? Is that what you want? Philip Innes running this place like his own private gulag?'

'I want you to do – your – job!' Helen grabbed her toddler and marched back inside, slamming the door in their faces.

Steel stood there, fuming at it.

'Wonderful.' Tufty let go. Stepped back. 'That went *really* well.'

'Just because she's too chicken doesn't mean everyone else is.'

'You've been spitting wasps since Jack Wallace phoned and it's *genuinely* not helping. We need more softly, softly, and less shouty ranty.'

'Arrrgh!' She stormed off, arms in the air, bellowing it out: 'SOMEONE IN THIS GOAT-BUGGERING TOWER BLOCK IS GOING TO TALK TO US!'

'I said no. Now leave me alone.' The old man thumped back inside and slammed the door.

* * *

'I didn't see anything, how many times do I have to tell you people that?' Little Miss Hairy shoved the door closed again.

A watery eye stared out at Tufty through the gap, the security chain stretched tight. 'Go away. I have nothing to say to you.' The door clunked shut.

Tufty knocked again. 'It's the police. Can you open the door please?'

A woman's voice came from the other side of the painted wood. *'Go away, I'm not in.'*

Roberta slumped against the wall beside the door. 'Why do we bother?' Ungrateful bunch of turdholes. You try to save them from a violent scumbag and do they help? Do they buggery.

'I know you're in, because I can hear you talking to me.'

'I'm not talking to you! I'm not talking to anyone. Now go away!'

She checked her watch. Ten past seven. 'We're achieving sod-all here. I'm calling it.' Then turned and scuffed towards the stairs. It wasn't even a *nice* tower block. Graffiti. Peeling paint. That faint, peppery-mouldy smell.

Tufty slouched up beside her as she pushed through into the stairwell. 'Maybe the labs will find something?'

'Honestly, why do we bother? No one here gives a stuff about Agnes Galloway but us. They're a bunch of selfish—'

Cagney & Lacey blared out. *Again.* Roberta stopped. Grimaced. 'You know what? That theme tune was fun for the first couple of days, but it's beginning to seriously get on my tits.' She hauled the phone out and answered it. Barked out the word with all the welcoming warmth of a shallow grave: *'What?'*

Big Gary tutted. *'You get worse, you know that? Your mobile phone man is in again, wanting his Nokia back.'*

'I don't care. Tell him to go shag a bollard!'

She hung up and rammed the phone back into her pocket. Stared upwards, through the gap between the flights of stairs, all the way up to the ceiling fifteen storeys above. Hauled in a deep breath. 'NO' ONE OF YOU BUNCH OF BASTARDS GIVES A TOSS ABOUT AN OLD LADY GETTING BATTERED HALF TO DEATH!' Another breath. 'AAAAA AAAAAAAAAAAAAAAAAAAAAAARGH!'

Tufty raised an eyebrow. 'Feel better?'

She stomped down the final flight of stairs, through the entrance hall, and out into the sunshine. Turned and stuck two fingers up at the tower block and its rancid occupants. 'Sodding, badger-ferreting, FUNKBISCUITS!'

A couple of old farts on the other side of the road stopped and stared at her, their cairn terrier yapping and twirling at the end of its leash.

She gave them the Vs as well. 'Oh, bugger off!' Then stormed away to the car.

The in-house forensics lab was awash with blue plastic evidence crates. They were stacked up everywhere – on the floor, on the filing cabinets, on the work benches, on the superglue/fingerprint cabinet, on the two upright fridges that stood by the door... The only bit that was crate-free was the central work table with its light boxes and magnifying glasses.

CSI Miami, it wasn't.

Tufty stood by the door, hands at his sides, shoulders hunched. Sniffing the chemical-scented air as if hunting for something that had gone off.

Roberta leaned back against one of the fridges – setting bottles inside it clinking. 'What if I said pretty please?'

'Urgh.' The lab technician picked a bloody knife off the light table, holding it between two purple-nitrile-gloved fingers, and popped it back into its tube. 'You know I can't do that.'

Roberta gave her a smile, piling on the charm. 'Come on, Gloria, there's a little old lady in intensive care because of this scumbag.'

A slow, sad sigh, then Gloria pointed at a stack of evidence crates. 'Husband came home and battered his wife to death with the iron.' Another box. 'Bus driver got pissed at lunchtime and flattened a motorcyclist.' Another. 'Bunch of teenagers gang-raped a grandmother.' Another. 'Brother and sister decided their parents were squandering their inheritance and took an axe to—'

'I get it. I really, really do. But no one's talking, Gloria. This scumbag's going to get away with it. Right now you're my only hope.'

Gloria's shoulders sank. 'I'll see what I can do.'

Roberta beamed. 'I could kiss you. And cop a feel of those magnificent breasts as well.'

'Don't you dare! Last time was bad enough.' A blush darkened her cheeks as she rummaged out an evidence crate from the stack by the storeroom door. Thumped it down on top of the work table. A hand-printed label was stuck to the lid: 'Galloway Mrs ~ 12-6 Cairnhill Court, Cairnhill.' Gloria opened it and peered inside 'And I'm not promising anything. If there's nothing there, there's nothing there.'

'Fair enough. But the offer of a grope still stands.'

Tufty eased the lab door closed and hurried down the corridor after Steel. Caught up to her just before the stairs. 'Doesn't really matter what she finds if we don't have anything to compare it with.'

'Blah, blah, blah.'

Through into the stairwell, their voices echoing back

from the walls. 'The whole floor could be covered in bloody footprints, but if we don't have Innes's shoes to match them against it's worthless.'

She blew a raspberry at him, thumping down the stairs. 'Are you being a party-piddler on purpose? Optimism, Tufty. Optimism.'

'Just being realistic. If we're going to pin this on Phil Innes we need a warrant first.'

'Do we?' She stopped and stared at him, eyebrows up, eyes wide, mouth hanging open. 'Wow. Twenty years in the job and I never knew! You must be some sort of idiot savant.'

'I'm just saying.'

'Well don't.' She started down the stairs again. 'Our luck's going to change, Tufty, I can feel it. No more dog days for us. Success: here we come.'

Yeah, right.

III

Tufty checked his phone. Twenty to nine and the only silly sods still silly enough to be hanging around the CID office were him and Steel. Everyone else went home ages ago. Lucky spods.

He was *stuck* here.

Waiting.

Bum was getting sore from all the sitting as well. He shoogled in his seat. Fiddled with his keyboard. Checked his phone again. Still 20:40.

Steel didn't look up from the notepad she was scribbling in. 'If you're needing the toilet, just go.'

He stopped fidgeting. 'We going to be much longer?'

'If you've finished writing up the door to doors: go home.'

'Yeah.' He stayed where he was. 'Finished those about half an hour ago.'

She narrowed her eyes and frowned at him. 'You're keeping an eye on me, aren't you?'

'Me? No.' Doing his best innocent face and voice.

'You're a terrible liar. And you can relax, Detective Constable Quirrel, I'm no' waiting for you to piffle off so I can go round Jack Wallace's place with a cricket bat and a blow torch.'

Oh thank God for that.

Tufty let out a long happy breath. 'Good.'

'I'm going to use a chainsaw.'

He stared at her. Sitting there with her hair all Albert Einstein. 'No, but really?'

She stood and grabbed her coat. 'I'm going home. You can follow me if you want.' A wink. 'But no tongues.'

Tufty followed the rear lights on Steel's MX-5 as she drove down Union Grove, her head rocking from side to side as she went. The sky was streaked with orange and scarlet, clouds fading from purple to black. Streetlights flickered out their yellowy glow. More light spilling from the windows of the granite terraces that lined both sides of the street.

She went straight across at the roundabout, onto Cromwell Road.

Tufty did the same, his Fiat Panda making its weird grindy-rattling noise again every time he changed gear. Probably should get that looked at. But what if the garage wanted to put Betsy down? What if they couldn't see the beauty in her rusty wings and hub caps? In that dangly bit at the back held on with half a roll of duct tape? In that burning-plastic smell that oozed out of her wheel arches if she had to navigate a bumpy road?

The playing fields drifted by on the right – all the floodlights on so some fat old blokes could pretend they were actually playing rugby.

Steel slowed for the roundabout with Anderson Drive.

OK, so it was a bit of a long way around, but they'd go right here, up the dual carriageway, and nip into... Nope. She wasn't indicating, she was going straight across.

Tufty leaned forward, making the steering wheel creak. 'Where are you going, you devious old horror?' He pointed. 'Your house is *that* way.'

An eighteen-wheeler trundled by, heading south.

Tufty nipped across the roundabout onto Seafield Road. A nice chunk of parkland on the left, fancy-looking granite semis on the right. He put his foot down, catching up with the Horror's MX-5. Flashed his lights.

Two fingers appeared in the little porthole at the back of her car.

'Daft old funkbiscuit...'

All the way up Seafield with its big houses and massive gardens. Past the Palm Court Hotel. Past the wee row of shops. And up to the junction. Straight through the green traffic lights.

'Where are you going, you monster? Some of us have boxed sets of *Buffy* to get home to!'

She indicated left and pulled into a car park beside a squat ugly little building and some sort of community centre. Crawled past a chunk of council recycling bins then stopped. Reversed into a sort of hollowed-out recess in the building painted all beige and brown.

He pulled up next to it. Checked his phone.

According to the map app, this was Airyhall Library. Open nine-till-seven Monday and Wednesday; nine-till-five Tuesday, Thursday, and Friday; ten-till-five on Saturday – shut for an hour at lunchtime; and closed on Sunday. So she wasn't here to borrow a book.

He climbed out of his car.

The sound of someone singing rattled out through the car's soft top.

> '*Got home today, and whadda you know,*
> *My TV's covered in electric snow,*
> *Got a "what devours, comes from below",*
> *And here's me missing my favourite show!*'

Was that Steel?

It was, belting it out. Singing along with the radio – the music all banjos and accordions.

'*Get gone,*

Get gone,

Get gone three times and turn to stone!'

He opened the door and slid into the passenger seat. Steel drummed away on her steering wheel.

'Got home today, and what do you say,

My lover's gone *Fifty Shades of Grey*,

He says we're gonna do things all his way,

And I said: "No way, Jose!"'

She was actually pretty good, in a smoky-voiced rock-granny kind of way.

She leaned over and poked him. 'Come on, Tufters, don't be shy.'

Yeah… No.

'Get gone,

Get gone,

Get gone three times, I'm on my own!'

An accordion solo wheezed out of the radio.

He poked her back. 'You said you were going home!'

'I say lots of things.'

Tufty peered out through the windscreen at the prison-wall-blandness side of the community centre. 'This isn't going to get me fired, is it?'

'Would I do that to you?' Still drumming along in time with the music. 'And we're singing in five, four, three—'

'Only I *really* don't want to get fired.'

'Got home today, but I can't see,

What the hell is wrong with me,

Why can't these crows just let me be,

Tormented for eternity!'

That was cheery.

'Sarge?'

'Get gone,
Get gone,
Cos this old world's all made of bones...'

She grinned at him. 'Come on, Tufty, all you've got to do is sing "get gone" a dozen or so times till the end. Ready? Here we go...'

He mumbled along, face getting hotter and hotter with every repetition. Till *finally* the DJ faded the bloody song out.

'An oldie but a goodie! Catnip Jane there, with "Three Times Gone".'

Tufty slumped back in his seat. 'Thank God for that.'

'Don't forget, Call-in Karaoke's coming up at eight, and we've got a special guest, talking about the protest this Saturday by the Northeast Farmers Union. But first here's some messages from—'

She killed the engine. 'You got a girlfriend, Tufty? Or boyfriend? Or favourite sheep?'

He took a look out of the passenger window – a big grey roller door, then a gap and the edge of a Portakabin kinda building. A tree-shaded path, a wee shed, and the back of a housing estate. The gap between the library's brick wall and the recycling bins looked out on the little car park. No sign of any cars, well, except for the manky brown van abandoned in the corner with two flat tyres, a crumpled bonnet, and a 'POLICE AWARE' sticker on the cracked windscreen.

Tufty sat back again. 'Jack Wallace isn't going to suddenly appear looking to return a copy of *Wind in the Willows* or something, is he?'

'Everyone should have someone to love. Someone they can trust. Someone who doesn't need shearing twice a year.'

'I am *not* shagging a sheep.'

'Takes all sorts.' She fiddled with the controls down the side of her seat, reclining it a bit. 'Now, then: I spy, with my little eye, something beginning with "L".'

Tufty pursed his lips and nodded. '...then I went out with Rebecca. She was nice. Sang in a country and western covers band.'

'No accounting for taste. You give up yet?'

'But she went off to university in Manchester, so that was that. "Bread Van"?'

'Nope.'

'Then there was Siobhan. Don't know why we ended up going out; she never seemed to like me very much...' A sigh. Didn't matter what he did, it was always wrong. *And* she snored. '"Big Vehicle?"'

'What about that perky Wildlife Crime Officer with the lovely breasts?'

'What about her?'

Steel leered at him. 'Are you shagging her yet?'

'God, you've got a one-track mind, haven't you?' He shifted in his seat. 'Anyway, I barely know the woman. "Brown Van"?'

'Well what are you hanging about for – go see her! You were meant to sort out that poor wee dog's funeral, you lazy sod.'

'*When?* I've been running about after you all day!' Honestly. 'Wait, is it "*Battered* Van"? The one over there that looks like they dropped it off a building?'

'About time you got that.' She gave her fake cigarette a couple of puffs. 'Your turn.'

'...but then I got home from work one morning and Lisa had broken every mug in the house, stabbed the fridge with an eight-inch carving knife, and ran off with my whole CD collection.'

'Pfff…' Steel slumped a bit further. 'Wish I hadn't asked now. Your love life's rubbish.'

Tufty turned in his seat. 'We could talk about something else then. How about black holes?'

'That a kinky euphemism?'

'No, listen: particles and antiparticles pop out of the quantum foam from time to time, right? Say it's an electron and a positron – normally they annihilate each other, but Stephen Hawking says—'

'Tufty, you—'

'—if it happens near a black hole's event horizon and the electron escapes, but the positron falls in, then—'

'Tufty!'

'—the positron's negative mass actually gobbles up a teeny bit of the black hole so it'll eventually evaporate. Course that depends on no other matter falling into— Ow!'

Then she hit him again. Right in the arm. And not a soft tap either: a full-on thump.

'Ow!' He rubbed at the stingy patch. 'Stop it!'

'I changed my mind. No physics. Go back to blethering on about your sodding love life. Only try to put a bit of spice into it, eh? I want at least a few vicarious thrills before you bore me to death.'

'…sick all down her front. She didn't want to speak to me after that.' He shrugged. 'And then I went out with Hannah for three weeks. Now she was *naughty*.'

Very, very naughty.

In all the right places.

And once on the top deck of a night-bus to Glasgow.

A warm smile spread across his face.

Steel poked him. 'Hoy!'

'Sorry. "Bendy Bus"?'

'You're supposed to be *sharing* the dirty bits. And no.'

'But her dad got done for drink-driving and suddenly every police officer was a "fascist bast"—'

She hit him. Again. Hard.

'Cut it out!'

'Shut up, you idiot.' She pointed through the windscreen.

A shadowy figure, all dressed in black with a rucksack on its back, crept out from behind the recycling bins. Ninja style. Assuming the ninja had a cold head, going by the massive black woolly hat she was wearing.

Ninja Rucksack Woman took a quick look left and right, but either Steel's car was parked in exactly the right place to be invisible or the Ninja was an idiot, because she crept across to the low wall separating the back of the library from the community centre. Hopped over it and did some more creeping to a red-painted door.

Another quick check, then she pulled a small crowbar out of her rucksack. A sharp thump at the lock and she slipped inside, closing the door behind her.

Steel fiddled her seat upright again. 'Well, I was hoping for something a bit more drug-dealerish, but it'll do.'

She climbed out of the car and closed the door without a sound. Looked in at Tufty with a finger to her lips. 'Shhh…' Then tiptoed to the wall, clambered over it and flattened herself against the bricks beside the jemmied door. Like something off of *Scooby-Doo*.

Woman was insane.

Ah well. Might as well.

He got out and wandered over. Swung his legs over the handrail and stood beside her, hands in his pockets. 'So far we've got "malicious mischief", "housebreaking with intent to steal", and violation of the Civic Government – Scotland – Act 1982: Section Fifty-Eight, Part One, AKA: "going equipped".'

'Shhh!' Steel stuck a finger to her lips again, whispering out, 'Will you shut up?'

She eased the jemmied door open and sneaked inside.

He scuffed in after her into a narrow corridor with raw breeze-block walls. A stack of cleaning supplies made it narrower still.

Another door at the end opened on a much fancier corridor, one with carpet on the floor and proper walls with framed posters and things. 'You CAN MAKE A DIFFERENCE TO YOUR COMMUNITY!', 'MUMS' BUMS & TUMS CLASSES AVAILABLE NOW!!!', 'TOGETHER, WE CAN DO ANYTHING!' Doors on either side.

Steel pointed.

Down at the far end, one of them swung shut on its slow closing arm thing, cutting off rubbery scraping sounds. Like a MASSIVE cat was sharpening its claws inside.

They crept over and peered through the glass panel into some sort of coffee lounge full of plastic chairs and little tables. A couple of highchairs. And a serving hatch off to one side with a teeny kitchen behind the counter. Notice boards covered in kids' drawings.

Ninja Rucksack Woman had dragged a stack of chairs away from the wall, which explained the scraping noises, and now she stood in front of it – rucksack at her feet spray-painting words across the breeze-blocks in big drippy red letters: 'MRS BROCKWELL IS A FAT STUPID COW!'

Poor Mrs Brockwell.

Tufty eased into the room.

The Ninja graffiti artist stood back to examine her work. Then added an extra exclamation mark and underlined 'COW' three times.

Steel made a loud, *'Er-h'r'm!'* noise. 'No' exactly Van Gogh, is it?'

Ninja Rucksack Woman froze.

'Yoo-hoo!' Steel waved. 'You do know we can see you?'

A whispered word floated through the silence. 'Shite...'
Then she was off: snatching up her rucksack and sprinting
for the only other exit, still holding the can of red spray
paint.

'Oh no you don't!' And Tufty was after her.

She leapt a row of tables with a parkour-style flip. Landed
and pulled the rucksack onto her back as part of the same
fluid movement. Not so much as a pause for breath.

Very cool.

Tufty hurdled the tables, sending a couple of plastic
chairs clattering. She battered out through the exit, but
he was right behind her, shoving into a big room with
rows and rows of plastic seats arranged facing a projector
screen.

She went charging through them, cutting diagonally
across the room, heading straight for the curtains that made
up one corner. The wake she left behind was right out of a
medieval battle film – overturned plastic chairs with their
metal legs pointing out in all directions like spears, waiting
to skewer an unsuspecting Tufty.

Yeah, *not* risking that.

He went round the outside instead. Further to go, but a
lot less chance of being impaled.

She yanked back one of the curtains, exposing an emergency exit. Grabbed the metal bar just as Tufty snatched a
handful of rucksack.

'You're going nowhere!'

The door must've opened far enough to trip the circuit,
because a shrill wailing alarm blared out of hidden speakers
somewhere. Loud enough to melt bone.

'GET OFF ME!' Ninja Rucksack Woman swung around.
Up close, from the front, she didn't really look like a

parkour kind of person. She looked like someone's mum: middle-aged, glasses, her hair escaping from beneath that black woolly hat in bouncy brown curls. Teeth bared. 'GRRRRRRAH!' She whipped the spray can in her hand up and pressed the button.

A hissing mist of bright red exploded in Tufty's face. 'AAAAAAAARGH!' Got his eyes clenched shut in time, but not his mouth. Now everything tasted of chemicals and turpentine.

He let go of her and covered his face with both hands.

She kept spraying, emptying the can.

It *cloinged* off the carpet.

Tufty squinted out through sticky eyelashes as she shouldered her way out through the emergency exit.

No!

He launched himself at her – a rugby tackle leap – wrapping his arms around her upper legs, sending them both crashing down on the paving slabs outside.

'GET OFF ME!'

Nope.

He crawled his way up her body – she slapped and punched at his shoulders and back.

Didn't stop him, though.

Tufty snatched out his handcuffs and grabbed one of her wrists. *Click.* A bit of a twist so her hand was facing the wrong direction, a teeny bit of pressure, and...

'AAAAAAAAAAAARGH! YOU'RE BREAKING MY WRIST! YOU'RE BREAKING MY WRIST!'

'THEN STOP HITTING ME!'

She went limp and he forced her other arm into place and finished snapping the cuffs on. Dragged her to her feet.

She was covered in smudgy red handprints.

Steel appeared, hands in her pockets. Grinning at him. 'You look like a baboon's bumhole.'

Tufty just glowered back, face all sticky and tight and stinking of paint.

The wee sod was still whinging by the time they got back to Division Headquarters. Muttering and moaning. Glowering and grumping as he manhandled their prisoner across the Rear Podium. Poor thing.

'Bloody paint, clarty everywhere, all over my poor little car...'

Wah, wah, wah, I'm all covered in paint, wah, wah, wah.

Roberta held the door open for him and he bundled their graffiti artist into the custody block. Just to cheer him up, she launched into a jaunty whistled rendition of 'Lady in Red'.

That got her a scarlet scowl. 'Oh you're so *motherfunking* funny, aren't you?'

Their prisoner snatched a frown over her shoulder at him. 'I need to go to the bathroom.'

'Oh ... shut up.' He shoved her towards the custody desk.

Sergeant Downie was on shout tonight, in all his fishbelly-pale, chinless glory. An albino worm in full Police Scotland uniform. Downie looked up from whatever it was he was reading and waved Roberta over.

Tufty thumped the woman's rucksack onto the desk. 'Assault. Malicious mischief. Housebreaking and vandalism by opening lockfast place. Going equipped. Resisting arrest. Failing to provide—'

'Now,' Downie held up a finger, 'just one moment, Constable, the grown-ups need to talk first.'

Tufty gave a wee snarl. Difficult to tell if he was going red in the face, because of the paint.

'My dear DS Steel, Big Gary said you were being obstreperous about someone picking up their stolen Nokia smartphone?'

She shook her head. 'I wasn't being obstreperous, Jeff, I was being pissed off.'

'Well, be pissed off no longer. I managed to track said phone down in the Productions Store, so you don't have to worry any more.' He placed a hand over his heart. 'No, don't thank me! It took forever and was a vast pain in my posterior, but at least he's got it back now.'

She stared at him.

He...

Tommy Shand's phone?

With all the *underage porn* on it.

How could anyone be so...

Roberta forced out the words like little burning lumps of cat poo. 'You let him have the *phone*?' Without the phone there was no evidence to take to the Procurator Fiscal. And it wasn't as if Josie Stephenson was going to clype on her boyfriend, was it? The whole thing was a complete goat-buggering disaster.

'He had all the correct paperwork.'

'Oh for...' Her head was going to explode. It was. Any second now: bang, pop, splatter! 'AAAAARGH!' She leaned forward and thunked it off the custody desk.

'If you didn't want the phone returned, why didn't you say something? There was no note or anything.'

'Arrrgh...'

Thunk, thunk, thunk.

'...aaargh, horrible, funkbiscuiting, awful...' Half an hour in the gents' toilet with a dirty big stack of paper towels and a bottle of turps and Tufty was *still* tomato coloured.

He stuck another towel over the open bottle and tipped it up, turning the paper a darker shade of green. Dabbed away at a scarlet cheek.

'Bloody, scumbagging, motherfunking, felchrabbit—'

The door banged open and Steel danced in. 'All hail the conquering heroine!'

'Rotten, badger-spanking—'

'You'll be happy to know that our guest has admitted everything.' She hopped up, plonking her backside down on the edge of the next sink over. 'Turns out Mrs Brockwell disqualified her Victoria sponge for having strawberry jam in it.'

He turpsed up another paper towel. 'I am absolutely sodding clarted!'

'Who would've thought passions ran so high in the WRI?'

Blearrrrg… A rancid petrol taste filled his mouth as he wiped at his lips. He scrubbed hard, then spat. 'Suit's *ruined*. And did you see the state of my car?'

A shrug. 'Well, we couldn't transport a prisoner back to the station in my MX-5, could we? Doesn't have a back seat.' She handed him another paper towel. 'And you think *you* got it bad? What about me? Was supposed to take Susan out for a nosh-up at that new French place. She'll no' be happy I stood her up.'

'Oh boo-hoo!' He turned on her. 'I got covered in *paint!*'

'That you most certainly did.' She winked at him. 'Come on Tufters: look on the bright side … at least *I* found it funny.'

He just scowled at her.

Roberta hitched up her trousers and leaned back against the windowsill. Smiled.

The ward was dark and quiet, all eight of the hospital beds occupied by a wee kid. Most were fast asleep, but a little girl's face halfway down was caught in the blue-green glow of a handheld games console. The only other light in the place was the Anglepoise lamp above Harrison Gray's bed. Harrison. What kind of monster called their kid 'Harrison'? Shouldn't be allowed.

He had his knees drawn up to his chest, the bags under his eyes darker and deeper in the harsh overhead light. Snot shining on his top lip.

She took out a hankie, spat on it, and wiped the bogies away. Kept her voice down to a conspiratorial whisper. 'There you go, much more handsome now.'

He stared at her with big black eyes. Not so much as a peep.

'The doctors say you're going to be in here for a couple of days, till they get those sores of yours sorted out. Then you can go live with a proper family. That'll be nice, won't it?'

Nothing.

'Proper family with proper food. No more "chicken and liver meaty chunks in jelly for a healthy coat and strong bones".'

He blinked.

'There's more to life than dog food, you know. There's pizza; and fish and chips; and soup; and steak pie and chips; and curry; and sushi; and sausages, baked beans, and chips; and egg and chips; and macaroni cheese and chips...' Roberta licked her lips, stomach growling. 'Pretty much anything you put with chips is good.'

Still nothing.

'I know you've seen terrible things, and having a horrible name like "Harrison" isn't going to help, but life gets better. It really, really does.' She gave his snotty nose another spit and polish. 'You just have to let it. OK?'

A shape appeared from the gloom. A little nurse with big hair, a squint smile, surgical gloves, and a tub of something. 'I'm sorry, but it's time to put some ointment on Harrison's sores. You like that, don't you Harrison? All nice and soothing?'

He just stared at her too.

216

'That's right.' As if he'd agreed with her. She turned her squint smile on Roberta. 'Don't worry, he's in safe hands now.'

'Aye, well I was just leaving anyway.' Roberta ruffled his hair. 'You behave yourself.' And off into the night.

Roberta rang the doorbell to her own house. Stood there with one hand behind her back. Waited for a count of ten, then rang the bell again.

Susan's voice muffled out from somewhere down the hall. *'All right, all right, keep your testicles on… I'm coming.'* Her shadow got bigger and bigger in the stained-glass panels flanking the door. Then the light in the peephole went out. *'Oh, it's you, is it?'*

A clunk and rattle as she undid the deadbolt and took off the chain.

Roberta stuck out her bottom lip and pulled on the puppy-dog eyes. 'Before you say anything…' She whipped out the bouquet of roses and chrysanthemums. 'Ta-da!'

'Stop by the petrol station on the way home, did we?'

'Tesco's, thank you very much.'

'What happened to my lovely night out at a posh French restaurant?'

'Operational difficulties.' She leaned in and gave Susan a kiss on the cheek. 'Now get your sexy bits upstairs and we'll see how I can make it up to you.'

Susan rolled her eyes. Sighed. Smiled. 'Roberta Elizabeth Steel: you're a terrible trial to your poor wife, you know that don't you?'

She buried her face in Susan's neck and made buzzing noises till Susan shrieked and giggled.

The downstairs was in darkness, but a light shone in the bedroom. One of those four poster beds. A bunch of mirrors and paintings on the walls. And those mirrors made it easy to see all around the room. At least they did from the other side of the street with a pair of binoculars.

What was taking them so *long*?

Ah, there they were. The wrinkly old lesbian bitch and her frumpy dyke wife.

Snogging away, in full view, like teenagers. No shame at all. Disgusting really.

The frumpy one danced over to the window and pulled the curtains shut, but not before the Steel bitch snuck up behind her and grabbed two handfuls of boob.

And that was it. Curtains shut. Nothing more to see.

A cat wandered past: big, fat and furry. Other than that, the street was dead.

Jack Wallace lowered his binoculars and stepped from the shadows. Took out the little metal tobacco tin with his dad's name scratched into the paint, and ground the stub of his cigarette to a grey powdery death. Adding it to the collection.

See, some people would be pissed off right now – standing there for two hours casing the joint, nothing to do but smoke cigarettes and not attract anyone's attention – but not him. The bit before. The calm bit. The quiet bit. The bit when they were so near every single tendon and sinew *thrummed* with it. That was the best.

You could shove your coke, heroin, and crystal meth: they had *nothing* on it.

Jack Wallace smiled up at the Steel bitch's house. 'Oh yeah, we're going to have *so* much fun.'

He turned and sauntered off, hands in his pockets, whistling a happy tune.

So much fun.

CHAPTER SEVEN

*in which we meet a Bad Man
and Roberta does a Very Naughty Thing*

I

The muster room was packed – nightshift and dayshift all crammed in together, uniform and plainclothes, all grumbling and moaning.

Standing in front of the door, Chief Superintendent Tony Campbell held up his arms and the angry muttering gave way to resentful silence. 'Look, I know it's not ideal, but we have reason to believe both camps have been infiltrated by violent elements.'

The grumbling started again.

Slumped against the lockers, Steel leaned over and hissed in Tufty's ear. 'You still look like a beetroot, by the way.'

Tufty gave her his best evil eye, but she just grinned back at him.

The Chief Superintendent let the complaining go for a couple of beats then stomped it into submission again. 'I will *not* have people coming into my city and treating it as a battlefield!' He gave them all a good hard stare. 'Attendance at tomorrow's farmers' protest is *mandatory*. All leave is cancelled. And *everyone* will be in uniform. That includes you, CID! There will be a kit inspection at oh nine hundred hours.'

Steel covered her face with her hands. 'Noooooooo…'

'We will be a united front. We will control the situation.

And we will arrest the living bejesus out of anyone who crosses the line!' He held out a hand and his deputy passed him a peaked cap. 'We have a duty to protect Aberdeen and its citizens. We're not going to let them down.' He stuck his hat on. Straightened it. 'Nightshift: go home and rest, you've got a green shift to work tomorrow. Everyone else: get out there and make a difference.'

He turned and marched from the room, back straight as an ironing board.

As soon as he was gone, the complaining started again. One by one the nightshift officers drifted away, moaning about having to work a double shift tomorrow. Then the dayshift slouched out, off to patrol the streets and all that kinda jazz.

Steel crumpled her face and stared at the ceiling tiles. 'Uniform! I haven't had to wear a sodding uniform since we buried DI Ding-Dong Bell.'

Oh boo-hoo.

The crowd of dayshift uniform parted slightly and there she was: PC Mackintosh, standing over by the vending machine, jabbing away at the buttons and hitting the thing with the side of her hand.

'Look at me!' Steel held her arms out. 'I'm no' built to wear a uniform like the rest of the plebs. I'm built for Armani, Gucci, Dolce and Gabbana…'

'Says the woman in the Primark suit.' Tufty pushed off the lockers and did his best impersonation of a swagger all the way across the muster room's scuffed floor to the vending machines.

PC Mackintosh thumped the machine again, voice a low bitter mumble: 'Give me my goddamned Lion Bar, you thieving hunk of metallic…' She froze. 'There's someone right behind me, isn't there?'

'Constable Mackintosh. No, I don't mean Constable

Mackintosh is behind you – that would be silly – *you're* Constable Mackintosh.' Yeah, this wasn't going all that well.

She turned and stared at him over the top of her glasses.

He tried for a smile. 'But you probably know that.' Tufty's mouth soldiered on, even though his brain was sounding the retreat. 'I mean, it's your name and everything.' Shut up. 'Well, not "Constable", who calls their child "Constable", and how weird would it be if they joined the police?' SHUT UP! 'I'm sure you've got a perfectly lovely first name. Nice. I meant *nice* first name. I wasn't trying to sexually harass you in the workplace or anything...' And finally, at long last, his mouth finally clicked shut. Leaving nothing behind but a high-pitched, 'Eek...'

Slick.

She pulled her chin in. 'What happened to your face?'

He licked his lips.

'Only it's a weird red colour and you've got a *massive* black eye.'

DO SOMETHING!

'Sometimes it helps if you give the machine a bit of thump-and-shoogle.' He bumped it with his hip and then his shoulder, rocking it on its feet.

The errant Lion Bar wobbled, then tipped off the end of its coil and into the dispensing tray. And, as an unexpected bonus, a bag of Skittles decided that if the Lion Bar was going – it was going too.

He jabbed both hands into the air. 'Yay!' Then lowered them again, heat flushing across his cheeks and up into his ears. 'That would've been a lot cooler if I hadn't done that last bit, wouldn't it?'

She dropped down and retrieved the machine's offerings. Stood and gave him the Skittles. 'I couldn't get a burial plot for Pudding, but I pulled in a couple of favours and the council *will* do us a cremation for free. We don't get an urn or anything, but they'll give us the ashes in a cardboard box so Mrs Galloway can scatter them somewhere nice.'

'Oh.' He frowned down at the Skittles. 'Given ... you know, what happened to him, don't know if cremation's maybe a bit...?'

Her cheeks went pink. 'Ah. Yes. I see what you—'

'No, but I'm probably being a little over—'

'—poor wee thing, but a coffin and a burial plot cost so much and—'

'Honestly I think it's a great idea. I was being daft...' He huffed out his cheeks. 'Sorry.'

Steel's voice came floating across the room like a vulture. 'FOR GOD'S SAKE, SHUT UP AND SNOG HER YOU IDIOT!'

PC Mackintosh's blush darkened a couple of shades. 'I better go.' Her glasses were steaming up a smidge too.

'Wait!' He stuffed the Skittles in his pocket and pulled out a Police Scotland business card. Scribbled his mobile number on the back. 'Call me.' Argh. Now it *definitely* looked like he was coming on to her. 'So we can work out the arrangements? Erm... For Pudding?'

She reached out and took the card. Her fingertips were warm and smooth, the nails short and bitten ragged.

'HUMPY, HUMPY, HUMPITTY, HUMP!'

Tufty turned and glared at Steel. 'You're not helping!'

But by the time he turned back, PC Mackintosh was already hurrying from the room. She thumped through the door, leaving Tufty alone with the Wrinkled Filthy Horror of Doom.

Steel grinned at him. 'Think you're in there.'

'I *hate* you.'

'Chocolate, chocolate, chocolate, chocolate...' Roberta nibbled the coating off the top of her Jaffa Cake, exposing the tangy orangey bit sitting like a rubbery splot on top of the sponge base.

Was there any finer word in the English language than 'chocolate'?

Well, except for 'Keira Knightley', 'nipples', and 'moist'.

Better yet, a combination of all four.

She had a lick of the orangey bit.

The CID office was abuzz with the sound of pointless policework.

Lund, Barrett, and Harmsworth were on the phones again – busy as busy buzzy bees being busy – reuniting stolen mobiles with their owners so DCI Pain-in-the-Rear Rutherford would take his pain and insert it in someone else's rear for a change.

No idea where the idiot Tufty was, though. Probably off having a stationery-cupboard fumble with his perky Wildlife Crime Officer. Dirty, *lucky*, wee sod that he was.

A list of the day's jobs was up on the whiteboard, along with the words 'CRUDWEASEL' and 'RIPPA!', two wanted posters: Lord Lucan and Philip Innes, and a drawing of a big hairy willy – which was hairy enough to be Harmsworth's, but no' small enough and no' floppy enough either.

Barrett ticked something off on his clipboard. 'Hello? Yes, I'm calling from Police Scotland. Has your mobile phone been stolen recently? ... Yes, that's right.'

The office door opened and Tufty backed into the room, carrying a tray laden with mugs.

Lund helped herself to one. 'Ooh, thank God for that. I'm gasping!'

Roberta gave him a squint. 'About sodding time! Running out of Jaffa Cakes here.'

He handed her a mug. 'If it's not spanky hot don't blame me. Got waylaid by DI Vine on the stairs.'

'Oh aye? And what did Buggerlugs McVine want?' She had a sip of her coffee. Bland and anaemic with a bitter edge to it. 'Urgh... Did you put sugar in this?'

'Two. And you're welcome.' He dumped a mug down in front of Barrett – got a thumbs up in reply. Did the same for Harmsworth.

'That's not my mug.'

'It's a mug and it's clean.'

'My mug has a thistle on it.'

'It wasn't there, I looked, OK?' Tufty helped himself to the last one, then perched his cheeky wee bum on the edge of Roberta's desk. 'Spoke to the hospital this morning: Mrs Galloway woke up.'

Now there was some *good* news for a change. 'Excellent. We'll pop over and—' Her phone *Cagney-&-Lacey*ed at her. 'Hold that thought.' She picked it up. 'This better be important, I've got Jaffa Cakes on the go.'

'Aye, it's Benny. You wanted to know next time Tommy Shand's spotted behind Airyhall Library? He's there now.'

Ha!

Her cheeks tightened as a massive grin snapped into place. 'Ooh, see if you weren't so ugly? I'd *kiss* you, Benny.' She hung up and grabbed her coat. 'Tufty: forget your horrible coffee, we've got a drug dealer to lift.'

The pool car snaked along Union Grove, engine growling as Tufty changed down and overtook a delivery van. Trees flashing past the windows. Grey tenements little more than a blur.

Steel leaned across from the passenger seat and thumped his arm. 'Come on, come on! Foot down!'

He kept his eyes on the road. 'I'm doing *fifty*.'

'Well put on the blues-and-twos.'

'Do you want to drive? Cos I can pull over, you know!'

She hit him again. 'You drive like an old lady.' Then reached across the car and honked the horn. 'MOVE IT, GRANDAD!'

The Volkswagen in front of them didn't.

'Oh for… Right. That's it. Pull over.'

Tufty kept driving. 'I'm not—'

'Pull over, you big damp jessie. It'll be Christmas by the time we get there.'

You know what? Fine.

He slammed on the brakes and pulled into the kerb. 'Happy now?'

She scrambled out of the passenger side and ran around the bonnet. Hauled open the driver's door. 'Shift over you idiot!'

Tufty groaned and clambered over the gearstick and handbrake. He'd barely got his legs into the footwell before the tyres gave a tortured-pig screech and the car fishtailed away from the kerb again. 'Let me get my seatbelt on!'

She jabbed the '999' button on the dashboard and the siren wailed, blue-and-white lights flickering out through the front grille – reflecting back from the Volkswagen's rear as they got closer, closer, closer…

'Too close, too close, too close!' Tufty clutched at the grab handle above his door, other hand fumbling with the seat-belt catch. 'Aaaargh!'

She wrenched the steering wheel to the right and they swung out around the Volkswagen, right into the path of an oncoming Clio.

'Car! Car! Car!'

They lurched to the left with only inches to spare as the Clio slithered to a halt in a cloud of blue tyre smoke.

'Are you *trying* to kill us?'

She didn't slow down for the roundabout onto Cromwell Road, throwing them around it like a runaway rollercoaster.

Finally! The seatbelt buckle clicked into its holder as they flew past the playing fields.

'I should never have let you drive!'

'Will you shut up whinging? I'm concentrating here.'

The houses screamed by and there was the roundabout with Anderson Drive. Anderson Drive the *dual carriageway*. The dual carriageway that was packed with traffic. Traffic like the dirty big articulated lorry just pulling onto the roundabout right now!

And Steel wasn't slowing down.

'No, no, no, no, no!' Tufty grabbed at the dashboard.

It was going to hit them, going to hit them, going to hit them! 'AAAAAAAAAAAAAAAAAARGH!'

Steel accelerated. '*WHEEEEEE!*'

The pool car roared onto the roundabout and everything slowed to a crawl. The shrubs growing in the middle of it, in vibrant shades of emerald and olive. The blue of the sky. The massive *enormous* lorry with its black cab – the driver's face pale, eyes wide, mouth open – big chunks of oil-industry machinery strapped to the back. The terrifying evil grin on Steel's face. The pebbly surface of the dashboard as Tufty braced himself...

And then it was back to full speed again.

There was a brief crunching noise, swallowed by the lorry's outraged horn, and the pool car flashed across the roundabout. Drivers on the north-bound carriageways hammered on their brakes, screeching to a halt halfway across the outside lane.

Oh God... They were still alive!

Seafield Road was a blur after that, the siren's wail barely making it through the pounding surge of blood in Tufty's ears.

Steel poked the '999' button again and the siren fell silent. Slowed to a more modest thirty miles an hour.

She turned to him and put a finger to her lips. 'Be vewy quiet, we're hunting dwug deawers…'

He peeled his fingers off the dashboard. 'You're completely and utterly *insane!*'

'Aye? Well *you* look as if you've just crapped yourself.'

'WE COULD'VE DIED!'

'But we didn't. So stop moaning.' She drifted across the junction with Springfield Road, right beside Airyhall Library. 'Where are you Tommy? Where are you…'

The pool car pulled into the library car park.

A neon-orange Peugeot sat beneath a tree, parked nose to tail with a lime-green Honda Civic – the drivers' windows level with one another. Both had stupidly huge spoilers and racing skirts, oversized exhausts poking out the back.

Tufty tried a few deep breaths. Wiped a hand across his damp forehead. 'Going to need fresh underwear after that one.'

'Here we go.' The pool car did a sweeping turn, coming to a halt right across the front/back of the two cars, blocking them in. 'Now, do you think you can act like a big boy, or does Aunty Roberta have to kiss it all better for you? No? Good.' She climbed out into the morning and thumped the door shut.

Horror. She was a cast-iron three-hundred-and-sixty-degree Horror, with a capital 'H'.

He reached for the passenger door handle, but there was no way he could actually open the thing – she'd parked too close to the other cars.

Great.

Tufty clambered back over the gearstick and handbrake again.

Complete and utter Horror.

Roberta sauntered around to the Peugeot's passenger window and knocked on it. A wee pause, then Tommy Shand peered out at her. Buzzed the window down.

'Hoy, shift your car, Granny.' He was wearing a baseball cap – the wrong way around – a pair of sunglasses perched across the top like a black plastic tiara. Tracksuit top, black polo-shirt, and jeans. A couple of gold chains glinting around his neck.

'Well, well, well, if it isn't Tommy Shand.' She flashed her warrant card. 'Keys. Take them out of the ignition and hand them over.'

'We wasn't doing nothing!' Voice getting higher and squeakier with every word. No' very gangsta.

'Give me the keys and get out of the car.' She snapped her fingers at Tufty as he finally struggled his way into the sunshine. 'You: search the other one.'

Tommy handed over his keys. 'This isn't fair!'

Tufty marched around to the Honda and banged on the roof. 'Out of the car.'

'Come on, man, this is harassment!' A pause. 'What happened to your face?'

'Out – now!'

The two cars were parked too close together to open the drivers' doors, so Tufty's idiot had to clamber out the passenger side.

Roberta grinned. Didn't matter how often she made people do it, it was still great. Especially the look on their faces when the gearstick nearly went up their bums.

What emerged from the Honda Civic was another rap-star wannabe. One of those stupid bowl haircuts that were shaved at the sides; a Manchester United football shirt – number seven with 'RONALDO' across the back; gold chains; and sunglasses.

She gave the Peugeot another knock. 'You too, Tommy: out you come.'

'But we haven't *done* anything.'

'I have reason to believe that you're currently engaged in

a criminal offence, Tommy boy. Now get your backside out
of the car.'

'Man…'

Ronaldo flounced in place as Tufty searched him. 'Wasn't
doing no criminal offences.'

'*Sure* you weren't.' Roberta snapped on a pair of blue
nitrile gloves. Stretched the rubbery skin down between her
fingers. 'You got anything sharp in your pockets I should
know about, Tommy? Any knives or needles or kittens?'

A pout. 'We wasn't doing nothing!'

'Hands on the car roof. Assume the position.' She gave
her gloves one last proctologist-style snap then started in
on his jeans pockets. 'You know how long you can get for
drug dealing, Tommy?'

'We wasn't *dealing* no drugs. We was just, you know …
talking and that.'

'Aye, right.' Nothing in the pockets or turn-ups of the
jeans. Nothing around the inside of the belt either.

'We *was*!'

'In the car park, round the back of the library? At half
nine in the morning? Aye, and all hours of the day and
night too. You've been spotted, Tommy boy.'

Time to give the tracksuit top a rummage.

'Wasn't like that.'

No drugs, in there, just a wallet, a lucky rabbit's foot, and
a big flat chunk of smartphone with a leather cover. No' the
stolen Nokia with the scratched case and dirty pictures of
an underage girl. Roberta gave the wallet a quick look
through – about thirty quid in cash and some bank cards.
A photo of Josie Stephenson grinning out from a laminated
window. No drugs.

She kept the phone.

Tufty waved at her. 'This one's clean.'

'So search his car!'

Honestly, did she have to think of *everything*?

Roberta held up the smartphone. 'What's this, Tommy, more porn?'

'Eh?' He pulled his chin in a bit. Frowned. 'Porn?'

'Right, let's check the vehicle, shall we?'

II

Ronaldo huffed and puffed, making a big show of straightening his Man United top as Tufty shut the Honda Civic's boot.

Roberta had a wee peek in through the back window. 'Anything?'

'Not so much as an aspirin.'

'*Told* you we wasn't doing nothing.' He was probably aiming for righteous indignation, but being a bowl-haircutted wee nyaff all he managed was 'sulky child'.

Tufty gave him a loom. 'Bit of advice? People who deal drugs get caught. Doesn't matter how careful you are, we'll get you. And you'll go to prison for a *very* long time.' Then a smile and a cheery wave. 'Drive carefully.'

Ronaldo clambered back into his car, through the passenger side, over the intimate prodding of the gearstick, thumping into the driver's side. Cranked the Civic's engine over and sat there with his oversized exhaust growling. Scowling out through the windscreen.

Roberta gave Tufty a poke. 'You'll have to shift the car, or he can't leave.'

'I know.' A nasty wee smile on his face. Arms folded. Going nowhere.

Fair enough.

Tommy stood leaning back against the horrible-orange Peugeot. Scowling and pouting all at the same time.

His spare wheel, tyre iron, and jack lay on the tarmac by the open boot, the cartridge from the CD changer balanced on top.

Tufty nodded at Tommy's car. 'How about you?'

'No.'

Roberta pulled out the confiscated smartphone and poked at the buttons till the screen came to life. Password protected. She held it out to Tommy. 'Unlock it.'

'God...' Tommy's shoulders drooped and he stared up at the bright blue sky for a moment. 'Dad's right, we're living in a fascist police state.' But he typed four numbers into the screen then handed it back.

Roberta found the pictures icon and went digging through the folders. Selfies. Selfies. Selfies. What the hell was wrong with kids these days? More selfies, but at least these had Josie Stephenson in them. Fully clothed, but it was a start. More selfies. For goodness' sake... How many photos did one seventeen-year-old need of themselves?

The last folder was a set taken at Aberdeen Beach. Josie starred in most of them, but the most racy shot was her paddling in the sea with her trousers rolled to the knee. Roberta flipped the cover closed. 'Where's the other one?'

'Other what?'

'*Phone*. Where's the other phone? The one you picked up from the station last night.'

A frown. 'Yeah... No idea what you're talking about.'

Roberta poked him in the chest. 'You're sodding lucky you're no' on your way to jail, Tommy.'

He hauled his shoulders back. 'I *told* you: Noel and me wasn't doing nothing!'

'Josie Stephenson is *fifteen* years old. The only reason I'm no' arresting you right now, is you got that phone back

234

before I could do you under Section Twenty-Eight of the Sexual Offences, Scotland, Act!'

He shrank back against the car. 'What?'

'She's fifteen, you randy wee shite! That means you should be on the Sex Offenders' Register.'

His eyes widened. 'I didn't... I... We never—'

'Don't bother, I've heard it all before. And delete those dirty photos off your phone, show some damn respect.'

'But I don't—'

'HER DAD'S DYING OF CANCER, YOU WEE SHITE!' Little bobbles of spit glittered and shone in the sunlight.

Tommy shrank down a bit, his weaselly little face just begging for a fist. 'What photos? I don't have no photos.'

'What photos?' Begging for more than just one fist – begging for a whole *army* of them. 'The photos on your phone! The phone that got stolen? The photos of you getting balls-deep in a fifteen-year-old girl, in a fancy bathroom!'

'Nah, I swear.' Tommy slithered along the Peugeot's side, hands up. 'I *swear* that's not me. That is *so* not me.'

'I saw them!'

He slid off the back end, retreated a couple of steps, till Tufty stepped right behind him.

'Where do you think you're going?'

'I mean, don't get me wrong, Josie's *lovely* and that, but...' Deep breath. 'Look, I haven't had sex with her, OK? I haven't. I'm...' He licked his lips, then his voice dropped to a whisper, barely audible over the traffic on Springfield Road, 'I'm gay. That OK with you? I'm gay. That's why I'm hanging about in a library car park miles away from home.' Getting louder and bolder with every word. 'I'm meeting my *boyfriend!*' He jabbed his arms out, as if he was being crucified.

Roberta stared at him. Then in through the windows to the Honda Civic and Ronaldo with his nasty bowl-haircut. Then back at Tommy again. 'You're *gay*? Oh...

Congratulations.' She patted him on the shoulder.
'Welcome to the club.'

He lowered his arms and drooped back against the car.
'Josie pretends we're all loved up, so no one finds out. You
don't know what my mum's like, she's all "born again" and
that. Thinks Graham Norton and Julian Clary are gonna
burn in hell...' Tommy paled, one hand clutching at his
stomach. 'Oh God, you can't tell her! She'll *kill* me if she
finds out!'

Poor wee sod.

Seventeen years old and too terrified of his mum to come
out.

Roberta stepped forward and gave him a quick hug.

He went rigid. 'What are you doing?'

'Being nice. Don't get used to it.' She let go, pulled out
her e-cigarette and had a couple of hard puffs on it. Hissed
pineapple-flavour vapour out of her nose. 'If you're Josie's
fake boyfriend, who's the real one?'

'She doesn't have one.' He pulled his chin in again. 'Why
are you looking at me like that? She doesn't. Says she wants
to concentrate on her exams. Josie's my *best* friend – she'd
tell me if she was seeing someone.'

Aye, you keep telling yourself that.

'So basically,' Tufty scowled across the car at her as Anderson
Drive drifted by the windows, 'we nearly got killed by that
lorry for nothing.'

'I'm on the phone, you divot.' Roberta put her feet up on
the dashboard. 'No' you, Gary, I was talking to *another* divot.'

'Don't you get all huffy at me!'

'I'm no' "getting all huffy", Gary, I just want to know who
picked up that sodding phone!'

'Yes, you are.' A crunch came from the earpiece and Big
Gary's voice went a bit chewy and muffled. The fat sod was

eating something. Bet it was biscuits. '*And how am I supposed to know? Am I psychic now?*'

The car paused for a second at the roundabout with Queen's Road to let a bendy bus grumble by.

'So ask Jeff Downie. He's the idiot who gave it away.'

'*Oh, I see. Why didn't you say?*' The biscuit muffling went away, replaced by a singsong tone – as if he was talking to a wee kid. '*Sergeant Downie was on* nightshift. *He's at home now, going sleepy bye-byes.*'

'Oh for … crudweasels.' She had a dig at the itchy bit under her left boob. 'Well, he must've written it down somewhere! Find it.'

'*With the greatest of respect, Detective Sergeant Steel, pucker up and French-kiss my fuzzy bumhole.*' Then silence: the cheeky biscuit-munching scumbag had hung up on her.

'Gah.' She stuck the phone back in her pocket. 'I miss being a detective chief inspector. People did what they were sodding well told, back then.'

Tufty overtook a car waiting to turn left into the business park. 'Think we should stop somewhere and buy Mrs Galloway a bunch of grapes?'

'Grapes are Satan's haemorrhoids, Tufty. *Chocolate*'s where it's at.'

'Oh, wow…' Tufty pointed. The brake light and indicator on the right of the pool car was a jagged hole fringed with broken plastic. So *that's* what the crunch was when they almost got flattened by the eighteen-wheeler. 'Look at it!' He pointed again, but Steel just wandered off, puffing on her rotten e-cigarette again. He locked the car. Hurried to catch up. 'I'm putting in the logbook that was *your* fault.'

'Don't be silly, little Tufty, I can't have been driving. *You* were the one signed the car out.'

'Oh no you don't!'

'Oh yes I do.' She hopped over the little wooden rail thing and marched out across the road towards the hospital entrance. Weaved her way through the clump of smokers. In through the main doors.

'How is that fair? You nearly kill me and I'm the one gets the blame for it!'

She smiled over her shoulder at him and slipped into the wee shop just inside the doors. 'You heard DCI Rutherford: my crimes will be *your* crimes. Might as well cut out the middle man.' She stopped and pointed at the shelves. 'Now, see if you can find the novelty teddy bears.'

Somehow, Steel didn't look so scary with a 'Naughty Nurse' teddy bear tucked under one arm; a big Toblerone, a couple of magazines, and an oversized get-well-soon card under the other; and a silver helium balloon with a happy face printed on it bobbing about above her head.

The lift doors pinged open and Tufty followed her out into the corridor. Institution-green with strips of duct tape holding patches of the floor together. Framed tapestry things on the wall.

They marched all the way down to the end, where the words 'AGNES GALLOWAY' were printed in wobbly red letters on a small whiteboard.

Steel breezed straight through into the private room.

Mrs Galloway lay huddled in the bed, a drip running through a blue boxy machine on a stand and into the back of one hand. If anything, she looked even worse than last time. The bruises had merged and aged, developing a patina of greens, blues, and yellows around the edges, dark plum-purple in the centre. They must have changed her bandages recently, because they were all shiny and white. That cast on her other arm was a dirty grey, though – a bright orange and green flower drawn on the fibreglass surface in childish felt pen.

'Hello, Agnes.' Steel arranged their purchases on the bedside cabinet with the couple of cards already there. Tied the balloon to the end of the bed, then sat on the edge of the mattress. 'You're looking well.' She took hold of two of Mrs Galloway's fingers, steering clear of the cannula. 'Be out of here in no time.'

Mrs Galloway stared down at her cast. 'I don't...'

Silence.

'And look at all the lovely cards you got.'

A floor polisher whummed past in the corridor.

Someone a few rooms down tried to cough up a lung.

Steel shoogled a little bit closer. 'I need a favour from you, Agnes. I need you to tell me what happened so Constable Quirrel here can write it down. And then we can go arrest the nasty flap of skin who did this to you.'

Tufty got out his notebook. Pen at the ready.

'I...' Mrs Galloway looked at him for a moment, eyes all bloodshot and swollen. Then went back to staring at her cast. 'I used to work on the railways. Was the RMT union rep. I ran marathons. I did karate...'

Steel shoogled closer. 'Who was it, Agnes? I need you to tell me their name.'

'When did I get so old and *useless*?' Her voice got a little mushy; a couple of tears pattered down onto the starchy white blanket.

'They won't give me a warrant without corroboration, Agnes. You don't want him to hurt anyone else, do you?'

She wiped her eyes on the sleeve of her hospital robe. 'In my twenties I could've kicked his arse from here to Stonehaven! Could've done it in my thirties and forties too.'

'Then help me kick his arse now.'

239

'I just… I just sat there…' A sob jagged through the words. 'He killed … killed my poor wee *Pudding!*'

'Hey, hey.' Tufty put a hand on her shoulder. 'It's not *your* fault, it's the guy who did it. He broke your arm. He…' Deep breath. 'We'll take good care of Pudding, sort everything out for the funeral. I promise. You just take care of getting better.'

'I just want it all to be over.' She put her cast across her eyes, hiding her face. 'The *real* me died years ago. I died and I went to hell. This is hell.'

Steel forced a smile. 'Come on, Agnes. We can beat him, I know we can.'

But Mrs Galloway turned away in the bed, face creased up into a bruised pain-filled knot. 'Please, just leave me alone.'

Steel barged out through the main entrance doors, yanked out her fake fag and puffed on it. Leaving a trail of fruity vape behind her. She got three steps out from beneath the portico and stopped. Stared up at the sky.

OAPs, pregnant people, people with various limbs in casts, one cadaverous man with a drip on a wheelie stand, clumped together on one side. All smoking. Some texting. About as much *joie de vivre* as an asthmatic hamster.

Tufty stopped beside Steel. Shrugged. 'Maybe she'll change her mind?'

A deep breath, then: '*AAAAAAAAAAAAAAAAAAARGH!*'

Everyone stared as she stormed off.

Yeah, she was definitely losing it.

He hurried after her. 'Look, maybe we should—'

'How the goat-buggering *hell* am I supposed to catch Philip Innes if no one will sodding talk to me? ARSEHOLES!'

'Actually, the word of the day is "crudweasel", so—'

'Do *not* fuck with me today, Tufty!'

240

OK...

She marched across the road, to the car park. 'Did you see the state of that poor woman? Am I supposed to just let that go?'

'Well, maybe we could—'

'Cos I'm no' letting it go!'

An Audi estate turned into the row from the boundary road and slammed on its brakes, scrunching to a halt inches away from hitting her. Its horn brayed out, the driver making watch-where-you're-going! faces through the windscreen.

She stuck two fingers up at them. 'Awa' an' boil yer heid!' She marched on till they got to the pool car. Stood there, snarling at it. Then turned. Narrowed her eyes at Tufty. 'You know what? There's nothing I can do to *make* people talk. Nothing at all. Nothing legal, anyway.'

'If we give her time, I know Mrs Galloway will change her mind. Innes killed her dog. She can't let him get away with that.'

Steel twisted her head, eyeing him the way a lion eyes a particularly tasty-looking zoo keeper. 'So maybe what we need is something that's *no'* legal? Maybe...' She drifted off into silence and stared into space.

A slow evil smile spread across her face.

Oh no.

Tufty backed up a couple of paces. 'Sarge? Please tell me you're not going to do what I think you're going to do.'

'Get in the car.'

III

Birdsong chittered through the garden centre, the *frrrrrrp* of little wings marking the passing of tiny little birds as they flitted from the rafters to the floor and back again. Tufty turned on the spot, following a chaffinch, or blue tit, or whatever it was popping along the back of a 'PARK-STYLE BENCH ONLY £159.99!'

The air was sharp with the smell of vegetation, underpinned by the yeasty-stale-bread scent of compost and fresh-turned earth. A coffee shop took up one corner of the massive warehouse space. The delicious welcoming aroma of something pastry-ish baking wafted out like a grandmother's hug.

The rest of the place was packed with bedding plants, fruit trees in pots, ornamental box hedges, roses in tubs, ferns, flowers and all the rest. A huge collection of ugly earthenware animals and uglier gnomes.

Yeah, not quite what he'd been expecting, given the evilness of Steel's smile.

She marched ahead, stopping in front of a young woman transferring seedlings from a tray into individual teeny pots. Hair pulled back in a pair of Heidi pigtails. The garden centre logo sat right in the middle of her blue apron, just beneath a big red badge with 'STACEY IS ALWAYS HAPPY To HELP' on it.

Steel knocked on the potting table and 'STACEY' looked up. Smiled.

'Can I help you?'

'Aye, Big Jimmy Grieve about?'

She pointed at a door in the wall at the end of the warehouse. 'Garden sheds and gazebos.'

'Cheers.' Steel marched off, past a display of water features and out through the door.

Tufty loped along beside her. 'Who's "Big Jimmy Grieve"?'

She kept marching.

A twelve-foot-high chainlink fence was lined with shelves of landscapy stuff – bags of gravel, fencing panels, rolls of wire, that kind of thing. They surrounded a collection of pre-built sheds that formed their own little shantytown, painted in jaunty outdoor colours.

An old man was fiddling about with bits of wood, building himself a gazebo on the outskirts of Jaunty Shed Shantytown. Doing a good job of it too. Which was just as well, because you'd have to be suicidal to tell him he was doing anything *other* than a good job.

He was huge. Grey hair cropped close to his head. Broad shouldered. Big arms and hands. Powerful. Like a rugby player and a boxer gave birth to a bouncer.

Steel came to a halt behind him. Leaned against a pastel-blue shed.

He didn't look round. Picked a nail from the box at his feet and pounded it in with three mighty blows.

She waited for the thumping to stop. 'Mr Grieve. Didn't have you down as the green-fingered type.'

He froze. Then turned.

Nyah... There was a face to frighten the living hell out

of Rottweilers. Chiselled with creases. Eyes of frozen granite. But when he opened his mouth, the words didn't boom out, they slid softly. Calm. Controlled. Still. 'Roberta Steel. What brings you out?' He didn't move either, didn't fidget. Just stood there impersonating a very menacing statue.

'Oh, just passing, Mr Grieve, just passing...' A shrug. 'How's Sheila and the grandkids?'

A smile deepened the lines around his eyes. 'They're good, thanks. Macy's at big school now. Says she's going to be a systems architect, whatever that is.'

'That's nice. Give them my best.'

A nod. He picked up the next bit of the gazebo kit, lining it up with the bit he'd just nailed on.

She stuck her hands in her pockets. 'You ever heard of a wee scroat called Philip Innes?'

'Should I have?' Still and menacing again.

'A wee birdie tells me he's loansharking at Cairnhill Court. You grew up there, didn't you?'

'Long time ago.'

'This Philip Innes attacked a little old lady. Put her in hospital. Microwaved her dog. Sad, isn't it?'

Big Jimmy Grieve's voice got quieter. Harder. 'So why don't you arrest him?'

'Can't touch the guy.' A sigh. 'You know how it is: everyone's too scared to say anything. Whole place has come down with amnesia, laryngitis, and a nasty dose of selective blindness.'

'I see.'

Something uncomfortable shifted in Tufty's stomach. Made the back of his neck go all clammy. This was definitely a very, *very* bad idea.

'Wasn't like that in your day, was it, Mr Grieve?' Steel shook her head. 'OK, so no one went clyping to the police, but they didn't have to, did they? They knew the building took care of its own.'

Big Jimmy Grieve stared down at the hammer in his massive hand. Like he was feeling its weight. Said nothing.

'You stepped out of line in those days – you smacked an old lady about? – you got slapped down. Hard. No' today, though...' Another sigh, then she reached up and patted him on the shoulder. 'Ah well, enough reminiscing. I better get back to work.'

He stood there, still and cold as a granite headstone, staring at the hammer.

'Tell Sheila I said, "Hi."' Steel turned and walked off.

Oh no, she was *not* leaving him alone with Big Jimmy Grieve.

Tufty scurried after her, not even trying to look cool.

He caught up halfway across the warehouse. Grabbed her arm. 'What did you just do?'

Steel turned and stared at him.

OK. Maybe no grabbing.

He let go.

She started walking again. 'I said hello to an old friend.'

'An old...?' Tufty dropped his voice to a hissing whisper as they passed 'STACEY' and her amazing pigtails. 'He looks like a serial killer!'

'Is it lunchtime yet? I'm feeling lunch-ish.'

'Why can't you do *anything* by the rules?'

'Lunch, lunch, lunch, lunch, lunch.' She pushed through the main door and into the car park.

'Who's Big Jimmy Grieve? What's he going to do to Phil Innes?'

'I'm thinking: fish supper, avec les onions pickled and peas à la mush.'

Tufty nipped around in front of her, blocking the way. 'What if he beats Phil Innes up? What if he *kills* him? Are we accessories to murder now?'

Steel smiled back. 'You worry too much.'

245

Then she stepped around him, sauntering away to where they'd parked the pool car.

Tufty stayed where he was. Risked a glance back towards the garden centre.

Big Jimmy Grieve's carved granite face stared out at him from just inside the main doors. Still and lifeless. Watching.

Oh they were *so* screwed.

CHAPTER EIGHT

*in which Tufty goes to the shops, and
we find out what happens
when you stand up to a Very Scary Man*

I

'*Oh, and I found the* cutest *set of antique golf clubs in a wee shop today, Robbie.*'

'Uh-huh…' Roberta scrubbed the soap into her hands, phone pinned between her ear and her shoulder. 'You really need more golf clubs?'

'*They're not for playing with, they're decorative. Six clubs in a lovely leather-and-canvas bag with a stand. I'm going to put it in the living room, next to the—*'

The rest of it was drowned out by the roar of the hand dryer.

'*—for dinner?*'

'Yeah, probably.' She hauled up her trousers. 'You know: my breeks are *definitely* looser than they used to be. Must be losing weight. Wasting away cos you don't feed me enough.'

'*You're* not *wasting away. And stop calling me when you're on the toilet, it's not hygienic.*'

'Ah well, better get back to it I suppose. Got an idiot waiting for me.' She hung up and thumped out of the ladies. 'And there he is.'

Tufty was slumped against the wall outside, looking bored. Poor wee sausage.

God knew what that Wildlife Crime Officer saw in him.

The pointy face with bits of red paint still stuck in the crevasses; the dirty-big thumbprint of a black eye. The sulking.

He did one of those teenagers' sighs. 'Can we *go* now?'

'Hey, when nature calls you can't just ask it to leave a message. Sometimes you have to...' Oh for God's sake.

That frantic nervous wee PC from before – the one running DCI Sodding Rutherford's errands – came clattering down the stairs and staggered to a halt right in front of her. Peching and heeching like a broken kettle. Face shiny and pink. 'Sar... Sarge?'

'No' *you* again!'

PC Sweaty-and-Nervous grabbed at the handrail to keep himself upright. 'Sarge ... DCI ... DCI Rutherford wants ... wants you ... both ... in his office.'

'I'm busy.'

'He was ... was very particular ... about it ... being completely ... totally *right now*.'

She narrowed her eyes and gave the PC a poke. 'I'm beginning to go off you.'

The boy Rutherford was standing behind his desk with his back to the room, staring out of his office window, hands crossed behind him. As if he was watching a parade marching across the Rear Podium car park six floors below. He didn't shift as Roberta wandered in. Didn't say a word. Ride git.

Rutherford wasn't the only one there, though.

Hissing Sid sat prim as a vicar's wife in one of the visitors' chairs. He gave her a teeny shake of the head and a disappointed look.

DI Vine had the other chair. Glowering. 'About time.'

Behind her, Tufty swore very, very quietly.

The wee loon wasn't wrong either: this was it, they were

dead. Hissing Sid wouldn't rock up in his fancy suit and leather briefcase if Jack Raping Scumbag Wallace hadn't made another complaint. And now Rutherford would make good on his threat – Roberta and Tufty, up in front of the firing squad. He'd given them one last chance, but now they were dead. Dead, screwed, buggered, spanked, wingwanged, crudweaselled, and completely and utterly dead.

Didn't mean she was going quietly, though.

She sniffed. Nodded at Hissing Sid. 'Going to be one of *those* meetings, is it?'

'Detective Sergeant Steel.' Rutherford kept staring out of his window, but you could've shaved your legs on his voice. Probably get frostbite doing it, though. 'Mr Moir-Farquharson tells me you've been hanging around outside Jack Wallace's house. WHEN I SPECIFICALLY ORDERED YOU NOT TO!'

That boomed around the room, bouncing off the filing cabinets and whiteboards before fading away.

Tufty licked his lips and backed towards the door. 'Maybe I should just—'

'Oh no you don't: you stay right there!' Rutherford uncrossed his hands – clenched them into fists instead. 'DS Steel, what did I tell you would happen if you screwed up again? That I would hold Constable Quirrel jointly responsible for your actions. Well *congratulations*.'

She jerked her chin up, shoulders back. 'Whatever Jack Wallace said, he's a lying wee turd.'

Hissing Sid sighed. 'Actually, in this instance, Mr Wallace has documentary evidence. To wit: a series of photographs of your car parked outside his property on no fewer than a dozen occasions.'

'Nah, don't believe you. They're fake photos.'

Rutherford turned around at that, face all dark and

trembling. 'For God's sake, Sergeant, you're not president of the United States; you can't just say *everything* incriminating is fake!' He stuck out his hand. 'Mr Moir-Farquharson?'

Hissing Sid dug into his briefcase and produced the same slimline laptop as last time. He placed it on the desk and opened it up. Tapped at the keyboard.

The screen filled with a photo of her MX-5, parked beneath the trees outside Wallace's house, the colours muted in the darkness. *Tap.* Another night-time photo: her car parked a couple of doors down. *Tap.* There she was, leaning against one of those trees, a cloud of vapour caught by a streetlight as she puffed on her e-cigarette. *Tap.* The car again, her face clearly visible through the rain-flecked windscreen as she stared up at the house.

Hissing Sid sighed. 'And last but not least…' *Tap.* In this one she was rummaging through Wallace's wheelie-bin, a torch clenched between her teeth.

Sod. He *did* have photographs.

Rutherford placed his fists on the desk. Looming over the laptop. 'Well?'

'I know this looks bad, but—'

'*Looks* bad? What did I tell you?'

'I was pursuing an ongoing investigation and—'

'I TOLD YOU SPECIFICALLY TO STAY AWAY FROM HIM!'

Outside a siren burst into life, fading away into the distance.

The sound of a phone ringing filtered through from the office next door.

Tufty shuffled his feet. 'Er… Can I…?' He pointed at the laptop.

DI Vine turned his glower on him. '*What?*'

'Well, I couldn't help noticing that DS Steel's wearing a green shirt and her blue suit in that last photo.'

'This isn't *Loose Women*, Constable, we're not here for bloody fashion tips!'

'No, yes, but we took her blue suit to the cleaners a *fortnight* ago, because Scabby George puked all over it when we did him for peeing off the top of Chapel Street multi-storey car park. She hasn't had it on since.' He inched his way forward and pointed at the laptop again. 'So can I...?'

Hissing Sid shrugged. 'I have no objection.'

Tufty fiddled about with the laptop's trackpad.

Rutherford stared at her. 'Is this true, DS Steel?'

'Scabby George? Oh aye. He'd been swigging down two-litre bottles of super-strength cider all morning. Said if society thought it was OK to piss on *him* the whole time, it was only fair he got his own back.'

Tufty held up a hand. 'Here we go. Look.' He stepped back from the screen. A window with file information sat on top. 'The image files' "created on" dates are weeks and weeks ago. The photos aren't recent.'

Ooh, you lovely wee spud of a man.

Roberta grinned. 'So we're off the hook.'

'I *beg* your pardon?' Vine poked at the arm of his chair. 'That doesn't change the facts at all.'

'Aye it does. These photos were all taken before our happy little meeting yesterday.'

'You were harassing Jack Wallace!'

Thicky McVine clearly wasn't getting it.

Try again, nice and slow. 'He took these photos ages ago, right? Then he came in yesterday and forgave *everything*, remember? You remember him forgiving everything? At the meeting? You were there?' Then she turned and snapped to attention in front of DCI Rutherford. 'You ordered me to stand down, *sir*, and down I jolly well stood!' She even threw in a salute for good measure.

Rutherford frowned at her for a bit, head on one side. Then nodded. 'Very well. So, Mr Moir-Farquharson, why is your client bringing this up now?'

She clicked her heels together. 'I can answer that one, sir. It's because he's a stirring wee shite.'

A smile flickered across Moir-Farquharson's face, before he caught and squashed it.

'I see.' Rutherford sank into his office chair. 'So you're no longer keeping Jack Wallace's house under surveillance?'

'And disobey a direct order from *you*, Guv? Wouldn't dream of it.'

DI Vine stood outside in the stairwell, scowling in at her as the lift doors slid shut.

Roberta gave him a wee wave and a wink just before he disappeared.

Miserable jobbie-faced crudweasel that he was.

It wasn't a huge lift to start with, but when you squeezed in one detective chief inspector, a very expensive criminal lawyer, a sexy bombshell detective sergeant, and a lovely wee Tufty-shaped star, it was more like a coffin that went up and down a bit.

No one said anything, just stood there in awkward silence, trying no' to rub up against anyone else in a faux-pervy manner.

Roberta leaned closer to Tufty and whispered in his ear. 'Hope nobody farts!'

The look on his face was thanks enough.

The lift doors pinged open and everyone spurted out like the contents of a squeezed pluke.

Rutherford turned and shook Hissing Sid's hand. 'Right, well, I'll leave DS Steel to show you out.' He marched off, arms swinging, back stiff. By the left, left, left – right – left.

Soon as he was out of earshot Roberta poked Hissing Sid in his immaculately suited chest. 'Aye, *thanks* for that.'

He brushed at his lapel, removing the freshly poked dent. 'Nothing personal, I can assure you, Detective Sergeant. My client asked me to present his photographs for Police Scotland's consideration, so here I am.'

Tufty fiddled with the keycode lock then held the door open for them.

She patted him on the back on the way past. 'Get the teas on. You earned yourself a Jammie Dodger the day.'

He mugged a wee smile. 'Yes, Sarge.' And scurried off.

An auld mannie in a tracksuit and hoodie was slumped in the plastic seating that lined the reception area. Other than that, the place was quiet.

'You no' a bit expensive to act as a messenger boy, Sandy?'

He followed her across the Police Scotland crest set into the terrazzo flooring. 'Thankfully Mr Wallace's associates are *very* generous with their support. And, to be honest, I enjoy a nice walk in the sunshine.'

'Generous...' She stopped, one hand on the 'Disabled' button to open the front doors. Frowned. 'What did you mean: my friends "came to my aid" and so did his?'

'Did I say that? Well, well, well.'

'Sandy!'

No reply.

'You told me you took my case pro bono, because of all those murderers and rapists you got off!'

'A small fiction. The individual who covered your legal expenses didn't wish to be named.'

Oh *sodding* hell.

She backed away. 'It wasn't someone dodgy, was it? A bank robber, or a drug dealer?'

'Quite the opposite. He merely felt that if you knew your benefactor's real identity you would have refused my help.'

'Aye, because I'd turn *that* down.' She pressed the button and the doors swung open. Sparked up her e-cigarette and wandered outside, puffing away with her hands in her pockets. Supposed to be 'Mandarin & Guava' but it tasted more like Fanta. 'After that two-faced back-stabbing sack of crap clyped on me to Professional Standards, I needed all the help I could...'

She stared at Hissing Sid.

He smiled calmly back. Then raised an eyebrow.

He didn't mean... He *couldn't*!

'No, no, no, no, no. You are... You have *got* to be taking the pish. It can't have been!'

'Inspector McRae believed your feelings towards him would cloud your judgement somewhat. He'd recently lost someone close to him and inherited a sum of money from their estate, that's how he was able to finance your defence.'

'Oh for *God's* sake!'

Tufty opened the door to the CID office and stuck his head in. Lund, Harmsworth and Barrett must've sloped off for lunch, because Steel was the only one in there, sitting with her feet up on the desk, frowning at the window.

Another four willies had joined the one on the white-board, but they looked sad and disappointed. Lacklustre willies whose hearts weren't really in it.

Bit like Steel, then.

'Sarge?'

She kept on frowning at the window. 'Ever get the feeling someone's just wheeched the tablecloth away, but instead of all the plates and glasses and stuff just sitting there, it all goes crashing down?'

Very profound.

'You'll never guess who's downstairs.'

'It was McRae. When his girlfriend died the life insurance

paid out big style. That's how he could afford to hire Hissing Sid to defend me.'

'See? Told you he was a good guy.'

Her face curdled, wrinkles getting wrinklier around her downturned mouth. 'Mind you: wouldn't have needed an expensive slippery lawyer if McRae hadn't landed me in it in the first sodding place!'

That's the spirit.

'Anyway: downstairs. It's Mrs Galloway's neighbour, the one with the wee kid.'

Steel went back to staring at the window. 'But why land me in it, then pay a fortune for Hissing Sid to come drag me out? Doesn't make any sense…'

'She wants to make a complaint.'

'Gah…' Steel's head fell back. She covered it with her hands and groaned. Sighed. 'Of course she does, because that's how this sharny horrible job works. No one helps, everyone complains.' A grunt and she stood, slouching and droopy. 'Might as well get it over with.'

A weird Pot-Noodley smell filled the small reception room. Maybe it lived here? Or maybe it had hitched a ride with Mrs Galloway's next-door neighbour? She sat with her back to the door, in an AFC away-strip tracksuit that looked a bit too shiny not to be a knock-off. Her toddler stood on the chair next to her, drawing swooping loops of red and green crayon on a sheet of paper.

Steel slumped into the chair opposite and sighed. 'You want to make a complaint.'

Tufty got his notebook out.

A nod sent her pigtail swaying. 'I do.' She took a deep breath and blurted it out: 'I saw Phil Innes kicking in Mrs Galloway's door. He's the one who attacked her. I heard everything.'

Tufty wiggled his eyebrows at Steel, mugging a huge grin. 'Wh…? Is…?'

The neighbour folded her arms. Swear to God, little crackles of static electricity glowed along those shiny track-suit sleeves. 'Well? You going to arrest him now?'

Tufty tapped his pen on his pad. 'Let's start at the very beginning, shall we?'

After all, it was a very good place to start.

'…and get on to the Sheriff's office.' Steel rubbed her hands together, Mr Burns style. 'I want a warrant to go through Philip Innes's place like a kilo of laxative.'

Tufty gave her a small salute. 'Yes, Captain, my captain.'

She turned to go, just as Big Gary lumbered up the corridor towards them.

'Hoy! Where do you two think you're going?'

'To do some actual police work, Gary. Don't know if you remember it…?'

He puffed out his chest, making himself even bigger. 'Not till you've seen to the bus-load of people cluttering up my nice clean reception area, you're not.' He pointed a finger at the keycode entry door.

On the other side of the toughened safety-glass panel, reception was packed. Twenty, maybe thirty people over flowed the rows of seats, wandering around the place staring at the 'HAVE YOU SEEN THIS MAN?' posters.

'And before you ask: yes, they *are* here to see you.'

Tufty stepped up to the glass. 'Wow. Looks like half of Cairnhill Court have turned up!'

He poked at the keycode lock and held the door open for Steel and Gary to squeeze past. Stepped through after them and let it swing closed.

An old man wobbled his way up from his seat and shook his walking stick at them. 'I want to complain about Philip

Bloody Innes. I was short twenty quid and he smashed my telly!'

A young woman shuffled forward, chunky in too tight jeans and a *much* too tight T-shirt. 'Phil Innes's been harassing my mum about a loan. She's fifty-three!'

A frizzy-haired woman with bags under her eyes and two snotty little kids on a leash: 'He beat the crap out of my husband.'

Steel held up her hands, mouth hanging open. A couple of blinks, then, 'Anyone here *no'* wanting to complain about Philip Innes?'

Not a single soul.

She leaned in and whispered at Tufty. 'We're going to need a bigger boat.'

II

'How much longer?' Lund peered out through the police van window at the lumpen grey bulk of Division Headquarters.

Harmsworth adjusted his knee and elbow pads – thick black plastic ones that crumpled his suit's sleeves and trouser legs. 'We're not going to get home on time. *Again*. I just know it.'

'Come on, come on, come on!'

'We're all going to end up in Accident and Emergency, you mark my words. Broken bones and stab wounds all round.'

Barrett checked his clipboard. 'No mention of Philip Innes ever stabbing anyone. Anyway, I think you should be more worried about ending the day with all your clothes on.'

'That's not funny: I was traumatised!'

'You were bare-arse naked.'

'Pfff…' Tufty's phone buzzed against his ribs. Text message. He pulled it out.

DC Quirrel, it's PC Mackintosh
Council can do us a crem slot tomorrow at
14:30 – cancellation

Half two, tomorrow? Hmm…

260

He typed out a reply:

> Mrs Galloway's going to be stuck in hospital
> for at least a week. Phil Innes REALLY
> battered her.

Send.

The phone buzzed in his hand.

> If we don't do it now, we can't get another
> pet slot for a fortnight and the Pathologist's
> complaining that Pudding's starting to smell
> up his fridges.
>
> Sorry :(

Ah. Suppose they could *freeze* him, but if they did, would he have to be defrosted before they could cremate him? Wouldn't want to screw it up…

And maybe it'd be better for Mrs Galloway if this was all done and taken care of? She was already standing out on the ledge. A funeral for her poor wee dog might be the final push.

> OK 14:30 tomorrow – it's a date

Send.

Oh no!

It's a *date*? What the hell was he thinking?

> Sorry! Didn't mean 'date' date – meant I'll
> see you there!!!
>
> Nobody goes on a date to the crematorium.
>
> Unless they're weird. And you're definitely
> not weird.

He stared at his phone's screen. No. Deleted the last three sentences and hit 'SEND'.

Lund nudged him. 'Time is it?'

'Ten past four.' He frowned, then slipped his phone back in his pocket. 'Steel said she'd be right down.'

'All together now!' Lund banged out the beat on the van roof, singing:

'Why are we waiting?
Owen's masturbating,
Davey's locating his arse – with – both hands,
Tufty's a numpty,
DC Lund is lovely...'

Finally Steel bustled out of the side door and in behind the wheel. The only one of them not wearing Method of Entry protective kit. Which probably meant she was planning on leading from the rear again.

She started the van and reversed out of the space – looking back over her shoulder at the four of them. 'Right, you horrible shower, listen up and listen good: Philip Innes is a violent wee crudweasel. He's got no qualms about putting little old ladies in intensive care. So I don't want any screw-ups, understand? I don't want to see so much as a broken fingernail on any of you. And Owen?'

Harmsworth's bottom lip jutted out. 'Here we go.'

'Try to keep your pants on this time, eh?'

The van swung around – narrowly missing taking the wing mirror off Chief Superintendent Campbell's Bentley – round the back of the mortuary, down Poultry Market Lane and out onto Queen Street.

The tyres squealed as they swung onto Broad Street.

Steel banged on the steering wheel. 'We are not at home to Mr Fuckup. What are we?'

The response was about as enthusiastic as the half-arsed willies on the CID whiteboard: 'Not at home to Mr Fuckup.'

She belted the steering wheel again, making it ring. 'I – CAN'T – HEAR – YOU!'

This time they all belted it out: 'WE'RE NOT AT HOME TO MR FUCKUP!'

Steel grinned.

*   *   *

Steel turned onto Cairncry Drive and put her foot down. The police van surged forward, shoving her back in her seat as they raced down the middle of the road – then a screech of brakes as she yanked the steering wheel left. Jerking to a halt just shy of Philip Innes's shiny black Jaguar. 'Release the hounds!'

Tufty hauled open the sliding door and Harmsworth leapt out – Barrett close on his heels. Lund grabbed the Big Red Door Key and ran after them, leaving him to bring up the rear. Leaping the two steps up to the garden path.

Harmsworth and Barrett stepped aside, leaving the door clear for Lund.

'Hot potato!' She swung the mini battering ram back as she ran, screeching to a halt just in front of the white UPVC and letting the thing smash forward. The whole door exploded inwards with a *BOOM*!

This was it.

Barrett was first inside. 'POLICE! NOBODY MOVE!'

Tufty and Harmsworth swarmed in after him.

Down at the end of the corridor, Barrett kicked a door open revealing a swanky kitchen.

Harmsworth charged up the stairs. 'POLICE!'

Tufty bashed through the first door on the right. 'EVERYBODY ON THE GROUND: NOW!'

The living room was a proper man cave: a full-sized pool table and massive entertainment system, a bar in the corner complete with optics, arty prints of naked ladies on the walls, two black leather recliners and a matching couch.

Phil Innes was sitting on it. Still and quiet. Head bowed. Shoulders quivering.

Tufty clacked out his extendable baton. 'Philip Innes, I'm detaining you under Section Fourteen of the Criminal Justice … Scotland?'

Innes wiped a hand across his eyes, sniffed, and stood.

Held both of his arms out, wrists together. 'I'll...' Another sniff. 'I'll come quietly.'

Lund poked her head into the lounge. 'Rest of the house is clear. You got him?'

Innes stared down at his proffered wrists. 'I just... I just want to say that I'm very, very, *very* sorry for what I did. I'm a... I'm a bad man...' His bottom lip went, followed by full-on sobbing.

'Er...' Tufty stepped closer and patted him on the shoulder. 'There, there?'

'Right, that's the lot.' Barrett eased past them with his blue plastic evidence crate. 'We've got about forty Post Office account books, hundreds of bank statements, twenty-one notebooks detailing loans and repayments, and sixty debit and credit cards. None of which are in Philip Innes's name.'

Tufty sucked on his teeth. 'Weird that he just gave it all up like that. Why didn't he ... I don't know, try to hide it instead of piling it all up on the kitchen table for us?'

'Hello?' Harmsworth peered around the edge of the battered UPVC door he was holding. 'I know it's only me, and hernias are oh-so-funny, but can we get this done please!'

'Oh, right.' Tufty fixed a Phillips-head to the cordless drill and held his hand out to Steel. 'Screw me.'

She stared back. 'Want to rephrase that?'

'I'm not kidding – this door is really heavy!'

Tufty tried again. 'Can I have a screw please, Sarge?'

'That's no' sounding any better.' She held out a handful of them, though.

'I'm going to drop this if you don't get a shift on!'

'All right, all right.' Tufty helped him manoeuvre the door back into the hole it was battered out of. 'Come on, Owen, hold the damn thing still.' The brass-colour screws bit through the UPVC and into the wooden frame.

Harmsworth sighed. 'It's nice not to get stabbed or bitten for a change, but all in all, it was a *bit* of an anticlimax.'

'Aye, that's enough about your love life, Owen. Keep your mind on the job.' She handed Tufty another couple of screws.

He turned to Tufty. 'You know what I mean? We get all dressed up and swarm out of the van and bash the door down and *really* put the work in.'

'Hold it steady...' Screw, screw, screw, screw.

'The least he could've done was resist arrest a little bit. Shown willing.'

Tufty gave the screwed-up door a wiggle – solid as a solid thing – and stepped back. 'There we go. All done.'

'Wasn't too much to ask for, was it? Little effort on his part?' Harmsworth stared at them for a moment, then shook his head and slouched back towards the van. 'But what does Owen know?'

Soon as the van door shut, Tufty had a quick look around to make sure no one was listening. Then leaned in close to Steel. 'Sarge, there wasn't a mark on Innes. Not a single one.'

'Course no'.' She took the drill from his hands. 'Why would there be?'

'So what did he do? Your mate, James Grieve? He must've done *something*.'

'God might move in mysterious ways, Tufty, but he's got nothing on Big Jimmy Grieve.' She dropped into a semi-squatting *Charlie's Angels* pose, firing off a few *vwwwwwwippps* with the drill. 'Now get your arse in the van. We've a couple of wee stops to make on the way home.'

Tufty climbed back into the van with his collection of paper bags, their white sides already turning see-through from the greasy treats inside.

He handed a bag to Barrett: 'One mince, one steak.' One to Lund: 'Sausage roll and a bridie.' One to Steel. 'Two steak.'

And one to Harmsworth. 'Chicken-curry pies aren't ready yet, so I got you a bacon butty and a fondant fancy.'

'Why does life hate me?'

Phil Innes stared over his shoulder at them from inside his grilled enclosure. 'That all smells really nice.'

Steel unwrapped a pie and took a big bite. 'Tough. You're getting nothing, cos you've been naughty.' She started the engine. 'Seatbelts, children.' Then stuffed the pie in her mouth, leaving her hands free to haul the van through a three-point turn, mumbling around the pastry case. 'One more stop.'

Steel hauled on the handbrake. 'Everyone remember where we parked.' She hopped out.

Tufty, Lund, Barrett, and Harmsworth clambered out through the sliding door and joined her around the back of the police van.

'Sarge?'

'Barrett, you and Lund are on prisoner escort duty. If you let him run away I will personally skin your intimate feminine areas with a potato peeler, are we clear?'

They nodded.

She clicked her fingers. 'Constable Quirrel, if you would be so kind as to fetch Mr Innes from the van?'

Tufty wiped the pastry crumbs from his fingers and unlocked the back doors.

Innes peered out at them. He was sitting in the middle of the three rear-facing seats, all handcuffed and seatbelted in. His bloodshot eyes drifted to what was behind them. Widened. He shrank back into his seat. 'This isn't the police station. This isn't the police station!'

'No, Philippy Willippy,' Steel grinned, 'it's the hospital. You're paying a visit and you're paying it *now*.'

'Please, don't! I wasn't—'

'Barrett, Lund: get that snottery sack of sick out of there.'

They stepped forward, Lund rolling her shoulders. 'Come on, you. Out.'

Tufty tugged at Steel's sleeve, keeping his voice down so no one would hear. 'Sarge, are you sure this is legal? Cos I really don't think it's legal.'

'Course it's no'.' She beamed at him as Phil Innes was hauled out of the van's cage. 'But Philippy Willippy isn't going to tell anyone. Are you, Philippy?'

Innes just bit his bottom lip and shook his head.

'Good boy.' She turned and sauntered towards one of the hospital's side entrances. 'Off we go.'

They frogmarched Innes in through the doors and over to a bank of scuff-fronted lifts.

The doors juddered open and they all stepped inside, Phil Innes squeezed between Lund and Barrett. Sweating. Fidgeting as the lift clunked and rattled upwards.

Lund poked him. 'Stand still.'

The lift creaked to a halt and the doors slid open again.

Steel was first out. 'From here on it's radio silence. No whinging, moaning, or making fun of Constable Harmsworth.'

He sniffed, nose in the air. 'About time too.'

'You can save that for the way back down again.'

'Hey!'

But she was off, marching down the corridor.

Lund and Barrett did their frogmarching trick again, scooting Innes along after her. All the way down to the private room at the end.

Steel stuck a finger to her lips then pointed at the lot of them. 'No' a sodding word, understand?'

Everyone kept their gobs shut.

'Good. Keep it that way.' Then she slipped into Mrs Galloway's room.

Tufty stepped up to the window.

Mrs Galloway made a thin frail figure in the bed, lying beneath the sheets, every visible inch of skin a rainbow of bruises. And Steel wasn't the only visitor. Big Jimmy Grieve sat in the chair on the far side of her bed, head buried in a book.

He looked up at Steel and nodded. Said something.

She said something back. Then turned to the poor battered old lady. Steel's lips moved, but it was impossible to hear what she was saying. Then she waved at the window.

They were on.

Lund gave Innes another poke. 'I'm watching you, sunshine.'

He *really* didn't look well. Pale and clammy. His whole body trembling.

They all shuffled inside, Tufty and Innes at the front.

Soon as everyone was in and the door closed, Tufty took out his key and undid the cuffs.

Innes made a little squeaky noise.

'Right.' Steel folded her arms. 'You've got something to say to Mrs Galloway, haven't you?'

'I'm...' Innes sounded more like a spanked child than a loanshark. 'I... I'm very, very sorry for what I've done. I'm... I'm a horrible, horrible person.'

Big Jimmy Grieve stared at him. 'Keep going.'

'Keep going... Right.' He licked his lips. Then pulled an envelope from his inside pocket. A standard one – the kind you could fit an A4 sheet of paper into if you folded it in three. Only there was a lot of paper in this one. It was about an inch thick. 'And ... and I want you to have this.'

He edged forward, the envelope held out at arm's length, keeping as much hospital bed between himself and Big Jimmy Grieve as possible. Placed it on the covers by her broken arm.

Mrs Galloway just looked at it.

Innes shrank back away from the bed again. 'Three thousand, two hundred, and seventy pounds. All yours. I...' His eyes drifted from the envelope to Big Jimmy Grieve for a second, then snapped down to stare at his own hands, clenched in front of his groin. 'I should never have charged you interest on a loan. That was illegal and I had no right doing it. I'm really, *really* sorry.'

A nod from Big Jimmy Grieve. 'And?'

'And I won't do it again?'

That quiet *still* note slipped into the big man's voice again. 'Try harder.'

'Right. Yes. Harder. And I ... I want you to have my car as an apology!' Babbling it out as he tossed his keys down beside the envelope. 'It's a Jaguar XJ with leather trim and heated seats...'

'And?'

Phil Innes's bottom lip wobbled, his eyes wet and glistening. 'And... And my watch too?'

'There we go.' Big Jimmy Grieve smiled. 'Now, doesn't that make you feel a bit better about yourself, Philip?'

He wiped a hand across his tear-moistened face. '*Please* can I go to prison now?'

III

Lund checked Phil Innes was all seatbelted in, then climbed out of the cage and locked the van's back door. She hooked a thumb at it. 'Ready to go when you are, Sarge.'

Steel nodded. 'Give us a minute, Veronica. Got some business to finish.'

Tufty shuffled his feet as Lund climbed in through the police van's side door and slid it shut, leaving him all alone with Steel and the horror that was Big Jimmy Grieve. 'Er, Sarge? Do you want I should...?' Pointing back at the van.

'You stay where you are. Might learn something.' Then Steel turned her back on him. 'Still got it, Mr Grieve?'

A modest shrug from those broad granite shoulders.

'As a gesture of our gratitude, I shall present you with your usual fee...' She held out her hand to Tufty for some reason. Like he had the slightest clue what was going on here.

'I have no idea what you're— Ow!'

She smacked him on the back of the head again.

'Ow!'

'Get the rowies.'

Rowies? They were all mad.

He hurried around to the passenger side, opened the door, retrieved the greasy paper bag from the dashboard, and hurried back again. Passed it to Steel. Who handed it to Big Jimmy Grieve.

'Half a dozen. You can count them, if you want?'

Big Jimmy Grieve weighed the bag in his hand. 'I trust you. Now, if we're all done here, it's Friday, it's half past five, and I have a bird table to put up.'

He turned to go.

OK, so it was now or never.

Tufty cleared his throat. 'Mr Grieve?'

The huge figure stopped, looked back over his shoulder. Made the kind of eye contact that caused perfectly brave detective constables' bowels to clench.

Right.

Here we go.

Deep breath. 'What did you do to Philip Innes? He was... It was like someone had run over him with a steamroller – squeezed the horrible right out of him. What are his defence going to hit us with when this goes to trial?' Tufty's chin came up: getting his righteous on with every sentence. 'I want to know what you did.'

Big Jimmy Grieve walked over until he was right in front of him – the tips of his boots pressing into Tufty's – and stood there. Not moving. Not saying anything. Just staring with those frozen granite eyes...

Yeah.

Maybe not.

Definitely not.

Tufty swallowed, backed away, pointing over his shoulder at the van. 'I'm gonna just... Erm...'

Big Jimmy Grieve looked at Steel. 'They don't get any brighter, do they?'

'I keep hoping, but no.'

Tufty hauled the side door open and clambered inside. Thumped it closed again. Locked it.

Sank into his seat.

And nearly jumped straight back out of it as a hand landed on his shoulder. He didn't mean to go, 'Eeek!' he really didn't.

Lund gave his shoulder a little squeeze. 'Did we try measuring willies with Big Jimmy Grieve? Did we lose?'

Outside, Steel stood on her tiptoes and kissed Mr Grieve on the cheek.

The hulking monster nodded, stared in through the police van windows for a heartbeat too many – like he was memorising Tufty's face and planning on rearranging it with his boot at some point – then lumbered off.

A shudder rippled its way down Tufty's back. 'That is, without any kind of doubt, the *scariest* motherfunker I have ever met.'

Tufty shoved the CID door open and bounded inside like a labradoodle puppy, belting out a one-man fanfare. 'Tan-tan-ta-ta!'

Barrett, Lund, and Harmsworth spun around in their office chairs as Roberta swaggered in, both hands up flashing the victory Vs.

She sang it out: 'We are the champions!'

Lund beamed. 'He cop to it?'

'Didn't even try to "no comment".' Roberta danced a couple of wee pas de basques. 'Shortest interview I've ever done: aggravated assault, animal cruelty, illegal money lending, harassment, and forty-nine other offences to be taken into consideration. CHAMPIONS!' Another two pas de basques, three high cuts, and done. She stood there grinning at them. Lowered her arms. 'We, my little love-monkeys, are off to the pub tonight to celebrate!'

Lund punched the air. 'Rippa!'

'Actually...' Barrett held up a hand. 'Remember we've got

that farmers' protest tomorrow morning? And the TV will be there, so we've got a full kit inspection first thing.'

'Aye, so?'

'So, perhaps, flaming Sambucas till three in the morning isn't such a *good* idea?'

Cagney & Lacey belted out into the room. 'Hold that thought.' She pulled out her phone.

'Unknown Number'.

Roberta pressed the button. 'Hello?'

Sodding Jack Sodding Wallace. *'Well, well: if it isn't my favourite demoted police officer.'*

The phone groaned a little as she squeezed it. 'What the hell do *you* want?'

'Did you enjoy seeing my photographs? Good, weren't they?'

She poked at the screen again, putting it on speakerphone. 'You know where you can stick your photos, Wallace?'

Everyone in the room gathered closer, staring at her mobile as his slimy voice slithered out of the speaker again.

'Oh, don't be so grumpy. I'm just here enjoying a nice meal at Doug's Dinner, with my mates, and thought I'd check in. We've been here, oh, at least, what?'

A muffled voice in the background: *'Hour and a half?'*

Tufty pulled a face at her, then scurried over to the whiteboard, wiping off the words of the day and the collection of willies scrawled up there.

'An hour and a half. Now we're off to see a film. Something exciting. Should take us till … oh, about half nine?'

'Yawn.' Roberta perched on the edge of the nearest desk. 'And I care *because*?'

Tufty yanked the top off a whiteboard pen, printed the word 'ALIBI!!!' in big red letters and underlined it. Made big pantomime gestures at the board.

Goat-buggering hell in a carrier bag: the wee sod was right. 'Wallace? What have you done?'

'*Me?*' A greasy little laugh. '*Nothing. That's the point.*'

And the line went dead. He'd hung up.

Roberta stared at the screen, then out at her team. 'Grab your coats and handcuffs: we're going out again. *Now!*' She marched from the room, scrolling through her contacts as everyone scurried into place behind her. Poked the button and set it ringing. 'Tufty: get us a Black Maria. Owen: you and Davey—'

A sharp impatient voice battered out of her phone. '*Vine.*'

'Aye, John – Jack Wallace is up to something.'

'*Oh in the name of... We've been over this! You can't just—*'

'Will you pin back your lugs for two minutes?' She barged through the double doors at the end of the corridor, boot heels echoing back off the concrete stairwell. 'Wallace just called me.'

Tufty squeezed past, taking the steps two at a time.

They all hurried down after him.

'*Look, I'm in the middle of an investigation here, so—*'

'Wallace wanted me to know that he'd been at dinner with his mates for an hour and a half, and then he was off to the pictures till half nine.'

Vine's voice got darker and louder. '*And you actually thought that was* important *enough to interrupt a—*'

'He's setting up another alibi.' Around the landing and down the next flight. 'Some poor woman's getting raped tonight!'

One last flight of stairs and along a corridor lined with 'WANTED' posters.

'John? You still there?'

She barged out through the door at the end and into the car park reserved for police vans.

'Detective Inspector Vine?'

Tufty came sprinting around the corner, waving a set of keys with a pink fuzzy fob dangling off them. 'Got it!'

The sound of a child crying came from the phone's speaker, then some scrunching noises.

'Did you hear me? Some woman's about to get raped!'

Tufty unlocked the van and they all piled inside. 'Buckle up, people!'

Roberta clambered into the passenger side as Vine's voice came back on. All flat – the anger drained out of it.

'I see.' He cleared his throat. *'You're too late.'*

'FUCK!' She punched the dashboard as Tufty hauled the van around the right way and roared away down Poultry Market Lane.

'Where am I going?'

'Union Square.' Back to the phone. 'I bloody well *told* you, didn't I?'

'Just … don't. OK?' That wee kid was still wailing in the background. *'Karen Marsh. Teacher. On maternity leave. I've seen some things in my time, but… Jesus.'*

The van burst out from behind Division Headquarters and onto Queen Street. Tufty hit the '999' button and the sirens screeched, blue-and-whites flickering back from the parked cars and shop windows.

'We're on our way to arrest Jack Wallace.'

Vine groaned. *'If he phoned you to boast about his alibi, what do you think the chances are it's waterproof? Because he knows we'll check.'*

'It's fake. It has to be.' She grabbed the handle above her door as the van screeched around the corner onto Broad Street. 'He claims he's at Union Square. We're going to pull the security camera footage and drag his raping arse out of the cinema.'

'Can you hear yourself? If he's on camera there, and he's still at the pictures, he – couldn't – have – done – this.'

'He's still involved! He knows!'

Right, onto Union Street, the traffic parting before them as Tufty gunned it.

'And how do we prove it? What magical bloody fairy wand do we wave to make that one stick?'

'We can't just sit on our thumbs and do nothing: women are getting raped!'

The traffic lights up ahead were red, Tufty pulled out onto the wrong side of the road, jabbing at the horn as a big blue Isuzu D-Max blocked the box junction, the bearded idiot behind the wheel grimacing at them as if that was going to help.

'No. We *can't sit on our thumbs. But* you *have to.*'

Finally the idiot reversed out of the way and the van roared forwards, round onto Market Street.

'I'm no'—'

'*Send two of your team to review the security footage. They can haul Wallace out of the cinema too: make sure he's not slipped out through a side door. But you go nowhere near him, understand?*'

Aye, right.

'He's involved!'

'*They're – going – to – fire – you, Roberta! Stay the hell away from Jack Wallace.*'

The van wheeched around the corner and onto Guild Street. The dark, rectangular, grey bulk of Union Square loomed up ahead. They eased their way around a cluster of buses, through two red lights, past the Jury's Inn and right up to the metal bollards outside Union Square.

'*Did you hear what I said? They'll* fire *you.*'

Roberta sniffed. Stared out of the window at the shopping centre's huge glass façade, bolted onto the side of the train station. 'Didn't know you cared.'

'*You're a good police officer, Roberta, you just … got obsessed and lost your way. This is your second chance, don't piss it away on a piece of dirt like Jack Wallace. We'll get him.*'

'Oh my…' She put a hand over her heart. 'Think I'm

tearing up a little… I mean, I'm a married woman, but yes! Yes, I will run away with you!'

'I'm serious.'

A sigh, then she sagged back in her seat. 'Fine.'

'Good. Let me know if your team finds anything.' He hung up.

She stuffed her phone back in its pocket.

Stay away from Jack Wallace. They'll fire you. You're a good police officer, Roberta. We love you, Roberta. Please don't leave us.

She scrunched her face closed. Took a deep breath. Bellowed it out: 'AAAAAAAARGH!' Grabbed at the dashboard, fingernails digging into the plastic as she wrenched herself back and forward six or seven times making it creak and groan. Then let go and slumped.

Everyone was staring at her, mouths pursed, eyebrows raised.

A shrug. 'I hate it when they're so sodding reasonable.' She waved a hand at the back seats. 'Davey: you and Veronica go check out Wallace's alibi.'

Barrett clutched his clipboard. 'Sarge.'

Lund hauled open the door and they both hopped out onto the cobbles. Marched away towards Union Square.

Harmsworth slid the door shut again then shoogled forward. 'Well done. It'll be good for them to handle a wee job on their own. They might learn something.'

Tufty tapped the steering wheel. 'Do we wait for them, or are we back to the station?'

'Pfff…' Roberta shook her head. 'No point hanging about. Might as well go back to the ranch.'

'Sarge.' He pulled the van around in a lumpy four-point turn.

Harmsworth changed seats so he was in the ones directly behind the front, facing the other way. 'And it won't hurt

DC Barrett to miss the first couple of drinks in the pub. He gets far too loud and irritating with six pints in him. And as for Lund? Pffff...' He turned in his seat, draping an arm around both her and Tufty's shoulders. 'We're the *heart* of the team. It's only fitting we—'

Roberta brushed his hand away. 'Sit your arse back down, Owen, and put your seatbelt on. They won't let me arrest Wallace, but I swear on God's fluffy slippers: I'm arresting someone tonight if it kills me.'

Roberta banged both the rear doors open and swept into the custody block like an outraged parent, Tufty scurrying along in her wake. A tubby PC in the full going-out kit was in front of the custody desk, holding onto a bootfaced middle-aged wifie dressed in fishnets, a short skirt, and a PVC leather jacket. Hair all Brillo pad.

Downie was on the desk again, peering at her over the top of his glasses. 'I see. And did the gentleman in question pay for these amorous services in advance, or does he have an account?'

'Oh aye, and a frequent flyer card and all. We give Nectar points these days, you know?'

'Hoy, Downie!' Roberta stormed up to the desk. 'Who did you give that mobile phone to? The stolen one? I want a name!'

The bootfaced prostitute stuck her nose in the air. 'Do you *mind*? Me and Sergeant Downie is having an intimate moment here.'

'Shove it, Dorothy.' Roberta jabbed a finger. 'Don't screw with me tonight, Downie: Susan swears I'm menopausal and I'm looking for a fight.'

He took off his glasses. 'If you'd checked your pigeon hole at the start of the shift you'd have found out, wouldn't you?'

She balled her fists. 'Don't say you weren't warned...'

His eyes widened, then he ducked down, below the desk – coming back up with a work book. Flicked through it. 'Phone, phone, phone... Ah, yes. Here we are.'

Downie spun the book around and pushed it towards her.

She squinted at it – all blurry and out of focus. 'How am I supposed to read that? Your handwriting's like two spiders fighting a hedgehog.'

'My handwriting is perfectly clear, thank you very much. It says, "Peter Stephenson, twenty-four Lochnagar Drive".'

Peter...?

Uncle Pete.

Married to horrible Aunt Vicki.

The scumbag who took those porn pics of Josie Stephenson was her *uncle*.

Roberta bared her teeth. 'Dirty ... GRAAAAAAH!' She thumped her fist down on the desk. Growling it out. 'Constable Quirrel: back in the van!'

IV

'YOU BASTARD! YOU FILTHY PERVERT BASTARD!'
Aunt Vicki lunged, swinging her claws.

Harmsworth grabbed her, holding on as Tufty marched
Peter Stephenson out of the living room. The place could've
starred in a supermarket magazine: a wallpaper feature wall
with ferny fronds on it, loads of Ikea furniture, themed
ornaments and throw pillows, pebbles and bits of driftwood
in frames above the fireplace, a fake log fire flickering gaily
away to itself.

And yes, they *could* have let Uncle Pete get dressed, but
sod it. Getting dragged down the station in his boxer shorts,
beige slippers, and an old T-shirt would be good practice
for him. Going to be plenty more humiliation where he was
going.

Roberta slipped the previously stolen Nokia into an
evidence bag. Glanced at Aunt Vicki. 'Do you want to tell
Josie's mum, or will we?'

'If I ever see that *bastard* again I'll kill him!'

No' a bad plan.

'So…?'

Aunt Vicki's chin came up. 'You do it. I'll never be able
to look her in the eye again after this. Because of that
BASTARD!' Still struggling in Harmsworth's hairy embrace.

'Fair enough.' Roberta turned and wandered out into the evening.

She'd barely gone halfway down the garden path before Aunt Vicki exploded from the front door. Screaming at the broken droopy wee figure of her husband as Tufty man-handled him into the back of the police van.

'YOU'RE DEAD TO ME, YOU HEAR ME, PERVERT? YOU'RE DEAD!'

Harmsworth bustled out after her. Grabbed her arms again. 'It's not my fault, Sarge, she bit me!'

'YOU'RE DEAD, YOU KIDDY-FIDDLING PAEDO BASTARD! DEAD!'

'Get her back inside.'

'Sarge.'

Every window had someone peering out of it, getting a good eyeful of the wee domestic drama playing out on their cosy middle-class street. The dinner-party set would be dining out on it for months.

Roberta scuffed over to the van.

Tufty was strapping scumbag Uncle Pete into the cage. Snapping the seatbelt over his handcuffs. After all, wouldn't want him hurting himself before someone got the chance to shank him in the prison showers.

Soon as Uncle Pete was all trussed up and cosy, Roberta hooked a thumb over her shoulder. 'Constable Quirrel, go give Owen a hand calming the wife down before she breaks something.'

He looked at her, then at the house, then back again, a worried frown on his weasely face. 'Sarge? You're not...?' Nodding at Uncle Pete.

'*Now*, Constable.'

'OK...' He scurried off back into the house.

She gave it a count of ten, then climbed into the prisoner cage and thumped the doors shut behind her. Glowered.

Uncle Pete was folded as far over as the seatbelt would allow. 'Oh God, I'm sorry, I'm so sorry...'

'Your brother's dying in hospital and you're *screwing* his fifteen-year-old daughter.'

'I'm sorry, I didn't mean to...'

'YOU TOOK PHOTOS OF IT ON YOUR BLOODY PHONE!' It boomed around the van like thunder.

He shrank back into his seat.

Roberta took a breath. Hissed it out. Calm.

'You pin back your lugs and you listen good: we're going to take you back to Queen Street and process you. You're going to call your solicitor and he's going to tell you to "no comment" the whole thing. He'll tell you if you keep your mouth shut he might be able to get you off with a slap on the wrists.' She held up the evidence bag with the offending DIY-porn-filled Nokia in it. 'And then we'll all have to go to court. They'll put Josie on the stand and make her tell the world how her uncle abused her. We'll have to show the photos. In court. In front of her *mum*, while her father's dying. You going to put Josie through that?'

'I ... love her.'

'Because either way, Good Old Uncle Pete's off to prison.'

He stared at his bare knees. Sniffed. Cleared his throat. Did his best to sound reasonable. 'It wasn't my idea. She got me drunk and—'

'DON'T YOU BLOODY DARE! You're a middle-aged man and she's fifteen.'

'But—'

'Let's count off how screwed you are, shall we?' She stuck out her thumb: 'Sex with an older child.' Forefinger: 'Sexual abuse of trust.' Middle finger: 'Making indecent images of a child.' Ring finger: 'Attempting to pervert the course of justice.' She stepped closer, looming over him in the back of the van. 'And you know what, Petey-boy? I'd *love* you to "no comment", because if you don't plead guilty before the trial we get to send you down for twenty-nine years.'

'Twenty…?' His cheeks paled, then his mouth fell open. A smear of snot glistened on his top lip.

'Twenty-nine years locked up with all the other paedos and rapists.' OK, so that wasn't *strictly* true – get a soft enough sheriff and they'd bundle all four charges into one concurrent job-lot, which meant fourteen years max – but Good Old Uncle Pete didn't know that. 'And if you tell *anyone* about this conversation, I swear to God the nonces in prison are going to be the least of your troubles. Understand?'

Uncle Pete collapsed into himself and sobbed.

'Good.' She climbed out, slammed the van doors hard enough to make the whole thing rock on its suspension. Turned, and marched back to the house.

Tufty was waiting for her. 'Sarge?'

'The wife any calmer?'

'Stopped screaming, which is nice.' He shuffled his feet and stared over her shoulder at the van. 'Er, Sarge, you didn't…?'

'When we get back to the ranch, you process and interview him.'

Tufty raised an eyebrow. 'You don't want to?'

'No. Because if I have to look at his slimy wee face once more tonight, I'm going to do what you think I just did. Only harder. And with a baseball bat.'

North Deeside Drive drifted by the van windows, the grumbling diesel engine no' quite loud enough to drown out Uncle Pete sobbing in the cage at the back.

Big houses, big gardens, big hedges, big trees, all painted in sparkling sunshine.

Roberta's phone buzzed at her, like a teeny ineffective vibrator. Text message:

Are you coming home tonight or not? You
still owe me a fancy French meal, you
workaholic bumhead!

True.

She was halfway through thumbing out a reply when the
thing launched into *Cagney & Lacey*. 'WEE DAVEY BARRETT'
popped up on screen. She hit the button. 'Davey? Tell me
you've got good news for your lovely Aunty Roberta.'

*'Sorry, Sarge. We've been through the security camera
footage and Jack Wallace was right where he said he was.
Doug's Dinner for an hour and three-quarters, then off to the
cinema to see* Once Upon a Time in Dundee.'

She frowned out at a chunk of parkland. Happy couples
strolling hand-in-hand along the winding path. 'Maybe he
slipped out?'

*'Nope. We went through the restaurant's footage too –
longest he's away from the table is a five-minute trip to the
loo. We rousted him from Screen Four, just as Ewan
McGregor was mid-shootout in the Overgate Centre. Got a
lot of swearing chucked our way when we had the lights
turned on. Him and his two buddies were right in the middle
of a row. No way they could've sneaked away with no one
noticing.'*

Gah...

The perfect end to the perfect day.

Roberta sagged back in her seat and covered her eyes
with a hand. 'Thanks, Davey. You and Lund write it up and
head off home.'

'Cheers, Sarge.'

And, no doubt, tomorrow there'd be yet another visit
from Jack Bloody Wallace and Hissing Sodding Sid. In to
moan about how the poor raping wee turdbasket was being
'harassed'.

Tufty poked her in the shoulder. 'Sarge, you OK?'

284

'No. No I'm not.' She deleted her text to Susan and composed a new reply:

Too late to get a table booked.
Stick the vodka in the freezer and get the
holiday brochures out.
Let's make a night of it.
Think they're going to fire me tomorrow.

Send.

And you know what? Good riddance to the lot of them.

Tufty was looking at her with that spanked puppy dog expression on his stupid face. 'Want to talk about it?'

'No. I want to go home and get very, *very* drunk.'

Whatever crap was coming tomorrow could wait.

CHAPTER NINE

*in which some tractors drive down Union Street
and Everyone Has A Bath*

I

'Urgh…' Roberta struggled her way into the itchiest black trousers ever invented by man. And it *had* to be a man – no woman would ever create something as horrible as Police-Scotland-issue uniform leg torturers.

Didn't help that they'd shrunk about two sizes since she'd last had them on.

She thumped back onto the floral-print duvet and puffed and wriggled, hauling them up.

Susan leaned back against the vanity unit, one foot up on the tartan chaise longue. Smiling away in her floaty Laura Ashley dress.

Rotten sod.

Finally the trousers gave up the fight! Roberta rolled off the bed, pulled in her stomach and did up the button. Zipped the bulgy bits in.

These trousers had *definitely* shrunk.

Susan sauntered over and brushed a bit of cat hair from the epaulettes buttoned to Roberta's black T-shirt. 'Oh, I do love a woman in uniform.'

'Surprised they still fit… Almost… Long as I don't breathe… And they're all *itchy*.'

'Well I think you look very sexy.' She threaded the black belt through the belt loops. Bit her bottom lip. 'Maybe you should keep it on when you get home? And don't forget your handcuffs. After all, I'm going to *cream* Marion Bridgeport on the golf course today: I'll be in the mood to *celebrate*.'

Roberta groaned down onto the chaise longue and pulled on her boots. Laced them up as all the blood above her trousers shoved its way into her head and the waistband made breathing impossible. Slumped back and sucked in a deep breath. 'Sodding hell...'

Really needed bigger trousers.

She looked up at Susan. 'Turns out Hissing Sid didn't defend me for free – someone paid him. It was—'

'Logan. He didn't want you to know and be all stubborn about it.' A small sad sigh as she brushed at the epaulettes again. 'It's a shame they had to swap the shirt-and-tie for a T-shirt. I always loved you in a tie.'

Wonderful. So everyone knew but her.

Roberta looked away. No' meeting Susan's eye. 'Why didn't you tell me?'

'Because I didn't want you to be all stubborn about it either. How am I supposed to get my kinky on with you banged up in prison somewhere?'

She pulled herself up with one of the bed's four posts. 'He ratted me out to the rubber heelers.'

'Plus, I really don't think I could trust you – locked in with all those naughty women, twenty-four hours a day? Communal showers? What *would* you get up to?'

'I trusted *him*.'

'I know you did, Robbie.' Then she reached around and took a good handful of Roberta's bum and squeezed. 'Now, get this sexy itchy backside downstairs. French toast for breakfast!'

'Hi.' He'd been aiming for cool-and-manly, but what came out was more of a testicularly ruptured squeak. Tufty cleared his throat and tried again. Much deeper this time. 'Constable Mackintosh.'

A faint pink tinge spread across her neck, where it poked out of her stabproof vest and high-viz waistcoat. 'Detective Constable Quirrel.'

Uniformed officers crowded the muster room, laughing, joking, moaning, whinging, talking about how great it was to be kicking off at nine in the morning instead of seven for a change.

'So... You all set for today?'

She nodded. 'You?'

He slipped his hands into the armpits of his stabproof. 'Nice being back in uniform again. Don't get me wrong, CID's fun, but it's not the same when you're running about in your own clothes. Like you're only playing at being a police officer.'

'Right.'

Yeah, this wasn't really going as well as he'd planned.

Tufty cleared his throat again. Safer ground. 'So... Half two this afternoon?'

'Yes.' A small smile. 'Looking forward to it. Well, not. Sort of. It's a wee dog's funeral and what kind of sicko enjoys that? I mean, it's good to be doing something nice for an old lady...' Constable Mackintosh straightened her equipment belt with its collection of limb restraints, handcuffs, pepper spray, and extendable baton. 'Shame we don't have an urn though. For the look of the thing.'

'Yeah. A lot nicer than getting your dog back in a shoebox.' He stared at his feet. 'After the funeral, do you want to—'

A voice boomed out from the doorway. 'All right, everyone, settle down.' Whoever was speaking, they were hidden behind the sea of heads. 'Chief Superintendent Campbell wants a word before you head out. Boss?'

'Thanks, Steve. Ladies, gentlemen, and Detective Sergeant

Marshall, social media is fizzing with posts from those who look at today's farmers' protest as an excuse to settle old scores. Independence: in–out. Brexit: in–out.' A sheaf of paper appeared above the waves of close-cropped haircuts for a brief shoogle. 'You should all have an information sheet – I want you to pay *particular* attention to Gareth Thannet and Angus Menzies. Last time this pair of individuals clashed, Glasgow city centre was turned into a warzone. And now they seem to think that they can come up to Aberdeen on a jolly and cause trouble on *our* streets. Are they right?'

They all thumped it out in unison: 'NO, BOSS!'

'They think we're going to just let them run riot in our city. Are we?'

'NO, BOSS!'

It was like electricity, crackling through the room, making all the hairs stand up on Tufty's arms.

'No we *bloody* well aren't. Now get out there and make me proud!'

A cheer belted out. This was it. They were ready. And if Thannet and Menzies tried anything they were in for a nasty shock. Because North East Division was pumped up. Energised. Ready to rock.

Hell, yeah: bring it on!

'Christ, I'm bored.' Roberta sagged, but no' very far. The stabproof vest squeezed her tight, as if she was an overfilled sausage, squooging her boobs and making every breath a struggle. Because the shrunken itchy trousers weren't bad enough.

Even rubbing her legs against the waist-high metal barrier that held back the unwashed masses didn't help. Swear to God they made these things out of ants, fleas and midge bites.

A massive seething mob filled the square outside Markie's.

Placards poked up above them, rehashing old arguments for and against everything from the last general election to farm subsidy payments. Those temporary metal barriers kept a clear patch in the middle of the square free, another two lines stopping them from spilling out onto Union Street, but the crowd stretched down past the Prince of Wales on one side, and all the way around to the Kirk on the other. There was even a crowd on the St Nicholas Centre's roof terrace.

The organisers had set up a stage outside the Clydesdale Bank, blocking access to the cash machines, big enough to fit a dozen chairs, a lectern and a microphone stand. And last, but no' least, about seventy-five percent of Aberdeen's police officers making a solid black-and-fluorescent-yellow line between the various factions. Big Tony Campbell had even managed to call in a couple of horse-mounted plods from Strathclyde.

Roberta checked her watch again. 'An hour we've been here. A whole hour, and no one's so much as trodden on anyone's toe.'

Lund smiled up at the blue sky. 'Still, it's nice to be out in the sunshine for a change.'

On the other side, Harmsworth grunted. Scowling. 'Probably getting a massive melanoma just from standing here. *And* my trousers are itchy.'

Roberta peered around his bloated lump of a body. Tufty was chatting up that perky Wildlife Crime Officer again.

Horny wee sod that he was.

Lund stood on her tiptoes. 'Ooh, I can see tractors. Here we go.'

Roberta had a squint, but the corner of the Royal Bank blocked off most of Union Street from here.

Pfff...

No' that there was anything particularly exciting about

tractors, but at least it'd be something to look at other than the motley collection of placards. And once you'd spotted the obligatory 'DOWN WITH THIS SORT OF THING!' and 'I'M SO ANNOYED I MADE A SIGN!' ones, there was nothing left to do but stand there in the blazing sunshine, dressed all in black, wearing a stone's-worth of equipment – sweat trickling down your back and into your underwear.

Fun.

Harmsworth had another dig at his backside. 'Itchy, itchy, itchy, itchy…'

Roberta thumped him. 'I'm no' telling you again: leave your arse alone.'

'It's itchy.'

'We're *all* itchy, Owen, that's how life works: you're born, you're itchy, then you die.'

He went in for another howk.

'Stop it!' She pointed across the square, where the media had set up camp. A blonde weather-girl-type was primping her curly hair in the mirror of a cameraman's lens. 'You want to be on national TV mining for bum-nuggets?'

'Oh that's right, poor Owen just has to suffer in silence, as usual.'

'Silence? You never stop moaning on about everything!'

Five people emerged from behind the Royal Bank, carrying a banner nearly as wide as Union Street: 'DON'T LET THEM KILL OUR FARMING INDUSTRY!!!' Waving at the crowds. Right behind them was a massive combine harvester, blades rotating slowly. Presumably as a warning to the banner carriers – don't slow down or fall over, or *else*.

Blondie finished primping and stood back a couple of paces, microphone up and ready. No' that she needed it – hers was the kind of voice that carried. A foghorn with a west-coast accent. 'You ready, Chris?'

*   *   *

Anne twisted the microphone around in her hand, so the BBC logo was visible from the front. Here we go. Deep breath. Red leather, yellow leather. Red leather, yellow leather.

She flashed her warmest smile at the camera.

You can do this, Anne. You can!

Just don't screw it up and everything will fall into place. They'll see that you're more than just a pretty face standing in front of a map blethering on about low pressure moving in from the west. That you've got what it takes to be a *serious* television journalist.

OK, so it's just a local interest piece for the twenty-four-hour news channel, but maybe they'll edit it down and put you on the six o'clock too? Maybe then someone will *finally* recognise all your untapped TV potential?

Maybe they'll send you to exotic places to interview important people like the Dalai Lama? Maybe they'll give you your own show? Then you're on *Strictly Come Dancing* and there's a *massive* book deal – not just a ghost-written autobiography either, a whole ghost-written series of best-selling children's novels! An OBE for services to literature. A spot of charity work and *BAM*: Dame Anne Darlington, beloved by millions. I want to thank the Nobel Committee for this peace prize...

And it all started right here, outside the Aberdeen branch of Markie's.

She pulled back her shoulders and sexied up her smile a bit.

Maybe that was *too* sexy? Approachable but serious, that was what to aim for.

She could do that.

Chris the cameraman looked out from behind his view-finder. Even with the sun blazing down he still had his bobble hat on, stubbled face pulled into a smile. 'Don't sweat it: you're going to be great.'

Yes. Yes she *was*.

He pursed his lips. 'Just as long as that copper in the background stops scratching at his arse.' Chris stuck his hand out to one side, counting her down one finger at a time. 'And we're live in five, four, three, two...' He made a swooshing gesture and she put on her approachable-but-serious voice to go with the approachable-but-serious smile.

'Tensions are running high in Aberdeen today as the local Farm Workers', Food Producers', and Livestock Handlers' Union protest about the proposed post-Brexit financial settlement.' She turned and gestured across the square at a bunch of officers in their high-viz bobby-on-the-beat costumes. 'As you can see, there's a *significant* police presence here, after rumours circulated on social media that a number of extremist organisations were planning to use the protest as an excuse for violent clashes.'

Bang on cue a vast combine harvester rumbled past, followed by a vintage tractor towing a trailer with an effigy of the Prime Minister being burnt at the stake on it – fake, tissue paper flames flickering in the breeze.

A tad sinister, but *great* television.

'So far, the demonstration has remained peaceful.'

Bill's voice sounded in her earpiece, all the way from the London studio. '*And we understand the Cabinet Secretary for Rural Affairs has challenged Ronnie Wells to a debate.*'

She put a finger to her ear. 'That's right, Bill. Ronnie Wells has become a controversial figure since he took over the FWFPLH last May. He's accused the Scottish government of abandoning Scotland's rural communities in favour of an easy deal with Westminster.'

The mock burning was followed by a jaunty pair of JCB diggers lofting a massive banner of their own: 'FARMING LIVES MATTER!!!' strung up between their raised backhoes.

A mixture of cheers and boos rippled around the crowd

as a handful of stodgy middle-aged men in bland suits clambered up onto a makeshift stage. The stodgiest and baldest of them shuffled over to the microphone.

'Of course this is the Cabinet Secretary, George Rushworth's, first public speech since the Arran-gate scandal, so we can expect some fiery rhetoric as he tries to put that behind him.'

There was a squeal of feedback as he tapped the microphone, then George Rushworth MSP's voice crackled out of the speakers. *'Can you hear me OK? Good. OK. Right. I know feelings are running high, but I want you to know that the Scottish government cares* passionately *about farming in this country!'*

More booing.

Alfie took one hand off the steering wheel, plucked the whisky bottle from the cup holder at his right elbow and knocked back a swig. It burned all the way down.

Should've bought some of the good stuff, really. But how was he supposed to afford that? That was the whole point of this buggering exercise – how could he, or any other struggling farmer afford anything?

Still. Would've been nice.

The peaty fire spread out across his stomach then up into his chest. Then his brain, making it swell and tingle.

I mean, take this big John Deere tractor, did anyone out there have the slightest idea how much it cost to keep one of these things going? The maintenance and servicing was bad enough, but what about all the diesel? And that was *on top* of the massive expense of buying the bloody thing in the first place. You could get a two-bedroom flat in Aberdeen for less than one of these.

Another swig.

Might as well enjoy it. There'd be sod-all whisky after

they caught up with him. They were probably quite strict about that kind of thing in prison.

Still, it wasn't as if they'd left him any option, was it?

They had no one to blame but themselves.

The JCBs in front were all shiny and yellow, their banner strung between them crisp and clean.

Not like the chunk of farm equipment *he* was towing.

Look at it: lurking in the tractor's wing mirrors. An evil black metal bomb. Big and dark and rusty at the edges. Ready to explode.

His radio bleeped at him as the Royal Bank's crisp granite frontage drifted by on the left – and there they were. Hundreds and hundreds of them, waving their silly little placards, as if that would make any difference.

Nope.

Only one thing *ever* made a difference. In a war you had to fight dirty.

Henry's voice crackled out of the set. *'Go on, Alfie, let the bastards have it!'*

Alfie checked his mirrors again – Henry was there, giving him the thumbs up from the cab of his Massey Ferguson.

It was time.

One more swig of whisky for luck.

Some of the crowd understood. Some of them were on the farmers' side.

Shame.

But in any war there was always collateral damage.

Alfie grabbed his radio handset and pressed the transmit button. Hauled in a big whisky-smoke breath. 'YEEEEEEE-HAAAAAW!'

He flicked the switch and pulled the lever.

And may God have mercy on them all.

II

'Scottish farmers have every right to be angry. It's vitally important that we sort this out, but we have to be realistic!'

Tufty shrugged. Playing it cool. 'So...' not quite shouting over the speech belting out of the PA system, but close. 'After the funeral, I thought we could pop round and see Mrs Galloway. I think she'd want to know that Pudding's in safe hands till she gets out of hospital.'

Constable Mackintosh nodded. 'That's true, but I don't think she'd want to see *me*. After all, you're—'

'Nope. You arranged everything. You sorted out the crematorium. This wouldn't have happened without you.'

She went a little pink again. 'It was nothing really.'

'You did a lovely thing for a poor old lady. That's not nothing, it's...' Tufty's eyes widened. 'Oh God!'

The huge green-and-yellow tractor – the one crawling along behind the banner-flying JCBs – the one towing a big black slurry tank – the one whose driver seemed to be swigging from a bottle of supermarket whisky – gave a grumbling clunk and unleashed HORROR.

The spray nozzle on the back burst into life sending out a massive brown peacock's tail of foul-stinking liquid. Its leading edge spattered down on the crowd and their placards, painting them with filth.

And that's when the screaming started.

The brown tide crawled forward.

Spraying and splattering.

Drenching everything it touched.

Filling the square with the bitter-sharp stench of fermented pig manure.

The people on the right-hand side of the square – the ones closest to the stage and furthest from the spray – struggled back, trying to get out of the way before the storm arrived. But there was nowhere to go. No escape. They just bunched up in a solid clump as the slurry rainbow got closer and closer.

PC Mackintosh stared at him. 'I don't want to be covered in poo!'

In the middle of the square, the steaming brown arc washed over the national media's representatives, smearing the right and left wing alike. A woman with blonde curly hair screamed into her camera as she became a brunette.

Oh no, here it came...

Up on the stage, Boring Speech Man stood rooted to the spot, his voice still belting out of the PA system as the slurry found him. *'AAAAAAGH! JESUS CHRIST! AAAAAAAAAAAAAAGH! IT'S GONE IN MY MOUTH!'*

Closer.

Closer.

Tufty took a deep breath, grabbed PC Mackintosh and bundled her into a crouch, covering her with his own body – back hunched as foul coffee-coloured rain pattered against his high-viz jacket and drummed on his cap. Soaked into the sleeves of his T-shirt. Trickled down the back of his stabproof vest. Slithered between the hairs on his arms.

Argh, the smell! The smell! The smell!

It took a count of three for the downpour to pass.

Tufty straightened up and PC Mackintosh came with him. Staring around her.

From here right back to the Royal Bank, people were yelling and spitting and swearing. On the other side – the as-yet unspattered side – everyone was backed up against the Clydesdale Bank, scrabbling to escape with nowhere to go as the slurry wrapped them in its stinky embrace.

And finally, the tractor and its evil tank were past – probably busy painting the front of the building instead.

Steam rose from the crowd.

Someone retched. Then someone else. Then it was an epidemic, spreading through the crowd.

PC Mackintosh blinked up at Tufty, mouth hanging open. 'That's the nicest thing anyone's *ever* done for me.'

A voice yelled out from the other side of the square: 'OH GOD, NOT ANOTHER ONE!'

The tractor right behind the slurry tank was hauling a muck spreader – it hurtled chunks of straw-studded manure at the crowd.

Steel was over by the barrier, standing like a scarecrow, dripping. 'Gaaaaahhh...'

Harmsworth, on her left, turned in small circles with his arms out – dancing with a large invisible bear. 'No, no, no, no...'

Lund, on her right, stood immobile and splattered, eyes wide as the dung thudded into the crowd opposite.

Then Steel shook out her hands and roared. Wiped her face. Looked around. And ran towards Tufty, boots slithery-slipping on the wet paving slabs. She grabbed him and pointed down Union Street, towards the rear end of the spraying slurry tank. 'You take that one. Arrest the dirty bastard. NOW!'

She let go and sprint-skated for the muck spreader.

Tufty stared at the back of the slurry tank. The guy driving still hadn't turned off the jets and the stinking plume was

301

wide enough to paint both sides of Union Street at the same time. Oh bumholeing motherfunker: to get to the tractor he'd have to run right through the spray.

Deep breath.

Yeah, probably shouldn't have done that, the air tasted *horrible*.

He ran.

Right at the edge of the crowd, a large woman in a duotone tweed jacket and skirt – grey at the back, brown and slimy all up the front – sat on the pavement making little squealing noises. She was still clutching her placard: a big one with 'SUCK IT UP, LIBTARD SNOWFLAKES ~ YOU LOST!!!' printed in big red letters.

He snatched the placard out of her hands on the way past, holding it up like a riot shield. Here we go: event horizon in three, two, one...

GAAAAAAAAAAAAAAAAAAAAAAAAAAAHHHHH!

Right through to the other side.

Oh God, it was *everywhere*...

He threw the placard away and pounded along the pavement, past the slurry tank and up level with the tractor's cab. Waved at the driver. 'HOY, YOU! STOP RIGHT THERE! HOY! POLICE!'

But the bulb-nosed, overall wearing, baldy-headed scumbag just stuck two fingers up and kept the whole thing chugging along at two or three miles an hour.

Right.

Tufty veered closer, till he was four foot from the steps up into the cab. 'POLICE! SHUT THIS DAMN THING DOWN, NOW!'

Farmer Stinky had a swig of whisky and put his foot down till the tractor chugged along at a steady jogging pace.

Nothing for it then – he'd have to get into the cab and shut it down himself.

Easy as pie, beans and chips.

Get a bit closer, jump onto the step, grab the metal bar holding the wing mirror on, climb up, and open the door. No problems. As long as he didn't miss. Or slip. Or fall. Because if he did *any* of those things he'd end up right under that massive back wheel, which would then grind him into the tarmac of Union Street like fourteen stone of mince in a stabproof vest and itchy trousers.

Urgh…

Come on, Tufty, save the day!

He went for it. Jumping at the last minute and scrabbling for the wing-mirror support, hauling himself up onto the step.

Not dead yet!

From up here there was a great view down Union Street to the council buildings and the Castlegate beyond. All closed to traffic with a line of metal barriers. The only other cars in sight were the patrol car parked at the junction with Broad Street and a shiny black Bentley with little flags flying from sticks either side of the bonnet and a swanky private number plate.

Which was a shame. Would've been nice if someone had been around to witness his historic leap. Oh Tufty, you're such an action hero! A kind of sexier Bruce Willis, only with more hair and not in a vest. And covered in shite.

Tufty took hold of the tractor door handle, pressing the button to open it… Nothing. The rotten sod had locked himself in.

Farmer Stinky grinned through the window and glugged back another mouthful of Sporran Rot McTurpentine's finest.

'Suit yourself.' Tufty whipped out his extendable baton and clacked it out to full length. Then battered it down, shattering the window, sending thousands of little cubes of glass flying.

He stuffed the baton back in its holder, reached through the gaping frame and grabbed Farmer Stinky, raising his voice over the engine's diesel roar. 'YOU'RE WELL AND TRULY NICKED!'

Farmer Stinky laughed at him, enveloping him in a barrage of whisky fumes. 'You're too late!' He slapped at Tufty's hand.

Tufty slapped back.

Another slap. Then it was *on*! Chins pulled in, heads stretched back out of the way as they went at it, two handed, like schoolkids in the playground. Leaving the steering wheel to its own devices.

The tractor drifted to the left, lurching as the front tyre bumped up onto the pavement.

Then a squealing crunch.

Tufty risked a glance: the tractor's front loader shoved its way into the wall of a bus shelter, deforming the metal supports and ripping them out of the concrete. The Perspex walls snapped and pinged out of their frames as the massive green and yellow monster crashed through the thing at a walking pace.

The structure peeled apart, buckling and crumpling its way along the bonnet, a blade of Perspex scraping at the paintwork. Getting closer to where Tufty clung on.

Eek!

It was going to scrape him right off the side of the tractor and under the back wheel. Mince. Squish. Pop goes the police officer.

He wrapped both arms around the wing-mirror stand as the Perspex tried to shove its way through him. Head down. Pressing himself in against the cab. Holding on tight as it grabbed at his stabproof and twisted him around...

'Aaaaaaargh!'

Then *poing*! And it was past.

A tortured squeal tore through the engine noise as what was left of the shelter got crushed beneath the back wheel.

The tractor lurched again, back down onto the road.

Farmer Stinky was laughing. Steering with one hand and swigging whisky with the other. 'Hike up *my* council tax, will you?'

What?

Tufty looked in the direction they were going: straight for the liveried Bentley.

Yeah … that looked expensive.

The tractor's front loader whirred up on its pneumatic rams, the scoop big and black against the blue sky. Then it crashed down on the Bentley's bonnet, crushing bodywork and flags alike. Farmer Stinky didn't slam on the brakes, though – he just kept going. Up went the front loader again. Down again – shattering the windscreen and flattening half the roof. The tractor's front end reared up as it mounted the ruined car.

Tufty grabbed the shattered tractor window frame and dragged his top half into the cab as the tractor climbed the Bentley, getting higher and higher and—

Something must've given way in the car beneath them, because the tractor's front end crunched down again.

Farmer Stinky dropped his whisky bottle.

Tufty wriggled his way across the guy's lap to the other side of the steering column. A set of keys poked out of the ignition. He grabbed them, twisted them left, then hauled them out.

The tractor lurched to a halt.

Silence.

Then the spattering slop of a *lot* of liquid hitting concrete and tarmac from a great height.

Then nothing but the pings and groans of the dying Bentley.

Tufty pulled his cuffs out. Urgh… He gave them a little shake to dislodge a blob of slurry. 'Let's try this again, shall we? You're *comprehensively* nicked!'

Oh God…

Everything. Was. *Ruined*.

Her Nobel peace prize. Her interview with the Dalai Lama. Her series of bestselling children's books. Dancing the tango with a perma-tanned man wearing too many sequins.

RUINED!

All around her, Aberdeen was straight out of a zombie movie – everyone shuffling around, groaning and filthy. Or huddled against the walls crying. Or just being violently and copiously sick in the background of the shot.

Anne blinked into the dead black eye of the camera.

Chris was just standing there, *horrible* brown stuff dripping off his bobble hat, filming.

That's because he's a professional, Anne, like *you're* supposed to be!

She wiped the slurry from her face, cleared her throat, and raised the microphone again – making sure the logo faced the camera. Gave the nation her approachable-but-serious face. 'Back to you in the studio, Bill'

III

Big Gary crossed his arms, blocking the doorway, keeping them all trapped in the car park. 'No.'

The hatred flowing in his direction was almost as strong as the stench. Twenty-five police officers, all in their Police Scotland slurry-splattered uniforms. More than enough to get a decent lynch mob going. Even if they would need an extra-strong rope and an extra-strong tree to string the fat lump up.

Roberta shoved her way through the stinky crowd to the front. 'Don't be such a *dick*, Gary! Let us in: we need those showers!'

Voices raised behind her: 'Yeah!', 'Out the way!', 'Shift it, fat boy!', 'I'm all covered in shite!'

Big Gary didn't move. 'You are *not* getting into my nice clean police station like that. No way. No, sir. No how.'

Roberta flicked a lump of dried-on dung off the back of her hand. 'Well, what the bloody hell are we supposed to do?'

Oooh, that was better. You know what? It was quite pleasant, standing there, round the back of the mortuary in a shaft of sunlight. All warm and tingly. A gentle breeze wafting its way across her naked flesh.

Well, mostly naked.

Roberta towelled her back off.

A double rainbow glittered in the spray as the pathologist and her anatomical pathology technician – dressed in plastic aprons, white wellington boots, green scrubs, purple nitrile gloves, and protective full-face masks – hosed down the next pair of candidates.

Harmsworth coughed and spluttered, both hands up covering his face as the water found him. 'Aaaagh, that's cold!'

Roberta moved on to drying her bum, patting the pale wobbly skin around her bright-red pants. Mind you, if she'd known she'd be stripping in front of half the dayshift, she'd have put on a bra that matched. 'Come on, Owen, you weren't this shy on Thursday morning. Gerremoff!' She gave him a wolf whistle. 'Or do we need to fetch a bunch of wee kids to help you undress?'

'Oh that's right, make off-colour remarks at poor Owen. He didn't bother you, did he? No, Owen was a gentleman, but does anyone care?' He undid his utility belt, holding it in the hose's glare till the water ran clear. He undid the Velcro on his stabproof vest, grimacing behind it, hiding from the tea-coloured backsplash.

Tufty was on his hands and knees, in his ThunderCats pants, dipping a sponge into a bucket of soapy water and scrubbing away at himself with it. 'Gah… Stinky, stinky, stinky, stinky, stinky…'

Harmsworth ditched his T-shirt and struggled out of his police-issue trousers till he had nothing on but his soggy underwear, cringing away from the stream of water. All those bite marks had turned into wee circular bruises, like he was wearing a pasty leopard-print onesie covered in wiry black hair.

'Hoy, Doc!' Roberta draped the towel around her shoulders and pointed. 'You missed a bit.'

The pathologist nodded and shifted the hose – water sprayed into Harmsworth's furry chest again.

'AAAAAAAAAAAGH!'

'There you go, *much* better.'

Roberta grinned.

Sometimes, when life gave you slurry, you just had to make lemonade.

'Urgh... I can still smell it.' Barrett sniffed at his naked arm and shuddered. 'One going-over with a hose, one scrub in a bucket, and a shower with carbolic soap and I can *still* smell it!'

Roberta adjusted herself and sank behind her desk. Amazing how quick you got chafed from a damp bra.

Harmsworth scowled away, slumped in his chair in his socks and pants, what was left of his hair sticking out in damp tufts. 'I'm never eating oxtail soup ever again.'

Lund shuddered, setting everything wobbling in a *very* interesting way. Either she was off on the pull later, or she was unbelievably organised: her bra actually matched her pants. And neither of them were denture-grey or looked as if they'd fall apart with one more washing. She caught Roberta looking and covered her chest with her arms. 'You're staring again.'

'Hey, I'm married, no' dead.'

The door thumped open and in backed Tufty, carrying a large cardboard box. He'd hidden his ThunderCats underwear beneath a pair of Aberdeen Football Club joggie bottoms. Top half covered with a Frightened Rabbit tour T-shirt, only the word 'Frightened' was spelled wrong.

He dumped the box on his desk. 'Roll up, roll up, get yer luverly knock-off clobber 'ere.' Then dug out a pair of dungarees and tossed them to Roberta. 'Faux Givenchy – with the compliments of those lovely loons and quines at Trading

Standards. They had some fake Louis Vuitton, but the MIT got there first.' He dug into the box. 'You want a counterfeit Tommy Hilfiger sweatshirt or a fake Calvin Klein polo?'

'With dungers? Has to be Gucci.'

He went a-rummaging, tossed her a red floral-printed chiffon thing with frilly bits. Roberta pulled it, and the dungarees, on over her moist underwear.

Another rummage. 'What do you fancy, Veronica: not quite Armani or not quite Fendi?'

'Armani.'

Harmsworth scowled. 'Oh that's right, let DC Lund choose first, don't worry about Owen, he's only been here four years longer than she has.'

Tufty tossed her a pair of jeans and a shimmery blue shirt. 'Manners, Owen. Ladies first. And you should be used to sitting about in the scud by now.' A grin. 'How about you, Davey?'

'Don't really care as long as Harmsworth gets something to wear sharpish. Was bad enough the other day: all that pasty grey hairy flesh. Urgh. It's enough to put you off sausages for life.'

'Hey!'

Roberta fiddled with the dungarees' shoulder straps. 'What do you think, both on, or one hanging off a bit flirty like?'

A knock on the door and DCI Rutherford marched in without waiting for an answer. Rotten sod looked every bit as clean and shiny as he had at the morning briefing. The joys of *no* being showered in slurry. He came to rest in the middle of the room, all stiff and erect, and looked down his nose at her. 'The Lord Provost is *very* upset about his car. And the bus shelter. Those things don't grow on trees, you know.'

She thumped back into her seat, scowling. 'Aye, well, the

Lord Provost can pucker up and kiss my recently sharny arse.'

Rutherford grinned. 'I, on the other hand, haven't laughed so much in *ages*.'

'Hoy!' Harmsworth had another pout. 'That's not fair. I got plastered in fermented pig manure!'

Tufty chucked him a pair of cargo shorts and a Batman T-shirt. 'Oh, boohoo. I had to run through it, so I got plastered *twice*.'

'And that, Constable Quirrel, is why I'm recommending you for a commendation. You too, Roberta – disabling that muck spreader saved a lot of people from a dung-based battering.' Rutherford clapped his hands. 'Best of all, the predicted riot never materialised! Apparently neither side was up for a fight after being liberally showered in slurry. We should recommend it to G Division next time there's an Old Firm game.'

Barrett rustled up a polite laugh. Crawly wee jobbie that he was.

'Now, under the circumstances, I think you and your team deserve to go home early. And if you pop past the Flare and Futtrit at half-three, you'll find two hundred and fifty pounds behind the bar as a special thank you from the Chief Superintendent. They're laying on a buffet for you too.'

Tufty stuck his hands in the air. 'Yay!'

'But, before you go.' He turned to Roberta. 'Detective Sergeant Steel, would you join me in my office please? Jack Wallace has made another complaint.'

Oh sodding hell.

Might have known it was too good to be true.

Vine was already there, sitting in the other visitors' chair, as Roberta followed DCI Rutherford into the office. He nodded at her. 'DS Steel.'

'Right, John,' Rutherford settled in behind his desk, 'do the honours, would you?'

Vine pulled the desk phone towards him and poked at the buttons, setting it ringing through the speaker.

She nodded at the vacant chair. 'Am I allowed to sit for this, or do you need access to my arse for spanking purposes?'

'Sit. Sit.' Rutherford leaned back in his chair and steepled his fingers.

She collapsed into the spare seat.

Oop!

Fake Givenchy dungarees got *way* too intimate if you sat down fast.

A woman's voice clattered out of the speakerphone, clipped and efficient. *'Moir-Farquharson Associates, can I help you?'*

'Yes: Detective Inspector Vine for Mr Moir-Farquharson. He's expecting me.'

'One moment please.' A pan-pipe rendition of 'I Shot the Sheriff' filled the silence.

Roberta fidgeted with the frisky dungarees' crotch. 'Whatever he says, he's lying. It's—'

Rutherford held up a finger as Hissing Sid came on the phone. *'DI Vine. I take it this isn't a social call?'*

'Your client has made another complaint against Police Scotland.' He pulled a sheet of paper from the manila folder at his feet. 'I refer you to the letter one of your interns delivered this morning.'

'Indeed. Your officers hauled my client out of a cinema in full view of the audience, causing him considerable anxiety and emotional distress. Not to mention reputational damage. They then proceeded to question him about a rape that occurred while he was at dinner with two friends, surrounded by witnesses.'

'And you hold Police Scotland responsible for that?'

'Well of course I do. Many though Detective Sergeant Steel's good points may be, her obsession with my client is both destructive and unhealthy.'

Roberta paused mid-crotch-fidget. 'Aye, aye, Sandy. How's yer arse for love bites?'

'Detective Sergeant. I'm afraid you've exhausted my client's capacity for forgiveness this time. We'll be looking for punitive damages.'

DCI Rutherford rapped on the desk with his knuckles. 'Mr Moir-Farquharson, I think that's rather unfair, don't you? You're implying that this was the result of a personal grudge perpetuated by DS Steel.'

'Ah, Detective Chief Inspector Rutherford, you're there too. How nice.' A sigh. 'I'm not implying anything, I'm stating it as a common fact. Your officers are harassing my client without any proof or justifiable reason.'

'No justifiable reason?' Rutherford frowned. 'That is strange. You see, your client phoned DS Steel to lay down an alibi for a rape that had just been committed. He was pulled out of the cinema because he made himself a person of interest.'

'Am I expected to believe—'

'Aye, you are.' Roberta stuck two fingers up at the disembodied voice. 'And I had the wee radge on speakerphone too – the whole team heard him.'

There was silence from the other end of the phone.

Then a bit more silence.

And some more.

She went back to howking wodges of denim out of her undercarriage. 'Maybe he's nipped off for a pee?'

Rutherford leaned in closer to the phone. 'Mr Moir-Farquharson?'

'I ... apologise. I wasn't aware that my client had precipitated yesterday's actions.'

'Ooooooh.' Finally, the last wodge howked free. 'Your client's no' hiding things from you, is he, Sandy? That's no' good.'

'I will, of course, be advising Mr Wallace that the sensible course of action is to withdraw his complaint and cancel any planned litigation.'

Roberta put on her best innocent voice. 'Because the jury's going to throw him out of court on his hairy raping bumhole and award us a monster bag of costs and damages?'

Vine held up a hand. 'All right, Detective Sergeant, I think Mr Moir-Farquharson gets the point.' And he was smiling as he said it, as well. 'Don't you, Mr Moir-Farquharson.'

A sniff. *'Now, if you'll excuse me, I need to talk to my client.'*

Aye, good luck with that.

Tufty powered down his computer and stood. Stretched. Sighed. Then grabbed his coat.

Steel looked at him. 'And just where do we think we're going?'

'You heard the boss – I get to go home early cos I've been brave.'

'Oh aye? And have we finished all our actions and written up our arrest report?'

'Emailed them to you and everything.'

She peered at her screen for a bit. 'Oh.'

'Anyway: need to run a couple of errands before half two.'

'And what happens at half two?' She tilted her head to one side, watching him the same way a cat watches an injured mouse. 'You got a hot date or something?'

'Kinda. We're taking Mrs Galloway's dog to the crematorium. They give you the ashes back in a cardboard box if you haven't got an urn. Thought it would be a bit … you know.' He mimed handing a cardboard box to a poor battered old woman. 'Hey, here's your dog.'

A dirty smile. 'And when you say "we", does that mean you and your perky Wildlife Crime Officer?'

The room got a bit hotter. 'It… Constable Mackintosh sorted out the crematorium, they're waiving their fee and everything.'

'Oh, Tufty, Tufty, Tufty.' Steel shook her head. 'I know we're no' supposed to promote casual sex, but if you're no' even on first-name terms you really shouldn't be shagging her.'

'I'm not… It's… I didn't…'

'You're a regular Casanova, aren't you?' She stood, pulled her dungarees up. 'Come on, then. I know a wee mannie who'll do us a good deal on a second-hand urn, no questions asked.'

'Is your underwear really chafing? Because mine's all hairy sandpaper.' Steel did a little step-shuffle dance, like she was trying to work something loose down there, then pressed the intercom buzzer again.

It didn't look very promising – a pair of big plain wooden doors, set into a featureless granite wall, buried halfway down Jopp's Lane, ten minutes' walk from Division Headquarters. Narrow, grey, and ignored.

Tufty shrugged. 'Took mine off and gave them a good blow-through under the hand dryer in the gents.'

She stared at him. '*Sod.* Should've thought of that.' Another go on the buzzer. 'Mind you, might've looked a bit weird: me standing there starkers in the gents' toilets. Getting everyone all hot and bothered with my raw sexual magnetism.'

Yeah…

A voice fizzed and crackled from the intercom's speaker. '*Viewing is by appointment only. Good day.*'

She mashed the button with the palm of her hand. 'Open up, Haddie, or I'll go pay your mum a visit.'

315

A seagull settled on the roof of a manky little Fiat, wings stretched out pterodactyl style. Pterodactyl size, too. Eyeing them.

Finally the voice was back again. *'Detective Chief Inspector Steel. Not heard from you in ages.'*

She looked up and waved at a security camera, mounted above a cracked vent. 'I'm no' joking, Haddie. Me and your mum have a *lot* of catching up to do.'

A sigh, then the left-hand door buzzed and popped open a crack.

'Good boy, now get the kettle on.' She pushed inside.

Tufty checked the pterodactyl wasn't following them and slipped in after Steel.

Down a short hallway to a set of solid-looking metal doors, the kind of doors it took hours to batter through with a Big Red Door Key. It even had a speakeasy hatch set into it.

The hatch clicked open and a pair of bespectacled eyes stared out at them. 'Is this all of you?'

'No.' Steel stuck her hands in her dungarees' pockets. 'I've got three hundred crack officers out there, a firearms team, and the force helicopter circling overhead. And we all want tea and biscuits.'

The hatch snapped shut.

Some clunks and rattles and scraping sounds, then one half of the big metal doors swung open, revealing a short, round man in blue overalls and dress shoes. A proper soup-strainer grey moustache and a few straggly wisps of grey hair poked out from beneath a tweed bunnet. Skin so pale it was almost blue in the flickering fluorescent lighting.

Steel sauntered past him. 'Constable Quirrel: Elinsworth Fredrick De Selincourt, AKA: Fish-Fingered Freddy, AKA: The Haddie. As in, "Have you seen thon big pile of nicked DVD players The Haddie's flogging the day?"'

'Oh I can assure you, Detective Chief Inspector, I indulge in no such practices these days. I'm a reformed character. I restrict myself solely to the pursuit of house clearance and estate sales.'

'Aye, right.'

Tufty wheeched through the metal doors into a long, low warehouse-sized room. It was stuffed with boxes and crates. Piles of things and heaps of stuff – solid and dusty between the pillars that held the ceiling up. A group of grandfather clocks ticked out of time with each other, making a background hiss like a thousand snakes eating ready-salted crisps.

Steel had a rummage in a tea chest. 'We're needing a favour, Haddie.'

'Why doesn't that surprise me?' He grabbed the massive handle on the back of the door and hauled it shut with an echoing *clang*. Snibbed three deadbolts into place, threaded a thick length of chain through its eyelets and over a hook bolted to the wall, then wedged a metal bar between a slot in the floor and another in the door.

Never mind a Big Red Door Key, you'd need a *tank* to get through that.

He folded his little arms over his massive chest. 'And what favour would that be?'

Tufty held up a hand. 'I need an urn. Something nice.'

'Hmm, I see. And you felt it was appropriate to come *here*?' Haddie shuffled off between the stacks. 'And I take it you weren't close to the deceased, Constable Quirrel? Well of course you weren't. You wouldn't be looking for a pre-loved urn for someone you actually cared about.'

'It's not for me. It's for a little old lady with no cash. Someone beat the living hell out of her and microwaved her dog.'

Haddie stopped. Turned. 'I'm confused, is the urn intended to hold the lady's remains or her dog's?'

317

'Yorkshire terrier called Pudding.'

'Well, there's no accounting for taste.' He reached into his pocket and produced a Stanley knife, clicked out a fingernail's width of blade and ran it through the brown packing tape holding a cardboard box shut. 'Here lie the mortal remains of... Well, I have to admit that I've rather lost count.' A thick dark urn, sort of bowling-trophy shaped, appeared in his hand. 'One thinks, when one dies, that one's ashes will be treasured by our loved ones. That they'll be handed down through the generations as venerated objects. That in this way we'll never truly die.'

He sighed and pulled out another urn. This one squat and brutal. 'Instead of which we end up in a job lot of Granny's old things, sold off at a car boot sale as soon as she's gone.' The next three urns were more like Thermos flasks. Then another trophy-style one. A couple of ornate vase-type ones. A wooden box with a brass butterfly on it. 'Stop me when you see something you feel reflects the deceased's personality.'

Tufty did a slow three-sixty. Boxes and crates and more boxes and more crates and the snakes-eating-crisps grandfather clocks... 'Did all this come from estate sales?'

'Sadly, when most people say something has immense sentimental value, what they really mean is they can't be bothered dusting it any more. Ah, here we are.' Haddie straightened up, holding out a blue enamel jar with golden swirls across it. 'The brass plaque says, "David Fairbairn, 1935 to 1994, beloved father and husband", but you could put a sticker or something over that. And, as it's for a good cause, you may have it on the house.'

Tufty accepted the urn. Cool in his hands. Heavy too. 'Erm... Is David...?'

'In residence?' Haddie's eyebrows popped up. 'Oh, very much so.' They sank back down again. 'Ah, I see. Of course, how insensitive of me. Please.' He held out his hands and Tufty gave him the urn back. 'I will be but a second. Feel free to browse.'

He turned and bustled off between the heaps.

Steel wandered up. 'You're no' going to put a sticker on it, are you?'

'Could go to that key-cutting/engraving place on Rosemount? Get them to do up a little plaque to glue over David's one?' He turned in place again. 'So much *stuff*.'

'I'm hungry. Are you hungry?'

'All those lives… You slave away, you save up, you buy stuff, and it ends up here.'

The muffled roar of a vacuum cleaner sounded in the distance.

'You know what I fancy? Noodles. No, ribs! Or maybe chicken?'

Tufty picked his way between a stack of oriental carpets and a rack of framed hunting prints. 'Hidden away in a warehouse, waiting for what?'

'Ooh, I know: Chinese.' Steel rubbed her hands together. 'We can go to the Manchurian, down by Mounthooly.'

A herd of bicycles, stacked on top of each other. A flock of standard lamps. Deeper and deeper into the gloomy recesses. 'You know what I think? I think Mr De Selincourt is fooling himself. He's banging on about your ashes ending up in a car boot sale, cos no one cares. What about all this stuff? Who's going to come in here and impulse buy a…' Tufty pointed, 'a treadle sewing machine from the Dark Ages, or a banjo with no strings? All this stuff's going to sit here growing dust till he snuffs it, then it's back to the car boot or off to the tip.'

The hairy grey layers on top of the boxes got thicker the further back Tufty went. An upright piano was almost mammalian with its pelt of fur.

'They do the most spectacular dim sum there. And the chicken wings! Oh God, the chicken wings...' Steel made a Homer Simpson gargling noise.

'Thought there was a buffet waiting for us at the Flare and Futtrit.'

'Aye, no' till half three, though.'

And right at the back, the most forgotten stacks of all: books. Hardback and paperback, leather-bound and slip-covered. They looked like they hadn't been touched in eons. *Pompeii* was buried under a thinner crust of grey than they were.

Well, not *quite* right at the back.

There were a couple of boxes tucked in behind the books. Completely and utterly dust free.

'See, Tufty, when you're off on the lash with your fellow officers, it's important to get a nice thick lining on your stomach first.'

Why would brand new boxes be hidden away back here?

'Oh, some people say, "eatin's cheatin'", but they're the ones who end up facedown in the corner covered in their own sick.'

They were sealed up with brown tape, just like the box the urns were in.

He nudged one with the toe of his boot. 'Does that look suspicious to you? All clean and shiny when everything else is clarty with dust?'

'Yoghurt's good, of course, but me? Dim sum. Nice and sticky and starchy... Are you even listening to me?'

'No.' And let's face it, Elinsworth Fredrick De Selincourt had form for resetting. Once a dodgy wee swine, always a dodgy wee swine. People didn't just give up selling stolen goods. 'Come on, it's not just suspicious, it's *hella* suspicious.'

'So open them. Take a peek.'

'I can't. It'd be inadmissible in court.'

'Oh, for God's sake.' She shoved him out of the way. 'Here, I'll do it, you damp—'

'Excuse me!' Haddie's voice boomed out from somewhere behind, getting closer with every word. 'You have no business being back here. I give you an urn out of the goodness of my heart and *this* is how you repay me? By snooping?'

'Mr De Selincourt.' Tufty pointed. 'Would you care to tell us what's in these boxes?'

Haddie licked his lips. 'Actually, I'm really busy this afternoon. Perhaps if you made an appointment for later in the week…?'

Steel sucked on her teeth, making them whistle. 'Oh, Haddie, Haddie, Haddie. No' *again!*'

'I… I haven't done anything wrong, and you don't have a warrant. Those boxes are from an estate sale. There's nothing illegal about them.' A blush breathed a bit of colour into those pale cheeks of his. 'You're not allowed to search my premises. If you do, it's inadmissible in court.'

'My ugly wee colleague here was just saying the very same thing, Haddie. But *you* said we were free to browse, remember?' She slapped a hand down on his shoulder, making him buckle slightly at the knees. 'And you're right: I *can't* search your Aladdin's Gloryhole. What I *can* do is tell Constable Quirrel here to stand guard over those boxes while I nip off and get a warrant organised. That'll take about an hour and I've no' had any lunch yet, so by the time I get back here I'm going to be very hungry and very, *very* grumpy.'

Tufty nodded. 'And she's in chafing underwear too, so— Ow!' He rubbed at his arm, squeezing down the burning jagged ache where she'd belted him one.

'Now, Haddie, my fish-fingered little fiend, you can cooperate right here, right now, and open these boxes of your own free will – or we can do it an hour later when I'm *probably* going to want to rip your arm off and eat it. Up to you.'

'But I don't… This isn't…' His eyebrows pinched up in the middle, shoulders drooping. 'I gave you an urn for *free*.'

She reached out and plucked the urn from his hands. 'Thanks for your kind donation, I'm sure Mrs Galloway will be touched.' She tucked it under one arm. 'So: friendly cooperative boxes now, or grumpy down-the-station boxes later?'

Haddie made a groany little wheezing noise then nodded. Got out his Stanley knife and slipped the blade through the pristine brown tape on both boxes. Sighed. 'This is what I get for trying to be nice to people.' He eased the flaps open on Box Number One, then did the same with Box Number Two.

Tufty peered inside and whistled. Reached in and pulled out a pair of brand-new-still-in-their-boxes iPhones. 'This must've been a very *strange* estate sale, Mr De Selincourt. As far as I can see, the dearly departed left about three grand's worth of state-of-the-art mobile technology.'

Steel helped herself to a boxed Samsung, turning it over in her hands. 'Let me guess: you got them from a thieving wee scroat called Billy Moon? Am I warm?'

'Detective Chief Inspector Steel, I—'

'It's Detective *Sergeant* now. They demoted me for dangling a fat wee resetter off the roof of his warehouse by the ankles. And dropping him. You want to see if we can make it two in a row?'

'But I'm cooperating!' Starting to whine a little now.

'So you are.' She tossed the phone to Tufty. 'Elinsworth Fredrick De Selincourt, I'm detaining you under Section Fourteen of the Criminal Justice, Scotland, Act…'

The woman in the burgundy apron huffed a breath onto the rectangle of thumb-smeared brass and polished it on the hem of her apron. Peering out of the window, down Union Street. 'You wouldn't believe it, would you? Two wee tractors, making all that *mess*.'

Tufty joined her, looking out between a display rack of key fobs and an animatronic plastic man pretending to hammer a nail into a shoe.

Four fire engines blocked the road outside Marks & Spencer – two of them sending out jets of thick white foam, the other two hosing the buildings down with water. The gutters were thick with brown froth.

'I'm just glad the shop's upwind.' She huffed another breath on the plaque. 'There we go, nice and shiny again.' She slipped it into a wee paper bag. 'That'll be six quid, please.'

IV

'Come on, *stick*, you horrible little...' Tufty shifted his fingers and pushed a bit harder. The brass plaque slithered side to side on the glue then *finally* got a grip. 'Right.'

He clambered out of his rusty old Fiat Panda, locked the door, straightened his tie and hurried across the car park. It was crowded: people filing out of the crematorium and into their vehicles.

He nodded at a thin man with red eyes and a trembling bottom lip. Giving the guy a 'Sorry for your loss' and a pat on the arm on the way past.

Aberdeen Crematorium looked like a nuclear bunker crossed with an unsuccessful airport terminal building. Only not so charming. A black roof sulked above concrete walls that sloped inward a bit as they rose. Dark glass panels either side of a big dark wooden door.

The last of the mourners were gathering up floral tributes to a backtrack of sombre music. Someone was still sitting down at the front, not moving, just staring up at the red velvety curtains. PC Mackintosh.

Tufty sorry-for-your-loss-ed his way past the mourners and slipped into the seat next to her. 'Sorry.'

'No, it's OK.'

'Had to go home and change. Didn't think it'd be right turning up in AFC joggies and a knock-off T-shirt.'

She looked him up and down. The shirt, the black tie, the black suit. 'I think you look very nice.'

He smiled back. 'You too. I mean, I know it's just police uniform, but it suits you and...' Why was everywhere so hot today? Oh, right, crematorium. Tufty cleared his throat. 'Anyway, I brought you this.' He held out the urn.

'Oh, Constable Quirrel, it's *lovely*.'

'There's a plaque.'

She ran a finger along the shiny brass rectangle. '"Pudding the Yorkshire terrier, a dearly loved friend and companion." That's very sweet.'

'I *was* going to put something about "now chasing the squirrels in heaven", but I didn't know if he liked squirrels or not. And...' He dug into his pocket. 'Ta-da!' He held up a Lion Bar and a bag of Skittles.

Mackintosh smiled, then reached out and took the Lion Bar. 'You remembered.'

'Of course, Lion Bars don't *actually* contain any real lion. And as chocolate's poisonous to all cats including lions – well, the caffeine and theobromine *in* chocolate to be pedantic about it – they can't really endorse it in good conscience, can they? The bar is a lie.'

'Oh yeah? Well Skittles say, "Taste the rainbow". Rainbows are an optical illusion caused by sunlight reflecting and refracting through water particles suspended in the atmosphere, relative to the observer, and have no intrinsic flavour. The *Skittles* are a lie.'

Ooh... Had to admit that was more than a little bit sexy.

Tufty turned to face her. 'Where do you stand on the topic of loop quantum gravity, because—'

She grabbed him by the tie. It came off in her hand –

clip-on – so she grabbed him by the lapel instead and pulled him into a kiss. Her lips tasted of chocolate and coffee and strawberries. Warm and soft and tingly. No tongues.

There was a thump and squeal right behind them, then, 'I hope you two are no' Frenching it up – this is a crematorium, no' a knocking shop!'

Aaargh!

They both flinched back.

PC Mackintosh dropped Pudding's urn, scrambling to snatch it up again before it hit the carpet.

Tufty lunged at the same time and their heads thunked together as the urn bounced off the floor.

Sitting behind them, Steel went, 'Nyuck, nyuck, nyuck.'

'Ow!' Mackintosh rubbed at her forehead.

He scooped up the urn. 'It's OK. Not even scratched.' And the plaque had stayed on too. He handed it back to her. Then turned.

Steel was beaming at him, still wearing her dungarees and floral-print chiffon top. Hair all anyhow. She winked. 'Ah: young love.'

He lowered his voice to a hiss. 'What the hell are *you* doing here?'

'Half two, you said. I'm here to pay my respect to poor little Pudding. No' like you, you randy sod.'

'I am not *randy*, I'm—'

'Excuse me?' A man's voice. They turned and there was a tall thin type in a dog collar and dark suit. Milk-bottle-bottom glasses and a wispy combover. 'I'm sorry to interrupt, but before we begin, does anyone want to say a few words about the deceased?'

'About time!' Barrett grabbed his coat and clapped his hands. 'Come on, everyone: up, up. The buffet starts in fifteen minutes.'

Harmsworth levered himself out of his chair and stood

there in his cargo shorts and Batman T-shirt. It *really* didn't go with his heavy police boots. 'Oh it's all right for you two to go off gallivanting, isn't it? Never mind about us, stuck here doing paperwork and interviewing *your* prisoners.'

Steel had a wee scratch at an itchy armpit. 'Prisoner singular, Owen. Singular. He cop to it?'

Lund pulled on her jacket. 'Mr De Selincourt has decided that assisting us with our enquiries is the cool and groovy thing to do. Especially if we'll cut him a deal for ratting out some of his rivals.'

'I'm down with that.'

Tufty lowered Pudding's urn onto his desk. Still warm. That was the thing about wee dogs – they didn't take long to reduce to ash. Poor Pudding. He patted the lid. 'You stay here where it's nice and safe. We'll take you up to see your mummy tomorrow, when you've cooled down.'

And maybe, if the DI Steel Horror Express could be persuaded to stay back at the station, PC Mackintosh might go with him? If he asked nicely. You know, for moral support. They could even talk physics on the way there. Like they had at the crematorium, when her warm soft lips tasted of—

Lund thumped him. 'What are you grinning about?'

'Nothing.'

Barrett clapped his hands again. 'Come on everyone, hop to it! No lollygagging.' He hustled them out of the office then locked the door and pocketed the key. 'Now, how are we getting there, foot or taxi?'

'Taxi?' Harmsworth pointed at the corner of the corridor. 'It's a ten-minute walk that way. It's further than that to the nearest taxi rank.'

'All right, all right,' he held his clipboard up above his head, 'and we're walking.' Leading the way down the corridor and into the stairwell. Lund skipping along behind him,

Harmsworth shuffling along beside her as the theme tune to *Cagney & Lacey* blared from Steel's pocket.

She stopped and dug out her phone, falling behind as she answered it.

Lund grinned at them. 'Just so you know: I'm going to get comprehensively blootered, pick up some stud, and ride him home like a rusty stallion.'

Barrett put a hand to his chest. 'Oh, my ears and whiskers!'

Yeah, it was definitely going to be one of *those* nights.

Tufty turned back to Steel.

She was standing on the landing, one foot on the top step, phone clamped to her ear. A scowl on her face. '*What?*' Her whole body tightened. She bared her teeth. 'No, *you* listen to *me*: I will skin you and wear you as a sodding posing pouch! ... Yeah? Well we'll see about that!' She hung up and rammed the phone back in her pocket. Turned and marched upstairs instead of down.

OK, that didn't look good.

He hurried after her, catching up as she reached the next landing. 'You not coming to the pub? Only I can't help noticing you're going the wrong way.'

She didn't even look at him. 'Got to see a man about a raping piece of crap.'

Oh, not again.

She thumped through the doors and into the corridor. Marching past the little offices and meeting rooms. Right up to DI Vine's door.

The sound of laughter came from the other side.

Tufty wheeched around in front of her. 'Maybe this isn't the best of ideas? You're angry, you've been showered in pig poo, we've been to a funeral! Maybe you—'

'I don't need you holding my hand, *Constable*.'

'Hey, I got showered *twice* for you, remember?'

'Idiot.' She shoved him aside and hammered on Vine's

door. Wrenched the handle and stormed in without waiting.

Vine was behind his desk and so were his sidekicks the Retro-Eighties-Ugly-Pugglers-Do-*Miami-Vice* Boys. The two of them leaning over his shoulder and laughing.

The uglier one pointed at Vine's computer screen. 'Play it again, play it again.'

'Ah, DS Steel,' Vine looked up and smiled at her, 'love the dungarees.' He nodded at whatever it was they'd been watching. 'You'll appreciate this – there's a lovely shot of you getting splattered.' He clicked his mouse and swivelled his monitor half-around.

A YouTube video filled the screen, the BBC News logo on a red band along the bottom with the title 'FARMERS' PROTEST IN ABERDEEN'. A baldy fat bloke in a wrinkly suit banging on behind a podium. *'Scottish farmers have every right to be angry. It's vitally important that we sort this out, but we have to be realistic!'*

She jabbed a finger at Vine. 'What's happening with Karen Marsh?'

'We care passionately about your future, because we care passionately about... AAAAAAGH! JESUS CHRIST!' The brown tide spattered its way across him.

Steel slammed her hand down on the desk. 'Karen Marsh, John!'

The smile died on his face. 'Ah... Not good. They're still trying to save what's left of her face. He...' Vine cleared his throat.

The screen shook, and there was the journalist again hunched over, screeching into her microphone. *'AAAAAAAAAAAAAAGH!'* A harsh bleeping noise smothered whatever she said next, then another one, *'[BLEEP]-ing, [BLEEP]-sucking, [PROLONGED BLEEPING] AAAAAAAAAARGH!!!'*

His hand found the mouse and Vine killed the video.
Silence.

He licked his lips. Looked away. 'The bastard made Karen's son watch. The kid's barely fourteen months.'

'Then why the hell are you in here watching internet videos? You should be out there making Jack Wallace talk!'

'How many times? We can't touch Wallace without evidence.'

'He was on the phone again. He was gloating – *again*! Two minutes ago.' Steel placed her fists on the desk, looming over it like a silverback. 'Wallace was talking about what he was going to do tonight. Dinner and a movie, same as every sodding alibi he's had for the last two attacks. Some poor woman is about to be raped!'

'We can't prove anything. We – don't – have – any – evidence!'

'Give me five minutes in a room with the bastard and I'll *get* you some.'

Now Vine was on his feet too, sidekicks backing away. 'Oh yes, because that's not a cliché, is it? And you don't need to be in the room with him to find evidence, do you? No, you just have to make some up and plant it, same as you did last time!'

'Don't you dare!'

'And how did *that* work out for you?'

The only noise in the room came from the central heating.

Finally Steel bared her teeth. 'FINE!' Shoving herself back from the desk.

She stormed out, slamming the door behind her, leaving Tufty abandoned in the room with Vine and his minions.

They were all looking at him.

Tufty pointed at the door. 'I probably should—'

'Aaaaargh!' Vine screwed his face tight, clenching his fists, arms trembling. 'Why does that woman have to be so *bloody* difficult?'

*   *   *

She was sitting in her MX-5, in the driver's seat, throttling the steering wheel and making the kind of faces a gargoyle would be terrified of.

Tufty sidled up to the car and clambered in the passenger side. 'So… Come on then: Flare and Futtrit. Drinks, nibbles, and a good old moan about—'

'No.' She kept her glare focused straight ahead at the windscreen. 'Get out.'

'I know Vine can be a patronising, fart-faced, hamster-molesting pain in the backside, but—'

'Get – out – of – my – god – damn – car!'

He sighed. Shook his head. 'Wallace isn't just screwing with you when he phones up with these alibis, he's screwing with every single one of us.'

'You don't want this, Tufty, you really don't.'

'Your crimes are my crimes, remember? If I'm going to get blamed anyway, I might as well commit the bloody things.' He fastened his seatbelt. 'Now: where are we going?'

Other than right down the plughole…

CHAPTER TEN

in which Everything Goes Horribly Wrong
and we say goodbye to NE Division

I

Steel parked right in front of Wallace's house, sitting there with the engine running as she stared out through the windscreen. Face like a scowl nailed to a breeze-block.

Tufty shifted in his seat, blood whooshing in his ears.

Maybe there was still time to talk her out of it?

Sunlight danced and swirled across the MX-5's bonnet, filtered through the leaves of the tree she'd parked under.

He cleared his throat. 'Wow, it's hot isn't it? Could really do with a pint right now. Couldn't you? Nice cold pint...?'

Nothing.

One more go. He reached out and put a hand on her arm. 'You *sure* we want to do this?'

She undid her seatbelt, climbed out and slammed the car door shut.

Tufty slumped a little. 'That's a "yes", then.'

Ah well, who wanted a career anyway?

He clambered out into the leaf-dappled sunlight.

A man was mowing his lawn a couple of doors down, humming a Flymo back and forth across his little green rectangle. A woman was on her hands and knees opposite, planting rose bushes. A little girl screeched from one pavement to the other, dragging a droopy kite behind her.

Steel marched across the road and up the path to Wallace's front door.

Tufty caught up with her just as she leaned on the doorbell. 'Only I notice we haven't actually got a plan...'

'We rouse him, we rattle him, and we ... something else beginning with "R" and ending with my boot up his arse.'

'Reprimand? Remonstrate?'

She gave up on the bell and hammered on the door instead. 'JACK WALLACE!'

No reply.

'OK.' Tufty shuffled his feet. 'Maybe he's not in?'

She banged on the door again. 'COME OUT HERE YOU WEE SHITE!'

'We could go away and come back later? Maybe Monday or Tuesday? Tuesday's good for me.'

Steel turned on him. 'You don't get it, do you? He – was – setting – up – an – alibi – for – tonight. And while he's off eating pizza and seeing a film, there'll be a woman out there getting raped!'

She banged on the door with both palms. 'WALLACE!'

Still nothing.

'He's not in.'

Steel turned and marched back towards the car. 'Fine. We'll wait!'

Even with the roof off, it was still baking hot in the car. Tufty took off his tie and stuffed it into his jacket pocket. Then took off his jacket as well.

Steel snuck a glance at him. 'You can stop right there. Seeing you in your pants this morning was quite enough for one lifetime.'

She could talk, sitting there with both straps of her dungarees unbuttoned and dangling.

'Sarge?'

336

'What.'

'This Jack Wallace thing, what we're doing here, don't you think it's a bit—'

'If one more word comes out of your mouth I'm going to write it in indelible marker on a coconut and shove it so far up your backside you'll be tasting Malibu for a month.'

Ah…

He rolled up his shirt sleeves. 'Change of subject?'

'Please.'

'OK. Vicarious love-life thrills it is.' Tufty smiled and sighed. 'I really like PC Mackintosh. I mean really *like*, like her.'

'Oh for God's sake, I'm sharing a car with a teenaged girl!'

'She's pretty, she's funny, she's into physics… Who doesn't love a woman who's into physics?'

Steel stared at him. 'You're an idiot, you know that don't you?'

The boy idiot tapped on the dashboard, as if it would make what he was saying any less boring. 'See, what *I* think is that they've got the question wrong. Gravity *isn't* a force like electromagnetism, or the strong and weak nuclear ones, it's an emergent property of squished space-time. So why should it have the same strength?'

'Honestly, if you don't shut up talking about physics I'm going to remove your scrotum with a fork and make you—' Her phone launched into *Cagney & Lacey*. 'Oh thank the Hairy God for that.' She pulled it out.

'BARRETT' sat in the middle of the screen.

'Davey?'

'*Sarge, are you remembering we're meant to be in the Flare and Futtrit? They've got a big buffet all laid out for us and everything.*'

'Aye, Davey, we're kinda in the middle of something right now. Be with you soon as we can.' Hmm… And just in case:

'You keep Owen and Veronica away from the kitty – that pair could drink their way through two hundred and fifty quid in five minutes flat.'

'*Well… I'll do my best, but I can't promise anything.*'

No prizes for guessing what *that* meant.

'…so maybe you simply can't combine quantum theory and general relativity?'

There was a *ding-ding*ing noise and Steel peered at her mobile phone. 'Susan wants me to pick up toilet paper, nappies, and a thing of athlete's foot powder.'

'Cos Einstein showed that gravity's an illusion, right? It's really just acceleration caused by mass distorting space-time and—'

'Tell you, Tufty, being a lesbian: it's no' all sex-swings and dildos.'

The guy had finally finished mowing his lawn and moved on to trimming his hedges with a massive electric orange swordfish thing.

Tufty sat up in his seat. 'Ooh, I know: "Motor Bike!"'

'No.'

'…and I wonder: what if he was right?' Roberta sagged a bit further, till Jack Wallace's house almost disappeared behind the car door.

The whole thing was all screwed up. And no' just Jack Scumbag Wallace – everything. From Detective Chief Inspector right down to Detective Sergeant. Two ranks. The biggest demotion Professional Standards were legally allowed to give her. One step up from taking her warrant card back and kicking her out onto the street.

All because she wouldn't … no, *couldn't* let Jack Wallace get away with it.

Planting evidence?

'Gah...' How could she think that was a good idea? *How?*

What a massive motherfunking moron.

Tufty stared around him, like a Labrador in a squirrel shop. '"Black Bird"?'

'"BD." "D", you idiot.' She rubbed a hand over her closed eyes. 'What would've happened if McRae hadn't clyped on me to the rubber heelers – would I have done it again? Fitted someone else up? Maybe forced a confession? Or beat up someone in custody? Taken bribes...' Oh aye, it was easy to say that'd never happen, but Hannibal Lecter didn't jump straight into the murdering and eating people, did he. Probably eased his way into it. Like getting into a hot bath.

She'd dipped her toe in the water.

'"Black Dog"!'

And Logan McRae had stopped her.

What if she'd been wrong all this time?

'What if he was actually saving me?'

Tufty poked her. 'Is it "Black Dog"?'

'No.'

'Erm ... Sarge?'

She kept her eyes on her phone's screen, thumbs poking away at the buttons. Maybe if she pretended she couldn't see or hear him he'd shut up about sodding gravitational lensing?

> How did you get on at the golf then? Are
> you going to be a grumpy old Susan when
> you get home?

Send.

Tufty poked her. 'Sarge?'

Don't give up – keep ignoring him and he'll go away.

Ding-ding.

Six under par! A personal best! Only Gillian
McMillan to beat & the Great Hazlehead
Ladies Challenge Cup is mine for another
year!
MINE!
My Precious!!!!!!!!
;P

At least *someone* was having a good day.

Another poke. 'Sarge? Hello, Sarge?'

Damn it – ignoring him didn't work. Ah well, it'd been
worth a try.

She gave Tufty a free sigh: nice and exasperated so he
knew what a pain in the ring he was. 'OK, OK: "Beech
Tree".'

'No. Well, yes it *is* "Beech Tree", but that's not what I'm
Hello-Sarge-ing about. Jack Wallace.'

'El Magnito del Turdo.'

'Yeah, him. What I was trying to say earlier, but you
threatened me with a coconut suppository: why are we here?
I mean, it's a waste of time, right?'

She glowered across the car. 'We are here because some
poor woman's going to be raped tonight!'

'I get that, but why are we *here*, here? Wallace called you
up with his pre-alibi, right? He's going out for a meal, then
off to the pictures. He'll make sure he's on CCTV so we
can't pin anything on him. Whoever does the actual raping,
it won't be him. And suppose he does come home and we
grab him – he *knows* we can't rattle it out of him. All Wallace
has to do is keep schtum and wait for his lawyer to appear.
He makes a complaint, we have to let him go, then DCI
Rutherford kicks us in the nads till we squeak and fires us
both.'

'Aye, I'll do the motivational speeches, thank you very
much.'

340

'But I'm right, aren't I? He knows we'll check, so his alibi's going to be tight as Harmsworth's wallet. All we can do here is cock it up and get ourselves chucked off the force. Wallace wins.'

Roberta ground her teeth for a bit, scowling out at the trees, the houses, the horrible blue sky.

Sodding hell.

The ugly wee spud *was* right. Wallace knew there was going to be a rape, but short of tying him to a chair and beating the living hell out of him with a sock full of batteries, how would they get him to talk? No' that the battery/sock thing wasn't appealing...

Hannibal Lecter, remember?

Gaaaaaah...!

There you go: Tufty was right and she was wrong.

No way she was admitting it, though. 'I spy, with my little eye, something beginning with "DM".'

'...so the two kids you found in that wardrobe are sorted.'

Roberta had a dig at an armpit. 'Good foster homes?'

There was a pause from the other end of the phone. *'No, crap ones. We like children to have a really horrible upbringing wherever possible. Keeps us in work.'*

God save us from sarcastic social workers. Mind you, was there any other kind?

'What about Harrison Gray?'

'Other than changing his name to something less bullyable? Going to take a while. But we should have something by the time he gets out of hospital. Maybe a family with a dog so he can find out what Pedigree Chum is really for?'

'Thanks, Pauline, I owe you one.'

'Oh you owe me several.' And Pauline was gone.

Tufty was staring at her. 'What?'

'You're smiling. Why are you smiling?'

'None of your business. And you've got three guesses left: "HP".'

'"Happy Police"?'

'No.'

Her phone *ding-ding*ed at her again. Harmsworth this time:

> I hate to disturb whatever important mission
> you're on, but is there any chance you could
> actually turn up at the pub? Or are you just
> hoping Owen will starve to death here?
> Because that's what I'm

Ding-ding.

> doing!!!

As if there was any chance of that happening. He had enough blubber reserves to last him till next Christmas. Still, it wasn't as if they were achieving anything here, was it? And surely Tufty would've forgotten it was his idea to leave by now, wouldn't he? The wee loon had the attention span of a butterfly.

Look at him, sitting there in the passenger seat banging on about sod-knew what.

'...and how can you come up with a theory of quantum gravity if gravity doesn't really exist? Stands to reason.'

So the choice was sit here – just to prove a point – or head down the pub and drink the Chief Superintendent's two hundred and fifty quid?

No contest, really...

She stuffed her phone away. Buttoned her dungers up again. 'OK, that's it. If I have to sit here for one more second I'm going to commit manslaughter. Well, idiotslaughter in your case.' She cranked the engine, setting it growling.

Tufty waggled his eyebrows. 'Pub?'

'Let's get *utterly* crudweaselled.'

II

A cheer went up from the table in the corner as Steel and Tufty pushed into the Flare and Futtrit. Lund and Barrett were on their feet, whooping and whistling in their knock-off Trading Standards finest.

Harmsworth stayed in his seat giving them a slow hand-clap. 'About time!'

The jukebox oozed smooth classics into a lounge bar that had probably been trendy around the same time as big hair and shoulder pads. Abstract neon shapes in pastel colours glowed around the grey checked wallpaper. A carpet that wouldn't have looked out of place on the seats of a bus.

A vast array of platters covered the table: deep-fried things, sandwiches, bowls of crisps, sausage rolls, wee individual quiches, more deep-fried things, wee individual pork pies, yet more deep-fried things.

Barrett toasted them with a half-full pint of something lagery. 'They say they'll do us some chips too, if you want?'

Lund whooped and knocked back a shot of something. 'Chips!'

'Now, if you *don't* mind,' Harmsworth peeled the clingfilm off a platter, 'can we *finally* start in on the buffet? I'm starving…'

'Hoy!' Steel chucked a beer mat at him. 'No' so fast, greedy guts. Got something to say.'

He crunched back in his seat and covered his face with his hands. 'Argh, what fresh hell is this?'

'Listen up, people: we did good today... Well, Tufty and I did good – tackling two jobbie-flinging tractors while the rest of you stood about dripping like spare socks at an orgy – but the important thing is: we prevented a riot.' She gave them all a good hard stare. 'Chief Superintendent Campbell, DCI Rutherford, DI Vine: they think we're a bunch of idiots. That they can keep us out of trouble by wasting our time with stupid stolen mobile phones. That we can't be trusted with anything else. Well, you know what? Sod them. Sod them in the ear with a stick!'

Yeah... If this was meant to be inspiring, it wasn't really working.

'We are damn fine police officers. We're the *best* police officers. Nobody has better police officers than I do! And we're no' going to let them village-idiot us any more. As long as there's rapey bastards like Jack Wallace out there, we're going to be the ones who get in their way. *We're* going to be the ones who catch him before he hurts anyone else. And if DCI Crudweaselling Rutherford thinks we're going back to returning mobile sodding phones, he can jam the lot of them up his motherfunking bumhole!' She banged her fist on the table. 'I didn't join the police force to be a glorified Christmas Elf at the Lost-and-Found Workshop, did you?'

Barrett shook his head. Harmsworth grunted. Lund stuck her chin in the air: 'Hell no!'

'We're going to make a sodding difference, aren't we?'

The response was a bit more enthusiastic this time. Dark mutterings and nods from everyone.

'We're going to show those felchmonkeys what *real* police officers can do!'

'Yeah!'

They were all on their feet now.

'Jack Wallace isn't getting away with it any more. We will find him in the bushes! We will find him in the nightclubs. We will find him in the streets and we will *never* surrender!'

Lund gave her a big-throated, 'WHOOOO!'

Barrett burst into applause. 'Damn right!'

Tufty punched the air. 'Testify!'

'Hurrah, etc.' Harmsworth sat back down again. 'Can we eat the buffet now?'

'Oh all right then, you unpatriotic sod.' Steel rubbed her hands. 'So: who's in charge of the kitty? Your Aunty Roberta's got a thirst on her the night.'

Tufty stuck one finger in his ear and moved over to the other side of the lounge, by the pool table. Kept his voice all smooth and sober. No slurring or sounding drunk at all. Nope, nope, nopeitty, nope. 'So, I was just wondering what you were doing tomorrow?'

A slow song slunk out of the jukebox and Lund was up dancing on her own. Wiggling and doing stuff with her hands that *bordered* on the obscene without ever actually crossing over.

'*Tomorrow?*' PC Mackintosh had a sort of doubtful sound in her voice, like she wasn't really certain what tomorrow was, or why some weird guy had phoned to ask her about it.

'It's DC Quirrel, by the way. From the crematorium?'

'*Yes, I know. You've said that three times already.*'

'Sorry. I'm not drunk or anything, we're just celebrating a little. Because of the tractors.' He was blowing it. He was *definitely* blowing it. Abort. ABORT! 'Sorry, I shouldn't have called. I'm… Sorry.'

'*I'm off seeing my mother tomorrow till five. After that I'm*' *doing my laundry. You can come over and help me fold, if you like?'*

Tufty's chest went all tingly and big. 'Cool. I would. Yes. Cool.'

'Good. Bring wine.' There was a small pause. *'How are you with ironing?'*

They weren't a bad bunch of spuds, really. Her team. Her minions. Her henchmen. And one henchwoman. Roberta smiled as Barrett placed a full shot glass in front of each of them. Even Harmsworth wasn't that bad once you got to know him. And as long as you didn't have to spend too long with the misery-faced old bugger. And could tell him to sod off and go be depressing somewhere else.

'OK,' Barrett knocked on the table, 'we go on three. Not three and go, *on* three. OK? OK.' His smile was getting a bit fuzzy at the edges, his eyes too. 'One. Two. Three!'

They all snatched up their shots and hammered them back. Thumped their glasses down on the table again.

The floral-bitter-chemical hit punched its way down through her chest, breath like a gas leak awaiting a match. 'Hoooo!'

Lund drummed on the table with her palms. 'More tequila!'

'You heard the lady.' Barrett dug a handful of change out of a Ziploc bag. 'Come on, everyone: another twenty quid each for the kitty.'

Because let's be honest, two hundred and fifty quid didn't go far split between five. Even at the Flare and Futtrit's special Police Scotland discount mates' rates.

And the night was still young.

Tufty poked her. 'You're snoring.'

But it didn't make any difference, Lund just stayed where

she was: slumped back in her chair, mouth open, making raspy chainsaw-in-a-metal-dustbin noises. Mind you, she wasn't the only one who'd had a bit much.

Look at Harmsworth – one arm wrapped around Steel's shoulders, shoogling her from side to side. 'No, I *mean* it. I love you. I do.' Another shoogle. 'You're the *best* DS in the world.'

Steel nodded. 'That's ... that's very true. I'm—' A hiccup. 'I'm lovely.'

Tufty nudged Barrett. 'I think Owen's a bit squiffy.'

Barrett didn't look up from the pair of chicken legs he was playing with – making them do the sword dance around a pair of crossed sausage rolls. 'Hippity, hoppity, hippity hop.'

'Did I tell you about her hair, Davey?' Tufty nudged him again. 'Police Constable Mackintosh's hair is like ... is like that wheat field at the start of *Gladiator*. Only ... only not full of dead people.'

'Hippity, hoppity.'

Tufty thumped his hand down, making the sausage-roll swords jump. 'Sambucas! We should do ... should do flaming Sambucas!'

'Oops.' Every time they tried to pour Lund into the taxi, she poured right back out again.

Didn't seem to bother her though, she just kept on singing as Harmsworth and Barrett scooped her up off the car park tarmac:

> 'My cowboy don't love cattle, he only shags
> his horses,
> He used to shag his sheep dogs, till his sheep
> dogs got divorces...'

The sun was slouching its way down to the rooftops, making everything all brown and yellow and orange – like an ancient photograph from the seventies.

They bundled her into the back. 'Stay. Stay…'

She started to slump doorwards:

> 'He's shagged his pigs and chickens too,
> One time he shagged a kangaroo…'

'OK.' Barrett clambered into Lund's taxi. 'Wait, we come too… Come on … come on, Owen.'

> 'One time he shagged a platypus, two times
> he shagged a duck…'

Harmsworth climbed in too. 'Whee!'

> 'One time he shagged a gerbil, he just doesn't
> give a—'

Owen thumped the door closed, cutting her off.

The taxi pulled away, the three of them waving out of the back window as it drove off, leaving Tufty and Steel all alone in the car park.

Steel patted him on the shoulder, the other hand out, palm up in front of him. Wobbling on her wobbly feet. 'No. Come on, gimme your keys.'

He squinted one eye shut. 'But—'

'No. *Keys!*' She patted him again, harder this time. 'Friends don't let friends drive … drive drunked.'

That made sense.

'Oh. OK.' He dug the keys out of his pocket and dropped them into her palm. Lurched a little to the side and back again. Was OK, though: no one noticed. No one, no one, no one. Tufty reached out and patted *her* on the shoulder. Cos it was only polite. 'Owen's a miserable poohead.'

'He is indeed.'

'But!' Tufty held up a finger. 'But he's right. He *is*. You're a very lovely defective sergeant. You are. Yes you are.'

A solemn nod. 'I am.' She wobbled a bit more. 'And you … *you* are a lovely defective connsable.'

'That's why… That's why we're gonna catch Jack Wallace.'

'DAMN RIGHT!'

'Shhhh!' Tufty had a quick check to make sure no one was eavesdropping. 'We gonna … gonna come up with a *plan* and … and nab him red-handed.'

'Right up the arse!'

'Right up the…' Tufty frowned. 'Wait, wait.' He pointed a finger at her clenched fist. 'I don't has a car here! Those… Those are *your* keys.'

'Oh…' She handed them back. 'Maybe we should taxi?'

'And … and I will see you to … to your door, because … is gentleman.'

Steel smiled, nodded, then let loose a window-rattling belch.

The taxi parked outside a big granitey house on a tree-lined granitey street. The sort of place investment bankers and hedge-fund doodahs probably lived. Up above, the sky faded from dark purple to wishy-washy blue, streetlights glimmering between the trees.

The taxi driver looked back over his shoulder. 'That'll be fifteen quid.'

Steel fumbled with the door and staggered out, sticking Tufty with the bill.

Which was typical.

He dug his wallet free and handed over the cash. Doing it nice and careful so everyone would know he wasn't drunk at all. 'Is fifteen.'

The driver took it. Counted it. Then gave him a good hard stare. 'Here, Min, I hope you're no' planning on taking advantage of that poor drunk auld wifie.'

'Oh *God*, no.' Tufty clambered out into the warm evening sun.

Steel whirled around on the pavement. 'Am not *auld wifie*: am LESBIAN!' She threw her arms out, crucifix-style, probably copying Tommy Shand. Then stood there, wobbling, in her dungarees and flouncy red chiffon top.

The taxi driver rolled his eyes. 'Police officers are the worst drunks…' He did a neat three-point turn and headed back towards town.

Bye, bye.

Tufty squinted up at the big granitey building. Something wasn't right. 'Do I live here?'

'No… No…' She lurched over to him, stiff-legged like a robotic chicken. 'My house. But… but we've got *whisky*.'

He held up a finger. 'Say it proper.'

'We does has a whisky?'

'Yay!'

'Shhhhh!' She grabbed his arm. 'Secret. Now gimme … gimme keys.'

He dug them out and Steel took a while skittering a brass Yale one around and around the lock, before finally clicking it home.

She eased the door open and crept inside. 'Shhhhh!'

Dark in here. No lights.

But the orangey glow filtering in from outside was enough to lift the gloom a teeny bit. It was a highfalutin hallway with a big wooden staircase on one side and lots of holiday photos all over the other. Steel and a pretty blonde woman in swimsuits and shorts and flip-flops and… Oh dear. That one was Steel in a bikini, pulling some sort of Marilyn Monroe pose – all pouty and suggestive.

Shudder.

Bad enough this afternoon, when she'd stripped off for the communal hosing down, but at least she wasn't trying to act all sexy and you couldn't really see any…

Oh, complete and utter *shudder*.

It was like catching your granny in stockings and suspenders trying to seduce the milkman.

Tufty slapped a hand over his mouth. Didn't say that out loud, did he?

350

Steel lowered her keys into a bowl by the coat rack, then turned and grinned at him.

Oh thank God for that: he hadn't.

'And … and Tufty said, "Let there be light."' He reached for the switch, but she slapped his hand away.

'No!' Her voice rasped out in a smoky whisper: 'Is … secret and quiet! Unnerstand? No telling Susan. Shhhh…'

Ah. He nodded. 'Shhhh…'

'Good.' She patted him on the cheek. 'You go kitchen and … and get glasses. I go kiss Jasmine and Naomi goodnight. And … maybe have a pee…?'

Peeing was good. But before he could ask where the room was for peeing in she was lurching upstairs, clutching onto the wooden handrail like it was the only thing keeping her upright.

Have to pee later, Tufty. Glasses now. Pee later.

Okeydoke.

He took a deep breath and crept deeper into the house.

Kitchen? Where are you little kitchen? Come to Uncle Tufty…

Oh, there it was: at the end of the hall and left a bit. Down a couple of stairs.

And it wasn't a little kitchen at all, it was Godzilla massive. Big shiny work surfaces gleaming in the light that filtered through the French doors and kitchen windows. A garden lurking in the twilight outside, complete with swings and a climbing frame. Ooh, that'd be fun. Hadn't … hadn't been on a climbing frame in *ages*.

No. Don't get distracted. Find the whisky glasses.

Right.

He reached for the light switch, then snatched his hand back.

Naughty Tufty. Secret, remember?

Stealthy time. He dug into his jacket pocket and came

351

out with his LED torch – long as a finger but much, much brighter. The narrow white beam swept the tiled floor and oak kitchen units. A breakfast bar and a table with six chairs. A dishwasher whooshing and buzzing away to itself. A great big American-style fridge freezer covered in truly terrible kids' drawings.

Was that meant to be a pirate Tyrannounicornosaurus Rex? Where was its parrot? Eh? Where was it? Kids these days.

Wait a minute, why was he…?

Oh, right: glasses.

'Come out little glasses, don't hide from Uncle Tufty…'

The cistern refilling hissed out of the bathroom as Roberta eased the door shut. Adjusted her dungers. That was the great thing about dungarees – lots of room. And they didn't creep down the whole time taking your pants with them. Should wear them all the time.

Bit of a cliché, but they were comfy.

Unless you sat down too fast.

Right: time to be all motherly and sober-ish.

She tiptoed her way down the hall to a pink door with a big sign stuck right in the middle of it: a skull and cross-bones grinning away above, 'JASMINE'S EVIL DUNGEON OF DOOM!'

It creaked a bit as she eased it open, but the figure beneath the Skeleton Bob duvet cover didn't stir. Had to be one of the best rooms in the house, this one. No' all chintzy and floral and stuff. A funky mix of decor and ornaments – like *My Little Pony* does *Game of Thrones* – all just visible through the gloom.

Jasmine lay on her side with a thumb in her mouth, one arm wrapped around Mr Stinky the teddy bear. All loved bald around the ears.

Roberta crept in and kissed Jasmine on the forehead. Then kissed Mr Stinky too, so he wouldn't feel left out. Then put a finger to her lips and shushed him, just in case.

Slipped back out of the room again.

Never mind Susan's Great Hazlehead Ladies Challenge Cup, *Roberta* deserved one for Mother of the Motherfunking Year. Right. One daughter down, one to go. Then it was whisky time!

She tiptoed over to the door opposite: bright orange with 'Naomi's Room' on it. Her fingers were inches from the handle when a floorboard creaked behind her.

Then a man's voice. 'Did you miss me?'

She put a finger to her lips. 'Shhh... I told...'

Oh sodding *hell*.

That wasn't Tufty.

That was Jack Wallace!

She spun around, snarling, fists ready to—

Something hard smashed into the side of her head, making the whole house rock and throb. Warm behind her eyes. Knees no' ... wouldn't...

Then the hall carpet jumped up and grabbed her.

Thump.

Darkness.

There was a thump upstairs.

Kneeling on the kitchen floor, Tufty wobbled his torch beam up at the ceiling.

And she had the cheek to tell *him* to be all secret and quiet? Charging about up there like a randy elephant on a pogo stick.

Well, as long as she was getting the whisky.

He lowered the torch back to the little cupboard. Glasses gleamed at him, caught in the hard white glare. 'Whisky, whisky, whisky, whisky.'

Be careful – don't break any. Careful as a careful fish.

Tufty eased two tumblers out, like they were nuclear fuel rods. Closed the cupboard door and stood. Crept across to the breakfast bar.

The tumblers clicked against the granite worktop.

'Whisky, whisky, whisky…'

Uh-ho.

His Tufty sense was tingling.

There was someone behind him, wasn't there? Someone—

'Peekaboo.'

Something whistled through the air and he jerked left, turning.

Whatever it was it battered into his shoulder instead of his head, sending barbed wire digging into the muscle.

A shadow-shape of a man loomed in the darkness, features just a hint of nose, mouth and glasses. Tufty broke them with his fist, snapping the scumbag's head back with a very satisfying grunt.

Shadow Scumbag grabbed at him, hauling Tufty down as he tumbled to the kitchen floor – the pair of them bashing into the tiles. Arms and legs. Elbows and knees. Rolling over and over.

Two quick jabs to the ribs had Shadows grunting again. They thumped into a cabinet, setting the contents ringing.

Back out onto the floor.

Fire shredded across Tufty's wrist as Shadows sunk his teeth in. 'AAAARGH!'

They rolled back the other way and *BANG*, right into the fridge, knocking the door open. A thin cold light spilled out across the room.

He was big, hairy, ugly. Scarlet streaming down his face from a newly squinted nose. Teeth bared, stained pink with either his own blood or Tufty's. Bitey sod. 'KILL YOU!'

A thick fist whistled past Tufty's face.

Oh no you don't!

He grabbed Shadows by the scruff of the neck and shoved his head into the open fridge, slamming the door on it over and over and over again, making the bottles and jars inside jingle and clink. Pats of butter and yoghurt pots cascaded out to thump and spatter against the floor all around them.

One more slam and Shadows went limp.

Tufty dragged him out of the fridge and shoved him onto his front. Hauled out his cuffs and grabbed the guy's wrist, pulling it up behind his back. 'You are comprehensively...'

There was that tingling again.

He twisted around. Too slow.

Just enough time to make out a fat bald shape in the fridge's ghostly glow before hard yellow lights exploded, wiping the kitchen from view. Didn't even hurt when his head bounced off the cool smooth tiles.

Fat fingers reached for him, and the world slowly disappeared...

Mnnnghfff... *DUNK*. Everything snapped up, then down again. *DUNK*. Up, then down. *DUNK*. Up, then down.

The alarm-clock was ringing, time to get up.

DUNK.

Or was it sirens?

DUNK.

Wait, that was... What was she doing on the stairs?

Roberta opened her mouth, but all that came out was, 'Unnnngggghhhh...'

DUNK.

And why was her leg...? Someone was pulling her down the stairs by the leg.

What?

A blurry figure oozed into focus. Jack Wallace. He smiled at her. 'Oh, we're going to have so much *fun!*'

DUNK.

DUNK.

DUNK.

And it all went black again.

III

Sleepy sleep. Warm cosy sleepy—

'AAAARGH!' Tufty jerked upright. Or almost.

His head moved, but the rest of him stayed exactly where it was: tied to a chair with his hands held tight behind his back. And from the feel of it, those were handcuffs. How did…?

Oh. Right, Shadows had a bald fat friend.

He blinked. Shook his head. But that only made things swoop and swing around from left to right and back again. The floor pitched and heaved. The ceiling rocked. The walls lurched.

Tufty screwed his eyes shut and gritted his teeth till the ferry-in-a-force-nine-gale subsided. Peeled one eye open again.

Oh crap.

It was a fancy-looking living room, with a collection of standard lamps, a pair of brown buttony leather sofas with matching armchairs, a fireplace with flowers in it, golfing trophies on the mantelpiece above. Happy family photos. An upright piano. A set of rusty old golf clubs in an elephant's-condom leather-and-fabric bag. A huge Middle-Eastern rug surrounded by polished wooden floorboards. Like he'd woken up in a photo shoot for a boutique hotel.

They probably weren't going to get five stars, though. Not with what was going on in the middle of the room. Three wooden dining chairs were arranged in a triangle. The blonde woman from the photographs – that would be Steel's wife, Susan – was gagged and tied to the one on the right, glaring out. Nostrils flaring. Steel was tied to the one on the left, hanging limp against her ropes. And lucky-old-Tufty was the pointy end furthest from the fireplace.

Jack Wallace was leaning back against it, sipping from a tumbler of deep amber liquid. The glass looked weird in his black leather gloves, but the smoky scent of whisky oiled its way through the air anyway.

Baldy McFatface was on one of the sofas, nursing a dram of his own.

A third man, vaguely familiar – maybe one of the guys from the security footage of Wallace going to the pictures? – poured a good stiff measure into another tumbler and passed it to a ruinous wreck in a bloodstained shirt.

Bright red leaked from the wreck's nose, ears, and mouth, dripping onto the tea towel he held in his other hand. That would be Tufty's old friend Shadows then. Which explained the fridge-door-shaped dents in his ugly-shaped head.

Tufty nodded at him. 'You want to put something cold on that. Like the fridge freezer.'

Shadows knocked back a mouthful of Steel's whisky, winced, then glowered at him through puffy squinted eyes. Oh, right: no glasses – those got all broken in the kitchen.

Diddums.

Wallace snapped his fingers. 'Richard: gag him.'

The vaguely familiar one put his tumbler on the piano and marched over, grabbed a handful of Tufty's hair and yanked his head back.

Needles and pins dug their way through his scalp. Then

a chunk of fabric was jammed into his mouth. Held in place with another bit – tied around the back.

Now everything tasted of fusty towels.

'OK, I think it's about time we got this party started!' Wallace gulped down his drink and stuck the empty on the fireplace. Flexed his gloved hand as he marched across the rug and slapped Steel, hard.

Nothing.

Still unconscious.

'Shall we try that again?' Harder this time – the whole chair rocked with the force of it.

She surfaced, coughing and spluttering. 'Gnnn…' Scarlet dripped from the side of her lips.

'Welcome back, sleepyhead! Did you have a nice snooze?'

She shook her head. Blinked. Then snarled – yanking herself back and forward against the ropes holding her to the chair. Going nowhere. 'GRRRRRRRRRRRAAAAAAAAAAAA!'

Wallace grabbed a handful of her chiffon top. 'You really thought you could get away with it, didn't you? What you did to me.' A laugh. 'Told you one day I'd tear your little world to pieces. Well, today's the day!'

Steel's voice was sharp as a prison chib. 'Get out of my sodding house!'

'All those months, locked up with dirty paedophiles and rapists.' He gave his mates a little salute. 'No offence, guys.'

'If you've hurt Susan…' Steel's eyes bugged and she struggled against the ropes again. Still nothing doing.

What they needed was a plan. Something clever. Something that ended with everyone currently tied up changing places with everyone currently *not* tied up. And Jack Wallace kicked in the balls three or four times.

Think.

Had to be something…

Ah ha! A plan!

Breaking the *chair* would do it! Break the chair and the ropes wouldn't be tying him to anything. They'd slither right off. Wriggle his arms down over his bum and get his hands back round the front again. Leap free and ... do something heroic.

Like punch Wallace in the throat. Then kick Baldy McFatface in the knee. Open-palm thrust to Vaguely-Familiar Richard's nose – shattering it – and they were done. Shadows was too busy scowling and bleeding to put up much of a fight.

Free Steel and Susan.

Oh, Tufty you're our hero.

Medals. A parade. And a promotion.

Yeah, *definitely* a plan.

Come on, Tufty: they're all depending on you!

He took a deep breath, shrank into himself, then bounced back. Hard and fast. LIKE – A – NINJA!

The ropes creaked. The chair creaked.

Come on, damn it: break!

...

But it didn't.

All that happened was his bitten wrist ached a bit harder.

Vaguely-Familiar Richard cuffed him over the back of the head. 'Sit still, you wee fanny.' He pulled out a Stanley knife and slid the blade out. Turning it under Tufty's nose, so the edge caught the light. Gleaming and shiny. 'Want me to start cutting bits off you? Cos I *will*.'

Ah... Right.

Wallace picked a book out of a leather holdall and turned back to Steel. 'One thing you *can* say for prison: gives you lots of time to read.'

She stared at him. 'If you let Susan go, we can talk about this.'

'They had this in the prison library.' He held it out to her for a couple of beats, then read from the cover. "'Take it a Mile", subtitled, "How a Detective Inspector went from chasing serial killers to making blockbuster movies." "A fascinating and heart-rending book…" says the *Scotsman*. "I can't recommend this book highly enough." *Daily Mail*. "Completely and utterly magnificent." William Hunter.'

Steel cleared her throat. Put on that faux-reasonable voice she sometimes used to get around DCI Rutherford. 'I mean it, Jack. Let Susan go.'

'He was a colleague of yours, wasn't he, this DI Insch guy? Ooh, you should see the things he says about you in here. Tsk, tsk.'

'Susan had nothing to do with it. This is just between us.'

'Oh! Nearly forgot: I've marked my favourite bit.' A wink. 'You'll like this.' He opened the book. "'Then Ken Wiseman said the most horrible thing I'd ever heard in my life. He was going to take my little girl, my Sophie, and sell her to paedophiles. That they would train her. That they would do whatever they liked." Oooh…' He shut the book. 'That's *harsh*, isn't it?'

Baldy McFatface shuffled his feet. 'Can we move this along, Jacky? Only I'm getting a bit … you know. Keen.'

Wallace didn't even look at him. 'Keep it in your pants for two minutes. We've plenty of time.' He squatted down in front of Steel, looking up into her face. One hand on her knee. 'See, thanks to *you*, they locked me up with all those sex offenders. And the funny thing is: paedophiles? On the whole, they're pretty nice guys. Well, other than the shagging little kids thing. And here's you with two *beautiful* baby girls.' He let go of Steel's knee, running his gloved finger up the inner thigh of her dungarees instead. 'How much do you think I'll get for them?'

Susan roared behind her gag, thumping against her ropes

and chair, making it rock. The chair legs bounced and skittered off the rug and onto the floorboards.

Richard marched over and backhanded her hard enough to send the whole chair tipping over backwards. It crashed to the ground.

Susan grunted. Something splintered.

He rubbed at his knuckles. 'And bloody stay down, you manky dyke bitch! You'll get your turn.'

Wallace took hold of Steel's face, turning it away from Susan and back to himself. 'All that time you wasted chasing me. But it was never *just* me, was it? Nah, it's a team sport. One of us on the pitch, the other three on the bench, being their alibi.' He pointed at Mr Bloodstains. 'Terry's the one did that teacher while her kid watched. Lovely work, Terry.'

Terry scowled at Tufty, voice all wet and slurred. 'That bastard cop knocked out half my teeth...'

Good.

'So here's what we're going to do. We're going to have some fun. Then you and your little friends are going swimming. With breeze-blocks chained to your ankles.'

Baldy McFatface grinned. 'Terry's got a fishing boat. And I've got this.' He clutched a hand to his crotch and squeezed the contents. 'Oooh, yeah.' Rubbing himself through his trousers. 'I know you lezzers are just gagging for a real man. Nice bit of cock to get you on the straight again.'

Wallace stood. 'See? *Told* you we were going to have fun. Eric is on sloppy seconds, Richard's on tacky thirds, and Terry's on filthy fourths. Which means *I* get first dibs.' He unzipped his trousers and pulled out his erection. Waved it in Steel's face.

Eric – Baldy McFatface – whooped. Clapping his hands as Wallace got closer. 'Go on, suck it you wrinkly old bitch. You know you want to. Suck it!'

Steel flinched her head away.

'Hoy!' Eric pulled out a six-inch hunting knife, serrated along one edge, gleaming sharp on the other. 'Suck it or I'll carve your frumpy lesbian bitch wife like a Sunday roast!'

Wallace gave his hips a twist, setting things swaying. 'He's not joking either. The mess Eric can make of a woman, it's quite something. Your dignity's not worth that, is it? Your pretty lesbo wife all slashed up?'

Tufty had another go. Shrink. And snap, LIKE – A – NINJA!

Straining.

Teeth gritted.

The muscles burning up and down his back…

Nope.

He collapsed again with nothing more than a creak to show for it.

Steel hung her head. Sniffed. Shuddered out a long breath. Then nodded and opened her mouth.

Wallace grinned. 'There we go! I knew you were gagging for it.' He took his cock in one hand, the other grabbing the back of her neck so she couldn't retreat. 'Now: here comes the aeroplane…'

Steel's head flashed forward teeth snapping shut with an audible *clack*. Tearing from side to side.

Wallace staggered back a couple of paces, staring at her blood-drenched chin, then down at himself as more blood pulsed out. A high, sharp, whistling noise scraped its way out of his mouth, then the screaming started. He hit the rug like a sack of tatties, rolling around between the two sofas, clutching his groin, bright red pulsing out between his clenched fingers. 'AAAAAAAAAAARGH! GOD, GOD, GOD, GOD!'

Steel spat the severed chunk out onto the rug at her feet. 'Was it good for you, *darling*? Thought you *liked* it rough!'

Richard slid out the blade on his Stanley knife again and lunged for her.

Oh no you don't!

Tufty snapped his foot forward, kicking it hard into the side of Richard's knee. Making something inside go *pop*!

He crashed to the floor, just short of Steel, shrieking, clutching his freshly deformed leg. The Stanley knife skittering away under the piano.

Steel jerked her left boot up and stamped the heel down on his face. Once. Twice. Three times. Bones snapping and crackling under every blow.

Two down, two to go.

Wallace rolled and screamed. Legs kicking out as he curled up even tighter. 'AAAAAAAAAAAARGH! JESUS, GOD, CHRIST, AAAAAAAAAAAARGH!' Painting the rug scarlet with his blood.

'You're dead, bitch!' Eric shifted his grip on the hunting knife, making little figure of eights with the tip, snarling his way towards Steel. 'Dead!'

Tufty raised his own foot, slamming it down and back into the leg of the chair he was tied to – the crack of battered wood muffled by Wallace's screams. Again. The leg snapped and the chair collapsed sideways onto the rug, the whole frame creaking as it hit. He thumped forward and back against the ropes.

Ha: it was working! They were getting looser. Just take a second more and he'd be—

Oh crap.

Terry loomed above him, ruined teeth bared: bloody stumps and ragged gums. He took a little run up and slammed a kick into Tufty's stomach. Flipping him and the chair over onto their backs.

A thousand burning spiders scuttled through his guts,

burrowing, scorching. He wheezed in a broken-glass breath, fanning the flames.

Then Terry was squatting over him, knees on his chest, hands around his throat. *Squeezing.* 'Think it's funny slamming people's heads in fridges, do you? Think it's funny?'

Susan reared up behind him, holding one of those rusty old golf clubs. Blood ran down from the corner of her mouth, dripped off the end of her chin. 'I am *not* frumpy!' She smashed the club down on Terry's head with a resounding *thunggggggg*!

His eyes went crossed, then dim, then he pitched forward onto Tufty.

'Mmmmnph!' God, he weighed a ton! Tufty hauled a breath in through the gag. Struggled and wiggled... But the fat sod just lay there, pinning him to the carpet. 'Mnnghfff mnngg mmn!'

But Susan didn't. Instead she tore her own gag off and turned – squaring up to Eric and his six-inch hunting knife.

She took the club in both hands, feet planted shoulder-width apart, the club's head resting against the rug. 'HEY, NUMB NUTS!'

Steel's eyes went wide. 'SUSAN, NO! RUN!'

'Think your wee golf stick's going to save you and your friends? Nah.' Eric grinned. Knife shining. Blade snaking back and forth through the air. 'I'm going to slash your guts open, then I'm going to—'

'FORE!' Susan swung back and then forward, *fast*, twisting her hips into it, the golf club's head whistling in a low flat arc and up, right between Eric's legs – *THUD* – so hard it lifted him up onto his tiptoes.

Oooooooh...

That *had* to hurt!

Eric's eyes bugged. Then he dropped the knife and toppled forward, squealing like a pig in a cement mixer. Tears streaming down his face. Mouth moving, but no words coming out.

Susan tossed her golf club on the couch and kicked him. 'Great Hazlehead Ladies Challenge Cup winner *three years in a row*, motherfunker!'

Blue-and-white lights strobed out, turning everything into a flickering mess of silhouettes and reflections. Three patrol cars and four ambulances were parked outside Steel's house, blocking the road, and every single window in the street was ablaze – a knot of people in expensive-looking casual clothes standing on the pavement to watch the show.

Logan pulled into the nearest parking space, two doors down. Stared through the windscreen.

Two stretcher trolleys were being wheeled out of the house, their occupants strapped-down motionless lumps wearing oxygen masks. Paramedics bustled them down the garden path, and into the back of the waiting ambulances.

OK, that *wasn't* a good sign.

He clambered out of the Audi and plipped the locks. Hurried up the pavement as the lead ambulance pulled away. Closely followed by the second one. Sirens wailing in the darkness.

'Excuse me...' Logan squeezed his way through the clump of people, then flashed his warrant card at the uniformed officer keeping them there. 'Are they still inside?'

'Inspector McRae?' The PC snapped to attention. 'DI Vine's SIO, the IB are processing the scene, DC Goodwin's CSM, and DCI Rutherford's ETA is twenty-two hundred hours. He's at some sort of black-tie dinner. Sir.'

'OK.' Not really what he'd meant, but never mind.

Logan marched over to the front gate. Shrank back as another stretcher trolley was wheeled out onto the pavement. A fat bald man with tears streaming down his face and a patch of red seeping out through the fly of his trousers. Making high-pitched squealing sobs as he got shoved into the back of Ambulance Number Three. Another wail of sirens.

The blinds were down in Steel's living room, but the indoor lightning strikes of flash photography lit up the room.

He hurried up the path, then had to step back into the gravel border as a fourth trolley was hefted out through the front door. Didn't need a Police National Computer check to know who *that* was.

Jack Wallace groaned behind his oxygen mask, skin pale as paper. he'd been handcuffed, trousers pulled down around his knees, a big wodge of blood-soaked gauze taped over his crotch.

The paramedic at the front shuddered. 'Oooh, makes you wince just to think, doesn't it?'

His colleague took up the rear, pushing. 'Shame we couldn't find the missing bit...'

Down the path, into the last ambulance, and away.

OK, that was ... weird.

Logan crossed the threshold into Steel's house and there was DC Goodwin, with his floppy hair and squint nose. 'What do you think you're doing, this is a crime... Oh.' He tucked his clipboard under his arm and saluted. 'Inspector McRae. Sorry.'

'Don't worry about it, Dougie. Is Steel still here?'

'Yes, Inspector. They're in the kitchen.' He pointed down the hall, as if Logan had never been here before. 'DI Vine's with them.'

Logan stayed where he was, staring down at Goodwin. 'And?'

'Er... DC Quirrel and Steel's wife's there too?'

'No: you're Crime Scene Manager. You have to make me sign in, remember?'

'Oh, yes! Right. Signing in.' He held out the clipboard and a pen. 'Sorry, Inspector. I just… Sorry.'

Logan filled in his details, then Goodwin flattened himself against the coat rack to let him past.

The flashgun flares clacked out of the open lounge door, reflecting back from the shiny wooden balusters and framed photos. He peered into the room.

Four Identification Bureau techs in the full scene of crime getup were measuring, tagging, and photographing things. Whatever had happened in there it'd been brutal: two smashed chairs, coils of blue nylon rope, blood all over the Persian rug. A six-inch hunting knife sticking out of the floorboards.

Yeah, that didn't look good.

Well, couldn't put it off any longer.

Logan straightened his shoulders and marched down the hall. Took a deep breath and pushed through into the kitchen.

Susan was on her hands and knees in front of the fridge, wiping up what looked like a massive bird-strike of yoghurt. Tufty sat on a stool at the breakfast bar, a bag of frozen peas clutched to his head, a massive shiner on his face, a ring of red around his throat, and a ring of bandages around one wrist.

DI Vine stood off to one side, doing his best Stern-Faced Police Officer impersonation. 'I can't believe you bit it clean off…'

'Urgh.' Steel swigged from a bottle of Smirnoff, gargled, swooshed it around her mouth, then spat it into the sink. 'Don't remind me.' Then tipped back another glug. Glanced at Logan. Spat. 'You took your time.'

'Control said Jack Wallace attacked everyone. What happened, are you all OK?'

'Logan!' Susan stood. Her lips were swollen, cracked in

one corner, the beginnings of a bruise darkening her cheek. She wiped her hands on a tea towel and hugged him. Warm and soft and smelling faintly of peaches.

'Jasmine and Naomi?'

'Oh, they're fine. Slept right through the whole thing.' One last squeeze and she let him go. Stepped back. 'Now, how about a nice cup of tea?'

Vine nodded at him. Formal. Wary. 'Inspector McRae.'

'John.'

'Well, I think we're about done here.' He turned to Steel. 'Come down the station tomorrow and we'll finalise your statements. Then I think you and Constable Quirrel deserve a couple of days off.' Vine held up a hand. 'No, don't thank me. It's only fair.' Then turned and stalked from the room.

Steel spat out another mouthful of vodka. Wiped her chin with a hand. 'Blah, blah, blah. Thought he'd never leave.'

'Ooh, ooh, ooh!' Tufty bounced up and down on his stool, peas still clasped to his head. 'You should've seen us, it was great! Jack Wallace tried to stick his willy in the Sarge's face and she's like, "No way!" And he's like, "Here comes the aeroplane!"—'

'That blow to the head didn't knock any sense into you then?'

Steel sniffed. 'I said that.'

'—and she's like, "BITE!" And then there's screaming and Richard's going to slash her with a Stanley knife and—'

'Tufty,' Steel put the cap back on the Smirnoff, 'give it a rest, eh?'

He stuck out his free hand, miming stabbing someone. '—but I tripped him up, and Eric's got this *massive* pointy knife, and Terry's trying to strangle me cos I banged his head in the fridge—'

Steel threw a scrubby sponge at him. Missed. 'Tufty!'

'—but Susan wriggles free and she's got this set of antique golf clubs—'

'CONSTABLE QUIRREL!'

'And POW! Then—' The second sponge found its mark, bouncing off his chest – leaving a rectangular damp patch on his shirt. 'Hey!'

She dried her hands. 'Give it a rest, OK? Just lived through it: don't need a blow-by-blow replay.'

'Oh…' His shoulders dipped a little, then he took a deep breath and rattled it out as quick as possible: 'Then she shouts, "Fore!" And WHANG! Right up the fairway. Gave him a hole in one. Popped it open like a squished grape.' Tufty sat back, smiling. Clearly pleased with himself for making it all the way through to the end. Then frowned. 'I'm feeling a bit dizzy. Is anyone else a bit dizzy?'

The garden stretched away back into the darkness, the short grass scattered with kids' toys. Bright plastic landmines waiting for the unwary foot. The lonicera was in bloom, filling the air with the sticky scent of warm honey.

Steel had parked herself at the picnic bench by the Wendy house, puffing away on her e-cigarette, making her own strawberry-scented fog bank.

Logan lowered a hot mug in front of her, then settled onto the bench-seat opposite. 'Horlicks.'

'Hmph.' She leaned forward and sniffed at it. 'Could at least have put some whisky in there.'

He stared up at the trees. 'Are you OK?'

'OK?' A small laugh, then a slurp of Horlicks. 'Someone threatened to rape my wife, sell my kids to paedophiles, and stuck their dick in my mouth. What do *you* think?'

'On the plus side, he's never going to do that again. Jack Wallace's raping days are over. If he ever gets out of prison, the tattered stump you left him with isn't going to trouble

370

anyone.' Logan snuck a glance. She had a *very* nasty smile on her face. 'You know they probably could've sewn it back on again, right?'

'I'm never going to moan about Susan spending all her time on the golf course again.'

'If they'd found the bit you bit off.'

'You should've seen her, Laz: she was magnificent. An Amazon with a six iron. Wonder Susan!'

A huge furry cat sauntered out of the darkness, big grey tail like a plume of smoke behind him. He wound his way around Logan's legs, then did the same with Steel. Purring. Hopped up onto the picnic table on large white paws.

Steel rubbed at his ears. 'You hungry, Mr Rumpole? Are you?'

'There's going to be an internal investigation – don't really have a choice after all the carnage here tonight – but it's nothing to worry about. Promise.'

'Who's my hungry little boy?' She stood and picked Mr Rumpole up with a grunt. 'Pfff… Ooh, you're a fat wee sod.' He hung in her arms: a bag of fur, smoky tail twitching as she carried him through the French doors and into the kitchen. Plonked him down on the breakfast bar.

Logan picked both mugs up again and followed Steel inside. Cleared his throat as she dug a sachet of cat food out of a cupboard and ripped it open. 'Roberta, I—'

'Don't. OK?' She didn't look at him, just squatted down and squeezed the food into Mr Rumpole's bowl. 'I know.'

'But—'

'You didn't clype on me because you're a traitorous bastard. You clyped on me because I was wrong. I should never have framed Jack Wallace, no matter how much of a rapey scumbag he is. I screwed up. If I'd played by the rules he wouldn't have come here. I put Susan, Jasmine and Naomi in danger.' She stamped on the bin's pedal and dropped the empty sachet in. 'You were right and I was wrong.'

Roberta Steel admitting she was wrong?

Dear Lord, that was a first.

He put a hand on her shoulder. 'I'm really, really sorry it worked out the way it did.'

'Me too.' She sighed, then turned to face him. Opened her arms wide, voice catching a little on the words 'Come on then, you big girl.'

He hugged her and she squeezed back so hard it made his ribs creak.

Steel sniffed. Let go of him and wiped her eyes with the heel of her hand. 'Gah...'

Logan smiled. 'A hug *and* tears? You're just a big softy, aren't you?'

'If you ever tell *anyone* I just did that, I'll castrate you too.' She reached into her pocket and dropped a little shrivelled bloody chunk of flesh on top of the cat food. Picked Mr Rumpole off the breakfast bar and set him down in front of his bowl. 'Dinner time.'

He wolfed the lot down as they watched in silence.

When it was all gone, Steel clapped her hands. 'Right. Now, how about we break out that whisky?'

IV

'COME BACK HERE!' Roberta shoved through a clot of halfwits in hoodies and puffy trainers.

'Hoy, watch it, Grandma!'

'"Grandma", nice one, Baz.'

Morons.

Union Street was almost solid with shoppers – old, young, men, women, rich, poor, and all of them IN THE SODDING WAY!

That red hoodie was getting further away, barging past families and oldies while she was mired neck-deep in a swamp of idiots.

Billy Moon glanced back over his shoulder and hooted at her, stuck his tongue out, then wheeched around the corner onto Market Street.

Cheeky wee sod.

She gritted her teeth and ran after him.

Tufty helped the old guy to his feet. Grey hair and damp eyes – the iris ringed in pale grey. Marks & Spencer ready meals littered the pavement all around them, a bottle of red smashed to curls of green glass. 'Are you OK?'

'He got my wallet and my phone!' The man waved a shaky

fist across the road, where Steel and Billy Moon's red hoodie and black backpack were rapidly disappearing downhill. 'You wee shite! I'll tan your arse for you!'

'Stay here.'

And Tufty was off, sprinting across the road, ducking and dodging the traffic to the other side. Steel and Billy Moon were legging it down Market Street, but Tufty had a clever. Instead of following them he turned the other way, running up Union Street towards the Trinity Centre.

It was time for a cunning plan.

Billy Moon jinked right, clattering down the stairs and into the Aberdeen Market shopping centre – a grey slab of a building with about as much charm as a litter tray.

He burst through the doors, trainers squeaking on the floor.

Roberta grabbed the stainless-steel handrail and swept around and down, after him. Through the doors and into a labyrinth of wee booth-type shops.

She hauled out her phone and thumbed the screen as she ran.

'*Control Room.*'

'Where's my sodding backup?'

Past places that unlocked mobile phones or flogged novelty balloons or sold underwear in six-packs.

'*I've told you already: we don't do backup for shoplifters!*'

Useless Spungbadgers.

She stuck her phone away again, whooshing past a home-made-jewellery shop, one selling ancient electrical equipment, tattoos while you wait, a greengrocer…

Billy was just visible up ahead: laughing, shoving through people, leaving a wake of fallen pensioners and their spilled shopping.

Arrrgh…

Roberta leaped over an auld wifie sprawled amongst a dozen packs of lacy pants as a clutch of 'HAPPY HEN NIGHT!' balloons – at least half of which were shaped like willies – bobbed against the ceiling tiles.

And past. Around the corner.

A two-storey atrium dropped away below her, a set of stairs descending to the floor below. Billy Moon was already halfway down them.

Tufty grabbed the edge of the Thorntons shop and swung himself around the corner and onto the Back Wynd Stairs, hammering down them two at a time towards the Green below. Arms out for balance, mouth wide. 'Aaaaaaaaaaaaaaaaaaaagh!'

Holy mother of *Fish* that was steep!

The granite steps were worn in the middle, acned with chewing gum, streaked with snotter-green moss and algae, but they were still hard and sharp enough to split a skull like a dropped Pot Noodle.

Across a small landing and down the other side.

'Aaaaaaaaaaaaaaaaaaagh!'

Billy Moon did a weird show-off twirling-jump thing over the edge of the stairwell, dropping onto the edge of a big wooden planter and back-flipping. Trainers squealing on the floor as he slid to a halt, both arms up, hands curled into fists, middle fingers out. Grinning.

Cheeky wee shite.

Roberta lumbered down the stairs.

He was backing away slowly. Actually, no he wasn't: the arrogant sod was *moonwalking* away. Letting her catch up a bit.

Well, when she caught up she was going to introduce the pointy bit of Mrs Shoe to the dark and stinky bit of Mr Bumhole!

He made a loudhailer out of his hands. 'Come on, Granny, you can do it!'

What the hell was it with people shouting 'Granny' at her? She was *no'* a sodding granny. Nowhere *near* old enough for a start! As Billy Cheeky Spungbadger Moon was about to find out!

Roberta put on an extra spurt of speed, thundered down the last flight of stairs and out onto the atrium floor.

'Woooo!' He turned and barged out through the doors.

She clattered across the atrium and out onto the Green.

A Mondeo estate slammed on its brakes, screeching to a halt on the cobblestones as Billy Moon danced past its bonnet, sticking two fingers up at the driver. Laughing. The Mondeo's horn blared.

And he was out of there, arms and legs pumping.

Roberta puffed and panted, sweat dribbling down between her breasts and buttocks. A tiny jagged knife jabbing away inside her ribs with every step.

She wasn't too old for this. She was just ... too important.

Chasing cheeky wee scroats was a job for detective constables, *no'* detective sergeants.

And where the hell was Tufty when you needed him?

This was *his* sodding job!

Argh...

Roberta lumbered after Billy Moon, but she was getting slower and he was getting away – looking back over his shoulder as he ran. Laughing. Hooting.

Young, fast, and never, ever going to—

Tufty appeared from behind the eating area in the middle of the Green, one arm out, and *THUMP* – Billy stopped dead, clotheslined.

His legs shot out in front of him, arse a good four feet

off the cobbles, hanging there as if gravity didn't exist. Then it grabbed hold again and he clattered down, flat on his backpack. Lay there groaning.

She staggered over, bent double, grabbed hold of her knees, and hacked up a lung. 'Aaaaaargh… Stitch…'

Tufty jumped up and down, like a thin ugly version of Rocky at the top of the Art Museum steps. 'I has a win!'

'Idiot… Ahhh… Spungbadgering hell…' More coughing. 'Argh…'

He hauled Billy to his feet. 'William Moon, I'm detaining you under Section Fourteen of the…' Tufty trailed off as Billy's bottom lip trembled, then the tears started. Snot making two shiny trails down his top lip.

'For goodness' sake.' Roberta straightened up. 'Don't be such a wimp.'

All that brash 'Aren't I young, and untouchable?' bravado had evaporated, leaving a teeny wee boy behind. What was he, ten years old? Maybe eleven at a push?

No' the big-time criminal he thought he was.

The crying got louder, damper, and snotterier.

Tufty shuffled his feet. 'Maybe just this once…?'

A ten-year-old boy, bawling his wee heart out on Aberdeen's cobbles.

Ah, what the hell…

She sighed. 'Go on then.'

He went through Billy's pockets, digging out mobile phones and wallets and watches and stuffing them into the backpack. Slipped the backpack's straps off and hefted it over his own shoulder. 'I'm confiscating the lot.'

Billy blinked at him and sniffed. Wiped his shiny nose on his sleeve. 'I'm sorry, Mister.'

'And stop nicking stuff off people! You want to end up like your mate, Charlie Roberts?'

He shook his head and sobbed some more.

Tufty pointed. 'Go on then, off you jolly well sod.'

Billy just stared at him. Sniffed again. Glanced over his shoulder, where Tufty was pointing, then legged it – away at full speed, the soles of his trainers flapping, arms swinging. Sprinting into the tunnel beneath the St Nicholas Centre, just like last time.

His voice echoed out from the gloom as he vanished. 'CATCH YOU LATER, MASTURBATORS!'

And he was gone.

Roberta stuck her hands in her pockets. 'Why do I get the feeling we've just been foolish and deluded?'

A shrug. 'Probably. Maybe we should—' The theme tune to *The Sweeney* belted out from his pocket and he produced his phone. Shrugged at her. 'What, you've got a monopoly on old TV show ringtones?' Hit the button. 'Kate?' A grin. 'Yeah...'

Ah to be young, stupid, gangly and in love.

He wandered off a couple of paces. 'Is she? That's great. Yeah. ... No... I know...'

Probably organising a threesome.

Roberta dug out her own phone, scrolling through her text messages. Logan's one was still sitting there.

> Jasmine's party: I can get hold of a bouncy castle, if you like?
> A guy I know has one shaped like a pirate ship and he'll do us a deal.

She smiled and thumbed out a reply.

> Perfect – it'll go great with the zombie theme.
> Just make sure you bring a LOT of booze with you. Going to be a LONG day.

Send.

When she looked up, Tufty was standing there beaming at her. 'That was Kate. She says Mrs Galloway's getting

378

out of hospital today. We're going round to make sure she's settled into the sheltered housing place OK. Want to come?'

'Why no'?'

They wandered back towards the Aberdeen Market.

Roberta kicked an empty plastic bottle, sending it skittering across the cobbles. 'And is Agnes keeping the car, or selling it?'

'Selling. Even second hand it's worth about thirty grand.' He shifted his grip on the backpack. 'Sarge, about the car?'

Her stomach made a wee rumbling grumbling noise. 'Ooh. Think I need a little smackerel of something.'

'Yeah, but the car, the cash, the watch. Big Jimmy Grieve...' A grimace. 'Do we owe him favours now? Only I don't want to owe gangsters favours.'

'Silly Tufty, Mr Grieve isn't a gangster, he's a retired cop. First DI I ever worked for. God, now *there's* a man who can drink. I could tell you stories that'd make your pubes go straight.'

'Oh thank God for that.' Tufty sagged a bit. 'Thought it was going to turn into one of those *Godfather* deals.' He flinched as her stomach growled again. 'Back to the station for tea and biscuits?'

'That's the first sensible thing you've said all day.'

'After all, must be nearly time for tenses,' he checked his watch, 'we can...' His eyes widened as he stared at the pale hairy stripe on his wrist. Then pulled up his other sleeve and stared at the wrist on that side. Then back to the first wrist. 'That rancid little spungbadger's nicked my watch!' He charged off towards the tunnel under the St Nicholas Centre. 'COME BACK HERE YOU THIEVING WEE JOBBIE!'

See? *That* was what you got for being nice to people.

Roberta shook her head. 'Foolish and deluded.' Then lumbered after him.

After all, he might be a useless wee spud, but he was *her* useless wee spud.

And some days, that was what counted.

BEFORE WE SAY GOODBYE

*in which Stuart says thank you to some
People Who Helped*

Thank you to: Fiona (partner in crime, maker of tea and naughty Fife person) – she knows what for; Grendel (fuzzy cat, companion, muse and advisor on all the gory bits) – so does she; Beetroot (teeny velvety cat) for trying to catch all the words on the screen as I typed them; Susan Calman (excellent stand-up, author, and all-round Radio-4-type funny person) for permission to quote the line 'it's not all sex-swings and dildos'; Chuck Imisson (bookseller extraordinaire and Death Watch frontman) for inspiring the CID team's 'Word of the Day' thing; Charlie Morrison (mechanical guru) for coming to the rescue on more than one occasion; Allan Buchan (AKA: Allan Guthrie, excellent writer of *proper* tartan noir) for all his input and feedback on this book and the shenanigans contained within; Terence Caven (production Man of Steel) for putting up with all my Oldcastle map-flavoured madness; Sergeant Bruce 'Brucie' Crawford (award-winning police-tweeter) who continues to be a font of many knowledges; everyone at HarperCollins but especially Sarah Hodgson (longsuffering editing guru, who's put up with my nonsense for years), Jane Johnson,

Julia Wisdom, Jaime Frost, Anna Derkacz, Sarah Collett, Charlie Redmayne, Roger Cazalet, Kate Elton, Hannah Gamon, Sarah Shea, Damon Greeney, Finn Cotton, the eagle-eyed Rhian McKay, Marie Goldie and the DC Bishopbriggs Naughty Monkey Gang; Phil Patterson and the team at Marjacq Scripts; everyone who works in a bookshop or a library also deserves a massive wodge of thanks, so often they're the ones who get people excited about books – they're Monsters of Fabulousness!

Last, but by no means least, I want to take my hat off to you – the person reading this book. If it wasn't for readers there wouldn't be writers, libraries, bookshops, or publishers. And what a crappy dreich grey world it would be.

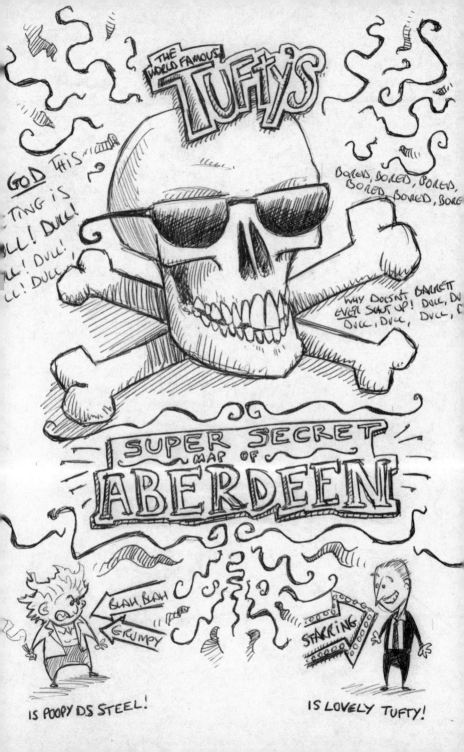